"An emotionally evocative, page-turning exploration of human corruption at its very worst. Chilling and riveting!" —Jonathan Kellerman

"Gregg Hurwitz sets up a compelling puzzle . . . Readers will be satisfied with and surprised by the conspirators." —*USA Today*

"Hurwitz starts the pressure early and never, ever lets up." —*Cleveland Plain Dealer*

"A deft, expertly plotted thriller driven by the kind of realistic suspense that will make any reader's heartbeat race." —Thomas Perry

"Beautifully written . . . if the ending doesn't bring on the full waterworks, or at least a slight misting of the eyes, you might want to double check that you didn't already lose your heart on the way there." —*New Mystery Reader*

"One of the best thrillers [of the year]."—*Shots Magazine*

"This thriller has everything—heightened action, fast-paced plot, well-rounded characters." —*Milwaukee Journal Sentinel*

"As suspenseful and as all important as any thriller you will read this year. The stakes are the highest you'll ever read." —*Crimespree Magazine*

THEY'RE WATCHING

"Riveting, emotionally rich, original, and beautifully written, this book kept me up too late reading, had me sneaking in pages the next day. *They're Watching* reminded me what it's like to be in the thrall of a great story: helpless until the end, loving every minute of it."
—Lisa Unger

"Rousing . . . intriguing . . . one shocking surprise after another . . . Always a master of the gripping setup, Hurwitz outdoes himself in this ultra-suspenseful thriller." —*Publishers Weekly* (starred review)

"Buckle up and get ready for a wild ride! From the anxiety-inducing first page to the nerve-wracking last, *They're Watching* will keep you riveted as one man fights for his family, his career, and his very life."
—Lisa Gardner

"A strong Hitchcock vibe . . . Hurwitz has the smarts and the writing chops to earn his suspense in a way that lesser writers simply can't . . . [he] has firmly established himself as one of the top writers in the suspense genre." —*Chicago Sun-Times*

"Invasion of privacy reaches sinister new levels in thriller maestro Hurwitz's latest. . . . With cinematic pacing and strong echoes of countless other twisty suspenses, this one is a natural for the big screen."
—*People*

ALSO BY GREGG HURWITZ

The Tower

Minutes to Burn

Do No Harm

The Kill Clause

The Program

Troubleshooter

Last Shot

The Crime Writer

Trust No One

They're Watching

You're Next

THE SURVIVOR

Gregg Hurwitz

St. Martin's Paperbacks

This is a work of fiction. All of the characters, organizations, and events portrayed in this novel are either products of the author's imagination or are used fictitiously.

THE SURVIVOR

For information address St. Martin's Press, 175 Fifth Avenue, New York, NY 10010.

Library of Congress Catalog Card Number: 2012013914

ISBN: 978-1-250-02943-0

Printed in the United States of America

St. Martin's Press hardcover edition / August 2012
St. Martin's Paperbacks edition / August 2013

St. Martin's Paperbacks are published by St. Martin's Press, 175 Fifth Avenue, New York, NY 10010.

10   9   8   7   6   5   4   3   2   1

To Lisa Erbach Vance,
simply the best

ON THE BRINK

Fear was absolutely necessary. Without it, I would have been scared to death.

—Floyd Patterson

Chapter 1

From this height the cars looked like dominoes, the pedestrians like roving dots. The breeze blew crisp and constant, cooling Nate's lungs on the inhale—none of that touted L.A. smog this close to the ocean. To the west, blocks of afternoon gridlock ended at the Santa Monica cliffs, a sheer drop to white sand and the eternal slate of the sea. The view would have been lovely.

Except he was here to kill himself.

The eleventh-story ledge gave him two spare inches past the tips of his sneakers. Balance was a challenge, but getting out here had been the hardest part. He'd shoehorned himself through the ancient bathroom window at First Union Bank of Southern California, wobbling for a solid minute on the ledge before daring to rise.

On the street below, people scurried about their business, no one squinting up into the late-morning glare to spot him. As he flattened against the wall, his senses lurched into overdrive—the smacking of his heart against his ribs, the sweat-damp shirt clinging to his shoulders, the salt tinge burning his nostrils. It felt a lot like panic, but somehow calmer, as if his brain was resigned to the circumstances but his body wasn't getting the signals.

Because he was unwilling to risk landing on someone—with his luck he'd pile-drive a pension-check-cashing granny through the pavement—he continued slide-stepping to the end of the ledge. The corner of the building gave him less trouble than he'd anticipated as he elbow-clamped his way around, and then he was staring down at the empty alley and the target of the Dumpster below. It was, if nothing else, a considerate plan. If he hit the bin squarely, the steel walls would contain the spatter, leaving him neatly packaged for delivery to the crematorium. He was sick of people cleaning up after him.

It had been less than ten minutes since he'd laid open that Dumpster lid, but it seemed like days. The chilly elevator ride up, the nod to the wizened black security guard, that final moment collecting his nerves by the row of urinals before muscling open the sash window—each had stretched out into a lifetime.

First Union of SoCal was one of the few West Coast banks located up off the ground floor—cheaper real estate, more space, better security. But only one high-rise perk held Nate's interest currently. Gauging his position, he slid another half step to the right, stopping shy of a casement window that had been cranked several turns outward. From the gap issued a current of warm, coffee-scented air and the busy hum of tellers and customers. Business as usual.

He considered his own dwindling checking account

within. His next step—literally—would void the million-dollar life-insurance policy to which he dutifully wrote a check every January, but even that wouldn't matter. There was no one who wanted anything of him and nothing ahead but increments of misery.

He took a deep breath—his last?—and closed his eyes. Spreading his arms, he let the October wind rise through the thin cotton of his T-shirt and chill the sweat on his ribs. He waited for his life to flash before his eyes, the ethereal song and dance, but there was nothing. No wedding-day close-up of Janie's lips parting to meet his, no image of Cielle dressed as a pumpkin for Halloween with her chocolate-smudged hands and dimpled thighs, just the teeth of the wind and a thousand needle points of fear, skewering him like a pincushion. The longest journey, according to Taoism and Hallmark, begins with a single step.

And so does the shortest.

He took one foot and moved it out into the weightless open.

That was when he heard the gunshots.

Chapter 2

For an instant, Nate wobbled at the fulcrum, seemingly past the point of no return, but then a subtle twist of his hip brought him back, fully, to the ledge. As he gulped in a mouthful of air, another gun snapped and a swath of crimson painted the window at his side.

Nate knew the crack of a nine-mil sidearm, but the next eruption, a resonant clatter, suggested that a semi-automatic was in play as well.

A gravelly voice floated out through the window gap: "Don't reach under the desks. Step back. *Back*. You saw what'll happen. Now *lay down*. On your fucking faces."

Gripping the frame beneath the swung-out pane, Nate rolled carefully across his shoulder to peer inside the bank. The blood-smeared glass turned the robbers' faces into smudges, but he could see that they were wearing ski masks. One stood a few feet away behind the teller line, his back to the window, automatic rifle cocked in one hand, the Beretta in his other, surveying the room methodically. Like the others he wore a one-piece charcoal flight suit, thick-soled boots, and black gloves. Duct tape wrapped his wrists and ankles so no hint of flesh peeked through. The burst of bullets had punched holes in the ceiling, and white dust clouded him like an aura, lending the scene an otherworldly tint.

The bank workers stretched flat at his feet, hands laced at their necks, foreheads to the tile, their labored breaths coming as rasps. On the main floor beyond, about fifteen customers also lay prone. The coffee trolley had been knocked over, cups resting in brown puddles. Two robbers patrolled the area on a circuit, stepping over bodies, handgun barrels moving from critical mass to critical mass.

By the entrance the black security guard lay sprawled, tangled in a vinyl banner announcing FREE WEB BILL PAY!, a fan of blood marring the money-green print. His pant leg was pulled up, exposing an anomalous striped sock.

Whereas his associates shouted and moved in quick bursts, the man by the window moved with a composed fluidity that suggested greater expertise. While the others barked orders, he remained unnervingly silent. Given the man's assurance and the fact that he commanded the big gun, Nate pegged him as the crew leader. And he was standing close enough that Nate could have reached through the window and tapped him on the shoulder.

To the right, a pair of armed men (five, that made *five* of them so far) dragged a middle-aged Hispanic woman toward the vault, her hands fussing at two knots of keys and making little progress. The bank manager. Dressed crisply in a wool pantsuit, pearl necklace, and matching earrings, she struggled to keep her legs beneath her. The steel vault door, thicker than a cinder block, rested open, leaving only the glass day gate to protect the nests of safe-deposit boxes beyond. As she fought two keys into two locks and swung the day gate ajar, a sixth masked man appeared from a rear corridor, dumped a black duffel off his shoulder, and announced, "Cameras are down." He removed a fierce-looking circular saw with a chain-saw handle. The teeth of the white-silver blade sparkled.

A woman's hoarse sobs echoed off the faux marble walls, and somewhere a man was pleading, a broken loop of desperation: *"—God oh God please I just got engaged I just—"*

Nate tried to swallow, but his throat had gone to sand. Forgetting where he was, he drew back slightly. The drop to the pavement below swirled vertiginously into view between his legs.

One sneaker lost purchase, his weight pulling out and away, and his stomach flew up into his throat and choked off a cry. His hand slipped a few inches before wedging in the corner of the window frame and firming him, panting, against the concrete.

The robbers kept shouting, oblivious to the minicommotion outside on the ledge.

"—anyone moves or speaks, and I mean one fucking squeak—"

"Three and Five, get going on those hinges. Four, that bitch better get you into the—"

All of them barking nervous commands except the crew leader, who stood mutely, projecting calm menace.

Nate had wound up clinging to the frame with his face filling the gap, peering down into the eyes of a teller crumpled just beneath the window. He was shocked he hadn't noticed her before. Her white blouse blotted a growing spot of blood. Her mouth guppied a few times, a bubble forming. She looked up at Nate, disbelieving, as if she wasn't sure how she'd been knocked over or why a stubble-faced angel had fluttered up to the eleventh-floor window.

One arm was slung back across her head, an ivory hand quivering in a sideways float. She stared at Nate imploringly. Watching the shallow rise and fall of her chest, he felt his breath catch. He reached down and took her hand. It was cool and smooth, carved from marble. A burbling sound escaped her, the bubble popping, leaving behind a speckled lipstick stain.

The crew leader consulted a stopwatch and for the first time spoke. Faint accent, utterly serene. "I would like to hear that saw, Three."

In reply, metal shrieked in the vault, sparks cascading into view. The manager backed into the hinges, her balled hands in front of her face. Her mouth formed an oval and veins bulged in her neck, but the metal-on-metal screech of the saw eclipsed all other noise. The biggest of the men had her by the hair. He smacked her head into the vault door, a smudge of blood darkening her forehead, but still the mouth stayed ajar, her fists trembling at her chin. The half-wall partition and open teller gate sliced Nate's view into horror-movie glimpses—straining arm, kicked-off high heel, hank of loose hair clutched in a dark glove.

It took the bite of the sill in his armpit to remind him he was hanging through a window. The cool hand tightened in his, grinding his knuckles together. He looked down at the woman beneath him. Her gaze went loose, looking through him instead of at him, and then her pretty green eyes turned to ice.

The saw paused, the manager came off mute, and Nate tore his focus from the death-smooth face below. Twisting his hand free, he withdrew his arm through the gap and tried to shake feeling back into it.

The manager's screams continued. The big man turned to look helplessly at the crew leader, who said with quiet authority, "She is near the duress alarm. Put her down."

"Look, Six, how many we gonna kill?"

Crew leader, Nate thought. *Number Six.*

The leader's boots tapped as he crossed the room. Sheetrock dust flecked his back. He raised his arms, and the automatic rifle coughed, tapping a line of holes through the woman's stiff suit, the percussion and horror nearly knocking Nate off the ledge. The woman remained grotesquely standing, propped against the open vault door, until Six placed two fingers on her shoulder and tipped her over. She slapped the floor, one arm unfurling, her rings clacking tile. A pearl earring skittered away, pinwheeling off a desk leg.

Several people yelped on the main floor, and a child began to wail, a single wavering note. A middle-aged man choked out a series of sobs, blurred against the floor into something feral.

"One dead or twenty—it carries the same sentence."

The crew leader's voice remained exceedingly even, almost peaceful. He brushed white powder from his shoulder. "I'll handle the vault. Empty the teller drawers." He handed off the automatic rifle and stepped toward the safe-deposit boxes, pointing. "Here next. Then here."

The big man moved obediently toward the teller line, Nate jerking his head back from the gap. As the footsteps neared, he pressed his face into his straining biceps. His wet shirt had gone to ice against his lower back, the wind riffling the hem. He realized he was biting into his own flesh to keep quiet.

The man passed by the window, shoving aside the teller's lifeless leg with his boot. He set his Beretta on a low file cabinet, looped the rifle over his shoulder, and began emptying teller drawers into a black trash bag.

A scream knifed through the bank, pronounced even out on the ledge. Nate risked another peek across the room, his face grinding the concrete to give himself a one-eyed vantage. A customer was bucking on her stomach, both masked men across the main floor oriented toward her. Nate wondered what the hell she was doing until a pigtailed girl, maybe four years old, popped out from beneath her and ran toward the exit. Two handgun barrels traced the girl's movement. The mother screamed again, lunging to a knee and grabbing her daughter's flailing arm. The man nearest kicked the woman in the face, blood erupting from her lip, and she fell limply, dragging the girl to the floor with her. The girl scooted away, hands and feet scrabbling for purchase, a streak of her mother's blood darkening the lobe of one ear. She struck a pillar, her feet still trying to propel her back until she realized she had nowhere to go. Shivering violently, she hugged her legs, buried her face in the bumps of her knees, and shut off like an unplugged TV.

The other man—Number Two?—walked over and stared down at her. "Get back over there with the others. Go on. Move it."

The girl remained motionless. He aimed the gun loosely at her head.

At the sight Nate pressed forward into the window gap, long-buried paternal instincts firing. The pane notched farther open against the pressure of his elbow. A few feet in front of Nate, the big man watched the scene unfolding on the main floor. He made a soft noise of deference in his throat and returned his focus to the next teller drawer, shoulder blades shifting beneath the charcoal flight suit.

Number Two firmed both hands on a Beretta, sighting on the girl. "You're gonna want to listen now, girlie."

The saw revved back to life over in the vault, a metallic grinding, and the ski mask pulsed again where Number Two's mouth would be—a final warning to the girl.

One dead or twenty—it carries the same sentence.

Nate looked down at the pretty green dead eyes aimed up at him. Across to the clip-on pearl earring resting on the dappled tile. Then over at the Beretta, sitting on the low file cabinet next to the big man's turned back, less than two steps from the windowsill.

Nate strained against the casement window, and it

gave another few inches, enough for him to worm his torso through. Headfirst, he cascaded down over the dead teller. Her body softened his landing, though the circular saw's teeth-rattling reverberation in the concrete walls obscured all sound. Three of the robbers were out of sight in the vault. The big man was a few feet away, his back still turned, rummaging in a cash drawer. The two across on the main floor stayed focused on the girl. Both pistols were now raised, their boots shuffling in at her. Still she didn't move, her head bowed, arms fastened around her bent legs.

Rising, Nate felt the complaint of his thirty-six-year-old knees. The listlessness of the past several months fell away, and for the first time in a long damn time he sensed himself moving without hesitation. With something like purpose.

Stepping forward, he reached for the Beretta on the file cabinet.

Chapter 3

Nate lifted the Beretta, swung the barrel to the back of the big man's head, and fired. The trigger hitched, a quarter-second delay, and somewhere between recoil and the flare of scarlet against the teller glass he registered that the first trigger pull had been double-action. From here on out, the Beretta would be single-action.

The gunshot was all but silent compared to the amplified screech of the saw within the vault. The big man's knees struck the ground as he collapsed, shuddering his shoulders and clearing Nate's view to the masked men on the main floor.

And theirs to him.

Both masks swiveled in puzzlement to take him in, the stillness of the moment stretching out in painful slow motion. The heads cocked slightly, an instinctive attack-dog tilt, sending an icy ripple up Nate's spine. He realized what looked off about the faces: There were no eyes. Mesh had been stitched over the holes so that no flesh was visible, an insectoid effect that smoothed the heads to disturbing perfection.

With detached tranquillity, Nate watched their gloved hands rise, blued steel glinting inside curled fingers. A bullet lasered past his face, close enough to trail heat across his cheek. He was, it struck him, utterly unafraid. In his indifference he felt a weight lift from his shoulders, felt a smile curve his lips, felt imaginary manacles release. And then his hands, too, were lifting. He reminded himself with alarming calmness that he had to keep his wrists steady as he'd learned in basic, that he should not anticipate recoil, that he was, if not an ace, a decent shot. The air around his head took form as more bullets rocketed past, and he aimed across the teller partition at the first man and squeezed, and half the masked head went to red mist. The man toppled out of sight. His companion was shooting, the muzzle flashing but still inaudible beneath the earsplitting action of the saw. Nate was firing, too, the far wall giving off little puffs of drywall, spent cartridges cartwheeling across his field of vision. He stepped forward through the laid-open teller gate into the incoming bullets, to his death, his senses alive with the thrill of freedom—no, more than that. The thrill of *liberation.*

Number Two's mask was stretched at the mouth—he was screaming—and his arms were trembling. Nate watched the bore winking into view like a black eye, and he stared back, his thoughts pounding a suicide urge:

Steady your hand. Hit me.

But the barrel jerked left, right, bullets framing Nate's silhouette. Nate replayed the man's growled threat—*You're gonna want to listen now, girlie*—and anger sharpened his focus. He felt the Beretta kick and kick in his hands until the flight suit's fabric did a little dance above the man's chest and he fell down and away.

Sometime in the past second or two, the saw had paused, leaving the pop of the bullets suddenly naked, and Nate turned quickly to face the vault door. A man emerged carrying the circular saw, hood pushed up atop his head, wearing an expression of mild surprise. Nate shot off his ear in a spray of black blood. The man swung his head back, and Nate put a bullet through the puzzled furrow between his eyes.

Really? That's the best you assholes can do?

The back-strap checkering on the grip had bitten into the web of his thumb. The scent of cordite spiced the air, dragging him almost a decade into the past, to burning sand and blood in his eyes.

He blinked himself to the present. Four down, two to go.

Moving again behind the teller line, he looked down at the automatic rifle on the floor, contemplating an upgrade. But he couldn't spare the time untangling the sling from the body, so he walked swiftly toward the vault door, stepping across workers' quivering bodies. "Sorry, 'scuse me, sorry."

Sobs and gasps answered him. A wail of sirens grew audible, faint enough to be imaginary.

A pistol reached around the vault jamb, firing blindly. Nate drew a careful bead on the gun hand and kept on, swift and steady, not because of courage or heroism but because he hadn't a thing to lose. He fired once, the round clanging off the vault door, and then he adjusted and fired twice more, a whirl of muscle memory, reaction, and instinct. The pistol flipped back, the fingers spreading comically wide, as if waving, and the hand vanished intact.

Five more steps brought Nate to the vault door, and he strolled through without hesitation. A man sat in the far corner, aiming at the doorway, locked elbows resting on the shelf of his knees. He took a clear-as-day shot at Nate's head, but the wind of the bullet kissed the side of Nate's neck, the slug bouncing around the vault more times than seemed plausible. Nate swung the pistol, figuring he was too close to bother with the sights, and unloaded two shots into the guy's gut. Simultaneously he heard the scuff of a boot in the blind spot behind him. He sidestepped, the coolness of metal brushing his neck and turning to a dagger of flame in his trapezius. Twisting, he shot, but the hammer clicked dryly—marking the fastest fifteen rounds he'd ever spent.

The blade tweaked the muscle down the length of his arm, barbed wire tugged through a vein. Heat poured into his little finger. A half turn of his neck brought the handle of a sleek metal letter opener visible, sticking up out of him like an Indian brave's feather.

He said, "Ouch."

His eyes tracked to the man who had stabbed him. The ski mask was still on, the mesh patches of the eyes shiny under the fluorescent glow of the vault lights, but from the man's bearing Nate recognized him.

Number Six.

Up close the crew leader seemed slight—slender-hipped and wiry, built for maximum efficiency. He couldn't have been more than five foot nine, shorter than his associates. Nate's eyes were drawn to a band of exposed flesh, the white skin striking against the comprehensive black getup. The man had peeled back the glove of his right hand, the meat at the base of the thumb pink from where Nate had shot the pistol from his grip. He held the palm up and at an angle, babying it, which gave Nate a flush of schoolyard pride.

They faced each other from a few paces, the masked man bare-handed, Nate holding a bulletless gun, Nate realizing with some disappointment that no one would be killing anyone else at the moment. He lifted his good shoulder in a half shrug, then drew back the Beretta and threw it at the guy's face. Number Six barely flinched, the gun clipping his forehead. He touched a hand to the black fabric at the point of impact, then rolled his fingertips together, a man accustomed to checking for his own blood. He gave off nothing resembling emotion.

The sirens, now louder.

That dead-calm voice again, the faint accent. "He will be greatly angered by you."

Nate said, "Tell whoever *he* is to take a number."

The man pointed at him. "You have no idea what you have done."

These words—even more, the gravity behind them—cut through Nate's exhilaration, an arctic chill. For the first time since climbing in off that ledge, he felt fear, cold and pure.

The man took a step back and then another, those patches of mesh trained on Nate. "He will make you pay," he said, "in ways you can't imagine." Then he slid past the vault door, his footsteps pattering off.

Dazed, Nate looked around, getting his bearings. Aside from the imposing wall of safe-deposit boxes, the vault was disappointingly ordinary. Concrete walls, file cabinets, the few freestanding Diebold safes no more impressive than airport lockers. A cardboard legal box on the floor held overflow holiday envelopes and stray staplers; Nate figured it to be the home of the letter opener protruding from his shoulder. One safe was cracked open, and the deposit boxes had been attacked. Thick metal hinges protruded in V-shaped ridges, bordering each column of boxes. Most of the hinges had been sheared off by the saw, leaving the metal door of each individual box embedded, its dead bolt still thrown. Red rectangular handle magnets, the kind used to lift sheet metal from a stack, remained adhered to the closest set of boxes, floating. Nate could see where someone had used them to pry off some of the little doors. A few freed boxes lay open on the tiles, foreign currency, jewelry, and legal documents scattered by the dead man's boots. A neat little scheme—attack the hinges, yank off the doors, and voilà—unearned wealth.

Muffled cries from the bank floor jarred Nate from his reluctant admiration. He thought of the kill order— *Put her down*—and his stomach roiled. *One dead or twenty—it carries the same sentence.* Human lives weighed against a cold efficiency. The terror that those people must have felt.

He walked back out to the bank floor. All of them still lying on their stomachs. Quiet sobbing. A few heads beginning to stir. The squeal of tires carried up from the street.

He cleared his throat. "It's okay now, everyone. Those guys are gone. Or dead, I guess. You're all safe. You can get up."

But they all stayed on the floor.

Nate wondered briefly if this was actually real and not some bizarre dream. "I promise you," he said, "no one'll hurt you now. Please don't be scared anymore." He took a pleading step forward, a lightning bolt of pain electrifying his left side. Wincing, he tried to reach back to grip the handle of the letter opener, but the movement just made it bob away from his fingertips.

Now came more sirens, the chop of a helicopter, a megaphone bleat. The phone on the New Accounts desk rang and rang. Nate stared at the motionless tableau, all those people, too afraid to rise.

The little girl crawled over to her mother, still unconscious from the kick to her face. Nate crouched above the inert woman, laid two fingers on her neck. Strong pulse.

"She's okay," he told the girl. "Your mom's gonna be fine."

He stood again, his knees cracking, and announced to no one in particular, "I'm gonna . . . um, go get some help. Medics. Okay? Everyone okay?"

More stunned silence.

The girl held up her arms. He looked down at her, the familiar pick-me-up gesture twingeing his heart in a place he'd thought had long ago gone brittle and blown away. One of her pigtails had pulled loose, freeing a cloud of hair. The blood on her earlobe had hardened, a black crust. Both cheeks glimmered with tears, but her face remained blank with shock. He crouched and lifted her, grunting against the pain, trying to use his legs instead of his arms. Her wrist brushed the letter opener, sending through him a wave of nausea so intense that he thought he might vomit. But he kept on toward the door, blood warming the back of his shirt.

The security guard had landed faceup, his head corkscrewed unnaturally, white eyes aimed over at them. Stepping into the waiting elevator, Nate turned so the girl was pointed away from the death sprawl. She took his cue, bending her head into the hollow of his neck, the scent of no-tears shampoo bringing him back to Cielle at that age in the bathtub: *We* don't *splash!*

The elevator hummed its descent. His skin tingled—the afterglow of that invincibility he'd felt staring down the hail of bullets. How long had it been since he'd felt like that? He'd cheated something in that room, sucked a last taste of marrow from the bone.

The elevator slowed, the girl's weight pulling at the crook of his arm. Her face was hot against the side of his neck, and he realized he'd been talking to her, whispering a quiet mantra: "—everything's gonna be all right everything's gonna—"

The doors peeled back, exposing the empty lobby. His footsteps grew heavier as he neared the tinted glass of the front wall. Beyond, cop cars, SWAT vans, ambulances, and fire engines crammed the street. Barricades and gun barrels alternated, a pattern of impenetrability. Sniper scopes winked from awnings and balconies.

The girl made a fearful noise and buried herself deeper in his neck. Firming his grip around her with one hand and raising his other painfully overhead, he shoved through the revolving door, staggering out to a reception of countless muzzles and the bright light of day.

Chapter 4

When Nate entered the emergency room, flanked by cops like an escaped convict, the TV in the lobby was already rolling footage from outside the First Union Bank of Southern California. Despite the bandages, blood trickled down his arm, drying across the backs of his fingers like an ill-advised fashion statement. The letter opener, removed from his trapezius and encased in an evidence bag, was handed off to a venerable triage nurse, who looked from it to Nate with an impressive lack of curiosity. She led him through a miasma of familiar hospital smells to Radiology, then deposited him in a room the size of a walk-in closet.

The doctor came in, scanning Nate's chart as Nate crinkled on the paper sheet of the exam table. "So you got stabbed with a letter opener."

"It sounds so unimpressive when you say it *that* way."

She hoisted her lovely eyebrows.

"Sorry," Nate said. "I just joke so people don't notice my low self-esteem."

"It's not working."

"It's a long-term plan." He exhaled shakily. The adrenaline had washed out of him, leaving him unsteady and vaguely drunk. Beneath the dull throb of a headache, a jumble of images reigned—a burst of red mist from a hooded head, patches of black mesh in place of eyes, the blood-sodden blouse of the bank teller whose hand he had clasped as she'd died. He was rattled, all right, but given what he'd just been through, he was surprised he didn't feel worse.

A page fluttered up. The doctor's pen tapped the chart. "Your liver enzymes are elevated. Taking any meds?"

"Riluzole."

She looked at him fully for the first time, her gaze sharpening behind John Lennon glasses. "So that's . . . ?"

The familiar image flickered through his mind—Lou Gehrig, the luckiest man on the face of the earth, against the packed grandstands of Yankee Stadium, his head bowed, cap clutched in both hands to rest against his thighs. "Yes," Nate said.

"Ouch."

"Yeah."

"And so you're . . . acquainted with your prognosis."

His prognosis. Yeah. He was acquainted. He knew he would soon have trouble gripping, say, a pen. Then one day he wouldn't be able to pick it up at all. He knew that his tongue would start to feel thick. Some slurring on and off, at first merely troubling, and then he wouldn't be able to communicate. Or swallow. He knew that he would in due course require a feeding tube. That his tear ducts would start to go, that he'd need eyedrops and eventually someone else to apply them. He knew that he would feel some general fatigue, at first inconvenient, then debilitating. That he wouldn't be able to get a full breath. At some point he'd need a CPAP mask at night. And then he'd go on a ventilator. He knew that the cause of the disease was unknown but that there was a significantly increased risk among veterans. There were no answers, and certainly no good ones.

"I am."

"Where are you in the course of illness?" the doctor asked.

"I was told I could expect six months to a year of good health."

"When?"

"About nine months ago." He couldn't help a dry smile—it so resembled a punch line.

"Any symptoms?"

"A little weakness in my hand. It goes in and out. The symptoms are intermittent. Until they're not."

She touched his forearm gently, a technique he employed now and again in his own job. "There are some experimental treatments."

"Don't."

"Okay." She moistened her lips. "I won't say anything comforting."

"Much appreciated."

She slotted the chart into an acrylic wall rack above a torn-loose *People* cover sporting an elegiac portrait of Elizabeth Taylor and wormed her pale hands into paler latex gloves. After poking and prodding at the edges of the stab wound, she slotted an X-ray into the light box and regarded it, chewing her lip. "You're lucky. The point bounced off your scapula instead of punching through to your lung. Mostly muscle damage. You current with tetanus?"

"Yeah."

"Then just antibiotics and Vicodin, you'll be back to form in a week"—she caught herself. "On this front, I mean." Chagrin colored her face, and she busied herself opening a suture packet. "Should we stitch you up now?"

Nate smiled wanly. "We could just let me bleed out on the table, save us all the aggravation."

"L.A.," she said, threading the needle. "Everybody's a comedian."

He sat quietly, enduring the pinpricks of the local anesthetic, then the tug of his numb skin.

"Everyone's talking about you," she said. "The bank. Where'd you learn to shoot like that?"

"The army."

"You don't seem the soldier type to me."

"I'm not. Just signed up for ROTC to pay for college. It was 1994. I was never gonna get called up to active duty."

She made a faint noise of amusement. A metallic snip as she cut the last stitch. "How'd that work out for you?"

"Not so hot," he said.

WHAT WAS LOST

There is a great deal of pain in life and perhaps the only pain that can be avoided is the pain that comes from trying to avoid pain.

–Unknown

Chapter 5

At UCLA the National Guard is not about training soldiers; it is about olive drab T-shirts, jumping jacks, and shooting-range practice one weekend a month. Nate enjoys the sense of belonging and participates with gratitude, if not the *hoo-ah* earnestness his superiors might prefer. The choice is primarily a financial one; he is on his own here. In high school he buckled down and studied hard, aware that that was the best way out of a house that had been lifeless since his mom had succumbed thoroughly, brutally, to cancer when he was in third grade. After her funeral his father vanished into an effluvium of scotch, a still life in a frayed armchair, the eternal microwave dinner resting on the eternal TV tray at his side. There will be no parent weekends for Nate in college, no palmed-off cash to help cover books.

Most of the time, Nate is a normal student. His roommate, a fellow ROTC cadet named Charles Brightbill, is pathologically relaxed and full of childlike wonderment. Charles has an unsurpassed appreciation of all things everybody else noticed five minutes ago, marveling at planes overhead, a classmate's cleavage, the color of his just-blown snot in a Kleenex. "Hey," Charles says. "Look at that rainbow in the sprinkler mist." Despite Nate's best efforts, he loves the guy. Charles who is incapable of deception, who dispenses the occasional nugget of inadvertent wisdom, who sleeps in the hall when he forgets his key rather than wake Nate, no matter how many times Nate tells him to bang on the door.

After a particularly soul-destroying exam in their junior year, Charles drags Nate out of bed, beach towels in hand. "Rise 'n' shine, podnah. Moping's like listening to Iron Maiden when you're hungover." That's Charles; he can boil down the world and put it in a fortune cookie. Nate relents. Ten minutes later he cranks open the window of Charles's Datsun 240Z and lets the salt-rich breeze wash over him. Sprawled on the hot Malibu sand, he basks, feeling the life creep back into him.

A distant waterlogged shriek startles him upright. A flailing feminine form, out beyond the break. Then a young man about Nate's age is disgorged from the sea, landing on all fours on the wet sand before them, surf seething up his forearms. He heaves up salt water, and then his hoarse voice croaks at the beachgoers— "Riptide. She's got a cramp."

There is a moment of utter stillness, people frozen on their towels. A few heads swivel to the lifeguard station far along the beach. And then Nate is up and running, dried seaweed pods crackling underfoot. Charles is bellowing after him, but Nate hurdles a wave and strikes out for the break. The undertow grips him, sweeping him toward the woman, who sputters and dips from sight. Muscles on fire, he strokes into a forceful current, and then, finally, her rubbery arm is in his grasp. He sweeps her into him, spinning her so her spine presses to his chest. She spits and struggles, and the back of her head cracks his eye. He lets go, and she goes under the green-black surface and bobs up again, choking. He says, "Stop fighting." He reaches for her arm once more. "Look at me. I got you." She stares at him, drops clinging to her eyelashes, and it occurs to him that she is quite beautiful. They are being swept along, the backdrop of the beach whipping by, and she gives a quick, youthful nod. He spins her like a dance partner, and she surrenders into him, her muscles going limp. Clamping an arm over her shoulder and across her flat chest, he lets them drift with the riptide, reading the water. Then he paddles, offsetting them slightly from the current. They reach the sand a half mile up the beach, with Charles, two lifeguards, and a cluster of onlookers sprinting to meet them. They both cough water and pant, and she rises first, tugging him to his feet, and then they are helped and dried and checked to the point of claustrophobia.

The young man who dragged himself to shore stands sheepishly at the outskirts of the cluster. Wrapped in a towel, the woman turns to thank Nate, providing his first full glimpse of her. Her lips are big, almost too big, and the shape of her mouth leaves them between a sneer and a smile. She has creamy white skin and a turned-up nose with a scattering of freckles across the bridge that seem out of place, like they've showed up to the wrong party. Her blond hair is cropped tight, short enough to be daring. Her features carry it off, but then Nate thinks they could carry off anything. One flash of that quick, wide grin and he'd not notice if she were wearing a Carmen Miranda hat piled with produce. She has her original, factory-issue breasts—a rarity in Los Angeles—and her body is lean, slim-hipped. Usually he gravitates to girls with a little more meat on their bones, but he is quick to realize that there isn't much sense in comparing her to anyone who came before.

She introduces herself as Janie. Hovering off Nate's shoulder, Charles stage-whispers, "Dude, she's *hot*," once again narrating the thunderbolt obvious.

Nate offers his hand. "Nate Overbay." And they shake, which feels a bit ludicrous given that their bare bodies have spent the previous fifteen minutes glued together.

At once Janie's date is by her side, asking Nate, "Can I give her a ride home? Or you gonna handle that, too?"

Nate thinks, *Now would be a really good time to not say anything.*

She and the guy begin to argue, Janie offering apologetic glances at Nate until the scene grows uncomfortable. Nate retreats from the commotion, Charles berating him all the way back to their crappy Westwood apartment for not getting her number. Lying awake that night, Nate realizes that Charles was once again dead-on and resigns himself to a lifetime of regret.

A few weeks later, Nate and Charles are eating Mama Celeste microwave pizza and watching *Melrose Place* when the doorbell rings. Nate answers and finds Janie outside, double-checking an address she has scrawled on her palm. Her short, wet hair sticks out at all angles, fresh from a shower, and she smells of lavender. Before he can figure out how to talk, she says, "I can't stop thinking about it. How you pulled me out of the water."

She has the faintest trace of a lisp, just enough to keep him in mind of her mouth, those lips shaping themselves around each word, however imperfectly.

Nate's heart beats a double-time rhythm. "I haven't stopped thinking about you either."

"I *tried*," she says, agitated. "I thought about all the things I probably wouldn't like about you. All the stuff we'd fight about if we ever actually were together. How you really aren't *that* good-looking."

"Why'd you do that?"

"Because of my boyfriend." Her hands tug at the back pockets of her jeans. A one-shouldered shrug. "*Ex*-boyfriend now." She lifts her fingers to the echo of a bruise around his eye where her skull cracked him in the surf.

They step into a kiss, and Charles's voice floats from the other room, "Dude, hurry up. Heather Locklear's in a frickin' *nightie*."

Janie and Nate are instantly inseparable. That weekend they sit cross-legged on his bed, nose to nose, engulfed in conversation about their childhoods, and, as is apt to happen, they start making out. He begins to move her horizontal, then stops himself.

She looks up, those lashes framing her large blue eyes. "What?"

"I can't decide if I want to have sex with you or keep talking to you."

"That," she says, "is the finest compliment I've been paid in all my twenty years."

Inevitably, sex wins out. They lie facing each other afterward, breathing hard, Nate's cupped hand tracing the flushed dip of her side. Her straw-colored bangs are now dark, sweat-pasted to her forehead. "What do you think about seeing other people?" she begins tentatively. "I know a lot of guys get weird around commitment. . . ."

"Commitment?" Nate says. "I *love* commitment."

Charles goes from scorned buddy to third wheel to joint best friend. Janie studies biology and French nearby at Pepperdine, but when she and Nate are apart, the half hour between campuses feels like a transatlantic separation. They are still young enough to pine as though pining were an Olympic event. Though they see each other almost every day, they pen indulgent letters, drunk on bad poetics. "Jesus H.," Charles says, uncrumpling a rough draft he lifted from Nate's trash can, "you're turning into a Celine Dion song."

On the occasions when Janie is dressed up and doesn't turn heads in a restaurant or bar, Nate is surprised. Yet this makes her somehow more special, that she is not as arresting to everyone, that her grace and manner put a hook in his limbic system as if she were designed for him and him alone.

They are engaged within three months.

* * *

She hails from Wisconsin, a normal childhood and family, with antecedents she calls Gammie and Papa. "What if your dad doesn't like me?" he asks, and she laughs. "He *won't* like you." Their circle of friends, however, is thrilled; they are the first to take the leap. They tell and retell their origin story, embellishing it by degrees, and he knows that by their fiftieth anniversary it will involve his rescuing her from a tidal wave in a tropical monsoon. Every time she gets to the rescue, no matter what company they're in, she takes his hand and quotes him back to him: " 'Stop fighting,' you told me. 'I got you.' "

They marry by spring. After the Olive Garden reception, exhausted and half drunk on bad Chianti, they collapse on the hotel mattress, Janie kicking off her heels, her white sundress unzipped. "Okay, Husband," she says sleepily, "we have to consummate this thing." That laugh. "You on top?"

Nate mumbles, "I would if I knew which direction that was."

"Give you a hundred dollars."

"I'm a grand, minimum."

"We have to. Or it's not legal."

"Right."

"And I might change my mind here."

By morning they are legal. They honeymoon at Nate and Charles's apartment, since they blew all their money on the fifty-person affair and their night at the Santa Monica Holiday Inn. Someday, they vow, when they have money, they will go to Paris for a makeup honeymoon, but until then they will always have Westwood. They spend their time drinking root-beer floats in bed and studying for midterms. It is like playing house without the house.

"Would you like Eggos in bed, Wife? On our finest paper plate?"

"Thank you, Husband. That would be delightful."

A week later she crawls under the sheets with him and announces, "We are having a baby."

All around him the world seems to pull itself into wonderful alignment. He blinks back emotion. "Are you sure?"

"The pee stick doesn't lie. And five of them *certainly* do not."

They move into a closet-size apartment of their own. Janie swells, her tiny frame accommodating near-impossible proportions. A former Boy Scout, Charles buys a pager for Nate. He is in Abnormal Psych when it goes off; her water has broken. Everything is a blur between Franz Hall and the delivery ward. She is growling and clawing the sheets, and when she takes his hand, she nearly crushes the bones of his fingers. "Look at me," he says. "I got you."

That night they crowd into her single hospital bed, a threesome. Two days later the infant remains Baby Overbay. As Nate steers Janie out in a wheelchair, the pink bundle in her lap, she says, "We'll name her after the first thing we see when we make it outta here."

Nate slows as they near the nurses' station. He says, "And how is little Garbage Can sleeping?"

Janie snorts, covers her mouth. "You know, it's been hard ever since Homeless Guy started teething."

A passing grandmother in the elevator gives them a dirty look, but they can't stop laughing. "Cat Ass really got your eyes," Nate says through tears.

Still laughing, they push past automated doors into daylight. Janie gazes up at the brilliant blue sky, and her breath catches in her throat.

"Cielle," she says.

They settle back into their tiny Westwood apartment. Charles brings a beautiful gift—a wooden stepstool with Cielle's name carved out, each letter a colored puzzle piece. They study, parent, juggle schedules, and somehow graduate. Nate starts a corporate job with a department store as a buyer of men's suits. Janie enrolls in nursing school.

A month before Cielle's third birthday, he manages a VA home loan, the incipient Paris re-honeymoon fund is happily reapportioned, and they get luckier than anyone could expect with a two-story bank-repo fixer-upper in a great part of Santa Monica. When they pull up in a U-Haul, Janie stops midway across the front lawn, crying with gratitude.

At night and on weekends, he slaves on the house, putting in floorboards, repainting, replacing iron pipes with copper. Every few months they mark off Cielle's height on her door jamb, the lines stacking up. One Tuesday morning Janie shakes him awake early and they sit in horror, clutching hands, watching footage of those 767s crashing into the towers again and again and again. Janie casts a dark glance through the open doorway to the laundry room, where his camouflage field jacket hangs drying from his last drill weekend. Upstairs, Cielle's bedroom door opens, and he rises silently to get her.

In the blink of an eye, Cielle is seven, her dark hair taken up in pigtails. The week after her birthday, they go for a long-overdue family portrait at Sears. Despite the photographer's entreaties, they can't get Cielle to focus. Isaac at school has introduced her to armpit farts, so every pose is bookended with: "Didja hear?"

Janie: "No."

"How 'bout now?"

Finally Nate swings Cielle upside down until she's red-faced from giggling, and the three of them topple over onto the plush blue mats, Janie sitting behind Nate, propping him up, Cielle squeezing her in a side hug, all three of them captured in the flash with indelicate open-mouthed laughs. After a family vote, the glossy portrait goes above their mantel. That night he and Janie read *The Lorax* to Cielle, then go downstairs, drink red wine, and watch *The West Wing*. He rubs Janie's feet and catches her looking at the portrait and shaking her head, and then they both crack up.

Nestled in the warmth of the couch, his wife's feet in his lap, his daughter soundly asleep overhead, he appreciates how their life is a quiet kind of spectacular, a bubble of bliss insulated from the horrors of the outside world.

In three days' time that bubble will pop.

Chapter 6

Standing with his ROTC battalion in neat formation on the pristine green lawn of the Los Alamitos Training Base, Nate senses a new kind of sharpness in the air. At his side, Charles casts him a wary eye and says, "There's no free lunch."

Sure enough the sergeant appears, grimacing beneath his patrol cap, and paces before them with the ramrod posture of a man who has seen too many war movies. "We've known this was coming for a long time now, gents. Yesterday I got the order that we're going to the Fight. We'll be deploying for an eighteen-month rotation."

Nate closes his eyes. He thinks of the family portrait above the mantel, Janie reclined on the couch with her feet in his lap, the Lorax lifting himself up, up, and away by the seat of his pants.

He tells Janie immediately, of course, but they wait for the weekend for him to break the news to Cielle. At bedtime she shifts beneath the covers and fixes her serious gaze on him. "I wanna go with you."

He forces a smile, though it feels plastic across his face. "It's a long flight, honey."

"Will there be snacks?"

Nate swallows around the bulge in his throat. "I'll miss you."

"If I go with you, you won't hafta miss me."

He stays with her until she falls asleep, and when he slips from her room, he finds Janie just outside, sitting in the hall. He offers a hand, and she wipes her nose and rises like a lady, and they head back to their bedroom.

The battalion is deposited on an air base in the middle of nowhere, positioned for missions into rural towns. In the Sandbox heat dominates every waking minute. The thermometer regularly creeps to 120; some days Nate pictures it making a cartoon bulge. The soldiers hump an unreasonable amount of gear—ammo and water, flak jackets and helmets, M16s and Beretta M9s coated with PVD film to withstand the sand, which rises into yellow-orange dust storms at the slightest provocation. Grit gets in their guns, their sweat; it turns the collars of their green-and-khaki ACUs to sandpaper. Nate's rucksack frame digs into his shoulder above the flak jacket, buffing the skin to an angry red. The moisture-wicking socks don't wick. No matter how much he drinks, he still pisses bright yellow.

A few weeks in, while sweeping a house, they come upon a retarded man-boy shackled to an outhouse. The weathered soldiers joke and laugh, and Nate, who has lost his breath at the sight, realizes that he will need to navigate a steep learning curve to make it here.

Somehow, despite it all, Charles's optimism remains undiminished. He is one of the rare few for whom war is not hell. On patrol he is laid back, deals easily with the locals, and has a sixth sense for snipers.

The months blend into a single sun-baked episode. They get shot at and do some shooting, mostly returning fire at sand dunes and heaps of rubble. They play policeman and janitor and try to avoid getting blown up by IEDs, car bombs, and booby-trapped corpses.

During morning formation one day, it is announced that their eighteen-month deployment has been extended to twenty-two months. That night Nate takes a very long shower. He buys an AT&T card at the PX and heads to the phone center. The booths are lined wall to wall, as in a prison, with hard wooden chairs. In the stall he is assigned for his ten-minute allotment, someone has scrawled, IF THE ARMY WANTED YOU TO HAVE A WIFE, THEY WOULD'VE ISSUED YOU ONE.

Janie's voice trembles when she hears him, as it always does. "Still alive?"

"I think so."

"Cielle keeps calling you on her play phone, having conversations with you. She sits there dialing and dialing."

His mouth is too dry to swallow. "Can I talk to her?"

"Of course. Hang on."

Some rustling, then Cielle says, "Knock-knock."

"Who's there?"

"Smell mop."

Nate smiles. "I won't do it. I shall not. I shall not be fooled."

Cielle giggles. Then her tone shifts. "Why can't I ever call *you*?"

"It's hard to get through here, baby. I have to call you."

"That's not fair."

"No. It's not."

"Zachary C called me Thunderthighs when I went up to write on the board, and everyone laughed. He had to say it all *loud*."

According to Janie, Cielle has been eating at a steady pace in the seventeen months since Nate's deployment. His guilt mixes with rage. He wants to cut off Zachary C's head and feed it to jackals, but all he can do here, in a prison-size phone booth on the far side of the world, is say, "I'm sorry, baby."

"That's okay. I drew you a picture at school. Come home and see it?" A pause. "Daddy?"

"I can't, baby."

"Why not?"

"It's too far. But I will."

"Promise? Promise you'll come home?"

He pictures her first beach trip—soggy diaper, pink suit, floppy hat, her standing against the backdrop of the waves, clear as a Kodak—and feels a mounting pressure behind his face. He thinks of his mother at the end. Her mouth, rimmed with cold sores, sipping ice water through a straw. The weight of her absence in the house. How his father crawled into a bottle and evaporated. And he saw himself at Cielle's age, alone at the kitchen counter, eating Cap'n Crunch for dinner.

"Yes," he tells Cielle. "I promise."

* * *

The next morning he is awakened by Charles at
oh-dark-hundred. They've been tasked with finding a
guy possessing critical information, who, judging by the
photograph, is not exactly distinctive in appearance.
Charles is not worried about the mission, however; his
biggest concern is his mother's cookies, which arrived
yesterday in a care package. Charles does not want to
eat the cookies but is too respectful to throw them
away. He owes much to his mother, not least his irrepressible good nature. A single parent, she lavished her
only child with endless love and support. But while
Grace Brightbill is a world-class mother, she is a terrible baker. Conflicted, Charles carries her package down
the hall as if he has been burdened with the custody of
a holy relic.

Rubbing his eyes, Nate trudges outside to where their
convoy patrol waits in the dark, the men stuffed into
Hummers. The interpreter, a bone-skinny teenager with
sleepy eyes, wears a too-big helmet, a threadbare rucksack left by someone from a previous rotation, and a
T-shirt with the sleeves cut off. The shirt features the
Adidas trefoil logo across the chest and, written beneath in the appropriate font, ABIBAS. The 'terp smiles
at Nate and Charles, showing a sideways front tooth,
and says, "What up, niggahs?"

Nate says, "Mah brothah," and they bump fists.

On the jostling ride, Nate is distracted by Janie's
words from last night, upset that he can't be on the other
end of his daughter's pretend phone calls. Charles is
still going on about his mom's shitty cookies, so finally

one of the guys says, "Give 'em to Abibas." The 'terp receives them with a smile, they vanish into the threadbare rucksack, and Nate enjoys a few hours of relative silence.

By the time they arrive at the town center, the sun has asserted its presence. They get out and scan the surroundings, their M16s aimed at the ground but tightly held. All around are cinder-block walls, street dogs, TV dishes nailed to corrugated roofs. And eyes everywhere. Windows. Rooftops. Doorways. People talking on cell phones, whispering, ducking from sight. A quartet of old women in burkas, all expanses of black cloth and jutting chins, stare from a front porch, as still and craggy as a rock garden, the skin under their eyes so dark it seems grafted on. Looking through the open door behind them, Nate sees a child-size coffin.

Nate's squad heads to a house with the front door busted off the hinges from the last raid. At least twenty people are jammed into the front room, which has a vague barnyard smell. A rug covers the cement floor, the walls are bare aside from piña-colada-size Iraqi and U.S. flags stuck in the cracks. Everyone inside is focused on a TV the size of a toaster. The men command the couch, holding hands. The women sit on the floor chewing flatbread. A little girl stands in the middle of the room, hitting a paddleball. *Whack whack whack*.

The men rise and offer tea, but the mood changes when the sergeant pulls the women into the next room, as is SOP. Nate takes off his Wiley X sunglasses so he can make eye contact as he helps settle everyone down.

He figures that ordering people around in their own house is disrespectful enough when you're not sporting shades on top of it. The girl continues—*whack whack whack*—but this seems not to bother anyone except Nate, who sees his own daughter in her deep brown eyes. The soldiers show the photo of the man they're after, but no one knows anything; the entire assemblage has gone as deaf, blind, and dumb as the proverbial three monkeys.

Charles comes in from the back with a skinny little man who has plastic zip ties around his hands. Shaggy hair frames the guy's drawn face, and he wears a white man-dress and black flip-flops.

"Found him hiding behind the generator," Charles says.

They get Abibas over to the man, who denies being whoever he is supposed to be. The dispute continues in translation, Abibas jotting down parts of the exchange in his notebook, and finally the sergeant lowers his radio and says, "They want him in *now*. I'm calling up a helo. You six get him to the meet point. Overbay, you're in charge."

The little girl trails the half squad out and follows at a distance, her face betraying no emotion or interest, the paddleball never ceasing its elastic dance. *Whack whack whack*.

They trudge under the heat, the houses turning to shacks, the shacks eventually giving way to sand dunes. The captive makes not a noise. Abibas is perspiring through his clothes, and McGuire makes a crack that maybe the sweat stain'll fix the spelling of his damn shirt. The little girl with Cielle's eyes crests the rise with them—*whack whack whack*—and there below, the Black Hawk waits. They pile in, Charles waving good-bye at the girl who stands silhouetted against the sun, her paddle in perpetual motion. The helo vibrates and shudders, revving to life.

Abibas shouts at Nate, "Damn eet to shit. I forget my notebook. Sarge tell me must *always* have notebook. At house. I go back."

He looks ill with concern, so Nate waves him off duty, figuring where they're heading there'll be professional interpreters, and the kid scrambles down and starts to jog away. The Black Hawk begins to lift.

"Hey!" Charles shouts after him, pointing at the threadbare rucksack wedged between the seat and the cabin floor. "You forgot my mom's cookies!"

Abibas stops and looks back at them.

Then he turns and runs.

The seconds slow to a molasses crawl. The Black Hawk hovers four feet above the sand. All six soldiers have gone as stiff as statues in a half rise above their seats, oriented toward the rucksack. Nate is nearest. It is right there across from him. Above the panicked roar inside his head, Nate hears the pledge he made last night to Cielle. *Promise? Promise you'll come home?* And he cannot unlock his muscles.

From the seat beside him, Charles leaps. He lands atop the rucksack, smothering it, and a brilliant white light frames his body as the bomb detonates. The Black Hawk pitches to the right, the pilot overcorrects, and they lurch into a nose-down spin. Nate sees the fan of the beating rotors kiss the sand, and then there is a great violence of physics and an eardrum-rending screech. Images and sensations strobe, rapid-fire: The slid-back door. Weightlessness. Nate's open mouth pressed to the sand.

He rises, uneven on his feet. An explosion surges behind him, a wave of heat propelling him to his knees. Atop the dune the girl bears silent witness, the *whack whack whack* lost beneath the roar of flame. There are parts everywhere, parts of flesh and metal. Half face-less, McGuire is screaming and holding his severed leg, and then he stops screaming. It is suddenly silent. Sand swirls, settling like rain. Though a whoosh of white noise streams in Nate's ears, he hears a ragged breathing coming from somewhere, and he spins in the cloud of grit and yells, "Charles! Where are you? Where the fuck are you?" and realizes he is stepping on his friend's hand. Charles is alive, his gut a muddle of tat-tered fabric and dark, dark blood. His hands press into his stomach farther than they should, and his eyes are wild and rolling.

Everyone else is dead. Nate's radio shattered. Sup-plies on fire. The nearest medic with the squad back in town.

Nate stands dumbly still for a moment, then crouches and hoists Charles over his shoulder. Charles gives off a sound that is not human. Nate staggers up the slope, past the girl silently watching with Cielle's eyes— *whack whack whack*—and Charles is howling and sob-bing, *"—don't leave me don't leave me don't you—"*

Nate runs. Pain screeches down his spine, ignites

his muscles. The heat rising through his combat boots and Charles's weight on his shoulder are oppressive; the burn spreads through his thighs, his calves, the taut muscles of his groin. He feels as though he is inside a pizza oven. Charles is sputtering and shrieking, the journey a jarring kind of hell—*don't leave me don't leave me don't you leave me*—and Nate's shirt is saturated with his friend's insides. He runs harder as if to stop the blood draining into his eyes. His vision is a painted haze of brown and red, red and brown, smudged together as if by a child's fingers.

"Help me!" Nate shouts. "Somebody . . .'elp . . . me. . . ."

Charles is quieter now: ". . . *don't . . . leave . . . please*. . . ."

Nate's lips are coated with dust, and his voice is gone; he can't generate saliva. He blanks out on his feet, still running. Then suddenly the squad is all around, the sergeant trying to pull Charles off his back, saying, "Let go. Nate. You can let go now. Let go of him. Let go."

Nate topples over, Charles landing beside him, long dead, the blank stare inches from Nate's face. And Nate is talking, but no one can hear him.

"He's okay," Nate pants into the hot sand. "He's okay. Just make him breathe again."

Chapter 7

When the ramp of the C-17 lowers, bringing into sight the wavering black tarmac of the Los Alamitos Army Airfield, a chorus of cheers goes up from the plane's cargo hold, and Nate spills out with a sea of camouflage into the temperate Southern California air. He spots Janie and Cielle on the runway, waiting behind the saw-horses. Cielle looks bigger, her face round and smiling. She and Janie are jumping up and down, beautiful. He runs to them, and they smash together in a three-way hug. "Welcome home, Husband," Janie tells him, beaming, and he says, "I missed you, Wife." But the jubilation quickly recedes, leaving behind a ponderous silence that lasts the car ride home.

Nate walks through every room in the house, the house he loves, trying to make it his own again. It does not feel like he belongs here, or anywhere else. A void has opened up between him and the rest of the world. He reminds himself it has been just seventy-two hours since his sprint across the dunes with Charles bleeding out on his back. How Nate feels here in Santa Monica—it's just temporary.

When his pacing carries him downstairs, Janie and Cielle are waiting in the family room, bursting with excitement. A large cardboard box sporting an oversize red bow sits on the carpet. Cielle says, "C'mon hurry hurry open it."

He lifts the lid and peers inside. A rustle of tan fur, and then a puppy head pokes into view. The pup scrambles up his arms into his face, slurping, and Nate holds him, running a hand down the strip of reversed fur on the spine.

Cielle says, "He's a Rhodesian ridgeback. They used to be lion hunters. He'll grow up huge, to a hundred pounds. He's yours, but Mom said I could name him. Wanna know his name? It's Casper. Like the ghost."

Janie adds, "They say it helps, I guess. Adjust. A dog. Unconditional love, no conversation."

Nate squeezes him, smells him, lost in the warmth, the quiet magnificence. He hugs his wife and his daughter, Casper squirming from lap to lap, and for a single moment, he forgets the burden he still carries on his back.

He sleeps fitfully, knowing the task in store for him tomorrow. Back on the eve of his redeployment, a gnawing need drove him to ask his lieutenant if he could serve the death notifications to the families of the men killed on his watch. His request went up the chain and was quickly approved—it was hardly a sought-after job—and he was handed a pamphlet to read on the flight home providing guidelines for Casualty Notification Officers.

It is not until he gets to the front door of the McGuires' house that he realizes how woefully unprepared he is. Every detail embeds thunderously in his brain—the paint peeling on the door frame, the sudden laxness in Mrs. McGuire's face at the sight of him, the rasp of the screen against his shoulder as he steps inside. McGuire's father, a hulking rectangle of a man, creaks the floorboards of the hall and then sits across from Nate, his dry hands cracking at the knuckles when he grips the armrests of his chair. Nate doesn't remember what he says, but then Mrs. McGuire's eyes are leaking and Mr. McGuire is asking him something.

Nate musters his voice. "Yes, sir, he died honorably."

"Was he in pain?" McGuire's mother asks.

Nate thinks of McGuire gripping his severed leg. The screams. He says, "No."

Mr. McGuire: "Did you kill the bastard who got him?"

"No, sir." Nate rises and, as instructed, delivers a small bag with McGuire's effects. His stomach burns as McGuire's mother sifts through the contents—a cross pendant, dog tags, a G-Shock watch with a smashed face—and feels the need to say, "I can't imagine what it's like to lose a son—"

"Two," the big man says sharply. "We lost both." He looks up and away, a distant glint in his eyes. "How's the war going, son?"

"I hope we've turned a corner, sir," Nate says lamely.

"Yeah, what corner is that?" He snickers at the silence. "We had a name for that corner, too, when I was in the Corps. We called it Clusterfuck Bend."

Nate cannot think of a response, so he keeps his mouth closed.

"His body?" Mr. McGuire asks.

"It's been well taken care of. It shipped from Ramstein, full honors rendered at each point of transfer—"

"I don't give a shit about that. What kind of shape?" A pause. "Well?"

"We didn't recover his whole body, sir."

"What's missing?" Mr. McGuire wets his lips. "Go on, son. If I can take it, you sure as hell can."

"A leg. And . . . and . . . part of his head."

Mrs. McGuire's eyes move abruptly to the ceiling.

"Who went down with him?" Mr. McGuire asks.

Nate lists the names, ending with Charles.

Mrs. McGuire says, "You tell their mothers and fathers thank you for us."

It is a full minute before Nate dares to speak again. Though he has been forbidden to offer any details about the activities surrounding the death, he hears himself start to spill: "It was an IED hidden in a rucksack. Right in front of me. I should've gotten to it before it went off. I could have—"

The deep voice cuts him off. "See, son. Now you're making *your* problems *our* problem. Don't ya think we got enough problems tonight?"

Nate's entire body is trembling. "Yes, sir."

"So act like you got some sense in you." The man's

face has turned ruddy. "Don't leave us with more to chew on. See, you'll go on home, eat dinner with your wife, tuck your kids into bed. You'll move on. We'll be here. So you think of us from time to time."

Mrs. McGuire says, softly, *"Jim,"* and he silences.

Nate looks down into his lap for a long time. "May I please use your restroom?"

She points. "Powder room off the hall there."

Nate runs the water to cover the sound of his vomiting. He splashes water on his face, dries his eyes with a pink hand towel that smells of floral detergent. Studying his reflection, he vows to learn how to do this better. He squares himself, emerges, delivers the necessary information as best he can, and shows himself out. As he drives away, his sweat-drenched uniform clings to him like a bad dream.

Johnson's family, next up, is kind and appreciative, and that is all the worse. Then comes Miles's step-mother, who says, "Well, then," and closes the door. Bilton's wife asks Nate to drive her to school to tell her son. The following day begins with a sad meeting in a church basement—stained coffeemaker, cinder-block walls, and unbroken wailing. Tommy K's mother takes her son's baseball cap from the bag of effects, presses it to her face, and inhales. By dusk the compounded effect of so much suffering has left Nate utterly void. He welcomes the numbness, because he fears that if he starts crying, he will crack wide open.

Arriving at Charles's childhood house, Nate real-izes he has saved this, the worst, for last. Inside, he sees Grace Brightbill bustling at the sink, a plump, pleasant-looking woman with dyed blond hair cut in a bob. He recalls her pride at every one of Charles's papers, no matter how bad. The report cards pinned to the fridge by photo magnets of Charles in T-ball. Nate sits in his car, replaying her son's voice—*don't leave me don't leave me don't you leave me*—and feeling the heat of the explosion, the sand raining down on him. How he himself couldn't leap for the rucksack.

And so Charles had.

Nate struggles to keep breathing. Self-loathing swells and washes over him, and he realizes he is too craven to proceed. Driving away, he dials headquarters to request that someone else be sent to serve Charles's death notice. He knows already that this will be a decision he will regret for the rest of his life, but he cannot stop himself from making it.

The next day, depleted and emotionally hungover, he takes Cielle to lunch as promised. She eats ten chicken nuggets and then five more. When she asks for a sundae, he says, "I think you've had enough, honey."

"But I can't get *full*."

As they walk out, a teenage kid accidentally pops a ketchup packet in his hand, and red goo snakes down his wrist, his forearm. All of a sudden, Nate's face goes hot and he is back in the Sandbox, spinning in the wake of the explosion, his ears ringing. McGuire is there holding his severed leg and—

"Daddy? *Daddy?*"

He has blanked out completely in the doorway of the

fast-food joint. He swallows hard, turns his head from the guy, and says, "Let's go."

There are other signs, too, in the weeks that follow. He cannot watch a plane in flight without bracing for it to explode. Despite the mounting bills, he cannot bring himself to go back to his job as a buyer of men's suits. He and Janie make love with more urgency, as if they're trying to hold on to something. They talk less afterward, Janie rolling over into a paperback, Nate staring at the ceiling, watching the fan blades spin like the rotors of a helo and reliving those instants confronting the left-behind rucksack. Night after night, lying beside his wife, he changes the dance steps, rewrites history. A thousand times he watches Abibas pause on the dune and stare back at them, then turn and run. Nate looks over at the rucksack. But in this alternate history, he puts his promise to Cielle out of his mind; he unlocks his legs; he leaps.

In the morning when Nate brushes his teeth, he hears Charles's voice in his head, sees him sitting on the edge of the bathtub. Charles is in his green-and-khaki ACUs and wears his combat helmet, but one thing is different: There is a massive hole blown in his stomach, and he is dripping blood onto the ivory bathroom tiles.

"What the fuck?" Charles says. "It's indulgent, all this moping and shit. Get over it already. You're *home*."

"I know," Nate says through a mouthful of toothpaste. "I *know* that. But I can't get it from my head into my gut."

Charles peers through the hole in his stomach wall.

He flexes, making the intestines wiggle, then looks up with a pleased smile. Noting Nate's expression, he assumes a serious face. "Don't get boring."

Nate spits foam into the sink, rinses. "Sorry. I'm hung up on killing you."

"That crap again?" Charles waves a bloody hand. "What could you have done?"

For the first time, Nate actually speaks out loud. "I could've jumped first."

He goes in search of work but inevitably winds up sitting with Casper on the curb by the car wash, watching the vehicles go in filthy and come out spotless, that toxic film reel throwing images against the walls of his skull, corroding him from the inside out. No matter how many times he works and reworks the equation he is locked inside, it is destined to tally up the same—two dead legs, three frozen seconds, threadbare rucksack five feet away.

Nate takes Casper out late when the neighborhood is still enough to mute the noise in his head. One night he arrives home to find Janie swaying on the porch swing. "Maybe you should bring Cielle on your walks. I'm worried about her weight."

He says, "I'm not home most nights until she's in bed."

"Maybe that's *why* she's getting so heavy," Janie says. "She's been comforting herself with food since you—"

"I know." He feels a burn across his face. "I just . . . can't clear my head right now. It's just temporary."

"Maybe if you were busier . . . ?"

He waves a hand, but the gesture loses momentum. "I can't buy men's suits again, Janie."

"I don't want you to buy men's suits. I don't care about the *money*. I'll pick up an extra shift at the hospital if I have to, to cover the mortgage."

"I will *always* make sure the mortgage is covered. I just need a little time. I've been home five fucking weeks."

Her face reddens, bringing the freckles into relief. "You know what?" She takes a deep breath, lets it out slowly. "We don't do this. We don't talk to each other this way."

He stares at her, and she stares back, unflinching. Agitated, Casper trots to Janie's side and whimpers until she pets him.

"I can't reach you, Nate. No one gets through to you."

"You do."

"Not anymore."

Her face holds so much sadness he has to look away.

Janie says, "I know you loved Charles—God, we *all* loved Charles. But you have to let go of what happened."

"I can't."

"Why?"

Though he never considered it, the truth is right there, waiting, and it comes out in a heated rush: "Because then I'd be abandoning him. Again."

She receives this, bracing into the weight of it. She nods once. The breeze blows through him.

"When you were gone," she says, "Cielle would

crawl into bed where you used to lie. How do I explain to her that now that you're home, you're still not home?"

He cannot lift his eyes from the porch boards.

Janie says, "You are the only man I want to be with. I feel like I dreamed you up playing 'boyfriend' when I was nine. I love you too much for us to turn into roommates. Some couples can do that, maybe. But not us. Doing that with you . . . It would be worse than not being with you."

He clears his throat. "You and Cielle are *all* I want. But I can't . . . I can't find my way back here."

Janie quotes him to himself: "Stop fighting," she says. "I got you."

His mouth is dry. "I don't know how."

Silence. The porch swing creaks, Janie's toes touching the wood as though stirring water. She says, "We build our own cells, brick by brick."

He thinks of his father shuffling around the house after his mom's funeral, how he'd blank out in front of the microwave sometimes, staring at the number pad, unable to proceed.

He says, "Maybe this is what I have to do right now."

She swallows hard, then says, "I have not a thing to say I won't regret later."

He walks upstairs into their bathroom, shuts the door, and sits on the closed toilet. A while after, her footsteps enter the bedroom, the sheets rustle, and the light clicks off. Through the thin door, he hears her crying softly, and though he wants to hold her more than anything, he cannot rise, cannot turn the doorknob. His courage is gone; he lost it back in the Sandbox in that goddamned helicopter. He lost it when he made his daughter a promise that he'd come home to her. He thinks back to the day Charles dragged him to the beach, Janie's cries carrying across the water. Nate was The One Who Had Jumped into the Riptide When No One Else Would. He had borne her to shore. And now he is huddled on a toilet, shuddering, scared to open a bathroom door.

He waits until her breathing grows regular, then sneaks out to slip into his side of the bed.

Later that night screams awaken him. He bolts off the mattress and his boots sink into burning sand and there is smoke in the air and he is yelling for Charles: "Where are you? Where are you?" The screams keep coming in the dark, and he stumbles and smacks his head into the corner of the wall by the door. Blood streams down his forehead, tacky and hot, and then his eyes are stinging and he lurches through the door, knocking it free of the top hinge and Janie is at his side holding his arm and then he sees Abibas staring with unreadable eyes and he shoves and Janie flies back and hits the wall and he is staggering down the hall, Charles's blood streaming down his face, bellowing, "Where are you? Where the fuck are you?" and the screams have stopped suddenly but Casper is barking and he fills his daughter's doorway but she is gone. Janie is behind him, yelling, her cheek carrying a plum-colored bruise and her words flood in: "Stop it! You're scaring her. You're *scaring* her!" and he follows her quaking finger to where Cielle has tried to wedge herself beneath her bed to hide. Janie goes to her and holds her.

He wipes his forehead, and his arm comes away dark. Quietly panicking at what he has done, he says, "No, no. I don't scare her. I don't. Do I scare you?"

And Cielle looks out from beneath the dark row of her bangs and says, "Yes."

His insides crumble. He stands, swaying, mouth ajar. His skin on fire, he retreats slowly into their bedroom, Casper at his heels. Nate washes the blood from his face. Uses Band-Aids to close the gash at his hairline. Finds an instant cold pack in the emergency kit beneath the sink. When he steps out, Janie stands watching, pale, silent.

He says, "I am so, so sorry I hurt you."

"You didn't know what you were doing. Cielle was crying. She had a nightmare."

"It is unacceptable what I did."

"I know you didn't mean it."

"It doesn't matter," he says. "I need to get myself . . ."

"What?"

"To a place where I deserve to live here again."

Janie looks away. Her eyes well. "It wasn't supposed to be like this."

He can't find any words. His throat clutches. Desperate for something to do, he cracks the ice pack, but she says, "I'm fine."

He holds it out. He can barely look at the growing spot of black on her beautiful pale cheek. "Please?"

She lifts the ice pack from his hand.

Casper follows him down the hall. Cielle is tucked in again, but wide awake. He sits at the edge of her bed. Casper curls up in the pink nest she has made for him from an old comforter. He keeps a wary eye on Nate, which shatters Nate's heart anew. When they are out, Casper will not allow strangers to get between him and Cielle, and that is how Nate feels now—like a stranger.

He says, "I'm so sorry I scared you."

She says, "It's okay, Daddy."

"No," he says. "It isn't." She stares up at him with her rich brown eyes, and he strokes her nose once with his finger.

"Why can't it be like it used to?" she asks.

He swallows around the lump inside his throat. "It just can't right now, baby."

"Why not? Don't I get a vote? I never get a say in *any*thing."

"We don't always get a say in what happens to us," he says gently. He kisses her on the forehead, breathes in the no-tears-shampoo scent of her.

He strokes her back until she falls asleep, then goes downstairs to try to catch his breath. As he paces the unlit living room, it strikes him that he is denying himself his wife and daughter as a punishment for cherishing them so much that he couldn't unlock his legs on that helicopter and leave them behind. He pauses before the family portrait. The three of them falling over, laughing, propping one another up. He vows to get back to that place.

What he's dealing with, it's just temporary.

And yet five years pass.

Five years that see further dismantling of the life he knew. Nate's journey through that time is weightless, stunned, much like his flight from the spiraling helicopter. The point of impact comes in a medical office, from a bearded neurologist with kind, wise features—precisely how one wants one's neurologist to look, particularly when he's delivering a diagnosis like this. And Nate realizes that up until that moment, when it came to bad news, he'd never had a sufficient yardstick for comparison.

He drives away in a daze, cloaked in a black cloud of dread. He pictures his mother languishing in her hospice bed, dying by millimeters, her features caving in on themselves. How his father, too, was eaten from the inside, hollowed out like a rubber Halloween mask, the eyeholes empty. As a nine-year-old, Nate had vowed that if he was ever lucky enough to have a family of his own, he would never, ever let it erode like that.

And so he tells no one—not Janie, not his daughter. At all costs he will spare them the suffering he learned all too well in his own childhood. Soon enough he will not be able to control the deterioration of his grip, the drying out of his eyes, the strength of the breath in his lungs. But he can pick a time and a date and a ledge high enough to offer a good view and a long drop.

He just has to do it while he still can.

And pray that nothing interrupts. Like, say, six hooded thugs robbing a bank.

Because then he might find himself sitting on an exam table with a neatly stitched stab wound, alive against his own goddamned will.

LONG WAY UP

Necessity has the face of a dog.
—Gabriel García Márquez

Chapter 8

Leaving the hospital, Nate rode shotgun in the unmarked sedan, ignoring the throbbing in his shoulder and doing his best to keep up. Abara—who'd given no first name—drove fast and talked faster. Easy confidence, slender athletic build, dense hair shaved to the bronzed flesh at the sides and back. He could've been thirty, or twenty-four. "So first of all, forget that shit you've seen on TV," Abara said. "We don't always travel in twos, we're not all dickheads, and"—a gesture to his charcoal golf shirt with the gold seal at the breast—"we don't have to wear suits and ties." He flashed an unreasonably handsome smile, complete with dimples. "Also, we play well with others. We do have juris, but LAPD's got a talented team over at Robbery Special, so I'm not gonna march in there and bark about how I'm taking over their case." He picked a speck of lint off the spit-polished dashboard. "You sure you don't need to go home, catch your breath, change?"

Nate looked down at his crisp new T-shirt, donated by the hospital. Crease marks at the chest and stomach from where it had been folded, presumably piled in a stack of other clothes awaiting stabbing victims. "Nah, I'm fine."

They reached the police cordon, and Abara slowed the Chevy Tahoe and flashed his badge. "Marcus Abara, FBI. I got the hero with me. Gonna go walk the scene."

The cop's eyes were hidden behind a pair of Oakley Blades, but he lifted the reflective band of glass to Nate and said, "Nice work in there."

Nate's heartbeat was quickening in proximity to the bank. He nodded. "Thanks."

Beyond the sawhorses, media and rubberneckers had massed. One woman was crying and kneading her sweater in her fists—a sister of a victim? It struck Nate that she could also be a relative of one of the men he'd killed this morning.

He had to rewind the thought: *One of the men he'd killed this morning.*

One head lifted higher than the rest, rising above the crowd as if on a stick. A man's rough-hewn face— lantern jaw, mashed nose, slash of mouth. Flat eyes fastened on Nate as his gaze swept across. Nate did a double take, but the face was gone.

Abara's eyes were on him and then on the sea of folks. "What?"

"Just a guy in the crowd. Looked . . . I don't know. Menacing, I guess."

He put it down to nerves but couldn't help noticing Abara file it away in some private place.

They drove through and parked on the sidewalk. Before leaving the hospital, Nate had filled in first a patrolman, then two detectives, and finally Abara on what had gone down in the bank—or at least a *version* of what had gone down. Assumptions had been made before Nate had been sutured up and available to correct the record. By the time he'd entered the discussion, he was already party to the lie, and the lie had ossified into something hard and immovable. It went like this: Nate had been in the bank bathroom; he had heard shots; he had climbed onto the ledge, inched his way around, and saved the day. The questions—which had been detailed and copious—had picked up mostly at the saved-the-day part. And he'd been happy to pick up there as well. Did everyone need to know he'd been planning to pancake himself into a Dumpster? He would be made the subject of a suicide interventionist, and then there'd be a seventy-two-hour psych hold—no, that wouldn't do at all. So rather than lay himself bare to be probed and picked at, he'd help through a few steps of the investigation, resort to Plan B, and let everyone figure it out when he wasn't around to feel stupid about it.

Walking toward the bank entrance, Nate was surprised to hear his name shouted out. Instinctively he stopped and looked at the swarming reporters, and the agent had to press a hand to the small of his back to keep him moving. In the elevator Abara knuckled the button for the eleventh floor. As they rose, Nate thought about the last time he'd ridden up in this car, how he'd been sweating through his shirt in anticipation of taking the leap. And yet, implausibly, here he was again, back in the same little box, ascending to the same floor, Sisyphus in the age of technology. Abara caught him smirking at himself, and it seemed to pique his interest.

"You seem remarkably steady," the agent said, "given, you know, everything."

"I must be faking it well," Nate said.

"Impressive stuff. The ledge, the window, the timing. I mean, *six armed men*." Abara whistled. "Guess that high-end military training kicked in."

Nate studied Abara back. Was that an accusatory edge in his voice? Or just Nate's guilt working on him, putting a paranoid filter on an ordinary observation? He knew the truth of who he was—Nate Overbay, failed suicide—and the hero routine was starting to wear thin.

"Look," Nate said, "I was a drafted dipshit. I don't know how to kill a guy with a chopstick or anything. I'm just an army grunt who learned how to shoot a gun."

"You laid low five trained gunmen."

"Element of surprise. And a lotta luck."

"I glanced through your military jacket," Abara said. "You went through quite a bit over there."

"Not as much as some people."

A familiar voice sailed out from behind him: "*I'll say.*"

Nate half turned, and sure enough there Charles stood, dripping on the elevator floor, chest blown open, heart visible through the bars of his ribs, hanging like a clump of grapes. He gave a big smile, dried blood cracking on his cheek. "You really stepped in it this time, podnah."

As always, impeccable timing.

Nate turned away, annoyed.

"*Someone's* uppity today," Charles said. "Prefers to hang out with his *alive* friends. No, really, it's cool. I get it. Ignore me. But can your alive friends do . . . *this*?"

Horrible moist sound effects from behind Nate. He didn't even want to know. It dawned on him that Abara was staring at him expectantly.

Nate did his best to look attentive. "Sorry. What?"

"I said, I had some buddies came back with PTSD. You dealing with anything like that that might be relevant to how things went down today?"

Out of the corner of his eye, Nate could see Charles poking his tongue through a hole in his cheek. "Nah," Nate said. "Got over that a long time ago."

The elevator doors spread to a panorama of cops, CSI, and bank security workers. Radios bleated, iPhones chimed, cameras winked. Charles had vanished—he hated commotions—and Nate found himself immersed in bloody memories of the morning. He moved forward on numb legs, the pill bottles rattling in his pocket, untouched. By the lobby, Abara held down the crime-scene tape, and Nate high-stepped over. The black security guard was gone, but evidence cones marked the outline of his body. The smudged pool of blood looked shiny and gelatinous beneath the overhead fluorescents.

A burly little man hurried over and blew out a breath, exasperated. He was balding, and the male-pattern swirl had lifted from his pate. It had been a long day. He introduced himself as the bank director of physical security, shook Nate's hand earnestly, then launched into the update.

"Looks like they dodged the parking-lot cameras downstairs, rode the service elevator up. So much for eleventh-floor security. As you saw, dark clothes, not form-fitting, big boots. Hard to read height, weight. No flesh showing anywhere, so witnesses couldn't get a read on their ethnicity."

"Considerate of them to leave their bodies behind," Abara said.

Nate was having a hard time lifting his focus from the crimson smudges on the floor tile. He thought of the guard's eyes, rolled back almost to solid white.

The security director continued, "Before they hit the vault, they broke down the door to the security closet and unplugged the DVR box that caches the digital footage."

Abara made a popping sound with his lips. "So they could work the vault with their hoods off."

"Right," Nate mumbled. He pictured the man stepping into sight in the vault doorway, gripping the circular saw, the hood pushed up atop his head. His ear, torn away in a spray of black blood. How he'd looked back and Nate had shot him again through the forehead.

He heard Abara's voice, as if from a distance. ". . . you okay?"

Nate nodded quickly. "Fine, fine."

"These guys were pros, moved fast and hard," the security director continued. "No one could get to an alarm. Our vault door's eighteen inches of steel, tool-resistant for thirty minutes, but it was, of course, open for the business day. So they sailed in through the day gate. They used a diamond-tipped rescue saw to hit one of the quarter-inch Diebolds, got a little over three hundo into a duffel. Which, thanks to you"—a nod to Nate—"is still sitting on the floor in there. They were razoring into the safe-deposit boxes when you went in guns blazing."

Abara was nodding along; he'd heard this all already. Clearly, repetition was a big part of the investigation— sifting through the evidence again and again, looking for flecks of gold.

The robbers' bodies lay where they'd fallen, hoods now tugged off, flight suits sliced open and peeled back like flayed skin. Nate walked where directed, minding the cones, the blood spatter. He found himself crouching over the first corpse in the lobby, regarding the clean-shaven face. *You're gonna want to listen now, girlie.* So much less menacing without the black hood and bug eyes. Younger than he'd have thought.

Nate wanted to reach down and touch the waxy features. "He's what? Twenty-seven, twenty-eight?"

"This one?" Abara checked a black leather notepad. "Twenty-six."

Nate wondered about the next of kin. Who would answer the door to the death notification? Sickly mother? Pregnant girlfriend? Nine-year-old son, home from soccer practice? Gazing at the bodies sprawled on the tile, Nate was all too aware of how the loss of these lives would ripple out. Awe settled in, a sense of the enormity of what he had done, but he expected to feel something more, too. A hint of remorse, perhaps. But no. There were too many other parts to this equation. Those bullets riddling the bank manager's stiff pantsuit. The cool white hand he'd gripped through the window. A young girl's earlobe, darkened with her mother's blood.

The security director had been pulled away, but Abara was still at Nate's side, asking a question: "You said the sixth man had an accent?"

"Eastern Europeanish," Nate replied.

"Russian? Polish?"

"More Russian, I'd say. But I don't know."

Abara gestured at the bodies. "Local dirty white boys, all five. Accent no makee the sense, hoss. You sure you weren't hearing things?"

"I'm sure. Do you know who they were? The dead ones?"

"Yup. They're an Inland Empire team. Been on our radar a little more than three years. But a few things don't add up. One: What the hell were they doing in Santa Monica? They've never even made it west of Victorville for a job. And two: What's with the sixth man? They've always run jobs as a five crew."

"Maybe they recruited," Nate said.

"I don't know. Five men's generally the most you see in a job like this. Six is the tipping point for logistics—more trouble than help."

"The sixth man seemed to be the crew leader."

"So you said. In that case why would a new recruit run the show?"

Nate closed his eyes, put himself back in the vault. The scuff of that boot behind him—Number Six, lying in wait with the letter opener. The whistle of movement, steel through air, and the hot pain in his shoulder. He heard the voice, a low rush of menace—*He will be greatly angered by you*—and couldn't ward off a shudder. "They were working for someone."

"Right," Abara said. " 'He' from 'He will make you pay.' " They'd been through this as well. Stepping past the teller gate, the agent gazed at the blasted drywall of the ceiling and ran a hand over his utilitarian buzz cut. "AKS-74U assault carbine."

"You can tell from the bullet holes?" Nate asked.

"No." Abara grinned. "Crime-scene report. Now can you walk me through it?"

"I already have. Several times."

Abara pressed his fingertips together. "I got this wife, yeah? She loses her damn birth-control pills. I'm talking two, three times a week. Not a good thing to lose. And I always tell her, I say, 'Honey. Retrace your steps.' And she argues and argues—Puerto Ricans, right? But when she finally listens? There they are. So what do you think. Can you do that for me?"

Nate said, "Find your wife's birth-control pills?"

No smile. Instead Abara pointed at the window, still cranked open as Nate had left it, a swath of blood across the pane. Nate took a moment, chewing his lip. Then he walked over, set his hands on the sill, and leaned out into the cool dusk air.

"Whoa, cowboy." Abara's voice sounded distant behind him. "Want to reel it back a little?"

Nate pulled himself in. Nothing was left of the teller with the pretty green eyes but a collection of evidence cones at his feet. He set about retracing each move, starting with his tumble through the window over her lifeless body. One detail at a time. The tiny puffs of drywall. The relentless screech of the saw. The bullet sailing past, so close it trailed heat across his cheek. Recounting all this now in relative solitude made it more real, and with every step he took, a black tide rose in his chest, threatening to choke off his words. He had shot two men on the main floor and was stepping back toward the vault when something glinted under a desk, catching his eye. He walked over, crouched, and picked up the pearl clip-on earring. Cradled it in his hand. Flashed on its owner's limp arm unfurling, her rings clacking tile. The black tide climbed into his throat, catching him off guard, and he eased himself down to sit on the floor. Several of the cops paused and looked at him. Then a few CSI techs. The movement around him ground to a halt, the focus of the room pulling to him. He swallowed hard, tried to keep the emotion from his face, but he could feel his cheeks turn to pins and needles.

"Sorry." He clutched the earring, the clasp digging into his palm. "Just give me a sec here."

Abara waved the others to get back to work and squatted next to him. "Take all the time you need."

After Nate caught his breath, he finished the walk-through, ending with his face-to-face with Number Six in the vault. Abara scratched his head with a pen. "Can you look at some security tape, see if you can pick out the crew leader?"

"I thought they wiped out the footage," Nate said.

"We got some in the service elevator and back hall before they pulled the plug on the digital feed."

Nate followed him to a rear office filled with monitors, where the security director and two Robbery-Homicide detectives waited, the screen before them fluttering on pause. The footage showed the robbers crowded in the service elevator, six forms covered with black fabric. The director clicked PLAY, and they all watched the men ride up, waiting to explode into action. Wrists jiggled. Boots tapped. Gun slides were racked, magazines reseated. Every man a jumble of live nerves.

Except one.

Number Six, the smallest of the crew, stood perfectly still, his head on a slight tilt, those patches of mesh staring directly up at the security camera. Staring directly, it seemed, at Nate.

Beneath the crisp folds of his T-shirt, Nate's skin went clammy. The man's quiet poise. No suggestion of what was to come. He might have been riding the elevator up to see a movie or visit a friend. That slender, compact build. The faint accent. *He will make you pay in ways you can't imagine.* The threat recalled sent a blade of ice up Nate's back. He was already dead, ready and willing to find the next opportunity to pull the plug himself. So why be scared?

Maybe because he sensed the promise hidden in that calm voice, the promise that whatever *he* would deliver would be worse than death.

Nate swallowed dryly and pointed at Number Six.

Riding down in the elevator, Abara said, "We're gonna need you at the press conference outside."

"Press conference?" Nate said. "So you're gonna *help* ID me for the guys who want to kill me?"

"The media's already dialed into the story. There's a picture circulating the Web of you walking out of the bank carrying that little girl—looks like a Bruckheimer one-sheet. If we don't trot you out, you'll have media crawling up your ass for weeks. Smile pretty for the cameras, satiate everyone's appetite, and no one'll remember you by tomorrow."

"The guy threatened me. Face-to-face. And I believed him. Whoever his boss is, I killed five of his guys and screwed up his robbery."

"I doubt they'll come after you. Bank robbers and cold-blooded murderers fit different profiles."

"A comforting factoid."

"I'd imagine not." Abara removed a business card and handed it to Nate. "My cell's on the back. Something freaks you out, anything you need, call me. And I'll make sure LAPD has a squad car drive by your place at intervals for a few nights until the scare wears off." Abara took note of Nate's expression and said, "What do you expect? A Secret Service detail?"

"Nah," Nate said. "If I get killed, I get killed."

Abara's smooth forehead wrinkled a bit at that one. They hit the ground floor, their footsteps ticking across the lobby. Abara spun them through the revolving door, and a wave of noise and heat hit them. Bodies and news crews everywhere. In the middle of a small clearing stood a podium. Before Nate could get his bearings, he was ushered forward to the bouquet of microphones, a police captain stepping aside. Nate blinked and gazed out. Above all else there were lights—bright lights that hid the faces of his interlocutors. Questions sailed out of the white blaze.

"When you took them on single-handedly, what were your thoughts?"

Nate moistened his lips. "I was just reacting to what was in front of me. I guess it took me thirty-six years *not* to think for once."

"Did you have a mission plan in mind?"

There was a particular chagrin, Nate realized, in being taken more seriously by others than he took himself. "Point and shoot?" he offered.

A feminine voice from the back: "Were you scared?"

"No, not really. I was angry."

"At what specifically?"

"They killed three people. Kicked a woman in the face. Seemed on the verge of shooting a little girl."

Bass voice in the front row: "So you think they all deserved a death sentence?"

Nate said, "I think if I hadn't shot them, they would've killed more people."

"Yes, but still. There are laws."

Clearly, the reporter intended to goad him. Nate thought about how in the past he might've responded with something appropriate. He sorted through all the replies he'd ordinarily think to make, the placating gestures, the tempered assurances. But then that feeling returned, the sensation he'd encountered as he'd floated through the teller gate, bullets carving the air around his face. *Liberation*. And he replied, "You want laws? Here's a law for you. Don't fucking rob banks and kill innocent people."

A hush descended. A reporter reached over to her cameraman's gear and clicked off the live feed. A firm hand hooked Nate's waist, politely conveying him to the side, and then the police captain replaced him in front of the microphones. "I think that's enough questions for the time being."

Biting off a smile with perfect white teeth, Abara led Nate off. Once they were clear of the crowd, they nodded good-bye, and Nate went to find his trusty, rusty Jeep Wrangler where he'd parked it an eternity ago this morning. Climbing into the driver's seat, he realized that he felt neither embarrassment nor regret over his final reply at the podium. He had said exactly what he'd wanted to. Just as this morning he'd done precisely what he'd needed to. No fear. No capitulation. No paralyzing self-scrutiny. He had—literally—nothing left to lose. He pulled on his seat belt, set his hands on the wheel, and the thought hit him: What a trite goddamned shame that he had to be dying to learn how to live again.

Chapter 9

Plan B: Nate would drive home and kill himself. Handful of Vicodin, some alcohol, a languid drift into the sweet hereafter. Given the press conference, news of his fake hero stint would spread quickly, complicating matters, making him answer questions he'd rather not. It would be best to handle business before opening up the whole can of worms with Janie and Cielle, especially since he'd managed to keep everything from them for this long.

After months with depression gnawing at his skull, he'd settled on a plan and had felt energized. Foot on the accelerator, a last burst of gas to take him over the cliff edge. He had to see it through now before he ran out of steam.

To fortify himself for what was to come, Nate stopped off at a diner for another last meal. The middle-aged waitress had tired eyes, crayon marks on the hem of her uniform, and a pale band of skin around her ring finger. "Triple-scoop hot-fudge sundae?" she asked. "That's it?"

He smiled up at her. "That's it."

He savored each bite and left her a $207 tip—all the money in his wallet. Where he was going, he wouldn't need it.

He was lurching between red lights on Wilshire on his way home when a dark Town Car pulled up beside him. It rolled forward, nosing dangerously into the intersection to bring a tinted back window even with him. He glanced across, sensing a presence behind it. Someone watching. A sheen of perspiration sprang up on his arms, the nape of his neck. He looked at the streetlight. Glanced back over. Menace emanating from that square of black glass. The tint was darker than standard, illegally so. The Town Car was too far forward for him to make out anything of the driver save a sliver of ear and an old-fashioned cap. He drifted up to get a better look, but the Town Car matched his movement precisely, pushing farther out into the red light, making a passing car honk and swerve.

He stopped. The Town Car stopped. That tinted rear window so close now he could reach across and knock on it. He rolled down his window and was proceeding to do just that when the tinted glass moved as well, lowering two inches. A hand emerged, a cigarette stub poking from between the index and middle fingers. A tattoo branded each knuckle, and yet the nails looked manicured, and three stripes showed at the wrist—pale flesh, cream French cuff, dark suit. The smoke reached Nate's nostrils. The cigarette burned down, and the hand adjusted, a quick pulse, and pinched the cherry between the two knuckles. A wisp of black smoke—burning flesh—then the hand let the dead stub fall.

An echo from the bank vault played in Nate's head, that accented voice: *He will make you pay in ways you can't imagine.*

Numbness spread through his body, a stand-in for fear. Slowly he became aware of a cacophony of bleating behind him, the din of horns, and he realized that the light had changed to green sometime ago. He stood on the brake pedal, a game of chicken, the two vehicles blocking a corridor of traffic.

A sharp ring issued from his lap, startling him into a jolt, sending his old-fashioned clamshell cell phone to the floor. He chased it around, and when he straightened back up, the Town Car was gone from its spot beside him, already way up ahead, shrinking to nothing. But one detail grabbed his attention before it vanished: There was no back license plate.

Enduring curses from L.A. drivers all around, he accelerated, glanced at caller ID, then fought the phone open. Jen Brown, his tough-minded boss, calling from downtown. Probably caught wind of the robbery. He said, "I'm okay."

"Good to know," Jen said. "But I wasn't asking."

Maybe word of his fake hero stint *wouldn't* spread quickly.

"I need you to pay a house call," she continued. "Sean and Erica O'Doherty of Encino."

"I don't know," he said. "It's not been the easiest day."

"Imagine what theirs is gonna look like."

He took a deep breath. Considered those pills awaiting him, and how he'd do well to get to them before the man or his bank robbery cohorts caught up to him as promised. "I don't think I can do it right now."

"Okay. Then I'll send Ken."

"Ken? Not *Ken*. Last time he—"

"I know," she said wearily. "He left a note pinned to the door. Let's skip the outrage. We're shorthanded, and you're the only guy who does it right. Blah, blah, blah. Pretty much every time you say you can't, you wind up doing it anyway. So let's just pretend we already had this part of the conversation."

He gritted his teeth. "You got the file?"

"Right in my pretty little hand."

He sighed, turned onto the freeway. "You know how to manipulate people."

"I'm not a cop for nuthin'."

Nate triple-checked the address before ringing the doorbell. At the side of the porch was a teak bench, its base lined with shoes. Loafers and sneakers and a pair of worn Converse high-tops with peace symbols Magic Markered on the sides. The stab wound throbbed in his shoulder, and he hoped it wasn't bleeding through the hospital-issue T-shirt.

Footsteps approached, and Nate closed his eyes, gathered himself. A pleasant woman in her forties answered, her husband behind her in gym clothes, a folded *Wall Street Journal* under his arm. The woman's eyebrows rose with surprise. "Hi . . . ?"

He took quick note of the marble floor of the entry. "I'm Nate Overbay. Are you Erica? Sean?"

"Yup." Sean glanced at a runner's watch with an angled face. He was a husky man, former athlete, with a wedge of dense copper hair. "What can we help you with?"

"I work with LAPD. May I come in?" Nate wanted to get them seated; Sean O'Doherty was a big guy, and it was a long fall to that hard marble floor if he fainted.

Erica nodded nervously. On their way to the couches, Sean let the newspaper drop. They sat, and Nate asked, "Just the two of you home?"

Sean said nervously, "Yeah, yeah, just us."

Nate set his hands on his knees. He hated this moment most, the moment before the world flew apart.

He cleared his throat. "At two-thirty today, your son Aiden was driving from his dorm room to guitar practice. He was struck by another car and brought into the USC Medical Center with severe injuries to his head and chest. He was unconscious. The medical staff did everything they could to revive him, but they failed, and he died."

A cry flew out of Erica. Her face turned red, and she leaned back into the cushions. Sean was standing; he'd moved so fast that Nate had missed the transition from couch to feet, and the man wobbled a moment and then sat down again. He was breathing hard, nostrils flaring. Nate gave them maybe ten seconds, which stretched longer than ten seconds seemed like they could.

"I am so sorry to be here," Nate said. "But I will help in any way I can and answer any questions."

The first reaction was often an unexpected one. Sean's mouth tightened. "Who did you say you are again?"

"Nate Overbay. I'm a Professional Crisis Responder."

The overblown title served to make up for the fact that he was not a social worker, a chaplain, or a paramedic. Though deployed by LAPD, he didn't carry a badge and was not a sworn officer. When he first started nearly five years ago, a social-services team was supposed to go out every time, but budget cuts had whittled down the cast until he was the last man standing. Now, when he wasn't available, death-notification service fell to whichever patrol officer drew the short straw. So Nate had done his best to be available for every call. To strive to better himself, to find one more way to diminish, however slightly, a family's pain the next time around. He was not so dumb as to be unaware that he was trying again and again for personal redemption but not so smart as to figure out how to break the cycle.

Erica's voice fluttered, so fragile that Nate could barely make out the words: "This is a mistake. How can you be sure there wasn't some mistake?"

Nate had pulled the incident report, gone to the morgue to talk with the coroner, sat with Aiden and held his cold hand. To make sure he didn't terrorize the wrong family, Nate had checked the driver's license in Aiden's wallet against the database in case the nineteen-year-old boy had been carrying a fake ID.

"I'm certain," Nate said. "Aiden was identified and pronounced dead at the hospital."

Experience had taught him that to overpower denial he needed to say to the bereaved, frequently and boldly, that the person had died. It had also taught him *not* to say that time heals all wounds, that he knew how they felt, that there was a reason for everything. He had learned when to pause, to let them breathe, when to lead and when to follow. But mostly he had learned to ignore everything he had learned, at a moment's notice.

Erica withdrew into herself, shoulders curling, chin dipping. Sean looked at her, his mouth downturning violently, almost a sob. "You're the cops," Sean said, his voice high, adrenalized. "He's a *kid*. You couldn't protect him from some idiot driver?"

Nate said gently, "No."

Sean was standing again, jabbing a finger down at Nate. "You should've done something. Someone needs to fix this. This is your fault. *Your* fault."

Nate rose. "Okay." He kept his hands out and his voice soft.

"I'm gonna sue the fucking shit out of you, this city. I'm gonna . . ." Sean's finger, inches from Nate's face, began trembling violently. His face flushed, and then he was sobbing, rent-open cries, loose on his feet. Nate lifted an arm, and Sean grabbed him and sobbed into his shoulder, and Nate held him for five minutes and then ten, until Erica rose and led her husband with great care back to the couch. Sean sat, holding her hand, tears streaming as Nate answered their questions and told them what to do next, writing everything down since recollection would be foggy—directions to the morgue, police case number, direct line to the coroner's office. He did all that, and then he shut up.

Erica broke the silence. "But it's so unfair. He's our only child." Finally she came apart, fist pressed to her mouth so hard that the skin went white.

Heat swelled in Nate's chest, and he looked down, the carpet blurring at his feet. Some responders believed they always had to be strong for the relatives, but Nate had found that the times his voice hitched or his eyes watered, family members had looked at him not with disdain but appreciation.

Erica caught her breath again, blew her nose. "What a stupid thing to say."

"No," Nate said.

"Life *isn't* fair, is it? Who gets to live. Who dies."

No.

"I want to see him," Erica said. "I want to see my boy. Where is he?"

Sean lifted the printout that Nate had brought—the route from their front door to the morgue. He raised his red-rimmed eyes to Nate and said, "Thank you."

Nate nodded. "Is there anything you'd like to ask me? Anything you want me to do?"

Shaking their heads, they rose to see him out.

He always made the second-day call himself, since the last thing a family in crisis needed to see the morning after was a new face. When a piece of jewelry or a watch was released, he'd take it home and scrub off the dried blood before delivering it. He'd be one call away, their guide through the rough terrain. So he started to say what he always said next—that he'd check in with them again tomorrow.

But then he remembered: For him there wouldn't *be* a tomorrow.

He paused on the porch, looking back at Erica and Sean, feeling that nagging sense of remorse. His mind moved to his best friend's body outlined against a brilliant blast of white. His failure of will in the car outside Charles's mother's house. That night in the house, his daughter trying to hide beneath the bed, his wife looking on, a bruise rising on her cheek. So much unfinished business. So much he still owed.

Since his diagnosis he'd done everything to spare Janie and Cielle any more trouble on his behalf. But maybe he owed them a final explanation before he punched out.

"He was just here last week," Erica said. "Standing where you're standing right now. He was tying his shoes, and the phone rang. . . ." She gestured toward the teak bench, at that row of sneakers, Aiden's beat-up Chuck Taylors waiting, one on its side. "I went to answer. Could be important, you know. A nail appointment." She gave a disgusted little laugh. "You know the worst part?"

Nate shook his head.

"I never got to say good-bye."

Chapter 10

For the whole ride, Nate alternated his gaze from the road to his rearview, searching for dark Town Cars with illegally tinted windows. After parking he sat, double-checking that no one had followed him, but also, he realized, stalling. It took all the courage he could muster to head up the walk of the beloved Santa Monica house. A corner brick at the base of the porch had come loose, and he paused to shove it with his heel back into alignment. Owning a house was a war of attrition. Sap holes in the gutters, birds' nests in the chimney, dry rot in the window frames. Tears of rust hung beneath the house numbers and he thought of the time he would have cleaned them with pride. He knocked, and a moment later the door swung open.

Pete looked out at him, doing his best to disguise his consternation. "Nate. Been a while."

"Right. Okay if I come in?"

Pete looked unsure. "Hang on." He leaned back. "Janie?"

A moment later there she was. She wore a flare-waisted Spanish gauze blouse, bright orange to pick up the flecks in her eyes. Not that Nate noticed. Her thin eyebrows lifted, disappearing beneath the bangs of her pixie cut. "What are you doing here?"

"I need to talk to you. And Cielle."

She raised her left hand to push a wisp of hair off her forehead, and he saw with great chagrin that her ring finger sported a diamond the size of a bran muffin. "It's been nine months, Nate. Nine months. Women make *babies* in that time. Not a visit. Not a phone call."

"I know. I want to explain—"

"And it's not like you came by to see her frequently before then."

"That wasn't just me. I would've loved nothing more than—"

At once there was a clutter of claws scraping floorboards, and then Casper was there, nosing through Pete and Janie, losing his mind at the sight of Nate. A hundred ten pounds of Rhodesian ridgeback backing up in celebration, wiggling, thick tail smacking legs and walls, turning to shove his hind end into the nearest set of knees. "Off," Pete said. "Off. Down, Casper. *Off.* Casper—"

Nate said, "Sit."

Casper sat.

Janie's face was flushed, hiding the freckles. "Did you at least bring the divorce papers?"

"They're at home. Signed."

"Why didn't you just bring them?"

"It's been an eventful day. That's why I want to talk

to you." He took a breath, unsure where to begin. "Did you see the news today?"

"No."

"There was a robbery this morning. At Wilshire and Ninth."

"I heard about it," Janie said. "Radio."

"I was sort of in the middle of it."

Whatever she and Pete were expecting, it was not this. Janie's expression softened with concern. The door creaked open, and Nate followed them in, Casper zigzagging underfoot like a patrol car slowing traffic. As they passed by the family room, Nate noted the new family portrait on the mantel—a trio, this time properly posed, with Pete replacing Nate. At the sight of the three glossy faces, he felt his last handhold at the cliff's edge crumble.

In the kitchen Nate perched on one of the stools that, in another life, he'd found at a garage sale, then sanded and repainted. He ran a thumb across the grain of the wood. Everything like a detail from a remembered dream.

Janie said, "I'll see if she'll come down," and headed upstairs.

Pete finished washing romaine leaves in the farmhouse sink, set them aside, and dried his hands on his Wharton School sweatshirt. Pete was a widower, an intrinsically decent guy, and a former neighbor whom Nate and Janie had known in passing. He had made a lot of money in commercial real estate, and when he'd moved in here a few months ago, he'd cut a check to finish off the mortgage, an act of generosity that Nate still resented. Nate might have been struggling with that bank note, but at least it had been *his.* Even when he and Janie had separated about three years ago, it had given him comfort to know he was keeping a roof over the head of his daughter and the woman he still wildly, ineffectually loved. Over Janie's objections he'd sent 70 percent of each modest paycheck to her until she stopped cashing every other one to make sure he kept some money for himself. Pete's arrival had dissolved the last sure way Nate had known to help his family. Since then he and Pete had harbored an affectionate dislike for each other. Back in the months after Pete's wife passed, Nate remembered walking Casper by his house and seeing him inside, eating dinner alone at that big dining table, and no matter how much Nate wanted to hate him now for sleeping with his wife and raising his daughter, he just couldn't bring himself to get there in full.

Nate sat on his former stool and fussed with the neat stack of mail before him. Brokerage statements, *Vanity Fair,* a Lexus service reminder—all the accoutrements of a robust, prosperous life. They had added a wine fridge beneath the microwave.

"One of the bricks on the porch is loose," Nate announced to the silence.

Pete laid the romaine leaves side by side on a paper towel. "How am I supposed to reply, Nate? I say it's no big deal, I'm insulting you. I say I'll fix it, you'll get pissed off since you think it's still your porch."

Nate wanted to say, *It is still my porch. I rebuilt it with my own two hands. I leveled the form, poured the concrete base, used a toothpick to scrape the mortar from beneath my fingernails.* Instead he said nothing. He had lost the right to have opinions here.

Pete distributed the romaine across three plates, setting fewer spears on the last. By way of explanation, he said uncomfortably, "We're trying to help her with her weight."

At a loss as to how to respond to that, Nate lined up the mail nervously and smacked the envelope edges straight on the marble slab. Two tickets fell out— *Turandot* at the Ahmanson Theatre. Nate lifted them to the yellow light. "Opera?"

"To celebrate our engagement. You saw the ring?"

"No," Nate said, "I didn't notice."

Janie entered, and he looked hopefully past her, but no Cielle. His disappointed gaze returned to the tickets. She took note of his expression. "What?"

Nate's mouth moved instinctively before he could stop it. "You hate opera," he told her.

Janie halted by the stove. "Huh?"

Pete paused from chopping. "It was a surprise."

"Oh," Nate said. "Oops. But she hates opera. You *hate* opera."

Janie's smile did not quite reach her eyes. "Not really," she told Pete.

"There is no 'not really,'" Nate said. "This is *opera*. There are two camps. You either love opera. Or you hate opera. There is no Switzerland when it comes to opera."

Janie's head whipped over to him. He showed his palms.

Pete looked confused and a touch disappointed. "You really don't like opera? I'm sure I can find someone to give the tickets to if you—"

"Look," she said, resting a hand on the small of Pete's back, "can we maybe not have this discussion right now, honey?"

Constantly with the pet names, as though they were afraid if they didn't label each other at the end of every sentence, they might find themselves estranged.

Nate said, "Where's my daughter?"

"She doesn't want to see you," Janie said.

The words like a slap. It took him a moment to recover. "Why not?"

Pete said, "She's probably afraid you'll disappoint her again."

"Don't take yourself so seriously, Pete," Nate said. "No one else does."

Janie was studying him, furrows texturing her forehead. It wasn't so much his words, he realized, as his tone that had caught her attention. She seemed less angry than mystified. "What's gotten into you, Nate?"

Pete leaned over the counter toward Nate. "Cielle is my responsibility now, too. And you can have all the smart-ass quips you want, but I'm gonna do right by her. Which—if you actually took a second to think—is probably what you want instead of some asshole step-dad who doesn't give a shit about her."

Nate thought about those abysmal first months after the separation. How on day four the sight of a girl riding her father's shoulders had nailed him to the pavement outside a grocery store. How one desperate night Janie had let him in just so he could sit in the darkness of his daughter's room and listen to the faint whistle of her breath as she slept. How Cielle, standing in the dim light of his tiny one-bedroom, had clumsily declared, "It's too hard when I see you and then you're gone." Then, a few visits later: "Sometimes it's easier when the person who leaves just leaves for good." And how, even though it gutted him, he'd given her more space and more space until their weekly dinner became monthly, then quarterly. And how after the diagnosis he'd torn himself away from her and Janie altogether, not wanting them to have to suffer anything with him, whether out of love, guilt, or obligation. Fair or not, he wanted to weaponize all that pain and loss and aim it right through Pete's gallant face, but instead he looked at Janie and screwed his jaw shut.

Casper lifted his square, Scooby-Doo head and compassionately took in Nate's discomfort. He wasn't an animal so much as a human in a dog suit.

Janie said, "You're bleeding."

He peered over his shoulder and saw where a crimson seam blotted the undershirt. "I'm okay."

She wet a hand towel, carried it over, and lifted his shirt in the back. Pete and Nate made an effort to avoid eye contact.

"Nice stitch work," she said, dabbing at the edges of the wound. He relaxed a bit under her touch. "The bank robbery," she reminded him.

Before he could speak, Cielle appeared in the doorway.

She still carried thirty or so extra pounds, though

her fullness didn't detract from her beauty. Those dark brown irises, almost black. Long bowed lashes framing her eyes, rendering eyeliner or mascara superfluous. Raven locks twisting this way and that, now streaked with maroon. Everything about her appearance, from the goth-girl highlights to the baggy charcoal sweater with torn thumbholes in the sleeves, seemed too angry for a fifteen-year-old girl. Or perhaps right on target. He'd forgotten how long ninth months was in the life cycle of a teenager.

"What's with the undershirt, Nate?" she asked.

"Show some respect, Cielle," Janie said. "Call him *Dad*."

"It's from the hospital," Nate said. "I got stabbed during a bank robbery."

Janie took in a clump of air.

"And I shot the robbers. Well, most of them."

Pete lowered his hands to the counter, and Janie's hands stopped moving on Nate's back, but Cielle didn't miss a beat. "Were any of them named Jason Hensley?"

". . . No."

"Then I don't care."

"Who's Jason Hensley?"

"My shithead boyfriend. Who thinks that buying a new guitar is more important than taking me to Magic Mountain as was promised for our three-month anniversary."

"Cielle," Janie said. "I love you, honey. And I know that in your fifteen-year-old brain, boy troubles are equivalent to your father's getting stabbed in a bank robbery, but can we please focus on him right now?"

"You don't actually *believe* him, do you?"

Pete said, "Whatever you want to think about your father, Cielle, he's not a liar."

She rolled her eyes. "Fine. Go ahead."

Nate walked them through the official version, leaving out the almost suicide and the threats that Number Six had leveled at him in the vault. When he finished, Cielle's mouth was popped open, exposing a wad of fluorescent gum.

"Aren't you worried?" Janie asked. "That they'll come after you? I mean, you killed five men. They have to have . . . I don't know, *associates*."

Nate thought about that tattooed hand curled through the gap in the Town Car's window, pinching off the cigarette between the fingers without so much as a flinch. Just slow, steady pressure, suffocating the flame. Nate tapped his palm to his pocket, felt the comforting weight of the pill bottle against his thigh. His exit plan. "I'm not concerned about it," he answered.

Cielle: "So you just came to . . . ?"

"I wanted to tell you before you heard about it somewhere else," he said. "And . . . um . . ." There was no good transition. "I'm sick. Too."

Janie had forgotten about the towel, which was dripping pink onto the floor tiles. She looked as though she were piecing herself back together internally, and he felt a darkening remorse for bringing this here, to her and Cielle. "As in . . . ?" was all Janie could manage.

Nate took a deep breath. Bit his lip. Here was that point before the world flew apart. The toughest death notification he'd have to serve.

He said softly, "I'm not gonna be around much longer."

Janie shook her head. More fat drops tapping the floor tile. "What . . . ?"

"ALS," he said. And then, for Cielle's sake, "Lou Gehrig's. That's why I cut off from you guys nine months ago. We were already . . . And . . . I didn't want to put you through it."

Though Janie's face stayed still, there were tracks on her cheeks instantly, as if they'd sprung through the skin. He felt an overpowering urge to take her in his arms, but then Cielle said sharply, "That is *so* unfair," and stomped away. They listened to her Doc Martens pound the stairs, and then a door slammed so hard that a magnet fell off the refrigerator.

Pete cleared his throat, then said, "I remember when Sally died, I couldn't find any sense in getting out of bed. But after a while . . ." His hand circled, trying to land on a thought. "Someone said once that whenever a door closes in your face, another opens farther down the hall."

"Which door is that?" Nate said. "To Valhalla?"

A sharp silence. Janie looked unsteady on her feet, and Pete pulled her in and rubbed her shoulders from behind. His face was heavy with sadness, and Nate felt a rush of regret.

He sucked in a breath. "Sorry. I'm sorry. I'm a jerk."

"No." Pete shook his head. "It was a dumb comment for me to make. I don't know what to say. I'm really sorry to hear about it, Nate."

Nate pointed upstairs. "Look, I'd better—"

Janie nodded, a quick jerk of the chin.

Upstairs, Cielle's closed door waited, as imposing as a prison gate. The pencil lines on the door jamb marking her childhood heights were fading; a few more months and that piece of their shared past would be as lost and gone as Nate himself. He'd wasted so many chances. Countless nights he could've just walked down the hall to this room, pulled out a board game, read a story, picked her up, and breathed her in.

Gathering himself, he tapped the wood with a knuckle. No response. He entered cautiously, expecting to draw fire. She sat at her desk, hunched over schoolwork, facing away. He hardly recognized the room beneath the magazine collages, the posters of boy-men actors, the scattering of teenager clothes. But there, half buried by a cast-off jacket, was the stepstool that Charles had sent as a baby gift, her name carved in wooden letters. It remained where Nate had positioned it a decade ago so she could step down from her big-girl bed and come wake him if she had a bad dream. He clung to the sight of it, let it moor him.

He cleared his throat. Where to start? "Your boyfriend. Is he a nice guy?"

"Of course not. He's an asshole who treats me like shit. I grew up with no positive male role model in the house, so that's what I get."

He watched her back, debated how to forge into a wave of sarcasm that thick. "Look, I get that you're angry with me—"

"No. I'm just sullen and withdrawn in general. Ironically self-aware, too, which insulates me further. I could do drugs or cut myself or get a shoulder tattoo of some Chinese symbol for vagina power. But instead I think I'll just stay pissed off."

"Cielle."

She whirled. *"What?"* Her face was fighting to maintain the tough veneer, but he saw right through the cracks.

"I'm sorry I'm not gonna be around."

"I'm not sure what the big diff will be. I mean, even before you split, our seasonal dinners were hardly a mainstay."

"You told me it was easier for you to see me less."

"I was *twelve*! I was a *kid*. You shouldn't have listened. You shouldn't have believed me. You should have *fought* me." Her voice was wavering now, on the verge.

"Well, honey, you were convincing."

"You *left*. I had no say. I had *no* say." She noted the effect her words had on him, and her scowl lightened, if only for a moment. "You know what? Never mind. Fine. It's all my fault." She turned back around. "Buh-bye now."

He stared helplessly at the clothes littering the floor, a black polo shirt catching his eye. Car-wash decal on the breast pocket, Cielle's name stitched above. "Wait a minute," he said. "You're working at a car wash? Why?"

"That's not really your concern either."

"Cielle," he said. "What's going on?"

She turned again. "Pete lost most of his money in the recession. Some real-estate thing crashed. Which means we can't afford my stupid private school. So I got a job. But it's still not enough."

He sank to sit on her bed. "Why didn't you tell me?"

She picked up her iPhone in its pink rubber case and poked at the screen disinterestedly. "Because you've been so available?"

"So you guys are . . . ?"

"We're fine. Or so Mom and Pete say. It's not like we'll be on the street or anything. There's just no money for *extras*. Which would be—oh, that's right—my education."

"How much is Brentwood Prep?" Since she'd started last year at Pete's urging, Nate was unacquainted with the price tag.

"Twenty."

"Twenty thousand dollars?"

"No. Twenty thousand glass beads. They're having a special."

"Do you . . . do you like it?"

"No." She tossed the iPhone aside. "The girls are all named Chelsea or Sloane, and if I have to hear from one more assclown that he's sooo brilliant he has to smoke pot to slow his brain down, I'm gonna puke on his worn-out Vans."

Nate was struggling to keep up with all this. "So you don't want to go there anyway."

"The thing is, I *do* want to go there. Annoying, sure, but hello? It's high school. At least the teachers are smart and there's honors classes and the students aren't as lame as they could be. Plus, it'll get me into a good college, too, not that I'll be able to afford that now either. So I'd better enjoy this semester, since it's my last hurrah before I move on to stitching wallets in some sweatshop."

Given his own experience joining the Guard to pay for college, Nate had always sworn he'd work until Cielle's education was squared away. Pete's arrival had seemed to take care of all that. Until now.

She glared at him. "Oh, c'mon. This isn't your concern. Any more than anything *else* has been these past nine months. Or three years, for that matter. You just . . . what? Moved on? Got over it?"

"No. I *never* got over it."

A cynical snicker couldn't quite hide the hopefulness. "What then?"

He studied his hands. "I always thought there would be time."

"There's never time. There's only right now. And you suck at right now."

He was running numbers in his head, but there weren't many to run given the anemic state of his bank account. "Maybe I can help with the tuition—"

"I don't want *anything* from you."

"What can I do, then?"

Once again she showed him her back. "Die somewhere else."

The words left a clean hole through him where his stomach used to be. He sat for a while and watched her shoulders, the back of her head. She was ostensibly re-immersed in homework.

His joints ached as he stood. "I wish I could've done better by you." He heard the faintest sniffle, but nothing more. "For whatever it's worth, I'm proud of everything you are and everything you'll be."

He took care to ease her door shut silently behind

him. Janie and Pete were where he'd left them downstairs by the sink, the salad plates sitting unmoved. Janie asked, "You wanna stay for dinner?"

He thought of his date with a handful of pills in the quiet dark of his apartment. Those inked fingers curling through the Town Car's window. "Nah. I have to get back."

The look of relief in Janie's eyes about killed him.

"I'm sorry to hear about the investments," Nate said.

Pete tensed a bit. "We'll figure it out. You have enough to worry about. Don't worry about this, too."

Janie added quickly, "She'll be fine in public school. We were."

"Okay." Nate wanted so badly to raise a hand to her cheek, to feel those lips one last time, but instead he tipped his head. "I just wanted . . . I just wanted to say good-bye."

Pete said, "If there's anything we can do . . ."

"You know what I like about you, Pete? You're a decent guy. And you've never let the fact that we don't get along mess anything up." Nate lifted his eyes, indicating the thunderous silence emanating through the ceiling. "Take care of her. When . . . you know, I can't."

They shook hands, and Pete pulled him into a hug. Janie said, "Honey, I'll just see him out," and Pete said, "Of course."

Janie walked Nate to the porch, and they stood there. Nate crouched and fussed with the loose goddamned brick. "There's a mortar bag in the garage with a little left over." When he stood, he saw that she had tears in her eyes again, and he said, "Janie."

"I want to say something comforting, but I don't know if it's for me or you. So I'll keep my mouth shut."

Afraid of what his face might show, he looked at his waiting car. "C'mon. It's not that bad. You still get to go to the opera next week with Pete the Fun Vacuum."

"You're a menace."

"I want you to know," he said, "there was never anyone else for me, Janie."

Her lips trembled, and then she nodded once, turned, and hurried inside. He walked to his car. He had the keys in the lock when he heard from behind, "*Fuck you.*"

He turned, and Cielle was standing there, her sweater sleeves pulled down over her fists, her face flushed. "I loved you *so much*." She spit it, like a curse. "I lit candles when you were away at war, and then, when you left us, I lit candles that you'd come back. 'Dear God, please bring my daddy back to me safe.' And even when you *were* with us, you were busy with your stupid job taking care of everyone else except for the people you were *supposed* to be taking care of."

"Cielle—"

"You can't have my sympathy. You *can't* have it. You don't. I don't care if you're dying." Despite her best efforts, tears were leaking.

He stood there, still, his heart coming apart for her. More than anything he wanted to go to her, but he knew if he took so much as a step, she'd bolt like a deer.

"You can't die yet," she said. "You didn't earn it. You left us, and now you get to die before I can get even."

When he trusted his voice, he asked, "How were you gonna get even?"

"I was gonna have a great life and get married and be successful and keep your grandkids from you. But you're dying and trying to make me feel . . . make me feel . . ." Her face wobbled all around. "Why'd you come tell us anyway?"

"I wanted to say good-bye to you. I wanted to have a chance to set things straight."

"Why now, *Nate*?" His proper name, like a projectile. "I mean, you found out *months* ago. And you're not sick yet. I mean, you still have months left at least, right?"

The weight of his bones pulled at him. "It might be sooner than that, Cielle."

She staggered a bit. Encased in her sleeves, her fists tightened. "Does Mom know that?"

He shook his head.

"Then why are you laying it on me?"

"It's too late for me and your mother."

She swiped at her cheeks angrily with her sleeve. "It's too late for me and you, too."

He watched her all the way up the walk, hoping for a final glimpse of her face, praying she'd turn around one last time.

She didn't.

Chapter 11

A scattering of envelopes waited on the doormat outside Nate's second-floor Westwood apartment. His mind flew to that dark sedan; were these written threats from the man attached to the tattooed hand? Not to worry—Nate was a handful of pills from being safely out of anyone's reach. Crouching, he saw the network logos brightening up the flaps and let out a thin breath of relief. Letters from a bunch of local news affiliates, requesting interviews about his "heroic" role in the bank robbery. Kicking them aside, he scooped up the morning paper.

Standing in the hall, he folded the *Los Angeles Times* back to the obituaries, as was his recent habit. There was Mary Montauk, a professor of linguistics who had helped design the first spell-check program. Gwendolyn Dawson, born crocheter and special-ed teacher. Arthur Fiske, heir to a textile fortune, World War II airman, and benefactor to the Getty. Nate pictured the man in a canary yellow sweater, reclining on a puffy down bed bleached with ethereal light as he drifted off, a faint grin touching his lips. He'd had plenty of time to adjust to the temperature, Arthur had, to ease his way into a place of nostalgic contemplation, a prince's view back over a life well lived. As always, Nate's eye snagged on the last line:

ARTHUR IS SURVIVED BY PAMELA, HIS LOVING
WIFE OF SIXTY-THREE YEARS, FOUR SONS,
AND ELEVEN GRANDCHILDREN.

Good on you, Arthur, he thought.

Entering his apartment, Nate dumped the paper and letters in the trash. Three years later IKEA labels remained stuck on the furniture, arrows and letters to aid assembly. He sank onto the foldout couch he'd bought in optimistic hope that Cielle would spend the occasional night. Two thumbtacked photos livened up the opposing wall. A candid, blurred shot of Janie and him from the wedding, dancing and laughing into the embrace of a private joke. And Cielle at six, all broad smile and crooked teeth, crouching with a soccer ball at her knee. On the coffee table before him sat the signed divorce papers and his suicide note. He lifted the note to the light.

To Janie and Cielle, my collective heart.
Janie, I wish you every happiness with Pete.
(Pete, please stop reading over her shoulder.
This is a suicide note—a little damn privacy,
please.) And Cielle. I've thought long and hard
about what I want to pass on to you. And I guess
it's that there are no guarantees, so don't waste

your time here like I did too much of mine. If you hold on to stuff too hard, you'll sink with it.

He paused and smirked a bit at himself. Nate Overbay, Armchair Philosopher.

I resent only one thing, sweetheart, and that's every minute I spent away from you and your mom. I had so many chances to do better, and I couldn't. But it was never for lack of love. You and your mother were the best part of me.

Were they ever.

To the cop reading this— First, sorry to the guy who had to scrape me out of the Dumpster. Or off the corner of Ninth and Wilshire if I missed. Second, when you serve the death notice to my wife and kid, please be patient and kind. Don't check your watch. Make eye contact and hug them if they need it. —Nate
P.S. There's half a ham sandwich in the fridge. Have at it.

Tapping the note to his lips, he sat awhile, thinking about his ill-fated visit to Cielle's room and running figures in his head. Three more years of high school at twenty grand a pop. Then college at twice that amount. A familiar pressure mounted inside him until he sprang forward, grabbed a pad and pencil from the drawer, and tallied up estimates, weighing his checking-account balance (not much), benefits from Uncle Sam (minimal), and projected income for the few months he'd still be able to work (meager) against upcoming medical costs to sustain him through his decline (colossal). A very large negative number stared up at him from the pad. How dismal to see his worth laid out like this, his life reduced to this sad figure. He was not much use at all to Cielle, but he was more use to her dead now than dead later.

He tossed down the pad, went to the kitchen, came back with ham sandwich in hand, chewing. He clicked on the radio, Lady Gaga still caught in that bad romance. Just because it was a suicide didn't mean it had to be depressing.

Taking another bite, he paused in the middle of the living room for a final survey. Everything was death. The unread books on the shelf, *Moby-Dick* staring out, unvanquished. The browning fern in the corner that would outlive him. That pillar candle that would be removed, half burned, from the shelf by a cleanup crew hired by his landlord. There was such a horrible self-centeredness to dying. Every detail, filtered through a gray lens. He'd been unable to break out of his own head. Until this morning in the bank when he'd floated past the bullets in a perfect suspended state of who-gives-a-fuck.

Grabbing a bottle of Knob Creek from the cupboard, he sat at the kitchen table, lined up his pill bottles, and took roll. Vicodin and antibiotics from the ER this morning. Xanax for sleep. Gold pearls of vitamin E. And his nemesis, riluzole—oblong tablets that left him alternately weak, fatigued, dizzy, or nauseous. Eleven

Xanax, eighteen Vicodin—more than enough to do the trick. He arranged them in a vast smiley face, poured himself a tall shot of bourbon.

The thought of his dead body bloating here sickened him. The stench would seep into the walls, and then some poor person would stumble onto him, maybe the landlord's wife— No, he couldn't have that. He thumbed open his cell phone and called the number on the back of Agent Abara's card. Voice mail. "Hi, it's Nate. You said to call if . . . Well, I remembered something that might help in the investigation. I'm out right now, won't be home for a few hours at least, so if you could come by my place late . . . ?" He hung up. Walked across. Unlocked the front door for Abara. Now. Now he was ready.

Sitting again at the kitchen table, he reached for the bottle of bourbon, but another hand gripped it suddenly from the other side, the fingers caked with blood and sand. Charles sat in the opposite chair, his torso a gruesome scramble. "They say suicide is a coward's way out."

Nate pulled the bottle irritably from Charles's grasp. "I'd like to see *them* stand eleven stories up and look down at the spot their body's gonna mark with a Rorschach."

Tendrils of black smoke lifted from the edges of his charred flesh. "Christ, you're touchy."

"Look, all I wanted to do is jump off a building."

"I get it. You got served a shit sandwich. Any way you slice it, you gotta eat the fucker. But still. I don't think you have to go all Jane Austen."

"Huh?"

"You know, the *Bell Jar* chick who offed herself."

"That was Sylvia Plath."

"Whatever. I'm just saying, look at the bright side. For the first time in your life, you can say and do whatever the hell you want."

"The *bright side*? I'm dying, I've still got PTSD or whatever the hell they're calling it these days as evidenced by . . . well, *you*. Plus, I'm one signature away from divorced, and my kid hates me."

Charles crossed his arms over the hole in his chest and did his best to look bored. "I won't sit here and listen to you whine. You can do that to a wall."

"I *am* doing that to a wall."

Charles shook his head with disappointment. "I'm outta here, then. I'm not sticking around for this."

"Fine."

"Fine." But Charles remained, looking away like a pouty child.

Nate banged down the bottle. "Look, I have to do this while I'm still up for it. Do you have any idea how pathetic it feels to be too depressed to kill yourself?"

"You're still sitting there talking to me. Which means you want *something*." Charles spread his arms, releasing a waft of smoke. "What do you want, Nate?"

Nate stared at the pills arrayed before him. "I want to die well," he said.

When he finally lifted his eyes, Charles was gone.

Leona Lewis had come on the radio, all soulful runs and sultry beat, a just-audible church organ running beneath the melody like bedrock.

Nate slid the pills neatly off the table into his hand and stared down at them. His heartbeat skipped, his brain spinning, throwing images. Janie's skin, pale beneath seawater. Cielle's baby gums, suckling his knuckle. The car-wash polo, her name embroidered at the breast. His daughter's education—her whole damn future. How could he not make sure he provided for that? His mind landed on the million-dollar life-insurance policy he was about to void with a single swallow. No payout for Janie and Cielle—his beneficiaries—in the event of suicide.

All he had to do to assure his daughter's future was put down the pills and die horrifically, one agonizing minute at a time.

His daughter's voice rang in his head: *I don't want* anything *from you.* He remembered as a child finding his mother's hair, too much of it to be stray, clumps and clusters like the residue of some violent act, loose on the pillow, twined in the teeth of her comb, lining the inside of that snug terry cap she wore. Cielle again, turning her back: *Die somewhere else.*

"Okay," he said. "Okay." He palmed the pills into his mouth.

On the radio Leona kept bleeding, she kept, kept bleeding.

The pills melted on his tongue, bitter and toxic.

He reached for the bottle, unscrewed the lid.

He thought of Cielle working at that car wash and its still not being enough.

The bottle was at his lips.

—*You cut me open and I*—

The bourbon pooled in his mouth, smoke and sweetness, the pills swirling.

A million dollars. All he had to do was suffer.

—*keep, keep bleeding*—

He turned his head and spit out the pills onto the cheap linoleum, leaning on the table, coughing.

His cell phone rang.

He said, "Cielle."

He darted across and snatched it from the counter. "Hello?"

An accented voice said, "Remember me?"

Nate's insides turned to ice. He looked down at the brown puddle dotted with pills. "Number Six."

"Go to your bedroom."

Nate could barely hear his own voice over his thundering heartbeat. "Why?"

"Something you must see."

Nate reached across and locked his front door again. Keeping the phone pressed to his face, he walked back, his steps slowed with dread. The room was as he'd left it, the bed neatly made, but one pillowcase was, oddly, missing. The striped ticking of the pillow stared up at him nakedly.

He halted in the doorway, gaping.

The voice jarred him. "Now look out the window."

His legs had turned to water, but he got himself across and parted the curtains. "There's nothing there."

"Just wait."

Something slipped over Nate's head, blotting out all light. Fabric yanked tight across his face, suffocating him. The last thing he sensed before dropping into a pool of black was that it felt an awful lot like a pillowcase.

Chapter 12

Before consciousness there was pain. In the thick soup of his head; in his feet, cold and numb; in his thighs, bitten lengthwise as if by a band saw. The sockets of his shoulders, tendons screaming. And his wrists, overhead. Oh, his wrists.

Nate's eyes opened tentatively. Vast, dank room, perhaps a warehouse. Little light. His own biceps crowding his field of vision. His arms, suspended above. His teeth chattered. It was colder than seemed reasonable for indoors, each breath frosting the linings of his lungs.

When he looked down, it seemed that his lower half had disappeared. Incredulous, he realized that his legs were, bizarrely, encased in ice. Claustrophobia crowded in on him, and he tried, stupidly, to lift his feet, to kick, to run, but there was nothing except the cold cast, enveloping him to the thighs.

Quick breaths, panic sweat freezing on his face. When he tried to wipe the beads off his cheek with his sleeve, he saw that his hands above were trapped inside matte black handcuffs and snared on a meat hook. The chain holding the hook rose several feet before vanishing into darkness—the ceiling might be ten feet above, or a hundred. Bands glittered at his wrists where the skin had been rubbed raw. And beneath everything else, pulsing like a heartbeat, was the dull pain of the stab wound in his shoulder, straining the stitches.

He will make you pay in ways you can't imagine.

He blinked rapidly several times, a trick he'd learned in the army that was supposed to hasten nighttime vision. First the rectangle of ice around his legs came clear—on its side, the size of a refrigerator. Mist rose from its surface, making the air waver as he peered into the darkness. Pallets. Boxes. Scattered tools. A rescue saw, like the one used to cut through the steel of the bank vault.

At the fringe of visibility, he became slowly, chillingly aware of four human forms standing idly apart, studying him with cocked heads. He gave a startled shout and reared back, the lip of ice biting his hamstrings, the meat hook's chain giving off a rusty abattoir rattle that scratched through the huge space and clawed its way back off the walls.

His vision clarified further, the men's facial features unsmudging. The tallest he recognized as the face in the crowd outside the bank—the man with the lantern jaw and mashed nose. Broad shoulders like a yoke. Stubble bristled on his bullet-shaped head. Beside him stood a stocky man with a red-and-white-striped *Where's Waldo?* sweater, frayed at the sleeves and collar. Rather than hanging regularly from his frame, the sweater sloped out a few inches over the shelf of his muscular chest before falling. Nate took in the next, a slender man with sharp features, shiny dark hair secured in a tight stub of ponytail.

And there, stepping forth for a closer look, was Number Six, the crew leader from the bank. Nate recognized his bearing—the short form with wiry muscles and a low center of gravity, built for fighting. He looked younger than Nate might have guessed. Blond hair carefully arrayed in a dated style, something just shy of a seventies bowl cut, and a forehead that, Nate noted with a stab of satisfaction, bore a bloody nick where he had nailed it with the empty gun. The puckish round face with blue eyes called to mind that of a youthful sailor from a Soviet propaganda poster, full of confidence and purpose and yet unnervingly flat, scrubbed of uncertainty.

He approached Nate, drawing disturbingly close, until Nate could feel the man's breath against his cheeks. Those blue eyes picked across Nate's face.

"He will stay conscious now," Number Six declared, the accent sounding more clearly Russian to Nate's ears.

Nate took it as a bad sign that they had not bothered to wear masks. "Who are you?"

The crew leader returned his focus to Nate. "We are Tyazhiki. Shadow people. We are not here. We do not exist."

"But you have names."

"Ah, yes. I did not introduce myself before. I am Misha. You wonder why you are here?"

"No," Nate said.

"He must collect from you. From your body, perhaps." Lazily, he touched Nate's chest with a finger and pushed. The chain creaked above, the ice again bit the back of Nate's legs, and he couldn't help but grunt.

He clenched his jaw to stop the chattering. Needles of pain pierced his bloodless arms. What they were going to do to him would no doubt be horrific, but in the end there would be death. He blew out a breath, trying to find that place of fearlessness he'd captured inside the bank. "Will you lower my hands, please?"

The man in the striped sweater spoke up: "Not yet."

"Look, Waldo, there's four of you, and I'm wearing ice-block pants," Nate said. "If I make a move, I think you got me covered."

The man looked confused. "Waldo?"

"He is called Dima," Misha said. "With the pony-tail, Valerik. And he"—a flick of the hand to the huge guy from outside the bank—"is Yuri." Despite the accent, his diction was perfect, if formal.

"His hands stay hooked on chain," Yuri declared. "More pain."

But Misha leaned close and unhooked Nate's wrists, their faces inches apart. He smelled of soap. Yuri sucked his teeth and looked away, displeased but unwilling to press the matter. The other two shifted uncomfortably, pretending not to notice Misha's power play.

Lowering his arms hurt more than Nate could have imagined. His shoulders throbbed. He fought off the pain, then asked, "Russian?"

"*Not* Russian," Misha said. The first fragment of anger. "Ukrainian."

Nate gestured with his chin. "What's with the ice?"

"Just wait."

Nate looked down helplessly at the freezing block. "You say that a lot."

"Do not wear yourself out," Misha said. "It is frozen solid around your legs. We chipped the hole, lowered you in."

"It take all four of you to think this one up?"

"A sense of humor. Impressive, given the circumstances."

"I'm ready to die," Nate said. "There is nothing you or your boss can do to me."

In response Misha smiled. The grin was all upper gums, as if someone had carved the slit of his mouth too high on his skull.

A bang of metal on metal boomed through the warehouse, Nate stiffening atop the block of ice. An unseen door slid on rusty hinges. Footsteps tapped slowly toward them through the darkness, Nate's apprehension growing with their proximity. And then a light flared, a directed beam, making Nate squint. Blotting the tunnel of light, the perfect silhouette of a male form. Standing still. Arms crossed high on his chest.

When the man began to walk again, his shadow preceded him, elongated across the floor, creeping up the ice block, Nate's torso, and finally his face. The man neared but remained perfectly backlit, so Nate could make out nothing of his features.

He halted several feet away, the culminating note of the big stagy entrance. "The width of a cheetah's canines match perfectly to vertebrae of its prey." His accent was much stronger, his gruff voice giving him away as decades older than the other men. "To sever the spinal cord." He made a single clean gesture, planing his hand to cut the air. In the cold his breath rose like smoke from his nostrils. "There are those who are meat and those who are fed. Nature's design."

He turned to pace, a slant of light falling across him. Weathered face, ridged and leathery, scored with wrinkles. Wide, rounded mouth. Sapphire eyes, hard as stones. He wore an impeccably tailored suit and, beneath, a form-fitting black thermal shirt with a boxer's notch at the throat. The fabric hugged his compact muscles; he looked dense, unbreakable, carved from wood. A few coarse gray chest hairs showed at his neck. Hands in his pockets. The sleeves of the suit, tight across his biceps. His skin looked to be nearing seventy, but his lean body and virile bearing seemed that of a man a half century younger.

No doubt, the man from the Town Car.

He halted again. Those stone-hard eyes bored into Nate. "I am *designed* to terrorize you."

Nate's heart drummed at the base of his throat. "I killed five of your men."

"Those were not *my* men. Except the one you did not kill." He showed his teeth, which were unexpectedly beautiful, and it took a few seconds for Nate to realize that they were of course fake. "My men do not get killed by someone like you. They are different. You do not make this kind of tough in America."

Nate's mouth had cottoned. His legs ached through the numbness, and he was having trouble keeping his own teeth from clicking together. "What's your name?" he managed.

"Pavlo Maksimovich Shevchenko."

"What are you gonna do to me?" Nate asked. "And can we just get it over with?"

Pavlo's lips peeled apart from those magnificent teeth again, then he held out his hand. It wore a black glove, but Nate would have bet that beneath the leather the nails were manicured and each knuckle sported a tattoo. Valerik stepped forward, sweat-darkened strands twisting loose from the pulled-back hair at his temples, and placed a few photos in Pavlo's palm.

"When the human body is severed and the torso placed on ice, the cold preserves the brain function. Sometimes for twenty minutes, half hour. So everything is felt and"—he mumbled a foreign phrase, searching out and finally finding a word—"observed." He held the glossy photos up to Nate's nose and thumbed through several.

Nate took in the slide show of pink and red. He said, "Excuse me."

Pavlo nodded like a gentleman, stepped back, and Nate vomited onto the floor. When he lifted his cuffed hands to wipe his mouth, his shoulders screamed. He noted how the ice stretched to his left like a tabletop, and when he looked back over, Yuri stood beside Pavlo, holding the rescue saw with its diamond-tipped circular blade.

Somehow, despite the ice, sweat trickled down Nate's face, his back. He fought his stomach still, tried to slow his gulps of air, kept his eyes from the saw.

Twenty minutes. Twenty minutes and then it's all over.

He composed himself. "Okay," he said.

There was a long pause. And then Misha asked, "Okay what?"

"Do it." It struck him that he'd rediscovered something in that bank, in the face of those bullets. He was once again the guy who'd saved Janie from the ocean, who'd pulled her through a riptide and delivered her to shore. A dark laugh bubbled out of him, edged with hysteria. "Kill me."

Pavlo's gaze moved across his face, as if searching out a way to bore in and crack him open. He stared back. The best part of having nothing to lose was that no one had leverage over him. There was nothing at stake anymore.

Pavlo seemed to read this, finally turning away. "There is little red diary," he said conversationally, "in the back of a closet. It is kept locked. In it are a girl's complaints. What she views as hardships. How life treated her unfairly. In last entry, on page eighty-nine, she recalls a childhood memory. Her father bursting into her room one night in the clutch of a nightmare, blood streaming down his face." He turned. The faintest pursing of his lips. Savoring a reaction.

Abruptly Nate became aware again of just how much the ice had chilled the air. The cold in the bones of his legs, aching. Each breath jerked his chest.

These men. In his daughter's room.

They broke into the house *today*. Between the robbery and now. They must have moved immediately after the shootings, while Pete and Janie were at work and Cielle at school.

"The ice is not for you. It is"—a black-gloved hand circled—"*demonstration*."

At once all pain was gone. "Let me be clear," Nate said. "If you lay one finger on my daughter, my entire life will narrow to the single focus of killing you."

Pavlo paced, frowning, deep furrows cupping his mouth. "There is a custom in our part of the world. If you step on someone's foot . . ." He turned and asked Misha a question in what Nate assumed was Ukrainian.

Misha replied, "Accidentally."

". . . *accidentally,* you must offer own foot for person to step on in turn. Just a light tap. And yet. We right wrongs at once, so resentments do not fester. Understand?"

Nate swallowed hard, his throat bobbing. Nodded.

"You and I, we require *razborka.* Settling of accounts," Pavlo said. "Much planning we spent for the bank heist."

Nate said, "I will figure out how to get you money."

"I do not want money. I have plenty of money."

"You robbed a *bank.*"

"I had an acquaintance, Danny Urban, no longer with us, God rest his soul. We had disagreement over fee and ownership of object. He place object in his safe-deposit box in First Union Bank of Southern California. We know it is there, but we do not know box number."

Nate thought about how the robbers had sheared off the hinges of all those nests of safe-deposit boxes and yanked off the tiny doors. How the safes and the cash had seemed like a second priority, an afterthought.

"So you robbed the bank as a cover?" Nate asked. "To get whatever Urban had?" No answer. "What is it?"

Pavlo stopped pacing. His gaze turned on Nate. "It

is what is inside the box." His teeth gleamed. "You interrupted my plan to get it. Now you will get it for me."

Nate felt his mouth fall open a little. "You're kidding, right? I can't do that. It's impossible. Plus, the bank's a crime scene. The safe-deposit boxes are sawed open—"

"Bank will reopen and have rebuilt boxes within twenty-four hours. They are bank. They cannot afford not to. Customers will be fearful."

"So you want me to . . . what?" Nate coughed out a note of incredulity. "Break in?"

"You are VIP at bank now. You play at being big hero. So use your special . . ."

"Status," Misha chimed in.

"Status." Pavlo repeated the word slowly, tasting it. "To figure out solution. We had our solution."

Nate stared frantically at Pavlo, but the man gave up nothing. "Just kill me. Let's handle this now, between you and me. Take it out on *me*."

Pavlo continued, undeterred, "You will find me at New Odessa restaurant. To deliver. In five days. Sunday at midnight."

"Sunday? It's Tuesday night. There's no way—"

The rescue saw in Yuri's hands revved to life, a deafening roar that faded back to silence.

Pavlo held up a finger. "Five days. The contents of that box in my hand. Or we will take your daughter, slice her in half, and place the top of her on this ice. Here. Where she can look across at rest of her. But you? We will not touch you." He rested a gloved hand on the surface beside Nate. "Is there any part of this that is unclear?"

Nate shook his head.

"If you run or we cannot find you, we do this to her also."

"How the hell am I supposed to . . . ?"

A long, patient blink, eyelids like crinkled paper. "If you talk to police or FBI and Agent Abara, we do this to her also."

The mention of Abara gave Nate a fresh stab of dread. So Pavlo knew about him already. How much access did this man have?

"Five days," Pavlo continued. "Or the precious handwriting in little red diary will never make it to page ninety."

He held up the handcuff key, which glinted in the faint light, then dropped it. A metallic ring, and then his dress shoe pinned it to the concrete off the bounce. He nodded, and Yuri revved the saw again. He walked up to Nate, forearms tensing to control the powerful tool, and drew the biting blade back over one shoulder. Nate tried to lean away, ice pressing into his hamstrings, and as the carbide teeth whistled toward his chest, he closed his eyes.

A scream of impact, frozen chips flying up at his face. The ice shuddered around him, and then the block shifted, a crack zigzagging from the incision and moving between his legs. As Nate blinked away the ice flecks from his eyelashes, the men withdrew. Their shadows crowded the beam of light. Then one of them kicked over the source, and the darkness was again all-embracing. Pattering of footsteps. The rusty door slid open, then shut.

Silence. Cold. Terror. Another reappraisal of what it meant to hit bottom.

Nate strained, shoving his numb legs this way and that, the ice giving by degrees. He fought one leg free and finally the other, sliding down onto the floor, where he lay for five minutes or thirty, panting, waiting for life to seep back into his lower body. His hands cuffed before him, he rolled painfully on the concrete, searching for the key that Shevchenko had dropped. At last he felt it beneath the numb tips of his fingers. It was an agony of cramped muscles and near misses until he finally guided it into the tiny slot and managed to twist. Freeing his wrists, he slung the cuffs away. They slid in the darkness a good distance, unobstructed.

It took several attempts to rise and a few more for him to feel his legs beneath him well enough to walk. Staggering in the gloom, pinwheeling off crates, he considered the task before him. And what hung in the balance. *Five days. The contents of that box in my hand.* Or they would kill Cielle.

There'd be no offing himself now.

Finally he groped his way to the door and stepped out, soaked jeans chafing him, T-shirt askew, into an alley. He limped toward an unfamiliar intersection. A few gangbangers sitting on the shell of a Camaro looked up from their brown-bagged forties as he passed.

He was, he realized, a long way from home.

Chapter 13

Pavlo Shevchenko woke with a knot in his throat and his lungs clutching for air. He drew in a screech of breath and rose, slapping off the sheets. He sat up, basted in sweat, eyes darting, making sure the walls were far away.

Space. There was space here.

His California king mattress sat centered in the two-thousand-square-foot bedroom that was the second floor. When he'd bought the mansion in the bombastically titled Mount Olympus community in the Hollywood Hills, the first thing he'd done was knock out all the upstairs walls to give himself more breathing room. He would've taken out the pillars, too, if they weren't needed to hold up the roof.

Floor-to-ceiling glass looked out at a steep stretch of canyon and the boulevard below, alive with light and movement. He rose and paced the vast room to show himself that he could, that he had the freedom to roam.

His history was defined by cages. His great-great-grandfather was a Cossack highwayman who'd died in the prison camps of Peter the Great, where the *vory v zakonye,* "thieves-in-law," first rose to power. Populating the sparse branches of Pavlo's family tree were more sworn criminals with allegiance to nothing but the thieves' world, the *vorovskoi mir.* A grandfather who survived the NKVD torture chambers only to succumb to the terrors of Babi Yar. An uncle who sliced off his finger in a corrective-labor camp in the Urals to show defiance to the conventions of the world outside the bars.

Pavlo was born on the day of Stalin's death in Donetsk, an industrial city in a bleak corner of Ukraine. At the time his father, who had taken the thief's vow—to turn his back on all family except for his fellow criminals—was busy dying of dysentery in the Omsk Colony, where he'd been sentenced to six decades of hard labor. By his thirteenth year, Pavlo had made his way to the black markets of Odessa, where he came up among the syndicate, rising to the prestigious position of pickpocket by the age of fifteen. He did the bidding of the old-school *vory,* growing skilled with a blade. For his first execution, he cut off a man's fingers, locked him in a car, and set it on fire. He never forgot how the man stared at him through the windows, never crying out. An early lesson taught by that hollow gaze: *There are those who are meat and those who are fed.*

By his seventeenth birthday, Pavlo was so feared that when he entered a room, grown men would put out their cigarettes and rise in respect. He did multiple stints in the Zone, coming out each time with more skills and more decoration, his service record tattooed into his flesh.

The Zone mocked the very conditions of existence. Cells built for sixteen prisoners were filled with sixty.

Not enough room for everyone to stand at once, so they took shifts on their feet, rotating by the slot of the window where they drew in a few precious lungfuls of oxygen. They slept in stacks on the bunk beds. One toilet for sixty men—a hole in the earth, no paper. Men died of the heat in the summers and of cold in the winters. They suffocated in plain sight. When Pavlo was punished for asserting order, he lived for months at a time in a cement-walled standing cell little bigger than a coffin. One hour a week, for exercise, he was allowed into a belowground pen with a mesh ceiling that looked up into cells, the caged run of a jaguar. Like everywhere else, it smelled of rot and death and the insides of other men.

Air. There was never enough air.

In the Zone he learned the truth of humanity, saw people as they really were. Downcasts, the lowest of the low, lived beneath cots, where they washed foot wrappings and ate crumbs. Their bodies existed only for the others; they were used until they were no more than living remains. Prisoners were trampled. Kicked to death. Beaten with dirt-filled socks until they urinated blood. The grumbling in their stomachs underscored the emptiness within. There was one rule only: survive.

And yet in the midst of all this, there was tradition. Honor. When there was an interruption in the order of things, Pavlo oversaw one of the *pravilki,* the thieves' courts. A man who had stolen from a *vor* above his rank was held on the floor, and the others took turns jumping from the top bunk until they'd shattered his rib cage. There was that potted plant in a prison in Perm that lived on the lip of the window grate. Each morning they would move it hand over hand through the room, each man allotted one sniff. There were chess games played with pieces of saliva-moistened bread and about once every season a ladle of fish stew poured over the kasha to make it edible.

Naked, Pavlo ran his fingers along the glass, staring down at Hollywood below. Notes from a rock concert at the Roxy climbed the hill, the thrumming of a bass guitar. He counted his steps. Two hundred eighty-three around the bedroom's perimeter. Just like last night. Just like the night before.

Pulling on a silk bathrobe, he walked up the floating staircase and emerged onto the concrete plain of the roof. Drew the nighttime air into his lungs. Free to walk, free to breathe. He was indestructible, as resilient as a cockroach. When the apocalypse came and the bombs fell, he would scuttle up from ground zero and turn his antennae to the toxic winds. He spread his arms in the darkness, reaching as far as his body allowed and touching only air.

After a six-year stint in Corrective Labor Colony No. 6, Pavlo had been released into a new age—post-Soviet Russia in the early nineties. The next generation of thieves didn't tattoo the markings of their trade on their flesh, but they respected and feared Pavlo and were savvy about the new system. A leader in the powerful syndicate, he was now a businessman, dealing in bank schemes, Japanese electronics, stolen Volvos and BMWs from Europe. The spoils of a nation were there for the taking. He bought factories, razed them to the ground, and exported the scrap metal. Aluminum to

Estonia, nickel to Latvia, titanium to Lithuania. He whored and gambled and ordered the deaths of judges who opposed his will. The time and his reach were *bespredel*—without limits.

He arrived at the edge of the roof, a sheer drop several hundred feet to the rocks of the canyon. The boulevard showed its full nighttime colors—the glitz of Ripley's Museum, the bronze pagoda and copper-topped turrets of Grauman's Chinese Theatre, the tall-wall billboard of the latest HBO star glowering over a Boeing-size pair of Ray-Bans. Commerce. Free trade. In the thawing of one empire, he had learned the rules and reaped the rewards of capitalism. He had come here, to the source, to enjoy them.

He walked the roof's edge, paying no mind to the harrowing drop inches away. His steps were sure and steady, his muscles taut. The fall was nothing compared to the beauty of all that space around him. He stopped and leaned over, his bare toes gripping the edge. Shout and there would be no echo. Drop a stone and he would hear no impact. Space. He turned and kept on. One hundred twenty steps. His to take whenever he liked.

The house was built into the hill, so the roof came level with the sloped street. A neighbor passing on a late-night walk lifted a hand in greeting. Pavlo stared until the man lowered his arm and hurried on. Pavlo walked along the property line as he did most nights, picking through the large, fine-grained granite rocks he had imported from the Urals. Sixty-eight steps, measuring the expanse of what was his. He reached the thick double front doors and tapped. Yuri opened and stepped aside, replacing his pistol at the small of his back. Pavlo entered, moving past the neat line of flannel slippers for guests; shoes were forbidden inside.

The downstairs furnishings were decadent. Cabinets of rift-sawn oak with ebony finish. Marble countertops with quartz for the glint. Dripping chandeliers, imported gold-leafed fixtures, patterned parquet flooring. A different life.

He pattered down the brief hall and turned into the girl's bedroom, opening the door quietly. The curtains were drawn, and it smelled of cigarettes and stale perfume. Nastya lay on her stomach across her bed, facing away, painting her nails, headphones on so loud he could hear the tinny echo of rock music. Tall and reed-thin, she wore a sleeveless T-shirt and jean shorts slightly bigger than bikini bottoms. Her legs were so smooth that it looked as though her skin had been spray-painted on. She was striking as only a Ukrainian girl could be. Expansive cheeks, pouting mouth, neck like a swan.

He remembered the first time he had seen her, a bundle of pink blanket delivered to his doorstep by a familiar whore, a girl herself. The infant's sapphire eyes, the shape of them, too—there could be no question that she was his. He'd taken her in his arms, and by the time he'd looked up, the whore had vanished.

As a *vor,* he could hold allegiance only to the brotherhood of thieves. He had turned his back on his birth family and sworn to have no family of his own save the *vory v zakonye.*

And yet.

Anastasia. Nastya for short. A daughter. Arriving

like Moses in the reeds. And him a weathered criminal aged by decades of crime and life in the Zone. When he'd held this infant, some part of him he'd long thought extinguished had flared to life inside his chest. She was pure. She was good. She was his last chance to be human.

He was revered enough that the brotherhood would honor this choice, but he could not be seen raising a girl in plain sight. To have her he'd have to leave the nation. Leave his life behind. And so he had, riding the wave of emigrants allowed out by Yeltsin in the late nineties. A stop in New York's Brighton Beach to organize his money through wires and offshore accounts, then on to Los Angeles, where anyone could be reinvented as anything. For her. All for her.

She was seventeen now.

He stood in the doorway and watched her. Long honey hair that reached the small of her back. Her legs were crossed at the ankles, one foot bobbing to the music. Fluorescent bands from various dance clubs encircled her wrists, each day of the week marked by a different stripe. He had spoiled her. He knew this and yet could not help himself.

He knocked gently on the open door. She turned, flinging the headphones down around her neck, her smile lighting the room. "Papa."

"Open these curtains," he said. "The view, it is free."

He could barely make out the faint etchings of the scars, a spiderweb just past her cheek. The imperfection only highlighted her beauty. He watched her in the liquid glow of the lava lamp.

"I like it dark. All holed up safe, ya know?"

She knew little of his past.

"Very well, Nastya." He discerned the faintest whiff of schnapps, that American syrup. "Have you been drinking?"

"Course not." She stretched, curling her back, her face screwed to one side, childlike. "What's with the new guy? Misha? He creeps me out."

"He is friend from the old country." The fan turned lazily overhead. "He makes you uncomfortable?"

"Yeah. He's always fucking *staring* at me. Why can't we just keep Valerik, Yuri, and Dima like we always have?"

"Misha, he does other things."

"Fine." She turned away and flicked her hair like a horse's tail. "I'm thinking of getting a tattoo. A little butterfly. Right here." She poked a finger at the base of her neck.

"We have discussed. You will not *ever* have your skin marked."

His tone, harsher than he'd intended. He remembered the time one of his *brodyagi* had brought him a monogrammed shirt, how it had reminded him of the ID tag sewn onto his prison uniforms. He'd excused himself and burned it in the bathroom sink.

Nastya looked at him, a touch of fear showing in her eyes. But he didn't mind if the fear kept her from marring her smooth skin. She covered with a pout and stretched languidly, rolling her shoulders, a great cat. "Okay, fine. But Jesus H. I mean, you're a fine one to talk. Head to toe."

"You are not me. And thank God you will never have to be."

"You're not so bad, old man." That smile. "Can I have some money? It's Tuesday night."

"The club again?"

"Yeah. It's Julie's birthday and the girls want to—"

Already he was peeling hundreds from the wad he kept shoved in the pocket of his bathrobe. "You know I cannot say no to you."

"Except about tattoos."

"Yes. Except tattoos." He set the money on her nightstand, next to an overflowing ashtray. "You will be driven. The Town Car."

"You're the best." Tugging the headphones back on, she returned to her nails. It was three in the morning and a school night, but when he thought about what *he* was doing at seventeen, he closed his mouth and exited.

Dima, Yuri, and Valerik were playing cards at the kitchen table. Misha sat alone at the counter, cleaning his gun and wearing the faint grin of a contented boy. They rose when Pavlo entered. He strode across to Misha.

"Do not look at Nastya again," he said quietly.

Misha nodded.

Pavlo moistened his lips. "I do not trust Nate Overbay. Watch him closely. And his daughter. At any sign . . ."

Yuri said, "What if he cannot deliver?"

"Any other plan will have a cost in lives and resources. We can afford to give him five days before we consider these."

"Why do we not just take the daughter now and start mailing him pieces of her?" Misha asked.

Yuri snickered. Misha swiveled his dead stare over at him, and the smirk dropped from the big man's face.

"This is not the old country," Pavlo explained patiently. "It does not work that way here. We must be more . . . subtle."

"I see no need," Misha said. "If you would free me to handle matters in the fashion I am accustomed—"

Pavlo leaned forward, setting a hand on Misha's shoulder, his stare making clear that the conversation had just ended.

Misha bit off his words, assembled his pistol with a deft twirl of the hands, and headed out.

Pavlo looked at Yuri. "I brought Misha because he is fearless. This is good but can also be bad. You are important. You understand how to play here."

Yuri's mouth moved around bunched lips, no doubt swallowing his objections.

Pavlo tilted his head toward the door. Yuri rose and followed. Valerik and Dima returned to their cards.

Pavlo walked upstairs. Fifty-seven steps. That empty second floor, room enough to breathe, to stretch. He walked the edges again, his shoulder rubbing the glass, counting and recounting his steps. Finally he lay on his mattress and stared through the skylight at the coal-black heavens, contemplating all that was at stake and what he was willing to do to protect it.

Chapter 14

Nate pried his wallet from his stiff jeans and paid the taxi driver with a credit card still cool from the ice block. Some UCLA frat boys ran by, hazing a pledge who was jogging with a bra on his head, all clamor and idiotic fun. The Westwood apartment, priced for students, had been the most that Nate could afford when he'd moved out, so a certain measure of shenanigans came with the territory. A block from campus again, but as a grown man. One step forward, nineteen steps back.

The cab pulled away, and he shouldered against a tree cracking the sidewalk and dialed. Of course, Pete answered.

"I wanted to check on Cielle. Make sure she's—"

"It's late, man. Really late."

"Sorry," Nate said. "Is Janie there?"

"She's asleep."

"Look, will you just go down the hall and check that Cielle's okay?"

"Just because you're sick doesn't mean you can pull this shit, Nate."

"Is my daughter fucking okay, Pete? Or do you want me to drive over to find out?"

Up until now Nate had never shown Pete an inch of anger, and the abrupt silence signaled the man's surprise. The phone hit something, hard, and then Nate heard footsteps thump away. After a few moments had passed, Pete said, "She's fine," and the dial tone hummed in Nate's ear.

He shot an exhale at the sky and limped upstairs, muscles aching.

In the shadows to the side of his door, a man waited, slumped against the wall. Bile rose in Nate's throat, and he froze midway up, hand clutching the rail. The head swiveled to him, an alertness piercing the darkness. They considered each other. Nate swallowed, a dry click, unlocked his legs, and continued up. As he crested the top step, the form came off the wall to meet him, stepping into the light.

Abara. Damn it—*Abara*.

The agent's curious expression turned into a concerned squint. "The hell happened to you?"

"What are you doing here?"

"You called *me*. Remember? Something you remembered from the heist?"

Right. He'd called Abara to come discover his own dead body. Back when life was simpler. "I– I . . . went for a walk. Fell into a puddle."

"A puddle? Where?"

Nate fought his key into the lock. "On the street."

"A waist-high puddle? On the street?"

"I fell." Nate's fingers felt loose and lifeless, and the keys slipped, clacking to the concrete. He crouched, but it took some concentration to get his hand to close around them. Maybe it was just the cold, not the illness.

Abara crossed his arms. "Here's where you probably want to stop digging. And tell me why, exactly, you called. And what the hell is going on."

The agent's confidence eroded Nate's resolve. Up against the Ukrainian mob, his daughter's life threatened, tasked with robbing a bank—there was no way he could navigate through this on his own. He *had* to get help from the authorities.

He turned to face Abara in the outdoor corridor. "Okay. Look, when I got home tonight—"

Abara shifted, and over his shoulder, beyond the brief throw of guardrail, a curve of street came visible down below. About a hundred yards away, a streetlight dropped a yellow funnel onto the sidewalk, encircling a man who stood motionless.

Misha.

He stood in the brazen open, his hands in his pockets, a statue. The night seemed to fragment, and Nate had to remind himself to keep drawing breath as he pieced it back together, shard by shard.

Abara, impatient: "You got home and *what*?"

Below, Misha moved his arms, letting them hang at his sides. Something glinted at his left fist, pointing down at the concrete.

Nate forced his eyes back to Abara. "I . . . called you because I was scared. I just made up an excuse to get you over here."

Abara ran his tongue along the inside of his lower lip, his eyes skeptical. "Don't waste my time."

Nate nodded. His gaze pulled right again, to the middle distance. Misha vanished behind a passing car, reappeared. The man was standing in the middle of the sidewalk gripping a gun, and no one seemed to notice.

"Okay. Sorry. You can go, then." Nate pointed to the stairs, a nice broad gesture so Misha could see that he'd refused to cooperate with the agent. Turning, he fumbled the key into the lock, his fingers half responsive.

"The bank manager who was killed," Abara said.

"Flores Esposita," Nate said.

"Her funeral's tomorrow. Forest Lawn, eleven A.M. Family asked if you could be there. You know, you being the guy who saved the day and all."

"I'll do my best."

"Yeah," Abara said, walking away, "you seem to have a lot on your plate."

Nate went inside, closed and locked the door, leaned against it, trying to catch his breath. Gripping his wrist, he flexed his fingers, balled them. More tingling. The living-room window beckoned. With dread, he crossed to it, the street drawing into view by degrees.

Misha remained, watching. Waiting for Nate.

Misha lifted the gun, aimed at the window, at Nate. A flush rolled beneath the skin of Nate's face like a breaking wave. Misha cocked his head. Tugged the barrel up an inch like a kid playing soldier. Even at this distance, Nate saw his lips move.

Pow.

Misha returned the gun to his pocket and stepped away from the streetlight, vanishing into the darkness.

Chapter 15

At first light, Nate emerged from the depths of a slumber, his cheek buried in the bare pillow. Despair washed over him, magnified by aches. Stab wound in his shoulder. Freeze burns on his legs. Chafe marks on his wrists. Concerned that his fingers were still weak, he sat up and tested his grip around his own forearm. Not great.

Trudging through the living room, he tapped the photos of Cielle and Janie as was his morning ritual. No matter how unpleasant it would be, he'd have to update them now in some fashion. He owed them the truth, but he'd rather not do it during the morning rush to school and work. This afternoon, then.

Reaching the kitchen, he confronted the puddle of bourbon and half-dissolved pills he'd spit on the floor last night when he'd decided not to go through with it. A pathetic postscript ensued—him on his hands and knees, wiping the mess off the linoleum with a dishrag. There'd be no easy way out now. Sitting, he took his pills, properly this time. Fifty milligrams, twice a day, on an empty stomach. Because deteriorating from Lou

Gehrig's wasn't unpleasant enough, he had to forswear alcohol and caffeine while taking riluzole. Sober, tired, *and* dying—a cheery little triad. He downed some Keflex—antibiotics for the stab wound—and sat, rubbing his eyes, trying to ratchet himself fully awake without the benefit of coffee.

The situation was surreal, beyond nightmarish. Had he really, ten hours prior, been ensconced in a Volkswagon-size block of ice? Had a Ukrainian thug actually threatened to murder his daughter if he didn't break into a safe-deposit box? He tried to formulate a next move, but his brain couldn't find traction.

When it came to robbing a bank, where did one start?

He grabbed the morning paper and read the account of yesterday's events. *"Local Man Foils Heist."* There he was in grainy black and white at the press conference, mouth ajar as if in mid-belch, being steered aside by the police captain. His current job was listed, Professional Crisis Responder for LAPD, and he was described as a former soldier. An Upstanding Citizen, brave and newsworthy. He wondered how the article might have read had the reporter known he'd slunk out onto that ledge to give up the ghost. No mention was made of his family. With that in mind, he flipped back a few sections. The obits were thin today. Henry Vivian White, global head of corporate development for a Century City–based investment bank, had died due to complications of a malarial infection he'd contracted while on safari.

HENRY LEAVES HIS BELOVED WIFE,
BEATRICE (POUNDSTONE), AND SONS ROBERT (24)
AND MICHAEL (22).

Atta boy, Henry.

After disabling the fire alarm, he retrieved his suicide note from the coffee table and burned it in the kitchen sink over the disposal. The words curled and vanished into black.

The ringing phone jarred him from his quiet desperation. A chirpy front-office woman was on the line, confirming his dental appointment for next week.

"Oh," Nate said, staring at the dying embers, "no thank you."

"Would you like to reschedule?"

"Nah. I'm gonna be dead soon, and one of the great benefits is not worrying about plaque." He thanked the puzzled silence and hung up.

Then he called to check in on Erica and Sean O'Doherty, the parents to whom he'd served the death notification yesterday. One advantage to still being alive was that he could do his job another day. Reaching voice mail, he left his information again should they need anything.

Into the shower, blasting the heat, flexing that left hand beneath the stream. Leaning into the burn, he thought, *I can still feel* this. *My nerves still function. My muscles still work.* Little victories. Little defeats. Breathing the steam, he contemplated his first step in dealing with Pavlo Shevchenko. He'd go into the office.

What better place to gather information than at LAPD headquarters?

Given that the funeral for Flores Esposita, the bank manager, was in a few hours, he pulled his suit from the back of the closet, brushing dust off the shoulders. His gaze caught on the gun safe buried beneath a pair of kicked-off trousers. Squatting, he twirled the dial, inputting Cielle's birthday. The safe clicked open for the first time since he'd lugged it into the apartment. With some hesitation he peered inside. There the pistol sat. An M9, the same model he'd toted around the Sandbox. Chewing his lip, he considered. What was he gonna do, gun down *mafiya* in the street? If it came to it. But not today. Today he had to go through a metal detector at LAPD headquarters. He kicked the door closed.

The suit still fit well, a pleasant surprise. Sitting on the bed, he leaned over to lace up his shoes, but his left hand had gone weak again, and he stared at it, willing it to clench, to obey. If it couldn't do this, how the hell could it grip a gun, pull a trigger, protect his family? His fingertips chased the laces around until he sat back up, winded with exasperation. He sat for a time, breathing.

Then he got up and retrieved his loafers from the closet.

When Nate stepped off the elevator at the Police Administration Building and entered the bull pen, the detectives and clerks rose and clapped—a tradition to recognize officers who'd closed tough cases. He literally stepped aside and glanced behind him, not getting it until Ken Nowak shouted out, "Look at Hero Boy all dolled up. You goin' on *Oprah* today?"

Nate moved into a sea of handshakes and backslaps, noting how odd—and enjoyable—it was to be recognized as an equal here on this floor, where, by dint of his unusual job, he'd never quite fit in. The only person seemingly unimpressed was Jen Brown, who remained hunched over her desk in her private office. Her center-part haircut had not been updated since he'd known her—nor, he suspected, for sometime before that. When he darkened her doorway, she did not look up from her paperwork. As a sergeant, she was tasked with overseeing the ever-diminishing Crisis-Response Unit, an added responsibility which bore little upside for her.

"So," she eventually said, not yet giving Nate the benefit of her gaze, "you shot a bunch of thugs. Good work, Overbay. And here I thought you only did touchy-feely."

"Look at you, getting all emotional."

She looked up finally, trying to stop a smile from forming. She liked him, he knew, no matter how much she tried not to, and he felt the same way about her. "Why are you here?" she asked. "No one died today. Yet."

"I wanted to do some more follow-up for the O'Doherty family. From yesterday." Telling a lie here, in the heart of LAPD headquarters, felt perilous. The first step onto a slippery slope. Jen was staring at him blankly. Or was that suspicion? "Remember?" he added. "Nineteen-year-old? Car crash?"

"Right. I forgot. Mr. Research. If my detectives did

half the legwork you put into holding people's hands, we'd have a ninety-percent close rate." She pulled off her eyeglasses, ducked out of the chain, and set them on her desk. Shoving back in her chair, she pinched the bridge of her nose. Her white blouse, as close to feminine as her wardrobe allowed, was tucked into severe wool pants. "Parents take it all right?"

"About as expected."

"Nineteen years old. What a thing." She sighed. Then her sergeant face snapped back on, and she waved him out. "Whatever you need for them. Just keep out of my hair. Oh—and, Nate?"

He leaned back through the doorway.

"The bank. Seriously. Didn't know you had it in you."

Nate went to his desk, a ledge of pressed wood floating above a swivel chair. If the half-partition walls hemming him in were more ambitious, he could call it a cubicle. Despite the cramped quarters, he couldn't complain about the work space or the building.

LAPD had finally upgraded its HQ after nearly sixty years, leaving behind Parker Center with all its scandals and transgressions. Two intersecting planes of mirrorlike glass, ten stories high, formed the new building. The city had gone to great lengths to have LAPD's kinder, gentler image reflected in the environmentally friendly building—plenty of glass to evince transparency, a café called LA Reflection, and a rooftop garden that the media releases referred to as "contemplative." Headquarters might have traveled merely the distance of two downtown blocks, but the move had allowed LAPD to enter the new millennium.

Nate sat at his desk and gave a nervous glance around. Across the aisle in his chair, Ken arched his back in a lazy stretch while one meaty hand scrabbled across the keyboard to refresh baseball scores. A Detective II, he was wide-shouldered, sloppy in demeanor but neat in appearance. Though disastrous when filling in to serve death notifications, he had proved to be a capable, even sharp detective—a fact that Nate found continually surprising.

He hunkered down, tucking into his computer and logging on to the databases. His job granted him low-level clearances—enough to pull up crime reports and case files, to check rap sheets and addresses. First he keyed in *"Pavlo Maksimovich Shevchenko."* A decades-old picture of the man came up, perhaps from when he first immigrated, along with minimal information. No driver's license. No gun license. Expensive address in the Hollywood Hills. Substantial taxes paid in California for a little more than a decade. He'd had surveillance placed on him by various detectives and the FBI, which at multiple points had tried to build a continuing-criminal-enterprise case. He was suspected of having served time throughout Ukraine and Russia, but his crimes were unknown, the files from Eastern Europe either lost, scrubbed, or made purposefully opaque by a bureaucracy eager to encourage his emigration. However, one detail had made the journey with him. His nickname, listed as Psyk, Russian for "psycho." Nate scrolled down to a series of surveillance shots, that predatory gleam in the eyes cutting right through the blurry photography.

His mouth, he realized, had gone dry.

A few drops of blood tapped the mouse pad, and he looked up sharply to see Charles there, his skin as gray as death. "Way to go, dipshit," Charles said. "You broke fortune-cookie rule number thirty-seven: Don't make enemies with a dude nicknamed Psycho."

"Not here, Charles. Not at *work*. Can't you just . . . I don't know, go back to being dead?"

But Charles was already leaning over him, staring at the screen. "Let's look up that hot girl with the huge rack from English 101. What was her name?"

Nate ignored him, checking the address of the warehouse in which he'd regained consciousness. The deed was held by a company that owned twenty-seven more properties in the Greater Los Angeles Area and Brighton Beach, New York. Slum apartments, a textile factory, scattered storage facilities. The company resided within a shell corp within a shell corp, and that was how many shell corps deep Nate was able to dig before his clearance hit a wall.

Charles had turned to sit on the desk next to him, resting an elbow atop the monitor. He snapped his fingers. "Mindy Scardina."

"Do you mind?"

Nate must have been making faces, because Ken glanced across, then turned back slowly to his desk, wearing a look of puzzled annoyance. He unclipped from his belt a cluster of keys the size of a hockey puck and tossed them on his desk, the gesture somehow conveying disgust with the state of his surroundings.

"Oh, what, your advanced Google search is more

interesting than Mindy Scardina's tits?" Charles slid over in front of the monitor and squirmed back and forth, making Nate try to read the screen through the hole in his torso.

"Move. Charles—*move*. You're disgusting. Would you grow up?"

"No can do. I'm frozen in time." He made spooky ghost fingers. "Stuck at twenty-seven years old. Like most men. 'Cept *I* have an excuse."

"If I don't figure out how to break into that safe-deposit box, they're gonna kill Cielle."

Charles's brow furrowed, a few grains of sand cascading down his face. "Maybe you can look up the bank?"

"That's what I'm trying to do." But Nate couldn't access any bank information whatsoever, let alone obtain a listing of safe-deposit boxes at First Union.

Charles's shoulders sagged. "Now what?"

Pavlo's dry voice ran in Nate's head: *I had an acquaintance, Danny Urban, who is no longer with us, God rest his soul.*

Already Nate was typing. "Let's start with the *owner* of the safe-deposit box."

Urban's digital file loaded, and they stared together at the text, mouths slightly ajar.

"You're kidding me," Charles finally said. "The guy's a fucking *hit man*. What next?"

Nate clicked a link. A file loaded, and then a crime-scene photo jumped out at them—Urban sprawled across a bedroom carpet, having clawed the patterned comforter off the mattress when he fell. A neat hole above his right eyebrow. One hand lay open, the two smallest fingers shot off, a defensive wound, and an assault rifle lay just beyond his reach. His thin lips were stretched wide in a death rictus, the glittering squares of his teeth spaced along the pink shelves of his gums. A subcompact pistol was placed deliberately beside his head, the barrel aligned neatly with his cheek.

An echo of that broken English: *We had disagreement over fee and ownership of object.* Clearly, this was how disagreements with Pavlo Shevchenko ended.

Nate scrolled down and lifted a finger to the screen, reading the lead detective's report of the ongoing investigation. Though an autopsy had been performed in short order, Urban's corpse remained in the perennially backlogged morgue, stowed for future tests. The hit man's private weapons cache had been taken into evidence, a small arsenal that included everything from frag grenades to AR-15s, ironic given Urban's low-tech MO for his murders: He used a ten-dollar lock-blade knife, available through any hunting catalog.

According to ballistics, the SIG Sauer P250 set down by Urban's cheek had fired the bullet extracted from his head. Leaving the gun behind with the body protected the killer from being found with the murder weapon. The move was also, the detective had noted, a calling card of elite contract killers hired by the Eastern European mob.

Misha.

Charles shuddered, sand falling off him like dandruff. "So a hit man killed a hit man? What's the story?"

"Pavlo hired Urban to do a job," Nate said. "To knock someone off and get something."

"Why'd he use an American killer?" Charles asked. "Why not one of his Ivans?"

"Maybe to make sure there was no connection that could be traced back to him."

"But then once Urban pulled a double cross or wanted to keep what he stole or whatever, our boy Pavlo went back to his roots."

"Which exposed him more. Then again, so did having Misha run a bank job. But Pavlo was willing to take the risk." Nate rocked back in his chair. "Whatever's in that safe-deposit box, he wants it bad."

"We don't even know which box it is," Charles complained. "What are we gonna do, break into all of them?"

"That was Misha's plan."

"What the hell could be in that box?"

"Incriminating photos. Family heirloom. A priceless jewel."

Charles shrugged. "I vote sex tape."

The floor creaked behind Nate, and he closed out of the screen quickly. Pivoting, he looked up at Ken.

"What you looking up?" Ken asked.

A flush crept hotly across Nate's face. His mouth opened, but his brain was still waiting to feed it an excuse. One second passed. Another. Then: "Just a word I overheard the other day. Tyazhiki." Nate grimaced. "I think it means—"

"Shadow people," Ken said. "They're enforcers brought in by the Russkies. No papers, no visas. Utterly lawless. They'll literally ship 'em in on container ships, route 'em through the Long Beach Port. They do a job and head back. Not a footprint."

Charles was standing behind the detective, imitating him, wagging his head importantly. Nate did his best to focus.

"The Russian mob's ruthless," Ken continued. "They'll shoot you just to check the sight alignment on their guns. If it's cheaper to bring in a hit man than pay off a loan, they put out a contract. Life means nothing."

"How about Ukrainians?" Nate asked.

"The Ukrainians?" Ken whistled, and Charles at last stood still at the ominous note. "Even the *Russians* are afraid of the Ukrainians."

Chapter 16

Flores Esposita's funeral at Forest Lawn Cemetery was a crowded, animated affair. Countless uncles and weeping second cousins and families from church. Among others, Nate was singled out by the stoic widower in the eulogy and had his hand shaken by numerous relatives after the casket was lowered from view. The outpouring of warmth only added to his silent regret at the fraudulent role he was playing here. He'd gone into that bank to take a coward's leap and had walked out a hero.

Head down, he moved between the plots back to his Jeep.

"You seem uncomfortable."

He turned to find Agent Abara, impeccably neat in a black suit.

"It's a funeral," Nate said.

"Right. I just thought that given your job, you know, you'd be used to . . ." A wave of his hand. "Events like this."

Nate thought about finding Flores Esposita's clip-on earring on the bank floor. How he'd squeezed and the clasp had pushed into the tender skin of his palm. "If I'd gone through the window earlier, maybe I could've kept her from being shot." It was a regret he hadn't made conscious until he heard himself saying it.

"But you said you climbed out the bathroom window right after you heard the shots."

". . . Yes."

"So how could you have gotten there earlier?"

Nate wet his lips. Shook his head.

Abara had fallen into step beside him. The lush grass, soft underfoot. "You know what happens when I see my kids?" Abara asked.

"You're reminded of the simple power of human love?"

Abara squinted over at him but didn't smile. "I wonder what they're *not* telling me. Maybe that's from being an agent, sure. But you know how teenagers are. Girls. I have two. And everything's a lie right now. Not 'cuz they're malicious. It's because their white matter's not grown in yet, you know?" He shook his head. "They're hard to get through to. It's like they're talking one language and I'm—"

"We're preverbal."

Abara laughed, a dimple indenting either cheek. "Right? So last night my oldest came in past curfew. And I asked where she was, and of course—she was at her friend's. And I know she's lying, and *she* knows I know she's lying, but we're doing this dance still, right?" He stopped walking, his perfect teeth shining in the morning brightness. "Ever have that? Where you're talking to someone and you know they're lying and they know you know? But there you are? Still talking?" The easy smile remained, but his gaze was suddenly intense.

The suit felt hot and tight across Nate's shoulders. He chose his words carefully. "With my daughter, sure."

"Yeah, kids. Sometimes they don't know what's good for them." Abara touched Nate's arm. "See you around."

Nate watched him pick his way through the headstones. When he turned around, he noticed someone among the graves just a few yards off. A worker with a bag lunch and neatly combed hair showing gray at the part, his mouth a line of forbearance. He'd paused for his break sitting respectfully at the edge of a little fountain beside a newly turned plot. A wet shovel rested against one thigh. When Nate approached, the man set down a remaining crescent of sandwich.

Nate stared at the fresh dirt, and the man looked at him with his sun-beaten face. "You family?"

"No," Nate said.

"Oh." The man set his cap on his knee. "Sometimes there's a big turnout"—a gesture to Flores Esposita's grave, around which a dozen folks and grandkids remained, consoling one another—"and sometimes . . ." He flared his half-chewed sandwich at the rectangle of soil.

Nate read the grave marker again, the name registering this time as belonging to the security guard from the bank robbery—the older black man with the striped socks who'd wound up twisted on his back in the lobby. "Wait. This is . . . ?"

The worker nodded. "The bank paid for his resting place."

"Jesus," Nate said. "Someone should be here. Someone should . . ." He felt suddenly weak, and he eased himself down to the fountain ledge beside the man.

"Bad way to die," the worker said. "When you won't be missed."

Nate tried to picture what his own funeral would look like. A few colleagues recycling the same stories. A hired shovel. A designated funeral coordinator, bowing his head mournfully and checking his watch.

Shirt untucked, tie loose, he sat, the sun heating his face. The man chewed quietly beside him for a while, then rose to get back to work, one callused hand rasping up the shaft of the shovel.

Chapter 17

When Nate approached the Santa Monica house, blaring music greeted him from the garage—less a song than a wall of noise aimed at his face. A masculine voice screamed the wrong lyrics to a Guns N' Roses song: *"Welcome to tha Jun-gul, we got funny games!"*

Nate passed between the cars, which had been pulled out onto the driveway to free up the garage, and a big doofy teenage kid drew into view inside, hopping around and flailing at an electric guitar. Cielle sat atop a low cabinet, flipping listlessly through a magazine, her fingers punctuated with black nail polish. Her private-school uniform—plaid skirt and white blouse— matched neither the fingernails nor her scowl, but it gave Nate a brief, inexplicable stab of pride nonetheless.

"Na na na na na na na na knees, knees! Come on, I'm gonna make you SPEED!" The kid noticed Nate and dropped the guitar, letting it dangle around his neck from the sling. He was at least six-four and thick, but he looked less strong than soft and uncoordinated,

all elbows and knees. The curse of the teenage male. A few spread-out dots marked his pale chin and cheeks where a five-o'clock shadow was trying to will itself into existence. An oversize hoodie with plush, checkered lining half covered a pair of Bermuda shorts so long and baggy that they hung in one piece like a kilt. He wore a slightly bemused smile and shaggy black hair capped by—of all things—a hipster fedora. Ear gauges had enlarged the holes in his lobes to the size of nickels.

Jason. The shithead boyfriend.

Cielle's dark pupils lifted, though her face stayed pointed at the magazine. "Gasp," she said flatly. "It's my screwup of a father."

Despite the reception, Nate took a moment to soak in the sight of her. Beautiful, safe, intact. She looked up at him, wrinkled her brow at the spectacle of him standing there gawking.

"Don't be disrespectful," he said, covering. "It's *Mr.* Screwup."

"Nice suit, Nate," she said. Jason ducked out of the guitar and extended it to Cielle, who gave him a withering glare. "I'm not a *coatrack*."

He set it down lovingly on the floor and turned to Nate with excitement. "Dude, you're the *man*. People are wearing WHAT WOULD NATE OVERBAY DO? T-shirts. I'm not kidding—Google that shit."

"What are you talking about?" Nate said.

"Have you watched the news? You're a celebrity."

"No. Steve McQueen was a celebrity. I'm Monica Lewinski."

Jason chewed his lower lip. "Who's Steve McQueen?"

"Who's Monica Lewinski?" Cielle asked.

"I give up," Nate said.

Cielle, back to her magazine. "Thank God."

Nate eyed the husky kid. "Jason, right? How old are you?"

"Seventeen. But I've been emancipated 'cuz my parents were screwups, too. No offense."

"None taken. You are aware that my daughter's fifteen?"

Cielle flipped a page harder than necessary, giving off a crisp snap.

"And a *half*," Jason said. The edge of a tattoo peeked up from his collar. "It's only like sixteen months' difference."

"I appreciate the math. But you're still too old for her."

"Or maybe you're just blinded by the radiance of my awesomeness."

"Or maybe that." Reminding himself that he had bigger fish to fry right now than an emancipated seventeen-year-old with gauge earrings, Nate backed out of the garage and headed to the porch.

Pete answered the front door, on his knees in the foyer, skinny bottle in hand. "Nate. How you feeling today?"

"Oh, God. Let's not start that, please. And what the hell are you doing?"

"Putting hot sauce on my dress shoes."

Casper watched cautiously from the kitchen

doorway. He lifted a stare in Nate's direction, his Rhodesian ridgeback brow furrowed in puzzlement. The
wrinkles on his forehead could convey a broader range
of human emotion than most human faces could.

Nate took in this standoff as Pete returned to the
task, diligently applying sauce to the heel of a two-tone
wing tip. "Of course," Nate said. Then: *"Why?"*

"The dog has chewed up half my shoes."

"So you're putting hot sauce on them."

"To dissuade him. Yes. An admittedly unconven-
tional approach, but I'm running out of footwear. At
least footwear that doesn't make me look like a home-
less guy."

Nate had to smile.

Pete got up. "Casper. Come. Here. Come. *Come.*"

Nate snapped his fingers low at his side, and Casper
trotted over. His hindquarters stayed offset at a slight
jag from his front legs, like revelers navigating a two-
man horse costume.

Pete took Casper's collar and pointed the dog's unwilling nose to the shoes. "See this? Steer clear." He
scratched Casper behind the ears, released him, and
dusted his hands. "He's a maniac. Ate a box of tampons
last week."

"This dog is an exceptional animal."

"That's what all dog owners say. You ever hear anyone say, 'Oh, *my* dog? He's really ordinary.' "

"A fair point." Nate looked at Casper. Casper looked
at him. They knew better.

"So what's up, Nate?"

"I want to talk to you and Janie, actually."

"She'll be right down." Pete started for the kitchen, then said reluctantly, "Listen, the U-pipe beneath the sink's leaking. I've checked it twice. What am I missing?"

"It's the drain, not the U-pipe. Plastic washer gets worn out. There's a box of them in the corner of the pantry."

"Thanks." A sheepish grin. "I'll take a look at it." Pete assumed his position behind the kitchen island. Ground turkey shaped into patties, corn bobbing in a pot on the stove, two glasses filled with soda and a third, presumably Cielle's, with water.

Pete drizzled olive oil into a pan, dropping in sliced onions as Janie entered.

Her head tilted as she took in Nate. Awkward. "You called late last night?"

"Yeah. Look. There's really no good way to lead into this. So . . . uh, I didn't just go up on that bank ledge to foil robbers. I was up there to jump." He kept his eyes on the marble island, but he sensed both faces go lax. "The disease, you know? And . . ."

"What, Nate?" Janie said.

"You need to be careful here. Keep an eye on Cielle. Keep her close."

"Wait. *Why*? You're scaring me."

"Just . . . be cautious. It's for your own good. And hers."

"We haven't seen you in *nine months,*" Janie said. "You don't get to tell us what to do. Certainly not without telling us *why*."

"Okay." He took a breath. Bit his lip. "I got knocked

out and regained consciousness half embedded in a slab of ice."

She'd been ready with a response, but his words must have caught up to her, because her mouth froze partway open. It closed with a little pop.

Still speechless, she circled a hand for him to continue, then listened intently as he spelled out his ordeal with the Ukrainians, ending with Pavlo's threat.

The onions sizzled, black wisps rising, until Pete picked up the pan and turned it upside down in the sink. Janie sank onto a barstool. Pete coughed out an angry one-note laugh, wiped his mouth.

"They threatened to kill my baby?" Janie finally managed. It seemed she was saying it aloud to try to get her mind around it.

"Yes. But I'm not gonna let that happen."

"All due respect, Nate," Pete said, "but it hardly seems like you're in control of the situation." He hurled a dish towel at the backsplash.

Janie looked catatonic. From the garage, muffled screaming: *"You can have anything ya want but yer a better mint taker for free!"*

"We need to just get in the car and start driving," Janie said.

"Not yet," Nate said. "These guys have shown that they have reach, resources. They'll be watching, and who knows what they'll do if you try to run. I've got a window to take care of this."

"So we're supposed to just *sit* here?" Janie said.

"You want them to catch up to us at a Motel 6 in Nevada?" Pete said.

The question bled through the air, and they breathed until it dissipated.

"Do we tell Cielle?" Nate asked Janie.

"Are you kidding?" Pete said. "It'd scare the living hell out of her. What's the upside in that?"

"She hates not knowing," Nate replied. "Not having a say in things. Janie? Are you okay?" Nothing. "Janie, look at me. I will take care of this."

"Give us a moment here," Pete said.

"Okay." Nate pulled his gaze reluctantly off Janie. "I need to check something in Cielle's room. I'll just . . ."

Heavy on his feet, he mounted the stairs. For all his concern about sparing them fallout from his illness, here he'd inflicted on them something much worse. In Cielle's room he headed for the closet. Parted the curtains of clothes. A mound of clutch purses in the back. He dug under them, and there it was.

A red diary.

Just as Pavlo had promised. His men had shown up so quickly after the bank shoot-out. They'd stood where Nate now stood, arms in his daughter's wardrobe, prying and digging and reading. Revulsion rose in his gorge, then something sharper. Rage.

Gathering himself, he breathed deeply, tapping the red leather against his thigh. Something in the closet caught his eye, mostly hidden beneath a black sweater. The edge of a wooden frame. Was it? He lifted the sweater tentatively to discover their old family portrait. The three of them laughing and hugging and half falling over. She'd kept it. Buried in her closet, but still. When he inhaled, he felt the slightest catch in his throat.

The door boomed open, and Cielle and Jason spilled in, Cielle mid-rant: "—just saying I can't believe you called a friend of mine 'Sewer Crotch' on your Face-book page." She halted two steps into the room, her eyes blazing over to Nate, who was bent into her closet, incriminating diary in hand.

Nate held out his hands, a felon at gunpoint, "I'm sorry. I—"

She flew across the room and ripped the diary from his hand. "I can't *believe* you. I get that you're dying and everything, but you can't just sail in here and start prying around in my stuff and reading my *journal*."

"Seriously," Jason added.

"Can we get this clown out of here?" Nate asked.

"Chillax." Jason showed him his palms. "I'm leaving." He kissed Cielle, keeping his eyes on Nate the whole time, a little power move that, on another day when Nate owed his daughter less, might have resulted in a broken nose. And then the kid was gone, thumping down the stairs whistling the chorus from "Paradise City."

Nate faced his daughter across a floor littered with dirty clothes and torn-out magazine pages.

She glowered at him. "Why are you back here?"

"What?"

"Why'd you come back again? I assume it wasn't just to read my diary."

He wanted so badly to be straight with her, to paint the whole picture, taking some of the edges off the gory points, but he wasn't sure what was best, and Pete and Janie certainly deserved a vote. He cleared his throat to stall, but Cielle was having none of it.

"What were you doing at the bank, Nate?"

Quite a lane change. He heard himself hesitate a beat too long. "Bank stuff. Making a deposit. But I was interrupted by the robbery—" A second late he caught his choice of words.

"*Interrupted?* From what? Making a deposit?"

"Yes," he said.

"In the news you said you were in the bathroom." Her gaze, steady beneath those long eyelashes. Questions and emotions whirring beneath the surface, slot-machine reels that wouldn't land. Did she know?

He chewed his cheek, not wanting to lie more but not willing to tell his fifteen-year-old daughter that he'd been planning on killing himself.

Finally she said, "At least do me one favor. Let's not pretend that either of us doesn't know you're lying."

"Okay."

Relief showed on her face, though she covered quickly, wiping her nose roughly on her sleeve. More silence.

He started for the door.

"You hate him," she said.

"What?"

"Shithead Jason. You *hate* him."

Nate paused, hand on the knob, trying to switch lanes. The dispute loomed ahead like a pileup. "He doesn't exactly make a glowing first impression."

"Jay is a *musician*. He's an artist."

"No. Eric *Clapton* is an artist. Jason is a mouth breather with a guitar."

"Who's Eric Clapton?"

Nate thought, *I'm gonna kill myself in earnest.*

She was already caught up in her objection. "Who do you want me to date? One of those is-this-gonna-be-on-the-test dorks from my AP classes? I like Jay because he's *different*. And you know what else? He's here for me. Unlike *some* people."

"I know you still like me a little." Nate gestured at the uncovered family portrait in the closet. "You keep the ridiculous picture of us in here."

She curled her broad shoulders, withdrawing into herself, her hands gone again in her sleeves, turning the cuffs to puppet mouths. "Nowhere else to store it."

He nodded. They were done here. As he passed her on his way out, his arm brushed lightly against hers, and he realized that this touch of fabric was the first physical contact he'd had with his daughter in years. How had it gotten here? The question weighed on him all the way down to the kitchen.

The smell of burned onions laced the air. Pete paced, circling the island, and Janie sat on the barstool. She was grimacing in pain, her head tilted and one arm stretched low with the wrist cocked back.

"I have an acquaintance who's a cop," Pete said. "We have to take this to someone who knows what the hell he's doing."

"And say what?" Nate asked. "What proof do we have? A pair of handcuffs in a warehouse? Even the ice has probably melted by now."

"This is out of our league, Nate. And certainly too much for you to handle. We need to enlist the help of folks whose job it is to deal with people like this."

"Pete, I researched this guy. He's a heavy hitter. He means what he says."

"He made a *death threat*. On a girl. They can move on him fast, get him behind bars."

"Investigations take time. A *lot* of time. And Pavlo Shevchenko is rich and connected."

"So he owns cops?" Pete's voice rose, fear and frustration masquerading as anger. "Federal agents? Who will do what? Call to warn him?"

"I work in a cop shop, Pete. It doesn't *take* a dirty cop. It takes one clerk with a big mouth. One IT guy willing to search a file. Trust me, I looked stuff up today I wasn't supposed to."

Jane lifted her head and pulled her arm across her chest, tugging at the back of her elbow, grimacing.

"I'm talking about one offline conversation," Pete said. "With someone I trust."

"Are you willing to take that chance?" Nate stabbed a finger up, aiming in the vicinity of Cielle's bedroom. "Given what he'll do to her if you're wrong?"

Pete stopped pacing, his long face looking even longer. The drain dripped invisibly beneath the sink.

"*No,*" Janie said. "Not yet anyway."

"Shevchenko gave me five days," Nate said. "I have until Sunday."

"To do what, Nate? Rob a bank?" Pete blew out a breath, ran both hands through his thick hair. "You make messes, Nate. That's what you do. And other people clean them up for you."

Janie gripped the top of her head, pulling gently to

the side, trying to stretch out the knot she always got on the right side when she was tense or upset.

"Her *shoulder*." The words came out more sharply than Nate had intended.

"What?"

Nate pointed at Janie. "Rub her damn shoulder, Pete."

A puzzled pause, and then it finally dawned, and Pete stepped behind her, massaging. Janie grimaced against the pain.

Nate took her hands across the island and looked into her scared blue eyes. "No matter what I have to do, I will not let them hurt our daughter. I promise you."

She gave the slightest nod. He started out.

Pete called after him, "Where are you going?"

"To handle it."

Nate passed Casper at the front door, gnawing on Pete's wing tips. He seemed to be enjoying the hot sauce.

Chapter 18

The Los Angeles County Department of the Coroner was closing up as Nate slotted the Jeep into a parking spot. The imposing administrative building, a majestic interlace of brick and stone, pinned down a street corner on North Mission at the brink of the USC Medical Center. The building had first been dropped into Boyle Heights, a not-altogether-pleasant East L.A. neighborhood, as the County General Hospital. Ceramic floor tiles still spelled out the original function. Given the surfeit of movies that used the location and the glut of tourists—yes, tourists—it was the only coroner's office, at least that he'd heard of, with a gift shop. Among the expected macabre paraphernalia, it sold coffin couches and chalk-outline beach towels. A sign by the cash register declared, CHECKS ACCEPTED WITH TWO FORMS OF ID OR DENTAL RECORDS.

It was Wednesday night, so Nate's favorite coroner, Eddie Yeap, would be toiling into the wee hours. Nonetheless, Nate put a spring into his step before the front door locked. As he had learned in his job: Always start with the body. In this case it was all he had. If he was ever going to figure out a way into Urban's safe-deposit box, he'd need to find out as much about the man as possible. And finding out as much as possible about the deceased happened to be what Nate was best at.

Department security had been beefed up since the O.J. trial had brought to light evidentiary chain-of-custody weaknesses. Winding down the corridors, Nate greeted the sets of guards by name, finally ending up in the doorway of one of the wide, cool autopsy rooms. Eddie stood hunched over a corpse, his wet latex gloves pulling up into view, gripping a pair of angled scissors. A soft little man with a nervous laugh, he inexplicably referred to all the corpses as "Jonesy."

"Mr. Overbay. Heh. Serving another death notification tonight? They're keeping you as busy as me. Heh."

The understaffed department processed over twenty thousand autopsies a year, and even so a crushing backlog waited in the wings. They were running out of space quicker than a state jail, the main lab and crypts jammed to capacity. Some years back there'd been a big stir when rats had gotten into the refrigerated annex behind the main building and chewed up the inert inhabitants.

"Yeah. Must be a full moon." The chill tightened Nate's arms, raised the hairs at his nape. "Did you work on Danny Urban?"

"Nine mil above the right eyebrow. A hit man. Heh. That got Jonesy fast-tracked."

"Anything unusual about him?"

"Guy had a whole damn armory in his closet, a real

gear queer. Cops took assault rifles and no foolin' C4 into evidence. Not yer average Jonesy." Eddie glanced up. "You give 'em all the treatment, don't you? Sit and hold their hands. Read the reports. Even a hit man. Heh. I guess if it helps you with the next of kin. Not their fault, I suppose."

Nate mustered a flat smile in response, glad to find Eddie focused again on his work. "Where'd you store him?"

"Dunno. Check the computer. I'm logged in. I'd do it myself, but"—he shrugged, gloves buried to the wrists in the Y incision—"got my hands full."

Nate checked the computer, then found his way to the appropriate crypt. A security guard unlocked for him the thick metal door, which released a waft of cold, medicinal air as it yawned open. The corpses were not stored in metal drawers but slotted in plain sight on trays that lined the walls like bunk beds on a submarine. Full to the rafters. Nate moved among the scattered morgue gurneys that accommodated the overflow, checking tags attached to body bags or to the flesh itself. A short ways in, he found Urban's gurney and nodded a thank-you at the guard, who left him alone with the body, as was their arrangement.

When Nate unzipped the body bag, it exhaled a puff of sweet rot and ethanol. As the vinyl fell away, Urban's face emerged, cold and firm. The ridiculousness of the task struck Nate. But he hadn't known where else to start.

"What's your safe-deposit-box number?" he asked Urban.

The unblinking eyes stared up at him.

Nate searched the corpse, taking his time. Hairline, toes, shoulders. One ankle was swollen and discolored; Urban had probably twisted it in the shoot-out. Nate didn't know what precisely he was looking for and discovered nothing of interest. Giving up, he sat beside the corpse and, more from habit than anything, took the intact hand in his own weakened grip. Alone with the dead, he considered the enormity of the job before him. A little more than four days to break into a safe-deposit box for which he had no number, to retrieve he knew not what. If he didn't figure something out, Cielle would be next on that slab. So much to accomplish before he could rest.

As he rose despondently, Urban's cool hand slid from his and he felt a slight rub on the finger. He turned over the hand, examining the white flesh. A thin seam of something sticky across the pad of the index finger. And a bit more under the nail. Adhesive?

The heavy door boomed back into place behind him when he exited the crypt, and he grabbed a few lungfuls of moderately fresher air as he crossed to the autopsy room. "There's something sticky on Urban's hand. Did you identify it?"

"I remember something," Eddie said. "Turned out to be insignificant. Report's on my desk, though, you wanna take a look."

The file was there in Eddie's tray, fifth down in a towering stack. Eddie had run the substance found beneath Urban's nail, the lab identifying it as duct-tape adhesive. Stuck to the adhesive was a strand of white carpet matching that in Urban's bedroom, where he was found.

Chewing his lip, Nate stared at the result, trying to figure out some way to make it relevant. Then he jotted down Urban's address and headed for the exit.

The sky above the row of town houses had turned charcoal by the time Nate arrived at Danny Urban's Van Nuys address. A shoe-box-size package waited on the porch, the orange-and-blue FedEx label frayed from transport. He toed it. Surprisingly heavy, it gave off a clank, its contents shifting. Behind a crisscross of crime-scene tape, the front door was locked. Judging from the way the door jiggled beneath Nate's hand, however, it was not dead-bolted. He took a step back, looked in either direction, then kicked the door in. Ducking through the tape, he entered, reached back for the FedEx box, and eased the door shut behind him in the damaged frame. Then he clicked on the flashlight he kept stored in the cargo space of his Jeep.

The bullet holes pockmarking the entry wall addressed a question that had been lingering in a corner of Nate's mind: Why hadn't Shevchenko's men tortured Danny Urban to force him to give up the number of his safe-deposit box? Answer: They hadn't had a chance to. That's the problem with trying to knock off hit men. They know how to shoot back.

Squatting, Nate opened the FedEx box, yanking and tearing until the cardboard gave way. When he glanced inside, the contents set his head ringing, and he glanced away and then back as if hoping to find something else there. Nested in the U of a curled hunting catalog were maybe twenty lock-blade knives. They looked so ordinary resting there, but Nate knew what they represented. Urban, stocking up for future jobs.

He left the box on the floor. The narrow flashlight beam restricted his view, so he progressed slowly, each movement a stomach-churning reveal. The town house's interior told the story of the assault. Bloodstains on the counter in the kitchen, where the fingers of Urban's left hand had been shot off. He must have had a weapon within reach when they'd burst in, for he'd returned fire quickly, punching divots into the entry wall and shattering a hanging mirror. Cupboards and drawers tossed, Shevchenko's men turning the place upside down in their search. Bloody handprint on the wall halfway up the stairs. Cabinets knocked open in the hall off the landing, side table shattered by bullets. Bedroom door ajar, painted with a stroke of red. And then the cluttered master suite, covered with porn DVDs, *Soldier of Fortune* magazines, and faux-antique furniture. Nate stepped over a fallen chair, taking in the lush white carpet marred with more handprints and finally matted down where Urban's head had landed once the triggerman—probably Misha—had caught up to him.

Tufts of foam poked through slashes in the mattress. A letter desk in the corner had been searched. The drawers were empty, half pulled out, papers rifled through by the Ukrainians or the cops or both.

Nate squatted over the amoeba of blood, which had hardened to rust in the thick carpet. Thinking about that white strand recovered from the duct-tape adhesive beneath Urban's nail, he looked at the handprint smudges leading from the door at intervals. Urban had been dragging himself to safety. Nate pictured him wounded and desperate, clawing forward with a hand and a half, bathed in sweat as footsteps grew loud behind him. If they'd done this to a hardened hit man, what chance did Nate have against them?

He spun, scanning the wall, the flashlight beam picking across a stack of army-surplus woodland-camo fatigue shirts, a dented DVD player, and a single dirty sock. Something shiny winked at him, half hidden by the leg of the letter desk.

A roll of duct tape.

A crackle of electricity moved through him, pricking his skin, trepidation and excitement rolled into one. He crossed the room and picked up the roll. One edge speckled with blood. A few indentations, millimeters apart. Teeth marks. Nate called to mind the crime-scene photo, Urban's square teeth spaced inside the terrible oval his mouth had formed in death. The man had needed to bite to tear the tape since by the time he'd gotten upstairs, he'd had only one functional hand.

With murderers on your heels, why go after duct tape?

Nate dropped the roll. Walked back to the blood splotch. Nothing. The flashlight beam moved toward the doorway as if of its own volition, illuminating the fallen chair. Then, slowly, Nate pulled it north to the ceiling above it.

A fan.

The electricity along his skin surged into a current. Urban had run up here not only to get away but to hide something. The thing Shevchenko's men were after. He'd stood on the chair and taped it to the fan. He'd fallen off the chair. Twisted that ankle. Tried to crawl to a position of cover. And then.

His heart thundering, Nate walked across the room. Righted the chair and stood on it. Reaching up, he felt along the tops of the fan blades. Sure enough, on the second blade his fingers touched a lifted edge of duct tape. He tore it free and held it under the flashlight.

Adhered to one side like a glittering jewel—a safe-deposit-box key. Stamped on the head, 227.

He blew out the breath burning his chest, his vision spotting. Clenched the key in his fist. Relief. Now all he had to do was impersonate a dead hit man, provide false documentation at the bank, get into the vault, trick a manager into using the guard key, and remove the box's contents while leaving no trace. Piece of cake. But still. He had the key. Which was further than Shevchenko and his team of expert thugs had gotten. Maybe Nate could find a way out of this yet.

The sudden ring of his cell phone cut through the silence, scaring him upright. He wobbled on the chair and had to take a quick step down, nearly turning his ankle in solidarity with Urban. His hands fumbled over the phone, finally opening it.

"Nate. Nate?" Janie's voice, thin, wrenched high with fear. "You have to get here *now*."

Chapter 19

Nate screeched up into the driveway, back tire swiping across the lawn. Flew from the Jeep, leaving the door ajar. He banged on the house door, shouting, and then hands fussed at the dead bolt and chain and Janie was there, her nostrils and the rims of her eyes red. He grabbed her shoulders. "Where's Cielle?"

"Cielle's okay. She was up in her room. With Casper."

Hearing voices, Nate charged back toward the kitchen. Janie had described the intruder in their brief conversation. Yuri, the giant from outside the bank. Yuri of the mashed nose and the rescue saw. "He came to the house," Nate said, still grappling with the fact of it.

"Yes, the driveway."

Nate rounded the corner and saw Pete sitting on the counter, cradling his hand, which he'd wrapped in a dish towel filled with ice. His mouth was clenched, lips bloodless and trembling, his broad shoulders drooping. Cielle stood before him, Casper leaned into the backs of her legs as he did when agitated or craving attention.

"I was in the car." Pete choked back pain. "Right in the driveway. Janie was inside."

Nate wheeled to Janie. "If he laid a finger on you—"

"No," she said. "I never saw him. I heard the noise outside." She carefully unwrapped the dish towel, and Pete's breathing quickened. "And then he was gone."

"What did he do to you?" Nate asked Pete.

"He grabbed my hand. Slammed it in the car door."

Cielle gave out a little cry. "Why? Who *was* he?"

Janie finished unfolding the blood-spotted towel, laying Pete's hand bare. It looked wrong, bent at the middle, his thumb lolling at an unnatural angle. His skin was pink, angry from the ice. "It's broken, honey," Janie said. "There's no question. We need a doc to reduce and cast it."

Pete said, "How will we explain it?"

"Fell off a ladder," Janie said.

"What are you talking about?" Cielle asked.

"Why'd he come here?" Nate asked. "Just out of the blue?"

Janie shifted with discomfort, and Pete's grimace tightened. "Pete called his friend," she said. "The cop. Earlier. From work."

From the set of her mouth, Nate knew that this had already caused a disagreement between them. He felt his pulse beating at his temples. "Despite what we agreed?"

Pete said, "I'm not really in the mood for a lecture right now."

"So they caught wind of it," Nate said. "You broke the one rule."

"Someone *please* tell me what's happening!" Cielle yelled.

"Don't lay this on me," Pete said. "This began with *you*, Nate. It's on *your* shoulders—"

Nate's voice rose to match Pete's. "You put my daughter at risk—"

Pete lifted his good hand, the fingers trembling. "I didn't. The guy, he said, 'Next time, we take her.' So she's safe now. At least as safe as she *was*."

Cielle screamed, a rush of fear and anger. *"What the hell is going on?"*

An abrupt silence, broken only by the *chop-chop-chop* of a sprinkler in the backyard.

"What?" With dread, Cielle glanced from face to face. "What are you keeping from me now?"

Janie looked over at Nate. Save the freckles across the bridge of her nose, her skin was washed of color. She gave a little nod.

"The guy behind the bank robbery found me," Nate said. "And he thinks I owe him for breaking up the heist. He wants me to steal something for him."

Cielle's eyes widened. "Or what?"

"He threatened to hurt you."

"Me? What did *I* do?"

Nate reached for her, but she jerked back as if he'd struck her.

"I will not let him touch you. I will do *any*thing—"

"So that guy, that huge guy you're talking about . . . ?" Cielle was shaking her head, still backing up, twisting away from him. "And you—you weren't gonna tell me? *I'm* the one at risk, and you kept it from me?"

"That was my fault," Pete said. "I didn't want to scare you."

"Well, guess what?" Cielle kept her glare on Nate. "I'm fucking scared."

With the longest of the kitchen knives held across his knees, Nate sat downstairs in his former living room on his former couch staring at his former TV, though it was turned off. In the dark rectangle of the flat-screen, he could see his pale reflection and the portrait of Pete, Janie, and Cielle on the wall behind him. Their frozen faces hovered ghostlike over his shoulder.

Since Janie had to take Pete to the emergency room, Nate had agreed to stay and keep watch over Cielle, who had retreated angrily to her bedroom. Twice he'd gone up to knock and talk through the locked door, but his attempts at comforting her were met with no response. The sounds of her frightened crying eroded something inside him until he'd put his back to the wall and slid to the floor. He'd sat in the hall outside her bedroom for a time torturing himself before taking up the more strategic position on the couch. His anger had spent the last few hours simmering as he contemplated what to do.

The rusty complaint of the garage door announced Janie and Pete's return. Nate rose to meet them, knife in hand. Janie helped Pete along, a white cast encasing his hand, his protruding index finger clamped by an additional splint.

"A couple metacarpal fractures," Janie said. "Spica cast for six weeks."

"I'm sorry," Nate said. "You're right. This did start with me."

Pete waved him off. He looked shaken still.

"Cielle?" Janie asked.

"Upstairs. Won't come out."

Janie nodded and started up.

Nate and Pete regarded each other awkwardly.

"I'm gonna take care of this, Pete. I'll keep you guys out of it. I promise. I'm gonna go see this guy. Tonight."

"Nate," Pete said, his eyes glassy. "Can I talk to you a minute?"

"Of course."

He gestured toward the garage, and Nate stepped out after him, puzzled. Once the door had closed behind them, they faced each other in the quiet.

"Look, Nate, I'll be honest with you." Pete shifted on his feet, uncomfortable.

"What, Pete? Spit it out."

"The guy, when he grabbed my arm, it was like I was a doll. I mean, Ukrainian gangsters. This is *real*."

"I know."

"And I mean, this is your mess, Nate. I've cleaned up after you before. But I don't know . . ."

"What?" The light from the garage-door opener clicked off, leaving them only with a faint throw of moonlight through the window. Nate could hear Pete breathing, see the outline of sweat on his cheek. "I don't get it. What are you saying?"

Pete cleared his throat. "I mean, what did you get me into here, Nate? It's your mess."

"Yeah. Yeah, it is."

"When Sally died, I barely came back from it. It took me months just to notice that the fucking sun was still in the sky, you know?"

"No one's gonna die here, Pete. Not Janie, not Cielle."

"I don't know that I could get through something like that again." More breathing. Something jangled in his hand, and Nate saw he was making a fist around his car keys. "I just moved in two and a half months ago."

"Wait," Nate said. "No. No, no, no—"

"I can't do it, Nate. It's not my mess. I paid off the mortgage here before things got tough financially—"

"This isn't about money, Pete. They *love* you. Janie loves you. And Cielle—think about how she feels about you. You *have* to stay."

"And I love them, too—" His voice broke in a half sob. "I'll go with nothing. They can keep it all. But I can't leave them knowing they're . . . you know. Alone."

It took everything Nate could muster to hold his mouth closed. Teeth clenched, lips pressed. And then he felt all the anger and tension leave, deflating him.

"Okay," Nate said. "I got it."

"I mean, you're in the middle of it anyway. You might as well—"

"Pete. I said I got it."

"Tell them. Tell them I love them. And I'm sorry." Pete shifted the keys in his hand, his face narrowed with grief. He shuffled to the car, cast drawn in to his stomach protectively. His fingers pulsed, and the car chirped, and when he ducked in, Nate could see in the dome light that he was sobbing silently.

The garage door whirred up, and Pete backed out, and then the door closed and Nate stood there until the overhead light clicked off again. He took a deep breath, his lungs aching. Blew it out. Went inside.

Janie sat cradling Cielle on the couch. They looked up, faces drawn. "I heard the garage door," Janie said. "I thought you left."

"No." Nate bit his lower lip. "Pete."

Janie's face broke.

Nate couldn't stand to see her grief head-on. He studied the tips of his shoes. "He loves you both very much. But it's a lot to handle. Too much, probably, for anyone." He couldn't believe he was defending the guy. "And he wanted to make sure you were taken care of financially, the house at least. He was broken up. He cares about you a lot, that much I could tell."

When he finally dared to lift his head, Janie had composed herself as best she could. For the moment she and Cielle were holding it together, but they looked utterly shell-shocked.

"My God." Janie blinked, tears finally spilling. She stroked her daughter's hair. "We're all alone in this."

Nate could hear the faintest click of the kitchen clock. "I'm still here."

Their faces showed that to be scant consolation.

Chapter 20

Passing a strip mall on a busy street in Tarzana, Nate spotted the illuminated sign with glowing ornate letters: *NEW ODESSA*. Pavlo Shevchenko's suggested meeting place. Granted, Nate was a few days early, but it was his best bet to find the man, and in light of Yuri's attack they had business to discuss. Janie was okay with holing up behind locked doors, 911 ready on speed dial. Vowing to check in on them later, Nate had stopped off at his place to pick up his gun and his medication, the two essentials he'd require moving forward.

He flipped a U-turn, the Jeep rattling into the lot, and parked at the far end. He popped the glove box and reached for the Beretta, but as soon as his hand touched the cool metal, something made him look up and across at the restaurant. A done-up middle-aged couple, the man with a cheap suit and skinny tie, the woman in a slinky sequined dress, approached a large oak door. A vast bouncer emerged from the shadows of the awning and patted them both down thoroughly, the diners submitting readily to the search as if it were a commonplace prelude to a meal. Nate looked back across at his hand buried in the glove box. Then he moved it from the stock of the handgun to the pill bottle. He gulped down his nightly dose of riluzole and antibiotics, adding Advil in response to the complaints of the stitched wound in his shoulder.

His heartbeat reverberated in his palms, his neck, matching the taps of his steps across the parking lot. As he neared the awning, the bouncer loomed.

"I'm here to see Pavlo Shevchenko," Nate said.

"Spread arms."

Nate complied.

The man's paws groped Nate's sides, his belt line, squeezing each leg and sliding from groin to ankle. As he knelt, his pant cuff pulled high, exposing a gun barrel strapped to the ankle. Satisfied, he rose and checked Nate's chest and stomach, presumably for a wire, untucking and lifting Nate's shirt without a trace of hesitation. "Come."

Nate followed him into a dim lounge, dense with smoke and sweet perfume and the tang of pickled fish. Couples and groups of men crowded the tables, animated voices speaking what Nate assumed was Ukrainian. A glimpse through velvet curtains revealed a brick-walled banquet hall to one side, a makeup-intensive singer swaying and crooning lyrics in a foreign tongue as partygoers slow-danced drunkenly, holding each other as if in grief. A momentary disorientation washed over Nate; he had stepped through a portal into a foreign country.

The bouncer put a broad hand on the small of Nate's back, steering him forcefully through. A table in the rear corner was framed by several pillars, affording it relative privacy and clear place of distinction. Drawing into view at the table's head, bent so his elbows framed his plate, was Pavlo Shevchenko. He wore a dark suit, slightly dated in style, with a thin, expensive-looking dress shirt. Hunched protectively over his food, chewing, he looked lean and hungry, his face angular in the faint light. His eyes lifted to freeze Nate in a cold stare.

Across from Pavlo in the other seat of honor sat a heavy older man, thick-lipped and wearing an expression of general displeasure. The rest of the chairs were occupied by men wearing velour warm-ups and chunky gold Rolexes, sipping vodka from weighty shot glasses. Right out of central casting. None of the henchmen from the warehouse were in evidence. Tyazhiki. Shadow people.

The bouncer had a brief exchange with one of the men, the words sharp. Pavlo interrupted, addressing Nate directly. "You have accomplished my task already?"

"No. I need to speak with you. About what happened tonight. At the house."

Pavlo leaned back, crossed his arms. "Sit." He gestured at the man beside him, who vacated his seat obediently. Nate slid down into the chair, the bouncer sidling behind him out of his line of sight. At the table's center stood a slender bottle of vodka.

Pavlo gestured at the man at the other end of the table. "Best Ukrainian restaurant, it is owned by a Georgian. Can you believe?"

Nate took a closer look at the restaurant owner. His jaundiced fingers twiddled with a thick black lock pasted across his forehead, arranging and rearranging it with a vanity befitting neither the matted hair nor his slovenly demeanor. He'd missed a spot shaving, a few coarse black threads at one corner of his mouth. The skin under his eyes was dark and flecked with skin tags, textured pouches like oyster shells. It was a magnificent face. A Depression-era photographer would have turned cartwheels to find such a face on a breadline. He appraised Nate sullenly, silently. Perhaps he did not understand English.

"Eat," Pavlo said. "Blini with red caviar. The Americans have with black caviar to spend more, but is better with red." He gestured at a mound of small half-moon dumplings beneath a dollop of sour cream. "And varenyky. Small, not like big China potstickers. Eat. You work for me now. One of my associates."

"I'm not hungry," Nate said.

Pavlo remained perfectly still, hands frozen at the sides of his plate. "The Georgian will be insulted that you do not eat."

"Then he'll have to be insulted," Nate said.

A chilled silence. The others set down their utensils.

"Your man came to my wife's house," Nate said. "He broke the hand of—"

Pavlo slid his plate to the side. "You did not make call to police. You did not break our arrangement. That is only reason your daughter still breathes."

Nate's gaze moved to a steak knife just beyond his elbow. Pavlo's eyes followed his stare, then rose again to his face, unconcerned.

"This man who called police, next time we will kill him. We know where he called. We know who he spoke to. His protest, it has been misfiled by police. We own many police. You do not know which ones in which departments. Every time you make phone call, you play Russian roulette with your daughter. Is this clear?"

"I will do what you want me to do. I will get you what's in that safe-deposit box. If you stay away from my family."

A glint of sturdy Soviet dentistry. "It is not anymore your family."

"Don't fuck with them."

Pavlo set his hands on the table's edge. Pushed back, his chair chirping on the faux-marble floors. He stood.

The men at the table were on their feet swiftly, even the Georgian. Nate became aware of uniform movement in the space all around him, and when he turned, his skin prickled at the sight. Every diner in the restaurant had risen, even those in booths, bending with difficulty from the effort. Their gazes stayed carefully forward, not fully turned toward Pavlo. Napkins fell from laps. The strains of music drifting in from the banquet hall only underscored the abrupt silence in the restaurant proper.

Nate, the only person sitting.

He had never seen anything like this. A headache thrummed at his temples. Every sense heightened. A spoon clattered to the floor across the restaurant; to Nate it sounded like drumsticks beating a snare.

Pavlo made a slight gesture with his hand, and the diners somehow noted this and rumbled back into motion, sitting, pouring wine, resuming conversations. His focus swiveled to Nate.

"You come here for *strelka*. Meeting. As if you are my equal." His voice, raised for the first time. Up until now he'd conveyed all his power and menace with little more than a whisper.

"I will teach you who I am." He pulled at his thin dress shirt, buttons popping off one after another, skittering across the table. At first his skin seemed bizarrely dark, but as his shirt fell away, Nate realized: It was covered with blue, slightly blurred tattoos. Pavlo lifted a thumb to a rose needled into the base of his neck. "My initiation." An eight-pointed star came next, just below his collarbone. "This says I am *vor*. Professional. I do not belong to myself. I belong to a code. To a world of thieves. I have no family but them." Below the star, a church with multiple domes. "And here. Each dome a trip to the Zone." He shed his jacket, his finger jabbing into a tattoo on his shoulder: a hand holding a tulip wrapped three times in barbed wire. "Convicted underage for robbery. Three years spent. Each barb on the wire one month. And this"—a cross and shackles with numbers and Cyrillic lettering—"second trip. Corrective Labor Colony Number Six. Here, isolation cell, Block Seven."

Nate said, "Look—"

"Close your mouth."

The sudden rage severed the words in Nate's throat.

Pavlo indicated a tattoo of a wolf with a bare-toothed scowl. "My promise to avenge those who put me inside." He tore his shirt off altogether, pointed to a gnarl of scar tissue in his side. "Derybasivska Street in Odessa. Stabbed." He translated a Cyrillic scroll across his ribs. " 'Mother, do not cry for me any longer. Let me be dead to you.' " He turned around. Two eyes on his back required no explanation, but he indicated an eagle on his shoulder blade. "This shows escape from Vorkuta Camp. And this"—a quarter-size patch of shiny skin—"assassination try in Kiev."

Nate risked a glance around the restaurant. Everyone eating and talking, dutifully ignoring what was happening in plain sight. Dozens of witnesses, none of whom would see a thing. He moved to rise, but a vise grip crushed his shoulders, sinking him back into the chair. The bouncer, breathing down on him.

Pavlo slammed his hands on the place mat in front of Nate, silverware and glasses jumping on the starched white tablecloth. Nate strained to lean back, but the pressure on his shoulders was unrelenting. Pavlo pointed at the fingers of one hand, ticking off each ring tattoo. An asterisk in a circle. "Fatherless. I become thief because of broken home." A white cross on a dark rectangle. "I survive the crosses. Solitary." A skull within a diamond, split by bars. "I serve in prison for violent criminals only."

Leaning forward, he gave off a waft of spicy cologne and old-fashioned shaving cream, the smell of a man from another era. His face inches from Nate's. His eyes fluttered closed. Words tattooed on his lids. " 'Do not rouse me.' For this the pricker insert a spoon beneath eyelid to firm it for needle." Pavlo straightened. One loafer hit the floor, then another. Shackle tattoos on his ankles, words on the insteps. He translated: " 'They drag me under armed guard.' " Pavlo tore at his belt violently. His pants fell, exposing boxer shorts of a blue that matched the ink decorating his flesh. His kneecaps sported stars. "I kneel before no man. And last."

With dread, Nate watched Pavlo's hands move to his boxers. Tattooed thumbs hooked the band and slid them down to midthigh. Nate shoved back violently in the chair, but the man whose seat he occupied stepped in to help the bouncer hold him in place.

He flushed, skin on fire. He felt like a child, utterly and comprehensively overpowered. The stink of the herring on the table was making him queasy. In the background he could hear the clink of silverware against plates, no one daring to stop eating.

Pavlo fisted Nate's hair with both hands and forced his face toward his bare thighs, toward the private smells of musk and talcum powder. The swollen bud of his head nudged out from a nest of gray wire. Cyrillic lettering low beneath his belly button. Pavlo leaned over, teeth clenched as he hissed the translation: " *'Let them hate as long as they fear.'* "

Anger burned in Nate's chest, evaporating any panic. He braced a foot against one of the table legs and shoved with all his might. The table skidded a foot or so, plates and glasses jumping, and the two men holding him down lost their grip. Nate twisted up and away from Pavlo's grasp, but then the bouncer palmed his head and slammed it to the table. A cool ring of steel pressed against his temple, and he heard the soft click of the gun cocking.

"You want to do it?" Nate said. "Then *do it*. But quit

wasting my time with the freak show. I've got a job to do."

A view of Pavlo, offset by forty-five degrees. Nate felt as though his skull might collapse from the pressure of the giant hand. One finger smashed his nose, another smeared his lips to one side. Vodka glugged unevenly from the toppled bottle.

Pavlo studied him calmly as he looped his belt, buttoned his coat.

The spilled alcohol was making Nate's eyes water. "Pull the trigger," he said, "or get off me."

The Georgian had barely moved. Overflowing his chair, now displaced from the shoved table, he uttered his first words in broken, barely intelligible English. "Take him into kitchen. I will haff cleaned up."

But Pavlo gave a small shake of his head, the ring of steel lifted, and the pressure came off Nate's temple. He straightened up.

"You are as crazy as Chechen nigger," Pavlo said. "I have seen many men in many circumstances. And you, my friend, are not correct in your head."

This, Nate thought, *from a man nicknamed Psyk*.

"We will see if you are still wise enough to fear." Though his pants were now buckled again, Pavlo set a hand above his groin where the slogan was tattooed.

"If you want any chance at getting what's in that safe-deposit box," Nate said, "then keep out of my way. And stay clear of my family."

"I will give you and family space if you obey. But we will be watching. You have four days. And then"—

Pavlo made a quick slashing gesture across his stomach with the blade of his hand—*"sffft."*

He pointed toward the door and sat down again at the strewn table.

Nate felt all eyes on his back as he threaded through the tables, his step quickening as he neared the big oak door and the fresh nighttime air beyond.

Chapter 21

Nate faced Janie across the kitchen counter, her hands cupped around a mug of chamomile tea. She'd drawn all the curtains, he'd checked all the rooms, and for the moment it was just them again in their old house, their daughter upstairs. But now, he realized, it was probably time for him to leave.

He got up from the barstool, withdrew the Beretta from the waist of his jeans, and set it carefully on the counter. "If they come again. You're here with Cielle."

"Is this real?" Janie's eyes were unfocused, dazed.

"What?"

"All of it. Your dying. The death threat on Cielle. Pete leaving."

"I'll make sure Cielle's safe and you're safe, too, and then Pete can come back and you and he can work it out, start over."

"How about you?" she asked. "The ALS?"

He smiled. "That I can't fix."

She reached across, slid the Beretta back to him. "I don't want the gun."

He made no move toward it. "I know you don't."

Her eyes went from the gun to his face. "Will you stay with it?"

He looked down, embarrassed that she'd see what this meant to him. He picked up the gun, tucked it in his jeans again. "I'll sleep down here on the couch. Keep watch."

"Talk to your daughter first. She needs you. Whether she knows it or not." Janie turned to wash out her cup and he looked at her back for a moment before starting for the stairs. Casper rose from his slumber to follow him up.

He confronted Cielle's bedroom door a moment before tapping. "Honey? It's me."

"What do you want?"

"I just want to see your face."

A long silence. Then she said, "I heard Pete say to Mom, 'I am not cleaning up his mess again.' Is that what I was to him? A mess?"

"Oh, honey. No." He leaned against the closed door. "He was talking about me and what I got us all into. Pete loves you."

"Then why'd he leave?"

"Because he was scared."

"I'm scared, too. And I don't get to leave. Because they're after *me*." Fear cracked her voice. "I never get a say in anything. Everything's just you guys making choices and doing things, and then I'm the one who has to live with it all."

He pressed a hand to the wood. "From here on out, I will tell you everything. Every move, every choice. And you will get a say. Deal?"

"What were you doing at the bank?"

Not a hesitation. The question right there, locked and loaded.

His mouth went dry. How could he tell her something like that?

"You said you'd tell me everything," Cielle said. "So?"

He struggled to find a point of entry. "Remember how I told you your grandma died?"

Her voice came through the door. "Yeah. Cancer."

"I never talked to you about what that was like. For me, as a kid. And so . . . with me now and what I'm looking at . . . I didn't want to put you through that." He took a breath. "That's why I was on that ledge."

He waited, palm against the door, listening. Nothing.

Just as he was about to turn away, the knob twisted and the door pulled open a little more than an inch. Her face, red from crying, filled the crack. She looked in his eyes, really looking at him for the first time since he'd come back. Then she nodded and closed the door.

Chapter 22

Waking on the well-worn couch to the sight of his favorite potted plant in the corner, the artfully distressed wood of the coffee table, and his dog curled in a spot of light beneath the curtains, Nate felt a momentary peace. Then he sensed the hard metal against his palm. He raised his hand, the pistol he was gripping came clear in the early-morning light, and the whole disastrous situation came flooding back in on him. Sitting up, he rubbed his eyes, and Casper padded over to him. He dug his fingers into the dog's scruff and kissed his head. How he loved the smell of his fur after it had been baking in the sun.

First order of business—Urban's safe-deposit key, which he dug from his pocket. The number 227 stamped unevenly on the head. He tapped it against his knuckles. Flipped it like a coin. Slid it back into his pocket.

He took his pills at the kitchen sink before walking down the hall to the bathroom. Passing the laundry room, he saw Janie's kicked-off clothes from last night, her underwear atop the heap. They were her favorite style from the Gap—pink, crosshatched. Not her most alluring pair, but still, the sight of them brought a rush of nostalgia. More times than he could count, he had watched her blow-dry her hair in them, had folded them out of the dryer, had slid them from her body. And now he diverted his gaze and kept on because noting them was somehow inappropriate. The shifting politics of intimacy.

When he returned to the living room, Janie was there, straining to reach above the mantel, the oversize Lakers T-shirt she slept in pulled high to the backs of her thighs. It took a moment for him to realize what she was doing. With a little grunt, she reached the frame and unhooked the portrait of her, Pete, and Cielle from the wall.

She turned, noticing Nate. "I bet this makes you happy."

"Not today."

She set the frame on the floor, leaned it against her legs, and stared down at it. "You were always messy. You infuriated me, and then . . . well, we could make love or fuck sometimes and I woke up mad next to you and woke up ecstatic, but I never woke up"—she searched for the words—"mildly contented. Pete was so safe after you, and kind, but there were times I thought, 'If I have to drink another glass of Kendall-Fucking-Jackson pinot noir, I'm gonna hang myself with one of his woven silk ties.'"

Nate couldn't help but smile. All humor faded, though, when he saw the weariness that remained on her face. She was voicing everything he'd dared to hope these past few years was true. And yet now that she was relating it, it felt nothing like how he'd dreamed it would be. An impression came over him—walking out onto thin ice, cracks spiderwebbing around his feet. Any direction he moved could put him under. He struggled to find the right next step. To find what was right for her.

He cleared his throat. "Pete had his good points, too."

"Yeah." Janie carried the portrait to the kitchen and set it against the back door. The spot for trash. "But I will *never* forgive him for walking out the way he did."

Nate recalled standing on the beach that fateful day as Janie, still dripping from her near drowning, argued with her date. He thought, again, *Now would be a really good time to not say anything.*

Still facing the door, she lowered her head, and her lovely shoulders rose once and fell. When she turned, her eyes were wet, but she held herself together. "I'm scared, Nate. I'm really goddamned scared." She stayed by the door way across the room from him, as if any human proximity were painful right now. "I keep wanting to get Cielle out of here while you do this, but a woman and a girl on the run from these guys? Might not be a safety improvement." She ran a hand through her chopped blond hair. "I suppose I'll do what I have to when I have to."

"I don't want to leave," he said. "Here." He felt a need to avert his gaze and realized he was no longer talking about safety.

"I don't want you to leave either." The scoop of skin

visible at her collar turned pink as it did when she was trying not to cry. Her chest rose and fell, rose and fell. The diamond glinted at her left hand. "But I'm afraid to count on you."

"You can."

"People don't change."

"I changed once."

"Yeah." Not quite a smile. "For the *worse*."

He sensed, over his shoulder, the empty space above the mantel where the portrait once hung. "Then I can change again."

Walking out, he felt her gaze on his back. He stepped over the loose brick on the porch and headed for the curb. As he reached the Jeep, a mangled hand snared the driver's-side handle and tugged the door open for him. Charles, bowing like a chauffeur, his smart-ass grin showing off a few chipped teeth.

"You're going to the bank?" he asked as Nate climbed in.

Nate tugged the door closed, turned over the engine. "Yes."

"To do *what*?"

Nate smiled as he pulled out, leaving Charles behind.

Chapter 23

A surreal elevator ride up to the eleventh floor, a numb walk through the lobby, and out onto the bank floor, the site of five homicides that he himself had perpetrated. Nate had timed his arrival to coincide with the lunchtime swell. Lots of customers, lots of distraction for the busy staff. The trolley housing the complimentary coffee had been restored to its upright position, though he noticed a ding in the metal side, no doubt where one of the gunmen had kicked it over. After pouring himself a cup of decaf French roast, he took his place at the back of the substantial line.

Which gave him plenty of time to relive where the bodies had fallen, how the blood spatter had misted, and countless other subtleties that left his stomach roiling. As he trudged forward in the teller line, his fingers worked Urban's key nervously in his pocket, digging his nail into the indentations of the stamped number—227. The damn box was less than twenty yards away, but the distance between here and there felt like a marathon.

When he'd finally made his restless way through the velvet-rope switchbacks, a tense young teller greeted him, bringing him up to speed on the policies for renting a safe-deposit box. Was he aware that a checking account was required? *Already have one.* Each time, he would need to show his driver's license and sign in to gain access to his box. *No problem.* His signature would be double-checked against the signature card. *Swell.* Safe-deposit boxes were either three by five, five by ten, or ten by ten. Which would he prefer?

"You know?" he said, tapping his hands on the lip of the teller window. "I'm a little bit superstitious. I have a lucky number, and I was hoping I could—"

"Happy to look for you, Mr. Overbay." She went back to nibbling at her thumbnail, a thin pendant cross jiggling against the front of her sweater.

"Two twenty-eight," he said. "My first street address."

She clicked around on the keyboard, her eyes darting at intervals from the screen to his face. Her jumpiness was making him uneasy, and yet how could she suspect he had an ulterior motive? "I'm sorry. That number's taken."

He feigned disappointment.

"I could get you *three* twenty-eight?" she offered.

He took a casual sip of coffee. "How about two twenty-nine? Two twenty-six or -seven?"

"Two twenty-six it is." She guided him through a few forms, then handed him a familiar-looking key—226.

He rubbed the number as if it were a lucky rabbit's foot. Then dropped the key into his left pocket. "Thank you."

"I'll buzz you through, and the guard will take you back to your box," she said. As he stepped away, she reached beneath the glass and rested her hand on his sleeve. "I didn't want to embarrass you, Mr. Overbay, but thank you for what you did for us Tuesday. I was here."

Her fingernails, on second look, were chewed to the quick. Her face raw from sleeplessness. He pictured that face pressed to the tile, gunfire erupting overhead as she'd prayed for her life. And here she was a few days later, doing her job as best she could and trying to put it behind her.

He touched her hand, and she nodded a few times rapidly and turned her focus to the next customer.

After leaving the counter, he noticed a stout manager at the end of the teller line staring at him, phone to his ear. Did he recognize Nate as well? The man offered a cordial little smile, and Nate returned his attention to the job before him.

Pausing before the teller gate, he made a fist around Urban's key in his right pocket. Squeezed. Cielle's life rested on the next two minutes.

A harsh buzz announced the gate's unlocking. He took a deep breath and stepped through. The security guard, an older gentleman with a fringe of blond mustache, nodded in greeting. As Nate headed toward the massive laid-open door of the vault, his steps slowed, the stutter of gunfire replaying in his head. There's where the bank manager had toppled over, roses of blood blooming on her stiff pink suit. The glass day gate creaked open, and Nate stepped into the vault, eyeing the corner where he'd unloaded two bullets into the robber's stomach. He looked down. His feet, precisely in the spot they'd been when he'd felt that letter opener sink into the flesh of his shoulder. *He will make you pay in ways you can't imagine.*

The security guard had said something.

"Sorry?" Nate said.

"You okay, sir?"

He took a nervous sip of coffee. "Yeah, fine."

He had to pull it together. Stepping forward, he eyed the nests of boxes. Everything repaired, just as Pavlo had promised. Nate ran his fingers across the small metal doors until he reached what he was looking for.

Danny Urban's safe-deposit box.

Directly below the one Nate had just signed up for.

The guard fussed among the keys fanning from an overburdened ring. "Let's see, two twenty-six, right?"

Again Nate slid his hand into his pocket. His *right* pocket. "That's the one."

The guard raised the master key, and Nate, pretending to juggle the key and the Styrofoam cup, dropped his coffee. It hit the floor, splattering on the guard's cuffs.

"Oh, man," Nate said. "I am so sorry."

"No problem." The guy swiped at his ankles with a handkerchief as Nate crouched over him. "It's fine," the guard said. "Come right out."

Nate rose and plugged Danny Urban's key into number 227. He waited patiently, holding the key so his hand blocked the number on the tiny door, his pounding heart seeming to reverberate in the hard walls of the vault. The muscle in his hand started to cramp, the faintest complaint of the disease. *Jesus,* he thought.

Not now. He fought off the sensation, forcing his fingers to hold in place.

Distracted, the guard rose, folding the handkerchief back into a pocket and sliding the master key home. He nodded at Nate, they twisted at the same time, and the door to 227 popped open. And then Urban's safe-deposit box was sliding out and—at last—in his hands. The spring-mounted door swung back and autolocked. They turned together, Nate gripping the box tightly, and headed for the private viewing rooms just beyond.

Five steps and they'd be clear of the vault. He counted them off, tried not to rush. Stepping through the day gate, he swept a gaze across the teller stations and the crowded lobby, and his muscles froze.

Agent Abara had just come through the bank doors.

Nate turned away reflexively, bumping into the guard. The long metal box in his hands gave off not so much as a rattle.

"Whoa, sir. This way."

Nate couldn't just reverse course and return the box without looking in it—too suspect. Plus, when would he have another chance to get to its contents? And yet he couldn't risk being caught with a stolen safe-deposit box belonging to a dead hit man.

The guard took the choice out of his hands, nudging him forward and indicating a door to the right of the vault. Keeping his face turned from the bank floor, Nate ducked through and closed the door swiftly behind him. The plain room crowded in on him—white walls, elevated desk, framed watercolor of a girl playing at the beach.

Nate pictured that stout bank manager watching him, phone to his face. Clearly, by the time Nate had reached the front of the line, the manager had alerted Abara, who'd been standing by somewhere close. Because he suspected Nate of *what*? More important, how long did Nate have before the agent tracked him to this room?

He set the box down hard on the elevated table. The long lid yawned open on its hinges. Inside, a plain, sealed business-size envelope. Nothing more.

He grabbed it, lifted it to the light. All this, for something that could fit inside an envelope. Based on its heft, it was no more than a single folded sheet. Its slightness only added to its menace. Did it contain something incriminating? As horrible as the glossy photographs Pavlo had held up to Nate's face in the warehouse?

He sharpened his thoughts to a single point: Get this envelope into Pavlo's hands and Cielle was safe.

But if Abara found it on Nate, he would certainly seize it. Which, however indirectly, would lead to the saw and the block of ice.

Frantically, Nate looked around the unadorned room. Where to stash the envelope?

He thought about Urban himself, desperate to hide key 227 as he stumbled bleeding into his bedroom.

Tape.

A plastic desk caddy contained a stapler, some paper clips, and a roll of Scotch tape. Spilling the paper clips in his haste, he yanked two strips of tape from the roll and slapped them on the envelope, leaving sticky ends protruding from either edge. Couldn't stick it beneath the desk—too obvious.

His gaze caught on the watercolor. Little girl at beach. He pulled the bottom of the painting from the wall, tilting it out. Reaching as far as he could toward the hanging wire, he pressed the envelope to the mounting board. He stepped back, straightened the frame with a tap of his finger, grabbed Urban's box, and bolted out the door.

Abara was ten yards away, at a window, talking to the manager. Through some miracle he did not glance over. Nate pivoted sharply, head lowered, rushing the vault door. The guard was waiting, hands clasped at his stomach. He cocked an eyebrow as Nate raced for the vault, somehow doing his best to look as though he wasn't hurrying.

The guard followed Nate into the vault. Nate got there first, stuck Urban's key in.

But the guard was just watching him, mouth shifting, making the mustache bristle. "I thought you were two twenty-*six*."

The cool air froze the sweat on Nate's back. "Nope," he said. "Two twenty-seven."

The guard's mouth pursed. He made a puzzled noise low in his throat.

A snatch of conversation drifted in from the main floor. "—believe he's in the vault, Agent—"

Nate tried to smile casually at the guard, though it felt like a death grimace. Footsteps approaching, the sound pronounced off all the metal. Growing louder.

The man's watery blue eyes took Nate's measure. Finally he lifted the master to the second keyhole.

Nate went to great pains to disguise his relieved exhale. They turned their keys in unison, and the tiny door swung open. Nate got the end of Urban's box slotted in the hole and was about to shove when a new realization struck him. If he was searched by Abara, he could not be caught with Urban's safe-deposit key. But where, inside a bank vault, was he supposed to hide it?

The spring-loaded door pressed against the back of his hand. He stared at where it dimpled his skin.

An autolocking door.

He lifted the long lid a crack and slipped Urban's key into the empty box. Slid the box home. The tiny door to 227 swung back and locked with a click.

And Abara entered.

Nate's breaths were coming fast and ragged. He did his best to muster a smile. "Agent."

"Nate." He wore a dress shirt, unbuttoned slightly to show off tan brown skin. "Happened to open a safe-deposit box today, huh?"

"That's right."

"Just . . . got a hankering?"

"After my brush here Tuesday, I realized I could stand to sort out my affairs a bit. Why not store some important docs away for safekeeping?"

"Why not indeed." Abara moistened his lips. "So you thought you'd handle this sudden bit of logistics at the same bank where you killed five men?"

"It's already been robbed. I figure it's the safest bank in town."

Abara did not smile. He flicked his head at the nest of boxes. "Which one's yours?"

Nate sensed the guard's head swivel over to him. Felt the heat of his stare as he waited on an answer.

Nate took a breath, tasted the metal of the vault. He had to say something immediately, and yet immediately had already passed.

"You know what?" His best approximation of moral indignation. "Is there some reason you're following me, harassing me? I mean, I'm the one who *took down* the robbers." He was almost yelling, the words ringing off the walls. "Shouldn't you be thanking me instead of stalking me at every goddamned turn?"

The security guard kept a steady gaze on Nate. Was he buying the act?

The guard had just opened his mouth to say something when the stout manager leaned nervously through the day gate. "Uh, Agent? Maybe you could take this line of questioning elsewhere? We have a bank full of customers."

"Sure thing." Abara's smile never faltered. His glibness seemed to take an uptick with every remark. "You have a private room?"

Of course they did.

They were led a few steps past the vault. Eyeing Nate, the security guard unlocked the door and returned to his post, letting the matter of the box number lie.

Nate stepped back inside the plain little room, confronting the watercolor of the little girl at the beach. With alarm he realized that despite his effort earlier, it hung crooked.

The door had barely closed when Abara stepped up on him. "Listen, I've done the nice-guy routine up until now. A little banter, a little innuendo. But let me tell you what I've learned from thirteen years on this job. I've learned to read liars. And you are lying. Now, I don't know why and I don't know what about. You're all wrong. How you handled yourself during the shootings. Your energy—when you're nervous, when you're calm."

Just over Abara's shoulder, the crooked watercolor hung there, screaming for attention. And taped behind it, the envelope that would decide Cielle's fate. Nate struggled to keep his eyes fixed on Abara.

"And yet," the agent continued, "I can tell you weren't part of the heist. You're not a piece-of-shit crook who decided to double-cross his team." He studied Nate's face. "I think you came here for something, and it wasn't to stow away Aunt Mabel's family photos in a safe-deposit box. I will search you. Either you can give your consent here and now or I will take you in to the Federal Building for questioning, where your person can be searched as you enter. Which is it?"

A long beat. Nate emptied out his pockets, slapping his wallet and cell phone on the desk beneath the watercolor, resisting the compulsion to reach over and straighten it. The key came next, number 226.

Abara lifted it to the light, made sure the number passed muster. "That it?"

"That's it."

"Mind if I search you?"

"I would *love* if you would search me."

Abara spun him, not gently, and nudged him between the shoulders so his hands thudded forward on the desk. The coerced lean brought his nose to within a foot of the painting. *Girl at Beach, Askew.* Abara's hands checked his crotch, his armpits, pressed his pockets flat to his thighs, the cold proficiency calling to mind not only the firm pat-down administered by the Ukrainian bouncer outside New Odessa but also the poking and prodding Nate had grown accustomed to in sterile exam rooms.

His body, less and less his own.

Abara's knees cracked as he rose.

Nate stared at the watercolor. "You done or are you gonna try to get to third base?"

"Now that you moved home," Abara said, "I'll leave that to your almost-ex-wife."

Nate turned around, the two men close in the small room, squaring off. "You watching me?"

"Nah." Abara backed off. "Drove by, saw the Jeep in the driveway." He opened the door, gestured graciously for Nate to step out. "Just keeping an eye, like you asked."

The walk across the bank floor seemed endless. Nate's clothes, damp with panic sweat, chafed him. His hand was on fire, wrist aching, a preview of what the disease would bring. He curled it to his sternum, cradling it like something precious as he stepped into the air-conditioned elevator for the ride down.

Outside, the benches were taken, so he lowered himself to the curb. Grit and hot air found his face, the texture of passing traffic. He sat for a time, trying to catch his breath.

Chapter 24

Doubt and fear swarmed Nate's brain, vying for attention. Had he pressed the tape hard enough onto the back of the watercolor? What if it didn't hold and the envelope fell out onto the desk? What if a janitor took the painting off the wall to dust and discovered what it hid?

It was almost six o'clock as he parked in front of the Santa Monica house and climbed out of the Jeep. Three days and six hours until he had to deliver that envelope into Pavlo Shevchenko's hands. At least it was out of the bank vault. Baby steps.

The sun had fallen behind the rooftops, clouds smudging the hot orange sky like a child's handprints. It would have been a beautiful evening had he been in a frame of mind to notice. Folded into his back pocket were the divorce papers he'd retrieved from his place before coming here. While in his apartment, he'd packed a few changes of clothes and swept the tiny forest of orange pill bottles from the bathroom counter into a grocery bag. On his way out, he'd plucked the thumbtacked photos of Cielle and Janie from the wall. Everything else he would happily leave behind.

As he entered, Casper barreled toward him, claws scrabbling against the hard floor. Janie swung through the doorway—"How'd it go?"—her face almost collapsing with relief when she read his expression.

He'd just set down the grocery bag and suitcase when Cielle descended the stairs, Shithead Jason at her heels. Nate did a literal double take at the husky kid before turning to Janie.

"She told him everything," Janie said. "And they think he's staying here."

"You what?" Nate spun to his daughter. "You told your *boyfriend*? This is life and death, Cielle."

Shithead Jason held up his hands calmingly, the picture of maturity. "And I am here for whatever you need, bro."

The muscles of Nate's left hand were contracting, and he did his best to shake out the knot forming in the meat of his palm. "Cielle, you need to—"

"*What?* Keep it a *secret*? You guys haven't. *You* told Pete, and look how *that* turned out. So why can't *I* tell someone important to *me*?"

"No one should know about this," he said.

"No, Nate. It's just that you want to make all the choices. Who to tell, who not to." She drifted down the final steps, on tilt. "*You* said I could make my own choices. Well, this is my first. And his."

She reached back for Jason, who took her hand and swallowed hard, his Adam's apple bobbing. He'd removed his small gauge earrings, leaving hole punches in his lobes through which Nate could see the sides of his neck.

Janie turned to Nate. "You told a *fifteen-year-old* she could make her own choices?"

"Not exactly," he said.

They were arrayed around the entryway like enemy tanks in a clearing, everyone ready to pivot and fire.

"I'm staying with her," Jason said. "That big guy comes back, I'll kick him in his Justin Bieber."

"You don't understand," Nate said. "These men, they don't care about anything. They are perfect terrorists. You need to stay away from this for your own safety."

"Far as I'm concerned," Jason announced grandly, "they can all go suck a bag o' dicks."

"Okay," Janie said. "Great. Thanks."

A rush of fury, burning Nate's throat with the words: "You think this is a fucking joke? Some kind of video game? Do you guys have any concept of—"

Cielle reddened. "I know what's best for me."

"Your inviting him here proves exactly how little you know what's best for you."

Cielle stormed upstairs, towing her boyfriend. Jason paused, pointing across at Casper. "By the way, the dog's showing his lipstick. I'm just sayin'. It's a little gross."

Cielle took up the slack, yanking him around, and then they were up and the bedroom door slammed, leaving Nate and Janie and an aroused Rhodesian ridgeback.

"Put that thing away," Janie said to Casper, who rose and padded off. She rubbed her eyebrows with thumb and forehead, muttering something unintelligible.

Nate's skin was tingling—the aftermath of the outburst. He looked at Janie. "What?"

"She's not *seven*, Nate. She is fifteen. You can't just pick her up and throw her over your shoulder. She has to be part of this. We need her to *cooperate*."

He tamped down a flurry of objections. "Okay," he said. "Okay. What do we do about it?"

"Absolutely nothing for fifteen minutes."

He followed her into the kitchen. Unfolded the divorce papers and dropped them on the island. "I brought these. You just need to countersign and mail them in."

The leak beneath the sink *drip-drip-dripped*.

Janie cast a weary gaze at the papers. "Thanks." She slid them off the marble, letting them clap to the side of her leg, and trudged over to her study, which was more of an alcove off the kitchen.

Nate found his tools and the little box in the back of the pantry and dropped a new washer in the flanged tailpiece of the kitchen drain to stop the leak. After tightening everything up, he brought the mortar bag down from the garage cabinet and reseated the loose brick on the porch. Janie worked quietly at her desk the whole time, and Nate found a familiar calm in their separate but harmonized routines. As he came back in from the front yard, he noticed a few spots of Pete's dried blood on the kitchen floor, which he cleaned up with a wet paper towel silently so Janie wouldn't turn around and notice. Finally he walked over and knocked gently on the wall behind her. When she pushed back on the rolling chair, he saw that she had out a calculator and a stack of bills.

She traced his gaze and said firmly, "Late bills are not a problem. They're a welcome distraction."

He nodded reluctantly. "Has it been fifteen minutes?"

"It has."

She rose, and they headed side by side up the stairs. Jason's deep voice was audible from the hall. "I wish I had like *ninety-seven* senses so I could love you with more of them."

And Cielle: "You are so lame. That's like a double trampoline bounce of lameness."

"Don't be a bitch."

Nate opened the door sharply without knocking. The kids were sitting on the floor, their backs to Cielle's bed. Jason played with a Zippo lighter decorated with a skull and crossbones, flicking open the lid, snapping it shut.

"I don't like the way you're talking to her," Nate said.

"Dude—you seen the way she talks to *me*?"

Janie's voice, strained thin enough to break: "Just . . . go home, Jason. Cielle will call you later."

He shrugged and lumbered out.

Cielle examined her cuticles.

Janie sat next to her and Nate against the adjoining wall. They looked at each other, united by parental helplessness. Janie made a gesture: *You first.*

"Look," Nate said. "About Jason—"

Cielle said, "I *love* him."

"I know, honey," he said. "And colors are bright, and music is subversive, and when you see him, he puts a hum in your chest. I *know.* And that's how it should be. But it isn't safe right now. I am one move away from extracting us from this mess, and we can't have any complications in the mix."

"He's not a *complication*," Cielle said.

Janie reached for her but thought better of it. "I know you think you know everything right now. What decisions you want to make."

Cielle's fists were at her temples, and she flung her hands, sending out flares of maroon-streaked hair. She glared at Nate. "You don't like Jay because he's more creative than you."

"No," he said. "I don't like Jason because he's not *human*. I wasn't either at his age. "

Cielle went back to her cuticles. Silence. Just beyond her line of sight, Janie regarded Nate imploringly.

He gritted his teeth. "Okay. Look, I'm sorry—"

Cielle's head snapped up. "So he can stay?"

"*No.*"

Cielle sank her chin beneath the frayed collar of her oversize sweater. "He could help if those guys come back."

"What's he gonna do? Scare them off with his music?"

With a sleeve bunched over her fist, she wiped her nose forcefully, as if to tear it off. "You don't get it."

"No." His voice was low, but hard as stone. "You don't get it. We could all get *killed,* Cielle. Him included. How you gonna feel if he winds up with a bullet in his chest?"

Her expression shifted abruptly, the wrinkles smoothing from her forehead. Reality slapping her. For a moment he thought she might start crying, but whatever twinge of guilt he felt was drowned out by the roaring necessities at hand.

His phone vibrated in his pocket, breaking the

silence. He stood with some difficulty, stiff from myriad bruises, and checked the ID.

Janie read his face and said, with all-too-familiar disappointment, "Work."

He pulled the phone open. "I can't," he said into it.

Sergeant Jen Brown sounded unimpressed with his opening salvo. "Pregnant woman raped and stabbed to death in Griffith Park a few hours ago. Picnickers just found the body."

"I can't."

"Husband'll be home from work any minute. Doesn't know a thing yet."

"I can't."

"He's on the Westside, ten minutes from your door. If you don't go, I'll have to send Ken."

Nate's head was bent, his neck tightening up, the heat of Janie's and Cielle's gazes boring through his back. Ken Nowak serving a death notification to a man who'd just lost his wife and unborn child—Nate's chest cramped at the thought of it. He did his best to stand still, to avoid squirming, to try to hold the course.

Instead he heard himself say, "Last time."

Janie blew out a soft breath of disappointment, and Cielle's head snapped away to face the wall.

He hung up, defeated, and turned to face them. "Look, I won't be an hour. It's an impossible one. This guy—"

Janie waved a hand. "I understand. Go ahead." She slumped back down next to Cielle.

Nate lingered a beat, but neither seemed interested in kick-starting this particular argument. He didn't blame them. Trudging downstairs, he breathed in the fragrances of the house—carpet cleaner, the lingering afterscent of a honey candle, a trace of ash from the fireplace. A faint rain tapped the roof, and the refrigerator hummed. He patted the dog on the head and stepped out onto the porch.

Halfway down the walk, he paused.

He turned around, gazed back at his house, at the square of his daughter's window. There was a movement at the curtain, and then Janie and Cielle appeared, looking down at him. Something inside him swelled and broke, and he felt weak and emancipated all at once. Squinting against the flecks of rain, he stood for a time, night air crisp at the back of his throat, staring up at them, them staring down, the three of them motionless and silent as if the slightest movement would shatter this unspoken dialogue.

Then he pulled out his phone and dialed.

Jen answered gruffly.

"I'm not going," he said. "I'm taking some time off."

"Ken left for home already. What if I gave you an order to handle this?"

"Then I'd tell you what you can do with your order."

A long silence, punctuated only by Jen's breathing. He could have sworn he sensed her mouth shape into a smile on the other end.

"Hear that crackling?" she said. "Must be hell freezing over."

He hung up and started back inside. His head was bent against the drizzle, but with each step home he felt the warm gaze of his wife and daughter overhead.

Chapter 25

Cielle's scream shattered Nate's sleep, and he bolted up from the couch, slamming his knee into the coffee table. For a moment he had no bearings—apartment or house? nightmare or real?—but then he snapped to awareness, clawing his way past the furniture toward the stairs.

Casper followed him up, two steps at a time, lunging as if fording water. Janie swung out of the master, nearly colliding with Nate at the landing, and then parents and dog were hurtling toward Cielle's door. They found her backed as far as she could get from the window, turned sideways as if trying to burrow through the wall.

"What is it?"

"Are you okay?"

Cielle was shuddering beneath her T-shirt and boxers. A fall of dark hair covered one eye, the other wide and glossy. Her mouth opened, but no words came out. She lifted a hand and pointed to the window.

Shoulders lowered, Casper slunk four steps toward the window and issued a growl seemingly too low even for his deep chest. Janie moved to Cielle and Nate toward the bare pane, setting each foot down slowly, heel to toe. He paused beside the dog, who hummed with menace, a stone grinder rumbling.

Four more cautious steps brought Nate to the sill. There lay the front yard, twin ellipses of mowed grass split by the snake of the front walk. The sturdy magnolia, its wrinkled, elephantine trunk dark with rain. Planters brimming with subdued lavender and juniper. And beyond, the wide street, the friendly façades of Craftsmen and Cape Cods looking on, observers at a parade. This panorama he knew in his bones, each lineament traced in memory, the curves and shapes of a cherished photograph. Comfort exemplified.

Except.

A dark figure stood centered on the patch of grass directly beneath Cielle's window. From the shadowed head, huffs of cigarette smoke rose, beaten flat by the rain. The face tilted up at the window. Legs confidently spaced. The man did nothing more than stand and smoke, but his presence there, at this hour, was invasive, horrifying. Large boots sank into the saturated sod—sod Nate himself had rolled onto the primed soil a few months after moving in. The sight pinballed around his insides, striking nerves at random, playing fears too primal to be named.

"I got up to pee and . . ." Cielle's words flared off.

"What is it?" Janie's breaths were audible.

Keeping his gaze locked on the dark oval of a face, Nate said, "Yuri."

The phone's ring sounded like a scream, scaring

Cielle into a yelp. After the second ring, Nate found his legs again and unburied the cordless from a sea of decorative pillows on the futon.

Mrs. Alizadeh's voice seemed to arrive from a different dimension.

"No, no," Nate said, moving back to the window. "Everything's okay. Yes, it's me. I'm back at the house again." Across the street, through the diaphanous silk of the old woman's bedroom curtains, he could make out her silhouette, down to the apprehensive curl of her shoulders. The two of them, like prisoners on their respective second floors, terrorized by a man on a lawn. The ridiculousness of this broke through his alarm, fired the breath in his throat. "It's probably just some lookie-loo, tracked me down after the whole bank thing. You heard about the bank thing?"

"No," Mrs. Alizadeh said. "I did not."

"Better just to ignore whoever it is," Nate said.

"He's scaring me. I will call 911."

"That's not necessary."

"I do not like this, Mr. Overbay."

"I'll take care of it," Nate said.

He hung up, threw the phone at the futon, and started for the door.

"You're going out there?" Cielle asked.

"Lock the door behind me."

Janie and Cielle followed him down. Stepping onto the porch, he waited for the thud of the dead bolt; seconds later two worried faces appeared in the living-room window.

His bare feet squished in the grass. The form waited

patiently as Nate neared, the face becoming recognizable by degrees in the dim light.

"Get the fuck off my lawn."

"It is not even your lawn anymore." The cigarette flared orange. "Pavlo will watch you and your family as he please. Through my eyes or through someone else."

Rain spit at them. Nate lifted his eyes past the big man's shoulders to Mrs. Alizadeh's perch by her upstairs window. She drew back slightly at his movement. Yuri's gaze ticked left past Nate, no doubt taking in Janie and Cielle. Two men squaring off on an unlit stage of grass, a can't-look-away spectacle. The wetness brought up the scent of the night-blooming jasmine. One wrong move and violence would explode here in the perfumed air of Santa Monica.

"You're scaring the neighbors. Someone'll call the cops."

"We don't worry about police. *You* must worry about police." The cigarette bounced at the brink of Yuri's mouth, a prop from a black-and-white movie. "You must pray we stay free men. If you let us get taken in by police, well . . ." His lips clamped the cigarette and curled up at the edges. The loglike arms made a slashing gesture, the fists gripping the handle of an imaginary rescue saw.

"Get off my property," Nate said. "Let me do the job you need me to do."

"No, I think I will stay awhile. Finish my cigarette." Yuri splayed a hand toward the house. "Go back to your beautiful women."

Nate took a step forward, and Yuri stiffened ever so

slightly, a gathering beneath his great dark coat. Standing ready, he made a scolding noise through pursed lips, a ticking of the tongue.

Nate's breath clouded about his face. He let the rain dampen his temper. Let it sizzle the rage until it was safe to move. To retreat.

Walking back, he kept his eyes trained on Janie and Cielle, their faces disembodied behind the pane. When he reached the porch, he finally turned.

The front yard, empty.

A cigarette butt smoldered in the wet blades, a last gasp before it was extinguished by the needling rain.

Chapter 26

Despite waking up on the couch, Nate felt as though it was almost a normal morning. He changed the dressing on his shoulder wound, took his pills, put coffee on for his soon-to-be ex-wife, and flipped through the soggy newspaper to the bleeding obits.

AN AVID GOLFER, KEVIN STRUTHERS LEAVES TWO
DAUGHTERS, NANCY AND OLIVIA, BOTH
PEDIATRICIANS, AND (AS HE TENDERLY CALLED THEM)
A "BROOD" OF SEVEN GRANDCHILDREN. HIS WIFE,
ELSIE, PREDECEASED HIM.

Nate raised an orange-juice toast to good old Kevin and washed down the bitter aftertaste of the riluzole and antibiotics.

Glancing through a window, he checked the front yard. Nothing there but two boot-shaped indentations in the soggy front lawn. He withdrew from the late-morning gloom and sat at the kitchen counter, listening to the coffee percolate and flexing his hand, testing the muscles. The numbness had crept from wrist to forearm. With mounting dread he regarded his arm. Maybe the stress had accelerated the disease. He wondered if his body would give out before he could get done what needed to get done.

After Yuri's intrusion last night, he and Janie had sat on Cielle's bed for hours to honor an unspoken agreement to stay with her until she drifted off. They were all three wired from the encounter, tension jumping from one to the other. It wasn't until the morning sun crept through the windows and overtook the shadows that Cielle had dozed off. After an awkward moment at the top of the stairs, Nate and Janie had parted ways.

She shuffled into the kitchen now, rubbing her eyes, a snarl of hair raised in the back. Drawn by the scent of coffee. Cielle was still slumbering; there'd been no question she'd miss school today.

"Don't you look all perky and ready to go," Janie mumbled.

"Got a date with the bank." He poured her a cup and slid it across.

Her gaze snared on something on the counter. His left hand, trembling slightly against the marble. Involuntary. He pulled his hand into his lap but in doing so knocked over one of his pill bottles, which rattled more loudly than seemed probable. The silence made an awkward return.

"You were really gonna do it?" Janie said. "Kill yourself?"

"Yes."

"Idiot." She took a sip. "Why? Because of the disease?"

He thought about it. Given the monumentality of the decision, it struck him as odd that he had no ready answer. "I wasn't killing myself because of the disease," he finally allowed. "I was killing myself because there was nothing left *but* the disease."

She leaned against the doorway to the study. "You couldn't find *something*? Anything? To make it worth it for another day, another week?"

"Like what?" he said. "I'm not researching the cure for cancer. I'm not Lou Gehrig—don't get to make a speech in front of a sold-out crowd at Yankee Stadium. All I had left was to inflict this on myself and others."

Her face stayed firm, whether from grief or anger, he didn't know.

He got up and started digging through the kitchen drawers, leafing through take-out menus, old receipts.

"What are you doing?" she asked.

"I need a pretense to get back into that private viewing room at the bank. Best bet is bringing something official-looking to put in my safe-deposit box, something I can just leave in there."

He was pulling together a few old pieces of mail when Janie said, "Take *this*."

Something in her voice sounded different, and he stopped what he was doing and looked up. She was offering up a stapled document. Even from across the room, he could see what it was.

He took a beat, because he didn't trust his voice. "You sure?"

"Of course not."

He stayed put by the kitchen drawer, unsure what to do next.

At length she nodded. "Yes. I'm sure." She shook the divorce papers impatiently.

He crossed and took them on his way out.

The line at the bank offered a good vantage to the private viewing rooms. There were two of them, an added complication that Nate was none too keen to account for. A wizened man stepped into the desired room as Nate neared the front of the line, forcing him to stall by pretending to fill out deposit slips. When the man at last shuffled back into sight, Nate hurried forward to the next available teller and was buzzed through. The security guard waited, the same older gentleman from round one. As they stepped into the vault, he studied Nate with eyes as small and hard as marbles.

"Two twenty-seven, right?" he asked.

Nate offered his best grin even as his hand left a sweat stain on the divorce papers. "Two twenty-*six*."

The guard said flatly, "Senility must be comin' on stronger than I imagined."

Nate got his safe-deposit box and strolled as casually as possible into the open private viewing room. The watercolored girl at the beach—still there. He hastened the pneumatic door closed with an elbow, then tossed down the box and rushed to pluck the painting off the wall, flipping it over.

At first he could scarcely believe it was still there. The business-size envelope taped firmly to the backing. So many worst-case scenarios had flashed through his mind in the past twenty-four hours that he'd half convinced himself he'd willed one into existence. But no, the envelope easily peeled free. Stepping out of a sneaker, he folded the envelope three times and hid the dense rectangle beneath the insole. He pulled the shoe back on, laced it tighter than necessary.

As he placed the divorce papers inside the safe-deposit box, bade them good-bye, and lowered the lid, he couldn't help but note how the contraption resembled a coffin. This was one burial he didn't mind a bit.

The security guard helped him deliver the box to its resting place within the vault, refusing to return his smile. As Nate headed out, the thrice-folded envelope dug into his arch, but he felt like he was walking on air.

Chapter 27

"Should we open it?" Janie asked.

"No," Nate said at the precise moment Cielle said, "Dunno."

The three of them were pulled into the kitchen table, the envelope sitting untouched on the otherwise blank surface like some unsavory dish. Outside, the hunched clouds seemed to be giving way to dusk, a transition from gray to grayer.

Janie's laptop glowed on the counter opposite, open to the home page for New Odessa restaurant, complete with the number for reservations. Beside the computer stood the cordless phone. Nate's impatience burned beneath his skin. He wanted to call the restaurant to see if Pavlo was there and willing to take early delivery.

"Did Shevchenko ever say anything about *opening* it?" Janie asked.

"He didn't even mention what it was."

Cielle took the envelope and held it up against the overhead light. They'd each given this a try, hoping for a better result. A single sheet, folded, no writing or typing visible.

"What could be so important that it could fit on a single piece of paper?" Janie asked.

"Doesn't matter," Nate said, rising. "Let's just get it to the man and call it a day." He'd reached the counter and was thumbing the area code into the phone when he heard a ripping behind him.

Cielle, sliding her finger beneath the flap.

Nate hung up.

She tilted the envelope, and the folded paper fell out. She reached for it delicately, laying it open. Janie rose, leaning over the table. She gave a faint, dismayed groan.

"What?" Cielle said. "I don't get it."

Nate's legs carried him across, and he stared over Cielle's shoulder, seeing what the paper held as Janie answered in a voice flat with regret, "A list of names."

There they were. Eight of them. Handwritten. And beneath each one an address in the L.A. area. The top name was crossed out.

Nate felt his stomach lift, as if he'd fallen off the edge of something. *"No."* His voice was loud, almost a shout. "You were *safe*. You were in the clear."

"What *is* it?" Cielle asked.

Nate took a mental snapshot of the first few names, turned back to the laptop, and typed furiously. The sole crossed-out name at the top, *Patrice McKenna,* and then her neighborhood, *Brentwood.*

"What, Mom? Why are you guys being so weird?"

Google spit out results, and he clicked the first link.

BRENTWOOD, CA—THE BODY OF THIRTY-SEVEN-YEAR-
OLD SCHOOLTEACHER PATRICE MCKENNA WAS FOUND
IN HER APARTMENT TODAY, WITH MULTIPLE STAB
WOUNDS INFLICTED BY A LOCK-BLADE HUNTING
KNIFE DISCOVERED AT THE SCENE.

He pictured himself in the dark entry of Danny Urban's shot-up town house, crouched over that FedEx
box. The clank of dozens of murder weapons inside.

At the table Janie was murmuring, her voice slurred
by her hands pressed to her mouth—*"my God, why
does it have to be—"*

His fingers had moved to the next entry, *Luis Millan, Marina del Rey.* A dozen Google links, none indicating a murder.

Because the name hadn't been crossed out yet.

The third—*Wendy Moreno, Westchester*—yielded a
similar nonresult.

Nate spun around, put his back to the counter.

Cielle said, "Someone tell me what this is. You're
freaking me out."

"Honey." Nate exhaled, hard. "Why would a hit man
keep a list of names?"

The answer struck, Cielle recoiling in her chair.
"Wait. No. What? These are . . . these are people he
was planning on *killing*? And this guy, the Ukrainian,
he wants the names to . . ."

Janie said, "To finish the job."

In his head Nate replayed Shevchenko's raspy voice:
We had disagreement over fee and ownership of object.
Given how badly the Ukrainian wanted this list, he

clearly didn't have the names on it, so he must have hired Urban to *identify* these people as well as kill them. But the whole venture had gone south when Urban demanded more money to keep going. Which raised a bizarre question: If these were people Shevchenko wanted dead, why didn't he know who they were?

"Eight people," Cielle said. "Eight *lives*."

"Seven." Nate pointed at the list. "One's already crossed out."

Cielle folded the sheet back up, stuffed it into the torn envelope, as if trying to rewind the past five minutes. "What do we do?"

The complications and ramifications raised by that single folded sheet seemed too vast to reason through. Hand over the sheet, kill seven strangers.

"We give it to Shevchenko," Janie said, "just as we planned."

"Mom! How can you *say* that?"

"For all we know, they're rival thugs."

"Or they could be innocent." Cielle whirled to Nate. "That first name. The woman who was killed. Did it say what her job was?"

He couldn't speak.

Janie said, "We don't need to know that. We don't. . . ."

Cielle glared at Nate. "*Answer* me."

"Schoolteacher," Nate said.

Janie dragged her elbows back off the table and fell into her chair.

"So what do *you* think?" Cielle asked him. "Turn over the list? Kill all those people like Mom says?"

Nate reached behind him, eased the laptop closed.

He could feel his heartbeat, pushing blood through his veins, one tiny surge at a time. He thought about a pink bundle in Janie's lap as he'd steered her wheelchair out of the maternity ward. Those faded lines in the doorway upstairs, marking off his daughter's height at each young age.

At his hesitation Cielle's face turned incredulous. "But what about those people?"

"I don't love *them*." The intensity in his voice, even to his own ears, sounded like fury.

"We can get the cops to help," Cielle said.

"Anything we do besides give that list to Shevchenko puts your life at risk," Nate said.

"I get a say in this," Cielle said. "It's *my* life. And I'm the one who'd have to grow up knowing . . . knowing . . ." She was starting to come undone, tears leaking. "You can't do this. You can't decide this for me."

A pressure built in Nate's chest, threatening to split him open. But at the sight of his daughter's face, he crouched and took her hands. "Okay," he said.

Janie's face was blank, shell-shocked. Cielle's warm hands squeezed his. Her tears fell, dotting his knuckles. Their fingers, locked. His knee ached against the floor, but he didn't dare to move, didn't *want* to move.

Until, shattering this moment of serenity, came the rising wail of police sirens.

Janie's head rose from where it rested against the union of her hands. "Are they coming—"

He saw her mouth shape the final word—"here?"—but the sound was lost behind the screech of tires in the front yard. He pulled free of Cielle's grasp and ran for the door, Janie close behind. His last glimpse back captured Cielle still in her chair, framed against the sliding glass door, head bent, envelope in hand.

Red and blue lights washed the ceiling of the foyer. He threw open the front door and spilled onto the porch, slipping on the wet brick.

Wearing a black guayabera shirt, Yuri stood beneath the magnolia, hands raised passively as four cops closed in on him.

He smiled broadly. "There he is. My friend. Tell them."

Nate stopped a few steps onto the grass, Janie back on the porch. Confronting Yuri again reminded Nate how *vast* the man was. Not beefy, but constructed like a cliff face, all ledges and hard outcroppings.

A female officer said, "We got a disturbance call to this address. A trespasser?"

Across the street Mrs. Alizadeh stood plaintively in her kitchen window, arms crossed as if to shiver, one arthritic hand clutching the telephone.

"I am not trespasser," Yuri said. "Tell them, Nate. Tell them I am your buddy pal." His smile was genuine. He was enjoying himself.

Nate glowered at him.

The officer nodded to the others, and they moved in another few steps on Yuri, a tightening noose. Their black gloves rested on holstered guns. Yuri's lips gathered above that lantern jaw, an expression of sheer menace pointed at Nate.

From the porch Janie called out sharply, "He's a friend."

The cops halted. Janie stepped down and walked over to Nate, threading an arm around his side. "I forgot to tell you, honey. I invited Yuri over."

Yuri said, "I was just haffing a smoke outside. They don't like me to smoke in house. They haff child."

The female officer peered across at Nate from beneath perfect curled bangs. "So he's a friend."

"*Old* friend." Yuri grinned.

Nate's smile felt like a baring of his teeth. "Neighbors around here get a bit jumpy."

The cops withdrew quickly and with annoyance, doors slamming, engines coughing. The patrol cars splashed off through puddles, on to the next complaint. The quiet reasserted itself. A slight movement across the street as Mrs. Alizadeh drifted from view.

Yuri tilted his large head to Janie, breaking the calm standoff. "Smart lady."

"Why are you here?" Nate said. "Just to fuck things up?"

A key fob hung over the edge of Yuri's breast pocket. "You went to bank today."

Between Abara and Pavlo's thugs, Nate wondered how many people were following him at any given time.

"You retrieve item?" Yuri asked.

Nate pictured Cielle inside at the table, clutching the envelope. Her fierce words earlier: *You can't decide this for me*.

"No." He had to force out the word. "Not yet. I'm maneuvering into position."

Yuri mulled this over. "Today is Friday. Bank closed tomorrow. You must deliver Sunday night."

"As you boys pointed out, I'm a VIP at that bank now. Special rules for the hero."

"How do you plan to get?"

"This isn't a joint effort. You'll have it by the deadline. If you can manage not to get arrested between now and then."

Yuri nodded once, severely, and lumbered away, vanishing past the Kerners' hedge.

Janie's arm fell from around Nate's side. "We could have just handed him that list." Her voice, heavy with dread.

They walked back inside in silence.

The door had no sooner swung shut behind them than Nate caught the scent. "You smell something burning?"

"Cielle?" Janie jogged into the house. "Cielle?"

Nate ran after her, a wisp of smoke coming clear in the kitchen. Cielle was leaning over the sink, her face flushed with emotion. A steady stream ran from the faucet.

"What'd you do?" Janie yelled. "What did you—"

Cielle opened one plump fist, and her boyfriend's skull-and-crossbones Zippo fell to the tile. "I couldn't do it. I couldn't let them get killed."

With horror Nate noted the empty envelope on the counter. A fleck of paper flew up from the sink, alight, orange turning to black. On weightless legs he moved forward.

The sheet of paper was no more than a delta of wet ash around the drain.

Chapter 28

Exhausted, Cielle shuffled toward her bed and sat. She was fully dressed—sweatpants and a black hoodie she wore low across her shoulder blades, like a shawl. She hugged her midsection, her eyes glazed.

Nate grasped her arms gently and lowered her to the pillow. She let him. He tugged the sheets up over her. Janie sat at Cielle's desk, fist propping up her chin, equally catatonic.

"What did I do?" Cielle asked hoarsely.

Nate could feel his fingernails digging into the flesh of his forearm. "Something brave," he said.

"Did I just kill myself?"

"No," he said. "It'll be all right."

"How will it be all right?"

"Because I'll make it all right."

Her blinks grew longer. "I screwed everything up. It was my choice. So I get it if you want to leave now."

"I'm never leaving you again."

Her face shifted, a softening. "What do you want?" she asked, not unkindly. "From me?"

"The honest truth?"

"Is there any other kind?"

"So many." He wanted to pet her shiny dark hair to soothe her to sleep as he used to when she was young, but he restrained himself. Instead he kneaded his palm, working the tiny bones, chasing the burn from the muscle. He was also, he realized, working up the courage to respond. He cleared his throat quietly. "I want the chance to mean something to you again."

But she was asleep.

He stared across at her doorway, all those pen marks notching off her height, Janie's scrawl recording a progression of key dates. First day of preschool. Fifth birthday. Elementary-school graduation. Would there be more? College, a wedding? He pictured the bulge of Yuri's muscles as he'd hefted the rescue saw, tendons shifting beneath pale skin and swaths of arm hair. An obscenity.

Janie's words were muffled by her hand. "Are you scared to death?"

"No," he lied.

He rose and walked down the hall into the master bathroom. Shut the door and sat on the floor. He pressed both hands over his mouth and set the back of his head against the full-length mirror behind the door. Pain radiated from his forearm into the crook of his elbow, tendrils of fire. His left hand had gone stiff and dead against his lips, and he squeezed his eyes shut and pictured those marks again in Cielle's doorway, how they stopped about waist-high. Panic unfolded inside his chest, a poisonous flower blooming. His ribcage heaved, and he pressed his hands tighter against his mouth.

When he dared, he opened his eyes and was not surprised to see Charles sitting on the closed lid of the toilet. His entrails were exposed, his hands charred and smoking, and for once he was not smiling. A feeling of overwhelming helplessness gripped Nate, the same as he'd felt in the car outside Charles's childhood house, watching Grace Brightbill bustle over the dishes, knowing he was supposed to walk to the front door to serve her son's death notification. The same he'd felt in this very bathroom, sitting where Charles now sat, unable to move his stubborn body into the next room to comfort his sobbing wife.

"What do I do now?" he asked his old friend.

"You know what you need to do," Charles said. "You need to keep going."

"My fucking hand hurts, Charles. I'm losing my *body*."

"You can do this."

"No. I can't. I'm the guy who froze on the helicopter—"

"No," Charles said. "You're the guy who dove into the waves to rescue a drowning girl when no one else would."

Janie knocked on the door, vibrating the mirror beneath Nate's shoulders. Charles lifted his face to the sound, smiled enigmatically.

Fear invaded Janie's voice. "Are you okay?"

"Yeah," Nate said, rising. "I'm okay."

* * *

Straining to steady his hand, Nate spooned tomato soup to his lips. When he'd admitted, under Janie's line of questioning, that he hadn't eaten in a day and a half, she'd heated some Campbell's. If ever there was a time for comfort food.

In his uncertain grip, the spoon handle rattled against the brim of the bowl, so he set it down gently. "We have forty-eight hours until that list is due in Shevchenko's hands," he said. "Our only advantage is that we know *now* I'm not gonna be able to deliver it."

"Two days to come up with an alternate game plan."

"Let's put you and Cielle on a plane tomorrow. Get you out of here. But we'll be cautious as hell. We'll buy tickets the day of, a few hours before the flight. Doesn't matter how much it costs. And we'll leave the house separately, at different times."

"And if Shevchenko finds out anyway?"

Nate pressed the edges of his teeth together. "The deal was that *I* wouldn't flee. Not you. I'll stay right here in plain sight."

"Doing what?"

"That FBI agent, Abara—he suspects me. But he also knows there's more to the story."

"So you'll go to him?"

"Right now what do I have? A story about a list that went up in smoke? I've got to get him something concrete. Something definitive enough that he can move on Shevchenko and his men and arrest them immediately. Something serious enough that they'll be held with no bail."

"Which means a murder charge," Janie said.

"Right. I need to find out *why* Shevchenko wants those people dead. I connect him to that murdered schoolteacher or those other names, I have something to bring to Abara that might actually save us. Shevchenko goes to prison, you and Cielle go into Witness Protection or whatever."

"Witness Protection. Jesus." Janie slid the pot from stove to sink and threw the faucet handle. Steam rose. "How are you gonna go about this now that Cielle burned the list? We don't even have the names anymore."

"We've got three of them." Nate slid his computer over and clicked on the history function in the browser. Sure enough, there were the last three Google searches. *Patrice McKenna, Brentwood. Luis Millan, Marina del Rey.* And *Wendy Moreno, Westchester.* "Tomorrow I'll start here."

Janie nudged his bowl closer to him. "Eat more."

He reached for the spoon, but his hand was vibrating, the strain of typing having taken a toll. He withdrew it, hiding it in his lap, but not before Janie had noticed. Again. She came around the counter, moving close enough that she pressed against his knees.

She beckoned, a nurse's impatient gesture. "Lemme see."

"It's fine."

"Come on. I owe you. That day on the beach."

He mustered a grin. "The tidal wave in the tropical monsoon."

"The very one. You saved my life."

"Nah," he said. "You saved mine."

Her teeth tugged at her lush lower lip, emotion working on her face. "Don't get philosophical. It doesn't suit you."

Their proximity made itself suddenly known. Her thighs pushing lightly against his knees. Her standing, him sitting on the stool, her mouth slightly higher than his, but close. They searched each other as if trying to read some hidden code. He prayed silently that she wouldn't step away, and she didn't.

She twisted the engagement ring around her finger, then became aware she was doing it. Her eyes moved to the diamond. "I think I knew somewhere," she said slowly, "even when I said yes, but it made sense, kind of, and then it was this *thing,* gaining momentum. . . ." Again her gaze found Nate's. "I'm glad you're here." She took a half breath. "He was never you."

He leaned forward on the stool, bringing his lips to hers. Tender, close-mouthed. She softened into him. Her fingers went to his cheeks, but then she stiffened, shrugging up and out of his embrace. "Sorry. Look, with everything going on . . ."

"What?" he prompted.

"What if this isn't real?"

"It's real," he said.

She smiled sadly, taking a few backward steps before turning for the stairs.

Chapter 29

High-end condos sprouted up along the water's edge in Marina del Rey, sturdy structures of tinted glass, rounded by a scalloping of balconies. The weekend was getting into swing, sorority girls shuffling from juice bars, surfers pedaling beach cruisers, their longboards tucked under tanned arms. Wafting inland from the small-boat harbor, the breeze carried salt and the faint sewer tinge of low tide.

Lincoln Boulevard ran straight through the class divide, the apartments to the east severed from the ocean view and the organic cafés. The complex where Luis Millan lived, at least according to several online directories, was three stories high, with bubbling pink stucco and wedding-cake railings. Work trucks proliferated in the parking lot, which backed on a body shop. Window air conditioners cantilevered out into space, dripping water and evoking calamity of the Looney Tunes variety.

After looping around the block a few times to ensure he wasn't being followed, Nate climbed the first flight of stairs, double-checked the address, and rang the bell. He had yet to land on a point of entry for the conversation to come, but having had plenty of practice knocking on doors and delivering bad news, he figured he'd wing it.

The guy who answered wore a porkpie hat, Bermuda shorts, and a V-necked undershirt. His facial hair was delicate and elaborate—soul patch, thin ridge lining either side of the jaw, strip along the upper lip that could have been stenciled on using eyeliner. His gold box-chain necklace looked like it had fallen out of a vending machine in 1983, all the more pronounced given that it was strung around a pillowy cervical brace holding his head regally erect. Though he was slight, his freckled shoulders bulged like softballs, masses of sinewy muscle. Two men on a couch were playing Xbox, working joysticks sophisticated enough to land a fighter jet.

"Luis Millan?"

The guy nodded. "That's me."

"Can we talk a minute? Alone?"

Luis's hand rose to his brace, which, Nate realized, was upside down. "You from the insurance company?"

"No."

"You look familiar. Did you go to North Hollywood High?"

"Nope." Nate glanced at his watch. Three hours before he'd attempt to get Janie and Cielle on a plane to Manhattan, where they'd try to lose themselves among 9 million people. "Listen, I'm sorry to walk in on your Saturday, but I really need to talk to you."

Luis stepped back, letting him in. "Go on, homeys. You heard the man."

His friends grumbled and rose, administering elaborate handshakes and shuffling out. Luis grabbed a Pacifico from the fridge and leaned against a cabinet in the galley kitchen. "You *sure* you ain't with the insurance company?"

"I'm sure."

He ripped off his brace with a groan, tossing it aside and rubbing the red skin beneath. "Screwed up my neck. Whiplash. Had to do rehab, all that. But the bullshit insurance companies don't believe you unless you look like Christopher Reeve, so my lawyer, he says I hafta wear the thing."

He palmed a few aspirin and downed them, which reminded Nate he was late for his own morning dose. Removing the riluzole and antibiotics from his pocket, he popped them in his mouth, then looked around for a glass. Luis tilted the beer bottle at him, and Nate shrugged, grabbed it, and washed them down.

Luis took back his bottle. "What's yours for? The meds?"

"Just some aches."

"The worst, isn't it? Not like when we was younger." He paused, thoughtful. "I got off lucky, I guess. Coulda been worse."

"Yeah," Nate said. "It could." He leaned against the fridge. "I have to ask you a bunch of weird questions."

"Shoot."

"Ever heard of somebody named Pavlo Shevchenko?"

"Nope."

"Do you know a Patrice McKenna?"

"Uh-uh."

"How about Wendy Moreno?"

"No, man. This one of those talk shows, you gonna tell me I got a daughter I don't know about or something?"

"No, nothing like that." Nate tried for another possible point of connection. "What do you do for work?"

"Auto-part sales." He gestured at the pass-through counter, stacked high with tool catalogs and invoices pinned to clipboards.

"You work here?"

"Based in Torrance. But I travel a lot."

Nate glanced around the small apartment. An antique L.A. Raiders poster sagged from tacks on the far wall. Pep Boys magnets pinned a variety of material to the fridge—Domino's Pizza coupons, an airport-shuttle brochure, pictures of Luis on a boat with several bikini-clad women, a Pacifico, and a grin wide enough to show his molars. A heap of wrenches lay on the spent living-room carpet like a scattering of bones, something about them recalling Urban's box of mail-ordered lock-blade hunting knives.

Nate decided to go at it directly. He took a breath. "Do you have any idea why someone would want you dead?"

The beer was almost to Luis's lips, but he pulled it to one side, the skin of his forehead twisting. Then he laughed. "Ex-wife count?"

"I'm serious."

"Why the hell would someone want to kill me?"

"I have no idea."

"You talking 'bout this guy? Pablo Shovechinko? What the hell? How's he know me?"

"I don't know."

With thumb and forefinger, Luis smoothed his pencil-thin mustache. "What'd you say your name was again?"

"I didn't."

Luis nodded once, slowly. He knocked back a last gulp and lowered the empty bottle to his side, his fist tightening around the long neck. "I think maybe you should go, homey."

"Okay. But you should know: Your name was on a list. Some people are looking to hurt you. I don't know why. I'm trying to find out. But if you can get out of town, take one of those business trips, now might be a good time."

Luis's eyes turned to slits. "Wait a minute. I recognize your ass. You're the guy from that bank shooting, lost his shit during the press conference."

"Nah," Nate said. "Wasn't me."

They stared at each other, blinking, both of them unsure of the next move. Nate trapped in the narrow kitchen. A standoff.

Finally Luis shifted to the side, opening up a slender gap for Nate to exit. Nate slid past him, smelling the beer on his breath. Luis kept a tight grip on the bottle but never raised it.

As Nate stepped outside, Luis lifted a black boot and kicked the front door shut behind him.

Chapter 30

They huddled together at the boarding gate, trying to blend in with the businessmen and students, the families laden with diaper bags and cameras. Janie had bought Nate a ticket for American Flight 4 as well so he could accompany her and Cielle right up until they crossed the threshold to the Jetway. He had been in a continuous state of alarm, scrutinizing every face, peering at every cluster of travelers, glancing over his shoulder every few steps. There'd been the predictable LAX tangle slowing them down at security, and groups three through six were already boarding. As he watched the throng leak slowly through the checkpoint and onto the plane, it struck Nate that these could well be the final minutes he'd have with his wife and daughter.

For most of the morning, Cielle had remained leaden and, aside from numerous whispered calls to Jason, silent. While Nate had paid the visit to Luis Millan, Janie had busied herself withdrawing wads of cash from the bank and making sure she'd have full remote access to her funds, dwindling though they might be. It wasn't exactly a long-term plan, and Nate well knew that if he found himself ensconced in another ice block come Sunday night, there would be no end of troubles accelerating to meet Janie head-on. Now she checked and rechecked her purse, her phone, her carry-on luggage, a nonstop cycle of small distractions that no doubt kept her from confronting the terrifying big picture.

The check-in agent called for group two, Janie and Cielle's departure now one announcement away. Time was scarce in another regard: Nate had to get to that next name on Urban's hit list, Wendy Moreno of Westchester, and hope he nailed down a connection to Shevchenko firm enough to bring to the FBI. The geography was convenient, Moreno's place just a few miles north of the airport.

Nate took a deep breath and stepped over to Cielle to say good-bye. She looked up into his face, her expression blurred with concern. He felt a faint elation that, at long last, she was going to say something warm and daughterly, but she wiped her nose and asked, "When can Jay come?"

The sensation was a bit like having a battering ram swung into his gut, but he covered as best he could with a lame parental standby: "Why don't you talk to your mother about that?"

And now group one was boarding, and they were out of time. He moved to hug her, and she half started for him, and they wound up clutching at each other briefly, like robots simulating a human custom.

When they parted, he bent so he could look at her directly. "When you were a baby, we got you home and we were gonna sleep you in our bed, between us. But you were so little and I was so big, I was worried I'd roll over and smother you or crack your neck. I was so scared I'd hurt you that I stayed awake all that night and the next, until finally your mom said she needed one of us to get some sleep, so we put you in a cradle by the side of the bed. And then finally I could fall asleep."

Cielle searched his face. "Why are you telling me this?"

His thoughts roiled; he could find no clarity in the heat of a dozen conflicting emotions. The remaining passengers were funneling toward the checkpoint, an hourglass down to its final grains. "I don't know."

Janie nudged her. "We have to go." Cielle started for the gate, Janie following, rolling her carry-on, Nate watching them walk away.

Janie got two steps, and then she let go, the handle cracking the speckled-tile floor as she spun, and then she was in his arms, squeezing him. "I'm sorry I never went to Paris with you for our makeup honeymoon and for all the times I yelled at you and for us fighting so stupidly and for the time I called you a useless asshole."

His hands remained raised in the air behind her in stunned flotation, as though he were fearful that if he embraced her back, she'd evanesce. "I don't remember you calling me a useless asshole," was all he could manage.

"You *don't*?" Her face was hot against his neck, moist with tears. "You can't imagine how many nights I've lost beating myself up over that and everything else I did wrong."

"Actually, I can."

Ahead, Cielle waited at the zipped-back stanchion, ticket in hand, chewing her gum impatiently and tugging on her purple-and-green Seuss-like scarf. The check-in agent gestured, a pert smile hiding her irritation.

Tentatively, Nate lowered his arms to Janie. She remained, firm and alive in his grasp. "Thank you for this," he said, and let her go.

She turned and boarded briskly, not looking back. He paced a bit before the vast windows as the crew loaded the luggage and unhooked the Jetway. Finally, the 767 pulled out of the gate and turned majestically for the runway. Nate watched, hands pressed to the glass, counting the airplane windows from the front. Row 7, Row 8—and there was Cielle, her frayed sweater a spot of black against the blinding white panels of the jet. She pressed a sleeve-covered hand to her window, and he waved back.

The plane drifted forward, the rest of its sleek body pulling into Nate's line of sight. In the row behind Janie and Cielle, a pale face loomed into view against the pane. Bullet-shaped head fringed with bristle.

Even from this distance, he could make out the displaced nose, the broad seam of the mouth twitching with something like amusement. Nate's fists ached, and he registered distantly that he was beating them against the window. Spittle flecked the reflection of his own roaring face.

Yuri lifted a hand in mock farewell, and the plane glided forward to the runway.

Chapter 31

"Sir, you'll have to calm down."

Nate leaned over the check-in counter. "I told you—"

"You want us to stop a flight? Because you don't like one of the passengers? Whose last name you can't even produce?"

"No, that's not why." He glanced through the giant windows. The plane, now taxiing to the end of the runway. "My wife and daughter's lives are at *risk*—"

"We've already left a message for them at the arrival gate. If they are uncomfortable in any way in the air, they can report it to the flight attendants. We have a very competent crew aboard, and—"

The rest of the agent's response was drowned out by American Flight 4 roaring into takeoff. Nate backpedaled from the counter despondently and watched the 767 mount the mockingly clear blue sky. Onlookers returned to their newspapers and laptops as the plane shrank to a speck.

Again he called Janie's cell phone and then Cielle's, but both were of course still turned off for the flight.

Arguing with himself, he vacillated between fleeing and staying, rising and sitting at intervals, a liturgy of panic.

What if Yuri killed them en route? Or right upon landing? Nate couldn't let his wife and daughter spend a five-and-a-half-hour flight unaware that their prospective killer was sitting right behind them. But what the hell could he do?

Flight 4 was now a memory lost to the cumulus clouds heaped at the horizon. Gone. Thin air and all. His lungs felt incapable of drawing a full breath, and for once he knew that the ALS was not to blame. What would Shevchenko have planned for Janie and Cielle when they set down in New York?

He turned from the window, nearly banging into a man standing behind him, facing away. As he started to apologize, the figure made a stiff, horror-movie pivot.

Charles.

He opened his mouth and puffed out a ghostly sheet of smoke from his charred insides. As it rose, he grinned, impressed with himself. "Know who my favorite officer always was?"

As usual, oblivious to the context.

Nate was almost too infuriated to reply. "Right now I don't give a *shit* who your favorite officer was."

"Lieutenant Spick-'n'-Span. 'Member him?"

Nate glowered at his dead friend, barely resisting the urge to inflict more bodily damage.

"One time we were rolling out for recon, and I stopped by his office to grab coordinates," Charles continued. "He was gone, but he'd left a note nailed to his door, said, 'In the absence of orders, figure out what those orders would be and execute aggressively.' " He took a step to the window, his fingers leaving red-wine streaks on the pane. "Funny motherfucker, LT was."

Nate followed Charles's gaze to the sky into which the plane had vanished, the vapor trail already starting to dissipate. Charles's ill-timed story bounced around in his head, two words sticking: *Execute aggressively.* That sounded about right.

He turned and walked briskly away from the gate, passing a continuous loop of storefronts—newsstand, Starbucks, McDonald's. Just before the escalator to baggage claim, he spotted what he was searching for—a white courtesy phone. Snatching it up and turning his face to the wall, he waited for the operator. When the pleasant voice came on, he said, "I'm calling about American Airlines Flight Four. There's a bomb on board, planted by the Ukrainian man in the tenth row. If you don't turn the plane around, it'll detonate."

He set down the receiver and, keeping his face lowered, strode the six steps to the escalator. As he descended, he dialed Janie on his cell phone, waiting for voice mail. "Janie, listen to me. I know you can't turn your phone on till you're taxiing in, but Yuri's on your flight, in the row behind you. Don't look back. Don't be obvious. But watch yourself. Delete this message now. There'll be security all over when you land. Get yourself and Cielle to them, and I'll figure something out by then. Okay. I—"

The question of how to sign off caught him by surprise. He was still searching for words when the escalator sank into the floor and he stepped out into the chaos of the baggage-claim area.

At once the phone was snatched from his grasp, an arm slid around his waist, and a point dug into the side of his lower back, pressing so hard it seemed his skin would pop at any quick move.

He grunted and jerked away, making out only the bill of a baseball cap just behind his shoulder. The arm tightened across his waist so that he and the small man moved as a piece, their bodies in lockstep. Twisting, he craned for a look beneath the cap.

Misha's boyish face peered up, dense bangs shoved down nearly to his eyes. "Keep walking or I will push the screwdriver straight through your kidney."

The pressure intensified, sending flames across the band of Nate's lower back and down the back of his thigh. "Okay," he grunted. "Okay. Where are we going?"

"To Pavlo."

"How do I know he won't just kill me?"

"Because you're still breathing."

They hadn't stopped moving, a brisk pace across the floor. People clustered all around, and yet no one paid them any mind. The automatic doors rolled open, the dry midday heat enveloping them. As they stepped to the curb, a white van pulled up, the side door rolling back with a screech. Valerik waited on a bench seat, gun resting flat against his thigh, the sleek stub of his ponytail so solid it looked carved from wood. The point of the screwdriver prodded Nate up and in, and a moment later Misha hopped up front with Dima.

Valerik pressed the barrel of the pistol to the top of Nate's knee, and they coasted out into the flow of traffic, Dima returning the traffic cop's polite nod as they passed.

Chapter 32

The van deposited Nate and Misha on a seedy downtown block where, with mounting concern, Nate was led up a set of cracked marble stairs into a sweat chamber announced as a *banya* on the sole sign providing translation from Cyrillic. They moved through several thick oak doors, passing hoary valets manning cash registers and towel booths, Misha's mere presence dispensing with procedure of any sort. Broad, hewn-featured men lounged naked on long benches before lockers, eating pickled fish, sipping chocolate-colored liquid from mugs, and arguing in rough Eastern tongues.

The temperature rising with every step, they passed a bank of urinals and a stone arch, entering an open antechamber where men of all makes and models sank into icy plunge pools, lolled corpselike in steaming claw-footed tubs, and rinsed beneath shower nozzles protruding from the walls at inexplicable intervals.

Misha shoved Nate onward through the furnace and a sturdy wooden door into a miasma of steam so dense that Nate choked against it. Bodies sprawled about the stone ledges framing the large room, glimpses of marbled flesh visible here and there through the mist. The men were naked, save a few who were absurdly accessorized with oversize mitts and bell-shaped felt caps. A worker fed a firebox with logs of white birch, the scent and taste as biting as eucalyptus, though less medicinal. The outside air from Nate's forced entrance blew a wavering corridor through the haze, revealing a masculine form sitting centered on the stained stone slab, his flesh an angry red beneath the elaborate ink.

Pavlo Shevchenko lifted a hand, and the room emptied. No rush, no ado. The others simply exited, sweat dripping, feet padding moistly, leaving them alone.

Nate's clothes clung to him, damp and oppressive. The heat was like nothing he had ever experienced. An approximation of hell within sweating insane-asylum-white tiles. What kind of men would subject themselves to this for leisure?

The steam reintroduced itself, rendering Pavlo's outline vague and ghostly, smudging the tattoos into bloodstains. The slab was elevated, thronelike. Misha shoved Nate forward, bringing him eye level to the stars tattooed across Pavlo's knees. *I kneel before no man.*

Pavlo's face was little more than an impression in the heavy air. "I know *everything* you do. I have eyes on computer screens in important offices. You file police complaint, you spend on credit card, you make flight arrangement, I will know."

Nate stepped forward again until he could discern the old man's eyes. "You *never* said my wife and daughter couldn't leave. You said *I* couldn't leave. And

I haven't. I'm still here, working on getting into that safe-deposit box."

"You had ticket, too. In your name."

"Just so I could make sure they got on the plane. I didn't go."

Pavlo stared, his face carved from stone.

"Where are they?" Nate asked.

"In Los Angeles. Flight was canceled thanks to your clever call. Everyone was questioned. And released. It is fortunate Yuri has proper work visa. I need one man who can travel."

"Don't hurt them. That wasn't the deal. I haven't broken the deal."

"Kneel," Pavlo said.

"What?"

"*Kneel.*" Shevchenko pointed down, a dog-training command.

Nate stood, dumbfounded, his shirt pasted to him. The cut on his shoulder from the letter opener gave off a healing itch so intense he wanted to reach back and claw it open with his nails. The heat was wreaking havoc with his symptoms, his hand and arm aflame, his legs weak, his lungs straining to draw full breaths in the soupy air. *This is what it will feel like soon,* he thought. *All the time.*

Pavlo sprang to his feet, causing a violent disruption of the steam around him. He towered, enraged, glistening with sweat. *"On your knees!"*

A blow from behind knocked Nate down, Misha kicking out one of his legs. Nate's kneecaps ground against the stone. His muscles screamed beneath the heat.

Pavlo leaned over him. "If you have hope of success to get into safe-deposit box, why do you panic and go to LAX?"

"I *have* a plan. I know Danny Urban's safe-deposit box is number two twenty-seven, and I've acquired the key. Agent Abara wants me to retrace my steps through the bank one more time to see what I can recall. For obvious reasons the bank manager wants to do it on a Sunday when the bank is closed. Tomorrow afternoon I'm gonna walk the crime scene again. I'll ask to be left alone when I get to the bank vault."

"You will need—"

"A master key. When I went to the bank Thursday, they gave me the VIP treatment, left me behind the teller bank alone." His brain raced a quarter second ahead of his mouth; he was lying as fast as he could speak. "I got to the master key and made an impression. I cast the duplicate Friday."

Shevchenko frowned, impressed. "If you can deliver, why do you put your wife and daughter on plane?"

Nate moved to rise, but Misha shoved him forward again, back onto his knees. He was having trouble breathing, thinking, his left arm trembling. Sweat stung his eyes.

He forced the words out. "My daughter is willful. She gets in my way. It's easier for me to do this with her gone. And"—he sucked in a moist breath—"I don't trust you."

The silence, dense as the air. Then Pavlo gave a resonant laugh. Genuine amusement that seemed to catch him by surprise. "These are first words of yours that are not lies." He chuckled a bit more, a deep sound that held little mirth. "You have daughter you struggle with. Who no longer cares for you. Americans let their children speak to them with disrespect. This is why they do not obey." For the first time, his face held a sentiment that Nate found familiar, human. "They are impossible creatures. Daughters. They wind barbed wire around your heart and tug."

He gestured mercifully for Nate to rise. Nate found his feet, stooping in the heat, his legs aching.

"You have a daughter?" Nate asked. "I thought you made some Russian-mafia promise to have no family. Only the brotherhood of thieves."

"Russian mafia." Pavlo chuckled. "Sounds frightening. Like your Marlon Brando. We are not mafia. We are not even Russian. The only real criminals from Russia live in the Duma and the Kremlin. There are no laws. Only loopholes, favors, bribes. We have been under the heel of war for generations. We fear no God. We believe in nothing. To survive you need muscle. And *will*. Here you need only lawyers. And I have them. A team of them—Jews—working in concert, burning midnight oil. They protect my businesses. My freedom."

His gaze sharpened, zeroing in on Nate's aching arm, which Nate had been holding against his stomach. He dropped it, letting it dangle, though the skin felt scoured by sandpaper. "Your guy twisted my arm at the restaurant," he said quickly. "Tore something."

Pavlo sneered at him. "We are not our bodies. We are more. Greater. This, our skin, is a cage. We must be *more*." .

The firebox leaked a steady stream of heat. Nate's vision dotted. He had never felt the disease so acutely, his muscles hanging about him like rags. *It's not always that easy,* he thought.

Pavlo's expression demanded a response, so Nate gestured at his tattoos. "But your body defines you."

"Because I am decorated? No. I am my body no more than you are yours. I have pride in my *code*. These?" His hands slid across his sweat-slick skin, moving from tattoo to tattoo. "They are my passport, my story. They cannot lie. In prison do you know what most valuable currency is?" His thumbs rubbed across his fingertips. "Pigment. One burns a boot heel. Sifts the ash through handkerchief and mixes with urine. The needle? A guitar string sharpened on strip of a matchbook. In the worst conditions, we find a way to speak our truth. To say, 'This is my promise. It is carved into my flesh.'" He slapped his flushed chest, leaving white handprints on both pectorals. "I fulfill every promise written here."

"Then fulfill your word to me," Nate said. "I didn't break the code. Don't touch my family."

"Go home. Your wife and daughter will be waiting. They must now behave. You do not know when we are looking." At last Pavlo sat, his bare flesh slapping the stone wetly. "Enjoy them for next thirty-six hours. The next time you see me, I will either release you or force you to watch your daughter die."

Chapter 33

Dima pulled up in front of the house, Valerik lifted the gun barrel from Nate's thigh, and Misha rolled back the door and prodded him out. A few shaky steps up the walk, Nate heard a whistle. When he turned, his cell phone was flying at him, and he moved to catch it in front of his face, but his hand couldn't clench in time. The phone bounced unbroken on the pavement, and he stooped painfully to pick it up. The door slammed shut as the van pulled away, leaving Nate alone in the thickening dusk with the smell of wet grass and a cell-phone screen showing seventeen missed calls from Janie.

Moving toward the front door, he sensed a tingling in his ankle and realized that his left foot was dragging, ever so slightly, along the concrete. The first sign of the dropped foot that heralded, for the afflicted, the beginning of the descent. No wonder Lou Gehrig started having trouble with grounders. With concentration, Nate returned his stride to normal, his pace quickening at the thought of seeing Janie and Cielle.

The front door flung open, two backlit feminine

forms crowding the opening, their bearings conveying distress and trepidation and—yes—relief at the sight of him. Firming his leg, he kept on, even as Janie and Cielle rushed out to meet him. His dread, as enveloping as the creeping nightfall, was penetrated by a single prick of light, a sharp gratitude for the embrace to come.

Three A.M.

Kneading his forearm, Nate sat on the couch with Janie, Cielle looking on with chagrin and flicking the edge of her scarf fretfully across her lips. Watching his daughter, he was reminded of what was at risk and had to look away to keep the dam of emotion from breaking inside him. It had been a day without beginning or end, just a prolonged episode of trauma, twisting through the hours like a trapped creature that refused to die.

After stumbling in from the coerced *banya* visit, he'd showered, changed into fresh clothes, and driven Janie's car down to find Wendy Moreno—that last name they had from Urban's list. His knock had gone unanswered, and he'd waited outside for six jittery hours until, assuming that Ms. Moreno would be spending the night out, he'd driven home in a state of exhaustion he could describe only as a stupor. While he'd been on his fruitless stakeout, Janie had scavenged every nook and cranny of the Internet to see if she could find anything about Patrice McKenna, the murdered schoolteacher from Brentwood, that might connect her to Pavlo Shevchenko. Janie had turned up little more than stunned testimonials from neighbors and relatives, variations on a common theme: Patrice was a pillar of the community, the last woman they'd ever expect something like this to happen to.

Twenty-one hours to zero hour, and Nate had not one scrap of evidence to bring to Abara. In fact, every dead end they hit reaquainted them with the alarming reality: They didn't even know what they were looking for.

Now they were rehashing the contingency to their contingency plan. First thing tomorrow he'd drive back to Wendy Moreno's and hope that he found her and could, through some Sherlockian miracle, scare up a piece of leverage that might flip the script on Shevchenko. Moreno's house was near the airport, so on his way he'd drop Janie and Cielle at LAX to retrieve his Jeep from short-term parking, where it had been languishing since he'd been snatched by Misha. Janie would get the Jeep home, pack it, stay visibly present in the house in case Shevchenko's men were watching, and wait to hear from Nate. Short of his finding the magical clue at Moreno's to bring to Abara and the FBI, he'd race home and they'd go on the run together well ahead of Shevchenko's midnight deadline.

"No credit cards," he said. "No flight or hotel reservations. No phone calls."

Janie looked across at Cielle. "That includes Jason."

Cielle's face wrinkled at the injustice of this, and she was about to reply when she registered something in Nate's face. "What's wrong?"

"Nothing, honey."

Her gaze hardened. "Remember our deal. No keeping stuff from me."

He looked down at his hands. "I haven't been able to

draw a full breath since . . . The heat, I think it screwed with me. My arm and then my lungs and my goddamned ankle now—" A glimpse at his daughter's face made him clamp his mouth shut. The words had flooded out, coming with more intensity than he'd intended.

He shook his arm gently, trying to force sensation back into it.

Janie gestured at it. "Do you need—"

"It's okay. I got it." He rested his arm on his thigh and dug at the muscle with his thumb.

Cielle curled her legs beneath herself on the couch. "Is it scary?"

"Being sick?"

She nodded. Her fists rose to her chin, elbows on her knees. She might have been six or ten. "What's it *like*?"

He could feel Janie, too, focused on him. The stillness was electric.

"It teaches you that no part of you is sacred," he said. "And that other people are."

Chapter 34

When the garage door lifted, revealing the gray morning sky, Nate heard Janie's and Cielle's breathing accelerate. The world had become a different place, full of dark vows and hidden eyes. He eased Janie's car from the garage, the street drawing into view, but there seemed to be no one there, no dark Town Cars or faces in the bushes. On the freeway, blazing toward LAX, he could feel his heartbeat still surging.

After dropping off Janie and Cielle to pick up the Jeep, Nate drove north toward Wendy Moreno's house. Idling at a stoplight, he glanced across at a board shop, a few kids skating outside and sucking on cigarettes, gliding through another world where cool still mattered. The surf-rat vibe reminded him of the Marina, where he'd paid the ill-fated visit to Luis Millan. Just a few miles farther north.

He felt a faint charge, the precursor to a thought. Pulling over, he grabbed a map and a pen from the glove box and circled the locations of Wendy Moreno's house and Luis Millan's apartment. Then the Brentwood residence of Patrice McKenna. They were in an almost precise line running north-south.

What the hell did *that* mean?

He tapped the pen against the tattered paper, considering, before folding the map and shoving it into his pocket. Three targets, all in a row. How could that possibly be relevant? Why would Shevchenko want to kill three strangers whose addresses aligned?

He pondered this question the rest of the way to Wendy Moreno's house. Though residential, her street was animated with a constant stream of through traffic. Keeping an eye on the rearview mirror, he drove around the block a few times. No one following.

On the porch, as he waited for an answer to the doorbell's ring, more questions hectored him. What if Moreno was out of town? What if Shevchenko's men had somehow identified her already? What if she hadn't answered last night because her corpse had been lying behind the front door, draining into the carpet?

He hardly had time to weigh these considerations when a Honda Civic pulled into the driveway and a bespectacled woman in her thirties climbed out and started for him. High heels looped around one finger, she tugged at an evening dress to straighten it. Her hair was a tangle. Her night out had not been a planned one.

"Wendy Moreno?"

"That's me."

"Can I talk to you a minute? I got your name through someone else, and I had a few questions."

"World of Warcraft?" She suddenly looked embarrassed. "Oh, shit, I thought you were a salesman. Come in. Gimme a minute. I just need to . . . you know."

He entered the small house and sat on the couch, listening to her bang about up the brief hall, closet doors opening, water running. Finally she came back out, more put together, and offered him something to drink. Sipping ice water, he ran through the initial questions. She'd never heard of Luis Millan, Patrice McKenna, or Pavlo Shevchenko.

"Wait a minute," she said. "You lost me. I thought you were from the crew I met at Blizzcon. Which realm are you playing?"

He held on to his next breath longer than necessary, contemplating the variety of ways the next moment, if mishandled, would likely combust. An airplane rumbled overhead, buying him another few precious seconds before he confessed, "I don't know you from World of Warcraft. I got your name off a list held by a very dangerous criminal. You did something to get on his radar."

She guffawed, hooked a strand of hair back over one ear. "You're kidding, right? Did Scytharian put you up to this?"

"No. This is real."

A back-and-forth ensued, different versions of the same questions and answers, until finally Wendy Moreno looked convinced. "What the hell," she said. "Do the cops know about this?"

"Not yet. Only I do. I wanted to warn you so you can get out of town, maybe, until you or I can find out what this is about."

"It should be easy to stay somewhere. I have friends all over the place from WoW. But still. I mean, Christ."

"You're sure you can't think of anything? Any reason you might have crossed—"

"A Ukrainian mafia guy? Uh, I think I'd've *noticed*. Unless maybe he's a pissed-off gamer?"

"Doesn't seem the type."

Her breaths grew shallow, and then all at once she was crying in short, suffocating spurts. After a few moments, she took a deep, shaky breath and pulled herself back from the edge. "God," she said. "Your life can just turn on a dime, can't it? Everything's normal, and then . . ."

"Wham," Nate said.

"Yeah. Wham's right." She pulled off her glasses, wiped the lenses.

His work instincts kicked in, that urge to comfort, to solve. "Is there someone you want to call to help map out the next steps?"

But her mood, it seemed, was more existential. "Fate's a bitch, huh? You ever think about it?"

He rotated his ankle, testing it. Since he'd awakened, the foot had been fine, as if healed by the few hours of broken sleep. That was the problem with ALS. It progressed in ebbs and flows. The spiral was downward, that much was promised, but you didn't know how many times the symptoms would loop-the-loop on the descent.

"More, lately," he answered. "I think about the bullets I've dodged. The ones I caught."

She set her glasses aside, her face wan, washed out.

"I saw this car crash a while back. This Jag came through an intersection and"—a nod to Nate—*"wham.* T-bone. Driver was some drunk girl, a scared, stupid kid so hammered she could barely stand up. Her face was all fucked up but she stumbled off. But the *other* car. Man. It was a Volvo. Supposed to be safe, right? With this family. A car seat, you know, the infant facing backward? It was a mess. Like a crumpled beer can. Just . . . *parts.* Right in front of us. I mean, *right there.* And I couldn't help thinking, that Jag missed us by two seconds. Maybe three. If I'd left the house a little faster, or if we'd accelerated quicker off the last stoplight, or if that girl had sneezed, even, and taken her foot off the gas for a sec . . ."

She chewed at a cuticle and kept on in a kind of trance, the words flattened by the weight of everything behind them. "I still see it. The dangly mobile from the car seat, little giraffes and elephants on the asphalt. And I think, That could've been me. And I think how lucky I was, and then I feel guilty for feeling lucky when that family wasn't. But I can't help it. I think, Thank God I missed that car. Well, you know what? That fucking car? It hit me now, didn't it?" She blew her nose into a tissue. "No one gets a free pass, do they?"

"No," Nate said. "I guess not." But his mind had wandered away from Wendy Moreno, locking on to a different image. Luis Millan and his upside-down neck brace. *Screwed up my neck. Whiplash.*

Pulses of cognition, words and images pulling into place quicker than Nate could process them. The plane's roar overhead. That brochure pinned to Luis's refrigerator with a Pep Boys magnet. *I travel a lot.* Shevchenko's ghostlike face in the steam, holding that first, faint glint of humanity. *They are impossible creatures. Daughters. They wind barbed wire around your heart and tug.* Nate pulled the map from his back pocket, looked at the addresses he'd circled. That neat line, north-south. He traced his finger down, connecting the dots, his nail ending at Los Angeles International Airport.

Wendy was midsentence: "—you think Chicago's far enough if—"

"You were in an airport shuttle," he said slowly. "When you saw the accident."

Wendy stopped, Kleenex halfway to her nose. "How could you *possibly* know that?" Her mouth came open a little. "I was going to the wedding of a girlfriend I met online."

"There were eight people in that shuttle," Nate told her. "One of them was a Hispanic guy. He hurt his neck."

"Yeah. One guy got whiplash. Our driver *stood on* the brakes."

"The girl driving the Jag. You all saw her when she fled the scene."

"She literally staggered right past the shuttle."

"The cops caught up to her."

"Yeah. Later. I gave a statement. I said I'd testify if they—" She went ashen. "Oh, my God. The guy. Pavlo Shevchenko. That was his daughter."

Nate stood, pulling the phone from his pocket. "You

need to get out of town. Immediately. Just get in your car and start driving. Shevchenko doesn't know your name yet, but don't take any chances."

Wendy called after him, but his ears were ringing and he kept on, moving mechanically, almost on autopilot. He banged through the screen into the front yard just as Janie picked up; not trusting the house line, he'd called her cell.

"The names on the list," Nate said. "Those people, they're all witnesses to a drunk-driving accident that killed some people. Shevchenko's daughter was behind the wheel."

"Holy *crap*," Janie said.

"I'm going to Abara. Keep lights on in the house, make sure it looks like you're home. Wait for me. I don't know how long it'll take with Abara, but I'll come for you well before the deadline."

"Wait—what if Shevchenko's men catch wind of you going to the FBI right now?"

"I'm covered —I told him I was going to see Abara today. That it was part of my plan to get to the safe-deposit box." Something seemed odd outside, but when Nate paused and looked up the street, it was peaceful and still. No suspicious cars. No loitering Ukrainians. He shoved the car key into the lock. "Keep the gun close," he said.

She agreed and hung up. He swung the driver's door open and was about to climb in when it occurred to him what felt strange about the neighborhood: It was perfectly still. When he'd waited at the front door earlier, traffic had been a constant background buzz. And now not a car. He shut the door and moved slowly to the center of the asphalt.

He looked up the street. Then down.

A few orange and yellow leaves scraped the sidewalk, the only movement.

A roar of engines shattered the silence. With stunned amazement Nate watched black SUVs screech into view from every side street, cascading in synchrony like stunt cars in a commercial, one after another, a ballet. They hurtled forward, sliding to within feet, corralling him, and then there were shouting voices and sunglasses and pointed guns.

Agent Abara broke through the vanguard, reaching Nate first, spinning him neatly to the ground, knee in back, zip ties on his wrists, frisking him high and low. "Nate Overbay, you are being taken into custody."

"For *what*?"

"Issuing a terrorist threat against a United States airliner." Fisting Nate's shirt between the shoulder blades and grabbing his belt in the back, Abara hoisted him painfully to his feet. "Forget third base, Overbay. Now you're gonna get fucked."

Shoved from behind, Nate stumbled and tripped, disappearing into the dark interior of a waiting SUV.

Chapter 35

When Pavlo entered the kitchen, Nastya was eating red caviar on borodinski, wiping crumbs of the black bread from her glossy lips with the back of her hand. Dima and Valerik sat with her at the table, shots of cloudy horseradish vodka set before them. She was in the middle of a story, her graceful arms gesturing comically, and the men were laughing, basking in her radiance. A black halter top and miniskirt displayed her woman's body, and yet she was still so much a girl, telling tales through a full mouth, laughing with abandon, wearing sunglasses even in the house, even at dusk. A razor-blade pendant, made of thick blunted steel, dangled on a black cord, resting against her flat chest.

Misha remained by himself at the counter, sipping tarkhun, the cheery bright green tarragon soda failing to lighten his dark expression. The fingers of one hand shifted and rubbed a set of matte-black handcuffs, working them like a rosary. He stared straight through a Russian soap opera on the wall-mounted TV, his thoughts as impossible to gauge as ever.

Six and a half hours to wait, and they would have resolution with Nate Overbay, one way or another. They would have the list, those names, and shortly thereafter seven hearts would stop beating and all would rest right in the world again.

Pavlo paused in the doorway, taking in the sight of his daughter. Young enough to be his granddaughter and yet ageless, timeless, the kind of girl-woman he'd chased around Kiev when he was twelve and twenty and forty. She was framed against a wall of plate glass that showed off the dizzying view. The lights of the Strip twinkled below, the wattage of Sunset Boulevard waging war with the encroaching night, whispering its age-old promise that it was not yet time to sleep, that there was more fun still to be squeezed from the residue of the day. Youth, beauty, and dangerous promises, all there in a single snapshot. Had there ever been a better encapsulation of the City of Angels?

Misha noticed Pavlo first and stood, the others following suit. Nastya smiled and removed her sunglasses, a sign of respect. The light limned the fringe of her face, the feathered seam of scar tissue along her ear in sudden, evident relief. He recalled coming into the back room of the club where she'd fled that night after the accident, her panicked, babbling phone call still echoing in his head. She'd been hunched over as if vomiting into a friend's maroon T-shirt, and it was only as he'd stepped closer that he'd realized that the cloth was not maroon at all, but had started the evening as a white undershirt. At the sound of his voice, she'd looked up, her face hanging off, hinged at one side.

He had known immediately that it was not severe. He had seen and inflicted injuries such as these and knew the ways that flesh could tear and mend. Her friends were shocked at his collected demeanor as he'd reseated the living mask and bundled her off. Then again, he was not like most fathers.

She'd had the best surgeons, one who'd been brought in to improve a pop star's nose, and within days the reconstruction had been complete. Swelling had diminished. Purple had faded to tan. Flesh had knit together, leaving only tiny cracks, like etched veins. In short order all that remained was the imprint of the accident at the back of her cheek like a manufacturer's stamp, a reminder that people were no more than toys that could be broken apart and occasionally, when luck and fate complied, put back together.

"Papa? What's wrong?"

"Nothing, my beauty." He crossed and took her face in his rough hands, holding it delicately, like a bird, kissing her softly on the scar. Nastya squeezed him in a hug, her mane of hair redolent of French cigarettes. A lovely smell, the closest thing to home these days.

Shotglasses clinked, and Dima cracked a joke, and there was laughter, muted in the soft glow of the kitchen. A haven up here in the Hollywood Hills, safe from the chill of evening and the world outside with its fangs and claws. Even Misha smiled and hoisted his glass in a toast, his boyish cheeks tightening into ovals.

Then Nastya stiffened in Pavlo's arms, all bone and angles.

Pavlo pulled back from their embrace, followed her gaze.

The television. A commercial. Plump diapered baby sitting in a car tire, floating safely along.

He looked back at his daughter. Frozen with remorse and horror.

The TV shut off—Yuri had the remote. Then the men faded from the room like wraiths, and there remained only the sound of Nastya's hard breaths.

"I forget it, like a dream. A drunken dream. But then images come back, here and there." Nastya's chest heaved. "The baby—"

"You hit no one. You were at the club all night. The Jag was stolen from valet there. You were struck in the face with bottle during fight on dance floor."

"I know," she said. "But no. This is you and me now. We can talk—"

"There is no need for talk. There is only what happened. You hit no one. You were at the club all night. The Jag was stolen—"

A thin, high-pitched noise escaped her throat, a stifled scream. Tears streaming down her face, she shifted her weight from boot to boot, as if the parquet flooring burned her feet. "I need to say the words. I need to know what I did. I need to know who I am."

She tottered back a step and collapsed into a chair. Her miniskirt stretched wide, and he saw, on the soft flank of skin beside her crotch, several dark lines. Rage bubbled up inside him, a familiar ally, there waiting in the shadows. He swept the plates from the table with his forearm and grabbed her throat, forcing her legs apart with his other hand.

"What is this? What did you do to yourself?"

She choked out a few words. "Papa . . . no . . ."

He dropped to his knees, peering up her skirt at the inside of her thigh. But the marks were not ink. They were cuts, a neat row of them. The top mark was mostly healed, the middle ones scabbed, the bottom slice still fresh.

He stared in disbelief. Cuts *there*? Why? He had forgotten he was still gripping her throat. He released, and she coughed and hacked.

"Who did this to you?"

She wiped her face on the inside of her collar.

"Who did this to you?"

"*I* did!" she screamed in a fury, her torso twisting away from him.

He was on his feet, stepping back from her, perplexed and oddly on edge. Coals in the pit of his belly. "You cut yourself? Why?"

"To *feel*. I just want to *feel* something. I just want . . ." She leaned onto the table, burying her face in her bare arms.

The air of the kitchen had grown thicker. He was having trouble inhaling fully. He needed the breadth of the floor upstairs, his perch atop the world. Her sobs trailed him up the stairs. Pacing the perimeter of his vast bedroom, counting his steps, he heard her cries still, rising through the floor.

The sound of her ripped him back to the night itself.

Quiet enough at first. A carved turkey served by a nameless maid who, like the others, spoke no English, the atmosphere in the dining room frigid with Nastya's mood.

"What's wrong?" he'd finally asked.

"I'm sick of this," she said. "Always us. Always alone. And I'm sick of *her*." She glared at the maid. "You can't even understand what I'm saying, can you? *Can you?*" The maid withdrew meekly. "She might as well not even be here." Nastya skewered a cooked carrot on the tines of her fork and held it before her face.

"You have no idea what you have," he said softly. "You have *everything*."

"It's like a mausoleum." She dropped her fork, which clanged against the fine china, chipping the twenty-four-karat-gold band at the rim. "Cold and empty."

He folded his hands, straining for patience. "What do you want?"

"I want to *belong*."

"We do belong. Here."

"No. We *float*. Above the city. Away from other people." She took a big gulp of red wine, the crystal throwing slivers of light across her face. Turning sideways in her chair, she stared at the wall. "What was my mama like?" she asked. "Tell me again."

He set down his silverware. Pushed his plate away. Studied the markings on his knuckles. Prison-ink asterisks in a circle, the symbol of a thief from a broken home. When he looked up again, he saw that Nastya had guzzled the rest of her wine.

He spoke the mantra. "She was simple country girl. Seamstress. She loved you very much."

Nastya's body sagged a bit, relaxing into a daze. "And how'd she die?"

"Diphtheria outbreak. She caught."

Nastya closed her eyes. "And she said . . ."

"On her deathbed she say, 'My daughter must always know I carry her in my heart. And she carries me in hers.'"

Nastya mouthed the last sentence with him. She pushed away dreamily from the table and drifted back toward her room.

He sat and stared at his knuckles, the table. Turkey and wine, stuffing and potatoes. A dripping gravy boat. All that American excess. He felt a hole grow inside him that could be filled with neither food nor rage. He thought about the bundle of pink blanket delivered into his arms by the whore. How the sight of those sapphire eyes had delivered him into another life.

His chair screeched when he pushed back from the table. He walked down the hall, the house staff shrinking into the walls as he passed.

Nastya's room, when he entered, smelled of schnapps and sweet perfume. A Gauloise protruded from an ashtray, sighing a wisp of smoke, and a plastic tumbler sat beside Nastya's hand on the mouse pad. At his footfall she started, then swiftly began clicking screens closed on the computer.

He'd come to comfort her, but now his steps across her lush carpet were hard, enraged. He brushed her aside, tapping the mouse around on pages with an un-skilled hand as file after file repopulated the screen.

"Papa, no," she slurred. "I was only . . ."

He stared at the monitor, doing his best to force the words to make sense. Requests made to a genealogy forum online. Subject line: *"American girl trying to find her mother."* A response to an e-mail she'd written to the U.S. embassy in Kiev. A database of victims of the diphtheria outbreak that had occurred after pere-stroika. Weeks, maybe months of searching and requests and secret communications. *"Is my mother dead?"*

His face glowed with heat, the pulse of an infection. He drew himself erect over the desk, gathering into himself. "You doubt me? *Me*? Who gave you every-thing? Who brought you here to give you this life?"

"I see the guns on the men. I know your tattoos. I'm not *stupid*." She wobbled on her stork legs, embold-ened by the alcohol. "I got a letter from the embassy. They said you served time. I don't know your story. I don't know my mama's story. I don't know *my* story."

"I told you your mama's story."

"I know it's fake. I know she wasn't a seamstress. I'm not a child. I'm *seventeen*." Her eyes were glassy, her breath ninety proof. "What happened to her?"

"It is history. No more."

"We *are* our history."

"No. We are who we are. *Now*. You and me. We have each other."

"It's not enough."

The hollow in his gut spread, devouring his intes-tines, flesh and blood, a black hole of pain. "I gave up *everything* for you. And this is how you show respect?" His mouth was moving, throwing words before thought. It felt like vomiting to say this. She was backing away from him, tripping over the furniture, terrified. "You want to know who your mama was? I do not even remember lying with her. I remember only when she dropped you into my arms like trash. She was a whore who died with a needle in her arm."

Nastya's mouth twisted open, emitting a startled moan. Then she was scrambling out, away, clawing across her bed to the door, pulling the sheets in her wake.

Her feet slapped the tile of the hall. Then the door to the garage opened and slammed harder than he believed a door could slam. The Jaguar fired to life in the garage, the roar of 470 horses. There came a scream of grinding metal, car scraping house, as she flew out into the night.

Chapter 36

Agent Abara's smooth, handsome face remained so blank, so noncommittal, that Nate, shivering in the cold box of the interrogation room, wondered if the man was devoid of human emotion. There were no windows here, but Nate knew he was somewhere high up in the Federal Building overlooking Westwood's National Cemetery. He'd noted as much through the windows earlier, before he'd been deposited in the proverbial chair before the proverbial table. Beside a digital recorder, a bolted metal bar protruded from the table, there to cuff suspects of less gentle demeanor.

Nate had endured the full rotation of the Joint Terrorism Task Force—a gruff supervisor sporting a broad, unironic mustache from an earlier era and a succession of female agents, each smarter than the last. He'd spilled all, directing his responses largely to Abara, praying that their previous rapport, no matter how strained, might accelerate the process. When he'd come clean about going out on the bank ledge to kill himself, he'd watched Abara do a *Sixth Sense* rewind and play the film over with the missing piece laid in.

The name Pavlo Shevchenko brought immediate color to the agents' cheeks and bought Nate a bit of back-and-forth. It quickly became evident that Abara had built impressive scaffolding around his suspicion of Nate. An interview with the bank security guard had led the agent to safe-deposit box 227, where he'd found Danny Urban's key bizarrely locked inside. And yesterday Luis Millan had called the cops after Nate had paid him the unsettling visit, a red flag landing the complaint on Abara's desk. These names—Danny Urban, Luis Millan—all connected now to lend some credence to Nate's tale of crazed Ukrainians and witness lists, but until confirmation worked its way through the maze of the system, Abara maintained a note of skepticism in his voice.

Abara's expression still gave up nothing, but through the course of the discussion he'd eased from the room's corner to point-man position, dispatching the others to make queries.

"We're running out of time," Nate said. "You have to believe me and do something *now*."

They'd confiscated his phone, and of course there was no clock in the room, but he could feel the minutes ticking down to Shevchenko's deadline.

"We need to verify that you're—"

Frantic, Nate let his hands slap to the table, an outburst he regretted immediately. Appearing calm and sane was a necessity.

Abara's cell phone chimed, a text message, and he glanced at the screen.

"What?" Nate said. "What's that?"

"Confirmation of your medical records." He replaced the phone in his pocket, some of the severity draining from his expression. "You want a cup of water, bathroom break?"

"No. I want you to tell me what time it is."

"Six thirty-seven," Abara said.

Nate pictured Janie and Cielle at home, waiting to hear from him. Pavlo's men on standby ready to swoop in. His knees bounced frantically beneath the table. "You *have* to let me out of here, or—"

A junior agent entered with a fat file and a concerned expression and asked Abara to step outside.

Abara rose. "One sec."

"I got five hours and change until my daughter gets cut in half with a chain saw," Nate said.

Abara paused, hand on the knob. "I won't dawdle."

For a small eternity, Nate drummed his fingers, paced the room, glared at the one-way mirror. Finally Abara returned.

"Here's where we are." He slid a sheet of paper across the table at Nate. A large stamp proclaimed, ATTORNEY WORK PRODUCT—CONFIDENTIAL. There was the witness list, the eight familiar names.

The whole black plot, confirmed.

"Anastasia Shevchenko had two prior DUIs and was driving on a suspended license," Abara said. "Which means they'll nail her on a Watson murder. She's staring at a life sentence. They have her dead to rights."

Finally they were into the meat of the matter. Nate

forced himself to slow down, to parse the matter properly so they could come out the other end rather than run frenzied circles. "So her only way off," he said, "is if Pavlo kills the witnesses."

"Pretty much. She smashed that family to shit and ran away, like you said. At which point her old man swung into cleanup mode, reported her Jag stolen, all that. So her lawyers—her dad's all-star *roster* of lawyers—are trying for the no-driving defense. It must be proved that she was behind the wheel when the car was moving for her to be found guilty."

"No other witnesses?"

"No." For the first time, Abara looked weary, his eyes puffy. But beneath the fatigue was something harder-edged—a calm fury. Knocking off a van load of witnesses to protect a drunk driver probably hit a level of lawless disregard that even an FBI agent didn't encounter every day. "After the hit-and-run, she ran to Nebesa, a Ukrainian club—she's there every fucking Tuesday. Given who her old man is, good luck reversing an alibi out of that joint."

"How did Urban get his hands on the witness list?"

"Not sure. He had some known associates who are skilled hackers, so maybe they cracked it out of the prosecutor's hard drive. It was confidential as hell, that's for sure. The prosecutor went to great lengths to protect the names. Blacked out the police report. All proceedings in camera—judge's chambers with only one side present, no transcript available to the defense. The judge had had a turn or two around the dance floor with

Pavlo, knew the colorful backstory. She figured the risk of witness intimidation was high enough to keep the names of material witnesses secret."

"And the trial is . . . ?"

"Next month."

"Thus the urgency," Nate said. "Why didn't the witnesses know about all this?"

"If they knew who they were testifying against, it might spook them."

"Might?" Nate said. *"Might?"*

"Never know. One of them might be a crazy-ass loose cannon. Like you."

Nate blew out a breath. "So what now?"

"We'll get to those witnesses right away, make sure everyone's safe until this thing settles."

"How quickly can you get Pavlo in custody?"

"A case like this takes a while to build," Abara said, "let alone file."

"Your confidence is comforting."

Abara's mouth tensed. "Believe me, crimes this . . . *flagrant*? The entire justice system is taking this personally. Whatever warrants we need, whatever resources we want, judges will line up to sign their names. But that doesn't mean a conviction'll be easy."

"What would you need to make it airtight?"

"A confession." Abara snickered at the thought. "Flipping his daughter, maybe, in exchange for immunity on the drunk-driving murder. Getting any of the club witnesses to change their story. In other words, shit that won't happen given who Shevchenko is and the power he has over these people."

"With what you *do* have, can you get to an arrest?"

"Probably. But with his lawyers? He'll be out on bail. Plus, his men . . ."

"What about his men?"

"We know some of the names in his orbit," Abara said. "The old-school blues with the tattoos, all that. Yuri Ivashko just applied for naturalization. Valerik Koval. Dimitri Zotov. Sure. We can roll them up, see if we can make something stick. But word is, Pavlo has a new hitter off the boat from the old country, a stone-cold pro."

"Misha," Nate said. "Number Six."

"We don't know who he is, let alone where to find him."

Nate's teeth ground, a muted shriek of frustration inside his skull. "My family," he said.

"We can dispatch agents to your house right now."

"If sedans pull up to our front door, you might as well paint a target on my daughter's forehead," Nate said. "Can you get her and Janie into Witness Protection?"

"We will make sure they're safe."

A cold flutter moved through Nate's stomach. "That's not what I asked."

Troubled, Abara pivoted aside in his chair and regarded his reflection in the one-way. "A lot of people have been waiting for a break on Pavlo Shevchenko for a long time, not least of all the DA's office. The head deputy of Major Crimes wants to press the strongest plays with the cleanest links and the most physical evidence—solicitation of murder for Danny Urban and the names on that list. As for you, your wife, your daughter, unfortunately, none of you are witnesses. You're not actually testifying to anything."

"That asshole *kidnapped* me. He made a death threat against my daughter." Nate's voice rang around the cold box for a while. He studied Abara's even stare and said, "Right. No hard evidence. For that."

"Not a scrap. It's your word against Pavlo's. Watch your average rape trial to see how well those cases turn out." Abara's even features tensed into a grimace. He smelled of cologne or scented deodorant. "Plus, no one's been killed."

"Yet," Nate said.

The two men stared at each other, the cold of the room chilling Nate's lungs. His arms were crossed, his left wrist giving off an ache that would have been agonizing if he were of a mind to focus on it.

Abara spidered his fingers on the table. "I have a buddy at the Marshals Service. I'll call him to look into WitSec for your family. But it's a long shot. And there's a process—"

"What the hell are we supposed to do in the meantime?" Nate didn't like the panic he heard creeping into his voice beneath the anger.

"As I said, we can roll a couple sedans right now."

"It's not *right now* I'm worried about. Right now they're home safe, at least for five more hours. I'm worried about what happens in a day, a week, a month, while you guys build your case."

"Look, we can send a patrol car around at intervals, keep an eye on them—"

"Like you did me after the bank robbery? Because within eight hours Pavlo had me ensconced in a fucking ice block!" The throbbing intensified in the bones of Nate's left hand. He clasped it under the table, but it refused to form more than a loose claw. "Given that man's reach, are you really telling me that half-assed police protection is a good idea?"

Abara pursed his lips. Said nothing.

"The FBI can't move into our house and play nanny indefinitely," Nate said. "I get it. Then let me out of here. *Now.* I've got just enough time before that deadline to get my family safely off the grid."

"You're wanted on charges. Remember? Terrorist threat to an airliner."

Nate stood quickly, his chair toppling, and Abara matched him, one hand raised calmingly.

"You're not keeping me in here," Nate said. "If *you* can't protect my family, *I* will."

"You gonna shoot your way out, Nate?"

"You saw what I did at the bank."

Abara's pulse beat at his temple. A tense smile. Then he said, "Why don't we sit a second."

"I don't have a fucking second. You put me in jail, Janie and Cielle are dead. Plus, tell me a guy like Pavlo can't get to me in jail. Easier than on the street. He'll have me gutted in there."

Abara eased back into his chair, strummed his fingers. "Despite all logic and reason, I like you, Nate. So I'm not gonna lie to you. Having a patrol car check on your family at intervals does carry some risk—"

"*Some* risk? It's like filing a restraining order when

there's a raving psychopath kicking down the door." Nate grabbed the edge of his rising temper, reined it in. He pulled out his chair, sat, folded his hands. "If it was your wife, your daughters, what would you do?"

Abara chewed the inside of his lip for a time. Then moved his finger a few centimeters and clicked off the digital recorder. "You're a dog guy, right?"

Nate tried for patience but failed. "Is this another heartfelt family anecdote with a not-so-hidden moral? Because if so, let's skip to the end."

"I have a dog, too," Abara continued, as if Nate had not spoken. "And he's a man-about-town. Likes to roam. Before I leave for work, I open our side gate and let him out for the day. But we have *years* of trust built up, the way trust is built up between a man and his dog. You feel me?"

Nate risked a hopeful glance at the turned-off recorder. "Yes."

"You're tangled up in some serious shit right now, with a lot of outstanding legal issues. And you're a resource, still, in the Shevchenko case. If I let you roam while I look into the Witness Security Program for your family, I have to trust that you won't go far in case I need you. You'll want to stay close anyway in case I can push WitSec through."

"How will we be in touch?" Nate asked.

"Your cell."

Paranoia swelled. "Can Pavlo track it?"

"I don't care who his contacts are, he's not gonna be able to triangulate a cell signal. That takes major resources. I can't get that done *officially* sometimes."

Abara moved to the door, then stopped. "I have determined that you are not an active terrorist threat. Which doesn't mean that the charges against you are dropped. While you're out in the cold, find a good lawyer." He produced Nate's cell phone from a pocket, held it out on his palm, an offering. "You'd better get a long-term plan in place."

"By the time this gets resolved, I'll be dead." Nate grabbed the phone from Abara's palm. "I don't need a long-term plan."

Abara nodded solemnly and stepped aside, shoving the door ajar.

Chapter 37

The rough October winds were acting up, fallen palm fronds littering the streets like knocked-off fenders. Dialing his cell phone, Nate urged the cabdriver to step on it. The house was mercifully close, mere miles from the Federal Building.

As they screeched onto Montana Boulevard, Janie finally picked up. "Nate? What happened? How'd it go?"

"Good and bad I'll explain later any sign of Pavlo's men?" The words came out in a rush, together, one long sentence.

"No. Cielle's been keeping watch at the windows. They don't seem to be—"

"I'm almost home. Finish packing up the Jeep. We're leaving *now*."

An abbreviated pause, but Janie read his voice and simply said, "Okay. Got it."

Rocketing past the multimillion-dollar houses with their lit front gardens and spit-polished sedans, he saw his situation in stark contrast with his former life. When had everything careened so drastically and suddenly off track? It was as if he'd taken a left turn and dropped into the Grand Canyon.

He asked the driver to let him off around the block. Then he cut through the Rajus' side yard, his left foot dragging through the fallen leaves. He'd been told that ALS symptoms could intensify at night, and so far he'd found that to be true, his body weakening as darkness encroached. His fingers fussed at the gate latch, numb and ineffective, until he knocked it open with an elbow and spilled into his backyard. Empty. No sign of anyone watching. The lights were on upstairs but not down, probably so no one could see Janie and Cielle loading the Jeep. He banged on the rear sliding glass door, and Janie rushed down the stairs, dropping a duffel bag, and let him in.

He slammed the slider behind him and locked it. Casper scrambled in from the other room, excited, slipping on the tile and ramming his muzzle into Nate's crotch. Nate scratched his ears, guiding him aside. "Where's Cielle?"

"Grabbing a last few things in her room. Go get her. I packed you already." Janie was flushed, breathing hard, tamping down her fear. The Beretta swung heavily in her jacket pocket, its etched grip protruding. The sight of it there, so out of place, did something painful to his heart.

Janie hoisted the duffel and started for the garage.

The phone rang.

Even across the kitchen counter, the illuminated LED screen was visible in the dark room: NEW ODESSA.

Janie stopped. The phone rang again.

Nate lifted it from its base. It shrilled in his hand. He clicked TALK. Moved the trembling receiver to his ear.

Pavlo's voice, rich with age: "Where is my item?"

"I have until midnight."

"No. It is done. Your time is up."

Nate's throat went dry. "We agreed that—"

"Your VIP trip to the bank to get inside box would have happened by now. Do you have what I want?"

Nate breathed through clenched teeth. "Yes. I have it."

"What is it?"

Janie's eyes were on him, wide and wild.

Nate tried to weigh his options, but time was moving too fast for him to keep up.

"Well?" Pavlo asked.

"A list of names," Nate said.

A sigh of pleasure came through the receiver, almost a hiss.

"I'll bring it to you. I'll leave right now." Nate gestured furiously for Janie to finish loading the Jeep, but she didn't move. She just stood there, the weight of the duffel tugging at her arm.

"No," Pavlo said. "Tell me names."

Any name Nate gave carried with it a death sentence. A drop of sweat ran from his hairline, stinging his eye. Casper whimpered at his side and shifted paw to paw.

"*Now,*" Pavlo said.

"Patrice McKenna," Nate blurted. The schoolteacher Danny Urban had already murdered. The one safe name to give—they couldn't kill someone who was already dead.

A pulse of excitement beneath Pavlo's words. "Yes. Now others."

Nate's last thought remained, banging about his head like a bird stuck in a room. *You can't kill the dead*—his personal theme since he'd come in from the ledge, the source of his fearlessness in the face of bullets, ice blocks, rescue saws, but there was something else, something—

"Aiden O'Doherty," he blurted. The last death notification he had served, the teenage boy who'd died in the car crash.

He heard Pavlo breathing through his nose, nothing more.

Nate cast his memory back to the previous six death notifications he'd served, naming the names of the dead.

Paula Jenkins, overdose.

Martin Padilla, drive-by.

Shin Sun-won, knife in the stomach.

Wally Case, suicide dive in front of a bus.

Clarissa and Frederick Frigerio, shot in a convenience-store robbery.

When Nate had finished, Pavlo said, "Fine. Now bring list to me. I want to see with my own eyes."

Nate hung up, and Janie sprang back into motion, hauling the bag to the Jeep. Nate took the steps up three at a time, Casper at his feet, calling Cielle's name as he charged down the hall. She was in her room, clutching an armload of photo albums, phone pressed to her ear.

"No, Jason." She tugged at a maroon streak in her hair. "I told you. Do *not* come over right now."

Nate grabbed her arm. "We gotta go."

"He's almost here, Dad, and—"

Casper's head jerked toward the door, his tags jangling. The patch of hair rose at the base of his ridge. His ears lifted, squaring off at the tops, then flattened back against his skull. He took several slow, stalking steps toward the hall.

Cielle still hadn't moved, but the cell phone bobbed beneath her thumb, giving a barely audible click as it turned off. Nate raised a finger to his lips and flattened a hand: *Stay here.*

He crept down the stairs, Casper a half step ahead, slinking like a great cat. The door to the garage was closed, and he could not hear Janie beyond. He started for her, but Casper moved swiftly across the kitchen and growled at the sliding glass door. Nate followed, flipped the lock, and had barely tugged the door open when Casper skimmed through. The dog stopped ten feet away at the near edge of the lawn, snarling down at something.

Nate moved out into the night air, took a few steps across the brief patio, and stared down.

Two oversize footprints crushing the grass, facing the house.

With mounting dread, Nate turned slowly and looked over his shoulder.

Yuri finished slipping inside and stood in the kitchen, staring out at Nate through the narrow gap in the door.

No gloating. No anger. Just an empty, gray-eyed stare.

A shushing noise as he tugged the sliding glass door closed.

The glass threw back only a reflection of the yard, the porch light a scorch mark in the corner of the pane. Before Nate could move, Yuri's chalky hand ghosted into sight behind the double panes and flipped the lock.

Chapter 38

Casper sprang before Nate did, swiping at the glass, barking furiously. Nate unlocked his legs and charged, crashing into the sliding door with his shoulder and bouncing back, landing on his ass. In the pane, he saw only a few feet of reflected patio, the uniform black sky, and his own expression of abject terror. Rising, he shoved his face to the glass to see inside, his breath clouding the view at quick intervals.

Indistinct in his massive dark coat, Yuri reached the door to the garage just as Janie passed into the house again, gun in hand, nearly colliding with him. Her expression clicked instantly from worry to horror, and then Yuri's massive hand palmed her face like a basketball and shoved her out into the garage, the gun spinning from her grip. She tripped, striking the still-opening door, tumbling off the step and out of sight. The door banged wall and wobbled back, slamming shut. Calmly, Yuri reached over and threw the dead bolt.

Crouching to retrieve the fallen gun, he turned and

looked across the kitchen, fixing his glinting possum eyes on Nate.

Then he rose and headed up the stairs.

Nate's skin caught fire, every nerve ending, every cell.

Casper's barks elongated into rumbling howls as he jabbed at the sliding door with his front paws, gouging up curls of wood from the frame. Nate spun, grabbing the nearest thing he could lay hands on—a wrought-iron patio chair. He hurled it with all his strength. It struck the pane, rippling the reflection, sending out a warbling sonar cry and bouncing back, narrowly missing his head. A thumbnail-size chip marred the perfect pane. Nothing more.

In a fury Nate swatted aside another chair, then kicked over a table, at last laying eyes on the cast-stone umbrella base waiting patiently for springtime. Squatting, he hoisted it, his compromised left hand useful only as a grappling hook. His back straining, he lifted the base above a shoulder and barreled at the sliding glass door, rotating to let the cast stone hit first.

The sound was limp, a muted cracking as the safety glass webbed. He punched through, sprawling onto his back, the umbrella base rocketing dangerously to bite up a chunk of kitchen tile.

From upstairs he heard Cielle's scream, *"Dad, help me!"*

Her voice, the terrified plea, the word at last—*Dad*—had him back on his feet as if he'd been yanked up by the collar. Trapped in the garage, Janie slapped and pounded on the door. Hurtling past to the foyer, he leaped at the stairs. In full gallop, trying to make the turn behind him, Casper skidded out, nails scrabbling helplessly across the floorboards. Nate seemed to fall up the stairs, four, five at a time, and then Cielle's door rocked into view, funhouse-tilting back and forth as his legs pounded the carpet. *"Dad! Daaad!"* He crashed through, catching one frenzied glimpse of Cielle recoiled against her window before Yuri's fist swung into view from nowhere, firmed around the handle of Nate's own gun, reverse brass knuckles flying at his forehead with dizzying speed.

A blip of blackness.

Then Cielle's ceiling staring down, a blank screen. Somewhere a fuzzy voice. Blood in his eyes. He tried to lift a hand to wipe it away, but his muscles did not respond. Blinking away the blood seemed to be the only movement he could muster. On the far side of the closed door, Casper was at the wood like a vampire, fangs and nails. The unique agony of face pain and the stunned moment of laid-out paralysis transported Nate to that dune, his mouth pressed to the sand, his eardrums thrumming, the heat of the helo explosion roiling across his back.

But no. This was worse.

Even over the snarls, Nate could make out the voice now, across the room, addressing Cielle: "I am bigger. I hold the power. This is way of the world. You will learn."

His head felt filled with concrete, the weight pulling at him. He let it fall to the side. The stepstool carved with his daughter's name had been kicked over, the letter puzzle pieces crowding his field of vision. Across the room Cielle was sobbing, black eyeliner streaking. Her round face lit with disbelief and shock.

Yuri spun her and pushed her brusquely against the window. "Undress."

She tried to look over her shoulder, a crescent of flushed cheek coming visible. A tiny voice. "Dad?"

Nate moved to rise, and daggers of pain shot through his skull. He coughed up a mouthful of vomit.

Yuri pushed the steel gun barrel against Cielle's shoulder blade so the skin dimpled. "Your father not help you now. Undress."

She crossed her arms weakly, gripped the hem of her sweater. Then she stopped, sagging against the wall, her knees giving out. "No," she said. "No."

"Relax." Yuri lowered the pistol's tip, grazing her kidney, menacing her. "I just want to see your insides."

Nate shoved himself up on his elbows, but static blotted his vision, and he knew that if he rose too quickly, he'd black out. He paused on trembling muscles, panting, the scene unfolding right across from him.

"I come right back, *pryntsesa*."

Yuri's footsteps creaked the floor, and then an enormous boot pressed down on Nate's trachea, pinning his head to the carpet and denting his windpipe closed. A long view up to that expressionless, tilted face. Nate gagged for air, his legs writhing like snakes. Nausea swelled, blotting out sensation, the breath gone from his lungs. His fingers curled around Yuri's boot, but his grasp was weak, his left hand worthless. In seconds he'd lose consciousness. Cielle's sobs kept on, a horrible background murmur.

Helpless, he rolled his head an inch or two toward the door, an arm's length away. The dog hurled himself against the far side, snapping and howling, but there was no way Nate could reach the knob to let him in. A rush of white noise hummed in his ears. The static came again, filling his eyes. Through the black and white specks, he noted a band of color running down, kissing the carpet.

Cielle's purple-and-green scarf. Hooked around the doorknob.

The *lever* doorknob.

He strained to reach the scarf. The tips of his fingers brushing the soft wool. Yuri smirked, amused. "You are going to hit me with scarf?"

He shoved down harder, and Nate's throat ignited. He could see nothing now but static, a great wide field of it. With a final burst of strength, he stretched, clinched the ends of the scarf in his weakened left hand. He commanded his fingers to close. They slid uselessly down the fabric, then finally clamped, the grip just firm enough.

Too late, Yuri realized what Nate was doing. The boot lifted, oxygen screeching into Nate's lungs even as he tugged. The scarf pulled the lever knob down, releasing the latch bolt. Before Yuri could take his first step, the door blasted open, an explosion of animal.

Chapter 39

It seemed at first that the dog was flying. His paws didn't touch so much as skim the carpet. There was a single superhero bound, a coiling of flanks and legs, and then 110 pounds of Rhodesian ridgeback went airborne. As Yuri swung the gun around, Casper rocketed directly up into his face.

The Beretta fired into the wall and the floor beside Nate's cheek, before kicking free from the big man's grasp. Casper didn't reestablish contact with the ground. His paws digging into thigh and throat, he stayed in a horror-movie flotation, driving himself continually up into Yuri's face. The big man stumbled, bellowing, swinging blindly, crashing into the bed, the wall. He finally managed to bat the dog away, and he lurched toward the door, his flailing arm throwing an arc of crimson drops against the stark white wall. Casper landed on his side but rotated immediately onto his paws, and then he was gone, shot from a cannon down the hall, clawing up the fleeing man's back.

There came a crashing on the stairs, a tumble of man

and dog, then a high-pitched animal yelp. Thunderous footsteps, the front door swinging open. A masculine shout outside and a secondary crash. Nate was on hands and knees, hacking, the air so fresh it burned. He forced himself up, wiping at his face. Cielle was slid down beneath the window, balled up, hugging her knees, her face streaked with tears. He went to her and held her, and she clutched at his arm hard, finally sobbing, letting go. He cradled her head and arm even as he pulled her to her feet, her dark hair sticking in the blood of his forehead.

"Baby, we have to go. We have to go."

She nodded rapidly, like a little kid. On the way out, he snatched up the pistol. Her legs were loose beneath her, but he braced her down the hall. Casper waited at the base of the stairs, one leg raised and bent delicately back to protect the injured paw. His snout gleamed darkly with liquid. There was blood on the stairs, the walls.

Not his.

Casper turned to trot beside them. Calling for Janie, Nate rushed to check the garage. It was empty, the Jeep there and loaded, the big door raised. As they spun back for the kitchen, Janie shoved through the jagged mouth in the sliding door, glass pebbles cascading over her shoulders. She ran to them, grabbing Cielle's face, checking her.

"You're okay," Janie said. "You're okay." Her knuckles glittered white, skinned from hammering at the locked door to the kitchen before she'd thought to open the big garage door.

"The Jeep," Nate said. "Right now. Let's go."

They rushed to pile in, Casper hopping into the

backseat with Cielle. Nate reversed, leaving streaks of rubber on the concrete.

As they blasted backward into the driveway, a body came into view in the bed of azaleas, mashing down the magenta blossoms. Yuri? Nate hit the brakes. The body stirred. Rolling her window open, Janie pulled the lever on her seat, dropping back to clear the way. Nate lifted the pistol, taking aim past her face through the open window.

Next to Cielle, Casper licked his paws, a moist lapping. They watched, waiting, Nate aligning the sights, casting his mind back to the shooting range during basic. Slow, steady pressure. Even exhale.

The flowers rustled again, and then Shithead Jason pulled himself up from the bed, brushing dirt from his flannel. He spotted Nate and threw his hands in the air, stickup style. "What the fuck! Don't shoot me!"

Even from that distance, it was clear his eye was swelling, mauve creeping in around the socket. His lip was split, too, probably from the fall. A guitar case and overnight bag lay in the flowers where they'd dropped.

Nate thought of that masculine shout he'd heard outside. The secondary crash. Yuri punching the boy and knocking him off the porch as he'd fled.

Nate lowered the gun, exhaled through clenched teeth as Jason grabbed his stuff and bounded toward them. "Where'd that big fucking guy go?"

"I don't know," Nate shouted. "But you've got to split. Go home."

"Where are you guys going all loaded up? Are you . . . are you just taking off?"

Nate craned his neck, looking around, expecting Yuri to lunge from the bushes, snarling saw in hand. "Jason, it's not safe here. Get the hell gone."

Cielle was leaning out her window, crying. "Jay, you have to go!"

Nate started to reverse again, but Jason was jogging alongside the vehicle, guitar case rattling against his knee. "Hang on! I'm going with you."

The Jeep chirped to a halt again, Nate shouting out the window, Janie now chiming in. "You *can't*."

"*Go,* Jason. You have to get out of here."

"Wait!" He banged the side panel. "Just wait. If you don't take me, I'll camp out right here. And I'll tell those guys and . . . and I'll say who I am, and they'll kill me, and it'll be on your head. I'll sleep on the porch. I'm not leaving." He was blubbering, snot and blood streaming down his chin. "I love her, okay? I love her."

Cielle made a noise in her throat indicating, somehow, that she found this romantic.

Jason stood there hunched pathetically in the driveway with his bag and guitar case and sad-sack eyes. "If you leave me here, you might as well kill me yourself."

Nate looked at him a moment longer, then stomped on the gas pedal. The Jeep lurched backward out of the driveway, leaving Jason there, his hands extended plaintively.

When Nate stopped in the street to yank the gearshift into drive, Janie was looking across at him. "*What?*" he said.

"They've seen him now," she said. "They could

come after him. No matter how much of a pain in the ass he is, it's our fault."

"He's a kid!" Nate said. "He's got parents. We can't just—"

Cielle now, from the backseat: "He's *emancipated*. His dad's dead. He hasn't talked to his mom in *months*."

The words flying. There was no time to discuss this and even less to decide. Jason was shuffling toward them, his hands still out as if catching rain.

"Mom, *please*," Cielle said.

"Oh, for the love of Christ." Janie cranked down her window. "Get in."

The waterworks shut off immediately, and Jason hopped in, tossing his bag and guitar into the back. Grimacing, Nate took off, eyes rotating from wing mirror to rearview. Five blocks away. Ten. On the freeway now, exits sailing past.

He almost dared to breathe normally.

"So what went down back there?" Jason asked, one hand covering his eye. Silence. He glanced around. "O-*kay*." He leaned forward, taking in Nate's face. "You're all bloody."

Nate's mouth was sour, laced with the bitterness of spent adrenaline. "Yes, Jason. I'm all bloody."

"Dude, you can call me Jay already. Jason sounds like you're all *angry*." He blinked a few times, awaiting a response that Nate withheld. "Where we going anyway?"

"*We*," Nate said. "Great." A big green freeway sign flew by overhead. He squeezed the steering wheel, the nerves of his fingers giving off a worrisome tingle. On the lam with a deteriorating medical condition. Hardly ideal. "We can't use credit cards. Can't make reservations. Can't book flights. So just this second, Jason? I don't know."

"Huh." Jason chewed his lip. He turned to Cielle. "Gimme your phone."

She passed him her iPhone, and he clicked around. Nate watched in the mirror, irritated. Janie kept her thin arms crossed, doing her best to stop them from shaking. Cielle cried silently, tears slipping down her cheeks. The trauma catching up to them.

The gentle iPhone tapping continued, and finally Nate said, "What the hell are you doing?"

"Facebook, dude."

"Do you really think this is the best time for—"

"I'm looking up my friends in the Los Angeles network. Well, it used to be a network, but now it's listed as 'current city.' Lame."

"Quiet would be good right now, Jason," Nate said.

"Like this dude. Status update: 'Can't wait for two weeks in Maui.' Then it links to his Twitter account for the real-time skinny. See? Cool. Here's his latest tweet: 'Rocking it with the Ps at the Grand Wailea.' Ps stands for 'parents.' "

"Yes. I figured."

"Then there's the location-map icon with the tweet. Here. Yup. Dude's in Maui all right."

"Fascinating, Jason. We just squeezed out of that house with our lives, and now you're—"

"And I'll scroll back a few tweets to find an old one.

Like this. 'Dear Funky Smell in my sock drawer. Please go away.'" He brayed a quick laugh. "Now I'll click *this* location-map icon. And here." He shoved the phone at Nate.

"What?"

"It's a house in Silver Lake," Jason said. "With no one home for the next nine days."

Nate took the iPhone, glanced down at the screen. A neat little map. Janie looked across at the device, too, and then they looked at each other, and her eyes reshaped themselves with a touch of amusement, though they were still wet.

Cielle wiped her tears, leaned over, and kissed Jason on the cheek. He leaned back, crossing his arms, gangsta style. "*Boo*-yah!"

Janie, deadpan, her eyes still glassy: "He was kinda growing on me till the *boo*-yah."

"I hope they have a hot tub," Jason mused.

"I thought you said this was your friend," Nate said.

"Don't you know anything?" Jason snickered. "No one's really friends on the Internet."

They drove east in silence, Janie reading the electronic map and issuing directions in a flat, almost lifeless voice. Jason took Cielle's hand, giving her knuckles a quick kiss, and Nate was surprised to feel not disapproval but a tremor of appreciation. His daughter had endured an edge-of-hell scare, and Shithead at least knew to offer a bit of comfort. Drinking in the silence, they tended their private worries, the thrum of the tires carrying them into the unknown.

Nate exited at Silver Lake. Home to hipsters, slackers, aspiring artists, indie musicians, and other redundancies, the hilly, tree-intensive neighborhood sits east of Hollywood and north of downtown. Nate navigated through a gauntlet of cafés, boutiques, coffee shops, Pilates studios, gay bookstores, and martini clubs, each crowded with a full rainbow of patrons. They drove past the famous flight of stairs where Laurel and Hardy had lugged that player piano up and ridden it down a time or twelve, and then they were winding up toward the reservoir and the address marked on Cielle's iPhone by a virtual guitar pick.

The architecture varied, Spanish bungalows interspersed with sleek Neutra knockoffs and a few actual Neutras. They reached the house, a modern structure of glass and concrete, and Jason let out a whistle. Leaving the Jeep up the street, they zombie-shuffled back toward the front yard, bruised and bloody and hollowed out, dead on their feet. Circling like predators, they assessed the doors, windows, and gates for vulnerabilities.

In the side yard, Nate found an unlatched window letting into the laundry room and jiggled the pane up. No alarm. The smells of detergent and fabric softener wafted through the gap, a reminder of normal lives lived normally. Turning to call to the others, he found his voice missing. The circumstances had dawned, reality riding in on the household scents, rattling him into speechlessness. He swallowed hard, dried blood crackling at his hairline, and tried again.

Chapter 40

The sun broke the horizon, sending a plane of yellow through the floor-to-ceiling windows. Light crept across the great-room floor, claiming the Oriental rug, the paisley-shaped coffee table, Shithead Jason sleeping in a swirl of blankets, finally reaching the base of the couch, Nate's bare toes, shins, knees. At last he was squinting into the glare rather than watching it stalk him. After a fitful few hours of sleep, he'd awakened as if jolted by a live wire, and sat silent watch as Jason snored at his feet and his wife and daughter slumbered in the bedroom up the hall. He'd left the house only once, creeping outside to swap the Jeep's license plates with those from the Range Rover parked in the garage.

Now Jason stirred and rose, rubbing his black eye, his hair practically on end. Yawning, he regarded the furnishings. "Who knew MonkeyBiz12 came from serious dosh?"

Nate elected to interpret the question as rhetorical. He closed his eyes, breathed, tested his muscles. Left hand weak. Right hand tingly but functional. He raised his left foot and rotated it, as if stretching his ankle. It seemed to be back online, another morning semirecovery. Padding across the kitchen, he set down the Beretta on the counter, found a glass of water, and swallowed his pills. Antibiotics for the mostly healed stab wound in his shoulder. Riluzole to slow the ALS symptoms. Fat lot of good the latter were doing of late—not so much as a charitable placebo bump. If his condition worsened, it would be too risky for him to break cover and go to a doctor. He was over the crest already, the brake lines snipped; there wasn't much he could do now but buckle up.

Cielle and Janie shuffled down the hall, hungover from stress. The four of them regarded one another, at a collective loss. Casper's nails clacked against the floorboards next, a slight unevenness to the cadence as he favored one paw. Nate regarded him with empathy. Like father, like son. Given the fight in Cielle's room, he considered what he owed this animal. Crouching, he scratched the dog's underbelly, a hind leg springing into instinctive motion.

Janie spoke first. "Let's get everyone cleaned up."

They located towels and rotated through various showers, reconvening in the living room. With a nurse's frank touch, Janie tended to the various injuries. A flashlight check of Jason's eye for a corneal abrasion, then Advil for the swelling. Butterfly stitches from the Jeep's first-aid kit for the gash at Nate's hairline. She leaned over him, close, forehead furrowed with concentration, front teeth dimpling her puffy lower lip. The pinch of her fingers. Her soft breaths across his face. Those light freckles, stamping the bridge of her unimprovable nose.

Finally she leaned back. "That should do you till you run into the next Ukrainian." Despite the joke he could see the dread in her eyes, hiding just beneath the surface.

"What now?" Jason asked, sounding an inappropriate note of adventuresomeness.

"I'm *starving*," Cielle said.

Jason hugged her from the side. "You still freaked out?" he asked. "From last night?"

"If we get scared, the terrorists win," Cielle said. She was joking in a Fox News sort of way, but also not. Nate couldn't help but note the quaver in her voice.

"I checked the fridge already," Janie said. "The cabinets. Looks like they cleared out most of the food before they left on vacation. Someone should go on a grocery run."

"*I* will," Jason said. Before Nate could protest, he held up his hand. "C'mon, man, no one's looking for me, really. At least as much. Plus, I can go stealth. I took tae kwon do." He put more into the pronunciation than seemed necessary.

"Yeah," Cielle said. "A *yellow* belt."

"With a green stripe!"

"Kids, en*ough*." Janie peeled a few bills from her wallet. "Be careful. To the store and home, Bruce Lee. Don't stop anywhere."

"Except Nicky D's," Jason said.

"What's Nicky D's?" she asked wearily.

"*What's Nicky D's?*" Jason clutched for air. "Only the best pizza *ever*."

It struck Nate that Jason had the emotional maturity of Charles. Or vice versa. One frozen in time. The other painfully present. "I don't know about this," Nate said. "I think I should go."

"With your head all Frankensteined up?" Jason said.

"He's right, Dad," Cielle said. "You should stay here."

"Chillax, man. It'll be cool." Jason started for the door, then turned. "I'm a strict vegetarian," he declared.

Janie now, through a tight smile: "Of course you are."

"I'm just saying, I hope that's cool. With the pizza, I mean."

"Anything's fine, Jason."

"*Jay,*" he pleaded. Then: "Can Cielle come with me?"

"*No,*" Nate and Janie said at the same time.

"Okay, okay." With a cheery shrug, he headed for the front door. "And by the way, Mrs. Overbay. Bruce Lee practiced Jeet Kune Do, not—"

"Back door, Jason," Janie said.

He reversed course and headed out. Cielle thumped herself down on the couch, and a moment later a reality show blinked to life, strident women dripping with jewels and makeup, debating over Beverly Hills sushi restaurants. She called the dog over and hugged him, her savior, twirling his ears and baby-talking to him. His eyes closed in languid pleasure as he basked in her affection. He looked ridiculous, a dragon getting a pedicure.

Janie walked across to the wall of glass and stared out at the reservoir. Nate came up quietly beside her.

With the midday heat wavering through, warming them, they watched the scene below, a painting come to life. The sun slanted down on the water, turning it to a sheet of hammered copper. Cyclists circled the path around the perimeter, blurring by beneath them. Couples strolled and held hands. Dogs strained on leashes. Life in motion, everyone oblivious to the troubles of the three people on the near side of the glass—the depleted, tentative family doing their private best. Knowing that the world continued on with its quotidian pleasures and challenges was an unexpected comfort.

Nate sensed a burn in his left hand, as if he were clenching it, but when he looked down, it was hanging loose. He considered the traitorous muscle beneath the skin.

"I wish I could call my parents," Janie said softly. "My friends. But Shevchenko's men found out about the flight, didn't they? We don't know what or who's being monitored. So we're just here. In a bubble. Cut off from the world."

He couldn't think of what to say, so he said nothing.

"I'll withdraw more money," she said. "Stop at different ATMs in no particular pattern, hit the daily max. All that *Law & Order* stuff."

Below her words he could make out the faintest suggestion of her extinguished lisp, one of those imperfections that seemed to catch and distill the light of her.

She placed a hand on the pane, as if testing the heat. "We're safe here. For the moment. Then what?"

"I'll touch base with Abara," he said, "see if he can

give us a time frame for his answer about Witness Security."

"And if he *can't* get us into the program?"

"Then you and Cielle should hit the road," Nate said.

"I won't leave," Janie said. "I feel safer with you. She does, too."

"Then let's hope it doesn't come to that."

Her throat jerked in a strained swallow. Then she was back in control. He risked a direct glance across at her. The sun turned her irises translucent, a postcard shade of blue, and he forced his gaze back to the reservoir before she could read his expression.

Behind them, from the TV: *"Bitch, you wouldn't know good hamachi if it bit you in the—"*

"Call Abara," she said.

He moved to open his cell phone, both arms giving off a dull ache, as if sore from lifting weights. He added the new symptom to his mental list and did his best to move on. There was no time for foreboding just now.

His fingers clawed weakly around the edge of the clamshell phone, finally prying it open, and he turned it on with a jab of his thumb. A voice mail waited from his boss. He knew that something was amiss when she used her title in the salutation.

"Nate, Sergeant Jen Brown here. It's been brought to our attention that you were detained as a person of interest in an ongoing terrorism investigation and that there are charges pending. Needless to say, you are suspended until the matter resolves. I need you to come in, clean out your desk, submit final paperwork on the last few notifications you served, and sign some papers from Legal."

The last one being, of course, the real reason she wanted him there.

He shook off the call and dialed Abara, who answered in a hushed tone. "Hang on." Some rustling as he moved around, and then Nate could hear wind whipping across the receiver. "You can't just *call* me, Overbay."

"When will you have an answer about Witness Security?"

"Soon. Look, sit tight. The DA is less than thrilled with me for releasing you before arraignment. I can't talk right now, and not over the phone."

"We barely got out of the house," Nate said. "We're twisting in the wind here, Abara."

A sigh blew across the receiver. "Give me twenty-four hours."

"How will we—"

"I'll text you a meet time, and we can talk through our next move."

The connection clicked off. Nate used his chin to flick the cell phone closed. He looked across at Janie and said, "Tomorrow," and she nodded solemnly and turned back to the view.

For a few moments, they stood quietly, the stillness gnawing at them—the first relative calm they'd had since fleeing the house. Cielle's face cracked, and then, unprovoked, she started weeping on the couch. Janie went to her and held her while Nate watched impotently from the kitchen, consumed by visions of bloody vengeance. They passed another hour or so in silence, Cielle zoned out on the sofa, Janie and Nate lost in various imagined scenarios.

Cielle was crossing to the kitchen with her water glass when the rear door flew open and a hooded form leaped in at her. *"Bleeeh!"*

Janie shrieked, and Nate all but levitated from the floor, grabbing for the gun before spotting the pizza box in the attacker's hand.

Shithead Jason pulled his hood down and grinned broadly. "Did I scare you?"

Cielle rolled her gaze to the ceiling, an exaggerated gesture that showed off swaths of maroon eye shadow. "That was so unscary it was *comfortable.*"

Jason looked disappointed.

"In fact," Cielle continued, "it gave me a warm, fuzzy feeling."

Janie was sagging against the wall, pale, twisting a clawful of shirt fabric at her chest. "If you do that again," she told Jason, "I will shoot you myself."

Jason looked across at Nate, breathing steam, holding the gun, and he reached over and let the pizza drop gently onto the counter. "Roger that." He licked his lips nervously. "Look, I'm sorry, okay? I didn't mean anything. You don't have to get all pissed off. I'm sick of being treated at like an asshole by you guys."

"Then quit acting like one," Nate said.

The blow registered immediately on Jason's face.

"Dad," Cielle said. "Jesus."

"No," Jason said. "It's fine. Whatever." He ambled out and returned with several bags of groceries—milk, orange juice, bread, a tub of Red Vines, cookies, dog food, spaghetti, ice cream, peanut butter, and Mountain Dew. Nate moved to pick up one of the white plastic bags, and the handles slipped right through his left hand. He tried again, focusing, but the weight tugged his fingers open, a carton of Ben & Jerry's rolling onto the floor.

Janie called across the counter, "Need a hand?"

"No thanks." He reached with his right hand but found it shaking. *Clasp and lift,* he told himself. But again his fingers pulled apart.

Cielle and Jason were playing around, enacting a sword fight with Red Vines. Sweat dripped from Nate's forehead. Nausea swept his stomach. He reached again.

Janie, at the fridge now: "Everything cool?"

"I got it," he said. "No problem."

The bag came an inch or two off the tile and fell, the jar of peanut butter bouncing free. He stared at his fingers in chagrin, Cielle and Jason's laughter washing over him from behind.

He straightened up and said gruffly, "Cielle, come put this away."

"You're right there, Dad."

"Just *do* it, please." Angrier than he'd intended.

Janie's head swiveled in his direction, taking in his face and then the fallen groceries. He pretended not to notice.

Crossing to the pizza, he flipped open the lid. Hawaiian style—pineapple and Canadian bacon. "Aren't you a vegetarian?" he said flatly.

"Oh," Jason said. "Yeah. Except for bacon."

A round of looks was exchanged.

"What?" Jason said. "Think about it. What makes everything good? Bacon. A BLT. Bacon. Salad? Bacon. A baked potato—"

"Right. Bacon. I get it."

"I figure if I just eat bacon, I can be a good vegetarian. Oh—*and* gyros."

Somehow they got through the afternoon, keeping clear of the front windows despite the pulled blinds. Sitting on the floor leaning against the sofa back, Nate dozed off in the fall of sunshine near the wall of glass, Casper curling across his thighs the way he had as a puppy, his paws and rump spilling over the sides; it had never occurred to the dog that he'd ceased being lap size years ago.

At some point between sleep and waking, Charles made a brief appearance, stroking Casper's fur with a bloody hand missing two fingers at the knuckles. "A bacon-eating vegetarian," he said. "If you don't punch that douche, I'm gonna."

"Okay," Nate mumbled. "Do it when I get up."

When he came to, it was dark; they'd agreed to keep the lights mostly off in the house so as not to attract attention. He slid out from under the heap of warm fur, Casper emitting a rumble of irritation.

With two spoons and one bucket of Cherry Garcia, Cielle and Jason were zoned out in front of the television. Nate paused by the doorway and took them in, the light flickering over their faces, turning the room into an aquarium, peaceful and blue. Their hands were intertwined on the cushion, and there was something about it so youthful and unconscious—chaste, even—that Nate skipped a breath. Cielle's spoon scraped the bottom of the empty container, and she peered down and said, "Rats."

Jason's spoon, en route to his mouth, paused. He moved it across to Cielle, and she took the last bite of ice cream. "Thanks," she mumbled through a full mouth.

He lifted her hand and kissed her knuckles.

Their eyes never left the screen.

Nate felt the faintest softening of the verdict he'd been carrying around since Shithead Jason's first appearance. Maybe, just maybe, these two weren't a universe apart from a young couple playing house and serving each other Eggos in a tiny Westwood apartment.

Nate drifted back down the dark hall in search of Janie. The light in the master bathroom was on, and he found her sitting on the lip of the tub, clutching tweezers, focused on her hand. A bottle of rubbing alcohol stood within reach on the sink.

She looked up and smiled. "Glad you got some sleep."

He came closer and took in her knuckles, shiny from striking the door to the garage during Yuri's assault. The diamond engagement ring had bitten into the flesh, bruising her finger. It struck him that she had spent the morning tending to everyone else's wounds and no one had taken care of her.

He took a knee before her. "Lemme see."

She put her hand in his, giving it a little southern-belle flair. He tilted it toward the harsh light of the vanity. Embedded in the pale white dermis, a scattering of splinters.

He moved her ring around so he could take stock of all the splinters.

She frowned down at Pete's ring. "It's in the way, isn't it?" She tugged the ring off and threw it. It clanged off the sink and wall, then rattled around on the tile for what seemed an unnaturally long time.

"They can consider it rental money for the house," she said. "Now get on with it."

He stuck out his hand. "Tweezers."

"Tweezers." She slapped them into his palm.

He looked at her. "This is gonna hurt."

"I know."

His grasp was suddenly, inexplicable steady. He worked at the splinters, her delicate hand jerking in his. "I'm sorry," he said.

And then, "I'm sorry." And, "I'm sorry."

He extracted the last one and reached for the alcohol and a bag of cotton balls that had fallen into the sink basin. He doused one of the balls, which shrank with the moisture, and then he was dabbing gently at the tender underskin of her hand. Janie bit her lip; her eyes watered; her bare feet twisted this way and that.

"I'm sorry," he said. "I'm so sorry."

And then it was done, and he kept her hand and he stayed there on one knee before her, his eyes downcast, and he was still saying it, the words having migrated to another meaning: "I'm sorry. I'm—"

She stilled his mouth with a kiss.

Tender and soft. And then less tender, less soft.

He rose awkwardly to a half crouch, and she leaned back on the tub, parting her legs to let him nearer. Their lips stayed attached as if they were afraid to break apart. Then they were standing, shuffling together toward the dark bedroom, knocking knees and half tripping, and she fell back on the mattress, one hand hooking the back of his neck to pull him closer, closer.

Rolling. Twisting. Pants tangled on ankles. The warmth of her laid bare against him—thighs, stomach, arms matching flesh to flesh, zippering up into one body. She gripped him tight, ankles crossed at the small of his back, her nails breaking the skin of his shoulder blade. Her mouth at his collarbone, blurring the words: "Why'd you make me wait so long?"

After, they lay, a cross section of legs and arms, breathing hard. Her blinks grew longer, and then she was asleep. Basking in the silent glow of her, he tried not to think of the seconds slipping away, heartbeat by heartbeat.

Chapter 41

As they ate cereal on the couch the next morning, a text arrived from Abara: 9PM. TRAVEL TOWN, GRIFFITH PARK. LOCOMOTIVE ENGINE NO 3025. The phone made its solemn rounds, from Nate to Janie to Cielle to Jason.

"Guess we'll know something tonight," Janie said. "One way or another."

The rest of the day, they stayed holed up in the house like fugitives, which Nate supposed they were. Though he did his best not to fixate on the upcoming meeting, he grew more antsy as night fell, his mood exacerbated by Cielle and Jason. The honeymoon had ended, and again they were quarreling like . . . well, teenagers.

Preparing dinner, Janie and Nate could hear them down the hall.

Jason's voice first. "I didn't say she was *hot*," he backpedaled. "I just said I didn't think she was *ugly*."

Checking the stove, Janie murmured to Nate, "He said she was hot."

Cielle's reply now, at equivalent volume: "*Christina Verducci*. As in, 'OMG, I would, like, so kill for a mani-pedi. Like, see how much time I save through my clever use of abbreviation?' If you find *that* 'hot,' what are you doing with me?"

Janie poured pasta into the colander. When the hiss died away, the debate had intensified.

"In telling *me* to shut up," Jason said, "you're clearly *not* shutting up."

Janie, again with the color commentary: "She *did* just tell him they both needed to shut up."

Cielle, back on the offensive, her voice echoing down the hall: "You're so wrong, I wish we had a tape recorder just so you could hear the extent of your total wrongness."

"I wish we had a tape recorder to rewind this conversation to prove I never said Christina Verducci was hot."

"If we asked, like, a hundred people, ninety-nine would agree with me."

"Sure. And Rosie O'Donnell is gay."

"She *is* gay, dipshit."

"I meant *not* gay."

Strident as it was, the youthful banter did provide, Nate had to admit, a respite from the oppressive heaviness of the wait. Janie handed him a stack of plates, and he set them on the wooden table, the knock of ceramic and the jangling of flatware momentarily drowning out Lincoln and Douglass. When he'd finished pouring water into the glasses, things had grown quiet down the hall.

Janie cocked her head. "What now?"

"Forest," Cielle was saying.

"Nah." Jason's husky voice, barely audible. "Too hippieish. Carson?"

"No. I knew a Carson in elementary school who used to eat his eyebrows. How 'bout Taylor?"

"I like it. Taylor Hensley."

"No, Taylor *Overbay*."

Nate thunked the final water glass into place. "Oh, Jesus. Are they . . . ?"

"I believe they are," Janie said.

They listened. Nothing.

"Silence is bad," Janie said, but already Nate was moving.

He stormed down the hall and into the study. They were upright, thank God, but making out on the leather couch. He cleared his throat angrily, and they scrambled apart and gave him Garfield eyes.

"No, okay?" Nate said. "Just . . . *no*. Now, come eat."

They followed him sheepishly, Jason muttering, "Dude, we were just kissing. We weren't all *boom-chicka-wah-wah*." Nate held up a finger, and the boy silenced.

In the kitchen Janie had lit candles to avoid turning on the overheads, the effect soothing and inadvertently elegant. The pasta steamed on the plates, but by some unspoken agreement none of them started eating. There was no sound save the faint crackling of the candle and Casper at his dinner, his collar dinging the salad bowl into which Nate had emptied a can of dog food. Nate stared down at the woven place mats, the folded napkins, and understood fully for perhaps the first time in his life why people said grace before meals. For a brief stretch, they'd managed to forget about what awaited them beyond the comforting walls of this borrowed house. Sitting down at a well-set table threw their situation into sudden relief. Even Shithead Jason kept his mouth sealed.

Cielle broke the stillness first, tentatively picking up a fork, and they followed suit, eating almost shyly.

With dismay Nate realized that his jaw quickly tired from chewing, soreness radiating out from the hinge of the bone. The first weakness to reach his face. The invasiveness of this—the increased proximity now of the illness to his brain—seemed dire and insurmountable. The irony was sickening; he'd finally found the will to crack free of the frozen suspension that had kept him from his family, and now his muscles were fighting to paralyze him. Struggling to contain his reaction, he set his fork aside.

"You okay?" Janie asked.

"Sure," he said. "Just not hungry." He dabbed his lips with his napkin. "Excuse me a sec."

He walked back to the master bathroom on wobbly legs and splashed water on his face. His fingers slipped over the faucet without purchase, so he knocked the water off with an elbow and stared at himself in the mirror. "Hold it together," he said.

He took a leak and used the heel of his hand to depress the flusher. He had trouble tucking his boxers back into his jeans, his hand gone numb, and he shoved at the fabric, frustration driving him to the verge of tears. He finally succeeded, but then the buttons wouldn't heed, and it struck him that he'd soon have to buy pants with elastic waistbands.

The time for his meeting with Abara was fast encroaching, and he needed his limbs to function if he hoped to get through it. His left arm was in worse shape, so he tried to use his right thumb to knead the muscle, pressing as hard as he could to feel something—*anything*—familiar. But no matter how hard he dug, the ache stayed foreign, a new shade of pain. In short order his right hand, too, began to lose its strength, and he stared it down, willing it to grip tighter, to obey the signals he was straining to send.

A faint knock at the door. He said, "Just a minute."

Janie pushed into the bathroom. "What's going on?"

"Nothing. I'm . . . I'm . . . Nothing." He was having trouble getting any strength into his voice.

Her stare moved across him. Belt unbuckled. Left arm curled to his stomach, his right hand still groping at it weakly. He was mortified to think what he looked like.

Stepping forward, Janie reached down and gently tugged the top button of his jeans through the hole, then fastened his belt. He stayed motionless, as if that might help him disappear. His arm shuddered against his stomach. His right hand clasping, clasping, yet barely denting the skin.

She took his arm firmly in her warm grasp. He pulled away from her, his hand quaking, but she held on tight.

"Look at me," she said.

Her gaze was steady, those blue eyes shining right

through him, forcing his gaze to meet hers. He and his arm were going nowhere.

"Stop fighting," she said.

His words from the riptide in which they'd met.

With effort he relaxed, releasing his arm to her, and she compressed his wrist gently. Stilling it. He drew in a quick, surprised breath. The motion of her hands resumed, working the muscles of his forearm, squeezing the feeling back into them.

A melancholy smile touched her mouth, faint enough to miss.

"I got you," she said.

Chapter 42

By the time he left, Nate felt better, the muscular fit having subsided under Janie's touch. His grasp of the steering wheel remained firm if stiff all the way up and through the dark bends and grassy slopes of Griffith Park. The municipal parcel of land, hemmed in by three freeways at the eastern edge of the Santa Monica Mountains, was L.A.'s answer to Central Park, only larger and more untamed. Nate passed turnoffs for the zoo and the merry-go-round, then the observatory where causeless James Dean had faced down a pack of baddies with a switchblade and his trademark smolder.

During the day the park was a democratic gathering place for the city, an explosion of movement and color. But at night shadowy foliage predominated. Every idling car and solitary wanderer took on an ominous cast before the headlights, a reminder that the city with its temptations and vices was as close as the obscured freeway pushing white noise through the California oaks.

A nine-acre sprawl at the northern bulge of the park,

Travel Town was part gymnasium, part museum, a place for kids to climb on retired cabooses, throw levers, or woo-woo around the wooded perimeter aboard a miniature Pullman.

Nate left the Jeep at the edge of the lot. Given his grip, he had difficulty scaling the wrought-iron fence and had to walk the perimeter until he found a shed roof he could use as a launch pad. He tumbled over and rose from the dirt, brushing himself off. The grand trains, perceptible only as impressions on the darkness, recalled nothing so much as an elephant graveyard. Moving among the freight cars and trolleys, he felt the place tug at his heart, all these battered servants saved from the scrap heap, put out to pasture here where they could soak in the laughter of children. It was a hopeful, sentimental interpretation, and Nate realized upon second reflection that it had less to do with repurposed machinery than with his own impending demise. Unsettled, he kept on, searching out Abara's meeting place.

The giant locomotive loomed ahead, number 3025, a hundred-plus-ton oil burner that had pulled a few presidential specials in its day, conveying Theodore Roosevelt and Woodrow Wilson up the rocky Coast Route to San Francisco. Years ago Nate had taken Cielle aboard this very engine for a third-grade classmate's birthday party. Pausing, he recalled the cone hats and plastic tablecloths, how her tiny fist had yanked the cord and made the big brass bell clang.

He thought about the two curved and worn photographs from his apartment, now tucked safely in the back pocket of his jeans. Janie and him laughing through their first dance at their wedding. And Cielle's childhood soccer picture, her eyeteeth missing, her face still slender. A year or so after that photo was snapped, he'd brought her here to that birthday party. And a few months after that, he'd shipped out to the desert. The distance between now and then seemed endless and minute at the same time, a long sleep or the blink of an eye.

He climbed aboard the venerable train, his eyes adjusting to the dimness. Abara's form resolved up front, reclining in the engineer's chair. Nate ambled up and sat beside him. The air was rich with oil and tasted of metal.

Abara glanced over, his stare snagging on Nate's forehead. "Nice butterfly stitches."

"Like I said, we got out just in time." Nate took a breath. "Where are we with everything?"

"I dug around, but . . ." Abara's tone torpedoed Nate's hopes instantly. "Witness Security is an even bigger deal than I thought. It requires a sign-off by the attorney general. As in *the* attorney general."

"So we're not gonna get it."

"You're not gonna get it." Abara rubbed his eyes. A thin gold chain fell from his collar, attached to a holy medal that glinted in the darkness. "I know it's faint consolation, but the witnesses to that car crash? They're out of danger for now. Thanks to you."

Nate managed a nod. "I'm glad."

"We got them into protection until they're needed to testify next month against his daughter. Luis Millan even sent along an apology to you. Let's just pray Shevchenko doesn't find out their names. It's much safer without him knowing who he's looking for."

"He knows *us.*" Nate made a faint noise of amusement. He wiped his mouth. "I don't suppose you could get my family the same protection. Even for a month." He already knew the answer, but he had to throw some words out to keep despair at bay.

"In short order you're gonna be charged with committing a terrorist act," Abara said. "You're not exactly beloved in the law-enforcement community right now."

"No," Nate said. "I suppose not."

"You wouldn't believe how much shit I'm catching for letting you go before arraignment. If the DA had it her way, you'd be in a cell waiting for—"

"Abara," Nate said. "I know this isn't your fault."

The agent paused, catching up to himself, his face boyish in the darkness. "There's something else."

"What?"

"There have been some unauthorized searches of your name in the databases. And your wife's name. And your daughter's. From different departments in different states. I backtracked a few, and the logins don't match up. Which means—"

"People are logging in under their colleagues' names. To cover their tracks."

"Right. Information like where you've checked in to hotels or used a credit card, it's not hugely classified. Unfortunately, people do favors like that all the time, whether running a background on a prospective nanny for a friend or trying to track down a cousin's deadbeat husband." He blew out an annoyed breath. "It's not hard to run a basic search."

Nate knew. Hadn't he done it himself on the databases at work?

His mouth had gone dry. "That's how they knew about the plane ticket."

Abara nodded. "I looked into the requests and got a bunch of fuzz and static." A labored breath. "So progress with the assumption that Shevchenko has a few purchased friends keeping an eye on various monitors."

"Where's that leave us?"

"Don't trust anyone."

"I was looking for something a bit more specific."

"I'm afraid you're gonna have to hang on till we can remove Shevchenko from the equation. Your family's not gonna be safe unless we can get this case tied up."

"How's it looking? The case?"

Abara's thumb worked the medallion's edge.

"Abara?"

"Not great. We pulled Danny Urban's financials, looking for payments from Shevchenko, but your boy, he knows how to cover his tracks. All we found were several wires originating in Moldova and you can imagine what the trail looks like from there. If we can't establish a connection between Urban and Shevchenko—"

"Then you can't get Shevchenko for the murder or solicitation."

"Right. It all stops with a dead hit man. For Pavlo we got motive. That's it."

"And given his lawyers, motive alone won't get you far."

Abara lifted his hand, palm up, then let it clap down on his knee. "I don't know how to help you, Nate."

As he gazed across the locomotive controls, Nate caught the faintest glimmer of an idea.

He remembered Abara's snicker when asked what the DA would need to make a conviction airtight. *Flipping his daughter, maybe, in exchange for immunity on the drunk-driving murder.*

And he'd told Nate earlier across that interrogation-room table, *After the hit-and-run, she ran to Nebesa, a Ukrainian club—she's there every fucking Tuesday.*

He pulled his phone out and stared at the date stamped across the blue LED screen: *October 30, Tuesday.*

"Maybe," Nate said, "I can figure out a way to help *you.*"

Abara's face swung around, and Nate could feel the weight of his stare. "I can't be party to involving you in an investigation."

"I'm not asking you to."

"Good." They sat in the locomotive, staring through the windshield, going nowhere. After a time Abara bobbed his head thoughtfully. "But you know my cell-phone number already. If you wanted to send me a text, there's not much I could do to dissuade you."

"No, I suppose there's not."

Abara rose, slapping Nate on the shoulder as he headed out. "I would say, 'Don't do anything stupid,' but that's *all* you seem to do."

Chapter 43

Gauche and trendy, Nebesa lived up to every stereotype of an Eastern European club. Movie-premiere searchlights swept the sky, Range Rovers and limos gleamed in parking spots, and the towering sign above the valets glowed violet. Many of the girls trickling in were indistinguishable from hookers, and the neckless doorman looked like an icebox in a knockoff suit.

With a neat stack of folded twenties in hand, Nate stepped past the red velvet rope and approached the overhang of the entrance, doing his best to firm his weak left ankle and keep his foot from dragging. The doorman gauged his approach, scowling, hands crossed at the crotch, one gripping the other at the wrist, a posture no doubt studied at bouncer school. He stared down at the bills, unimpressed, and then his eyes flicked up at Nate. His bearing and mien matched those of the other Ukrainian heavies, and sure enough the accent did, too: "Cannot come in."

"Why?" Nate asked.

"You are not pretty enough."

"Explains why you're out here."

The man had no eyebrows, but the glossy bulges of flesh above his eyes rose. He shifted slightly, his loafers inching out to shoulder width. Balancing his weight.

Another bouncer of equivalent size steamrolled out through the dark-tinted door. "Iss there problem?"

"No. Our friend is just leaving."

The man nodded and withdrew back inside.

"I'm here on behalf of Pavlo Shevchenko," Nate said. "I have a message for his daughter. He will be displeased if you interfere with his directive."

The doorman sneered. "You do not *look* like friend of Mr. Shevchenko. You do not *sound* like friend of Mr. Shevchenko."

Nate remained in place, keeping his stare even and, he hoped, menacing. Thumping bass vibrated through the walls of the club, and two women across the parking lot greeted each other with squeals of delight. The cut on Nate's forehead tingled beneath the butterfly stitches.

The doorman breathed down on him for a moment or two. Then, affecting a bored expression, he calmly removed a slender but wicked-looking knife from inside his lapel. He touched the tip to just beneath Nate's eye.

Nate didn't flinch, didn't take a step back.

The man let the point skim down across Nate's lips, his throat, and come to a rest on the ball of his shoulder. He applied a bit of pressure.

Nate stepped forward into the blade.

It broke the surface tension of his skin cleanly, a spot of crimson spreading on his white shirt. The doorman pulled the knife back quickly, alarmed, but Nate gave him no space, leaning in until the hard edge rested across his own throat. He stared up at the bouncer's wide face.

"Yeah," Nate said, "but do I *act* like a friend of Mr. Shevchenko's?"

"You act like crazy person."

Nate pushed into the knife a bit more, feeling the pressure against his Adam's apple. "Do you want to step aside, or do you want me to wake up Pavlo Shevchenko and ask him to handle this matter himself?"

The doorman withdrew the knife carefully and put it away. "She is in VIP booth on balcony." His bare skull glistened. "I'm sorry, bro. We do not always know Mr. Shevchenko's men—"

Nate moved past him, and the tinted door flew open as he neared, the backup bouncer nodding deferentially. The noise hit Nate like a truck, the strobe lights making him doubt his balance up the stairs. Despite the smoking ban, the air reeked of cigarettes. As he reached the landing, a girl with glassy eyes and a latex dress swiveled, lifting a maraschino cherry from an apple-tini and sucking it, twirling the stem languidly in his direction.

With its cabana-like drapery, cushioned benches, and rock-star view of the undulating dance floor, the VIP booth was clear enough. Boy-men clustered at the edge, bouncing, pumping fists in the air, and lifting their cell phones to record a scene blocked from Nate's vantage. Making his way over, he saw the cause of the commotion—a blonde and a brunette, so skinny they seemed almost elongated, making out with each other as the onlookers whooped and filmed. The girls were really putting on a show, bumping and grinding, tongues flashing into view, long red nails running along endless stretches of stockinged thigh.

Nate pushed past the guys, through an effluvium of spicy cologne. "Anastasia Shevchenko?"

The blonde lifted her head dreamily. "It's *Nastya*. What do you want?"

The guys with their cell phones bristled at the disruption, their complaints growing aggressive. Nate turned into them. "Get the fuck out of here. Go. *Go.*"

They took note of his stitched forehead and the coaster-size bloodstain on his shirt and dissipated into the crowd. The brunette slid out of the booth, plucking at her miniskirt, and Nastya turned her glazed focus to Nate. Her sapphire eyes blazed, accenting perfect features. Her appearance was so striking it seemed almost fake.

She straightened her too-tight dress, cinched at her tiny waist with a throwback eighties studded belt. Her hands fumbled at a cobalt pack of Gauloises, and she lit up lazily. "Way to ruin the party."

Nate slid into a seat opposite her. Took a breath to even himself out. "I know you were driving that car," he said. "I know you killed that family."

"Are you another relative?" she said, unfazed. "'Cuz I told you I can't talk about all that. I know you need to blame someone, but it wasn't me. It wasn't me."

She jerked an inhale, the orange flare casting a glow across the left side of her face and illuminating for an instant the raised scar tissue laid like a twig across her porcelain cheek. The damage was all the more evident given her flawless skin. Nate reached across, took her chin, and turned her head, exposing the seam back by her ear. "Yeah? Then what's that?"

She wrenched away, her first show of emotion. "I hit no one. I was at the club all night. My car was stolen from the valet here. I was struck in the face with a bottle during a fight on the dance floor." Her voice had turned stiff, almost robotic.

"We both know that's not true."

"I hit *no one*! I was at the club all night. My car was stolen from the valet here. I was struck in the face with a bottle during a fight on the dance floor." She punched the words, aiming them like bullets across the table at Nate, but he had dealt with his own teenage daughter enough to see right through the shell of fury. He could sense the denial in her face, behind her eyes.

"No," Nate said.

"I hit no one." Her voice trembled. "I— I was at . . ." The long cigarette held an inch-long tube of ash that defied physics, refusing to fall.

"Look at you," Nate said. "Can't keep your face straight here. Think what they'll do to you in court."

She sucked an inhale, fingers trembling around the cigarette.

"You fucked up horribly," he continued. "And it cost people their lives. I can promise you: You'll live with that the rest of your life. But I can also promise you: You can move on from this. You can figure out how to live again."

A tear clung to her mascara-dense lashes. "How do you know?"

"Because I know. But it's not over. Your father, he's ordered the killing of everyone who witnessed you in the Jaguar that night."

To gauge her reaction, he watched her closely, but he needn't have. Her eyes widened with surprise; she jerked in a half breath and then another, as if choking. "It's not true."

"It is. The first witness, Patrice McKenna, was already stabbed to death. He's trying to find the names of the other witnesses."

"There's no way. It *can't* be true."

"He is willing to murder more people to protect *you*. I have a daughter your age." Just saying the words made his chest burn, brought the whole flammable scenario roaring back to life. He fought away emotion, leveled out his voice. "And if your father isn't stopped, he's gonna kill her. In front of me."

Her lips parted to suck in another clump of air.

"He holds me responsible," Nate said. "He holds the witnesses responsible. He will do *anything*. To protect you. Which means you're the only one who can stop it. Talk to him. Get him to tell you what he's done."

Her radiant skin suddenly looked sallow. "He wouldn't do something like that. What you said. He just *wouldn't*."

"Wouldn't he?"

She looked anywhere but at him.

"If the lives of those people, my daughter, matter to

you, get your father to talk to you. And take what he tells you to the cops. They'll make it stop. If you do this, they'll probably be able to keep you out of prison—"

"Everyone is so concerned about prison, prison, prison. I don't *care* about going to prison."

"You're looking at a life sentence," Nate said.

The dance beat throbbed like something living, rumbling the booth, the floor, the cushion in the small of Nate's back. The ash fell, scattering across Nastya's knuckles. She took no note.

"Your daughter," she said. "Does she have a boyfriend?"

"If you can call him that."

"You don't like him?"

"No."

"Did you have someone threaten him? Bolt cutter around his knuckle. Like this?" She encircled one delicate forefinger with another.

Nate felt the shift in conversation as something physical, a rise in the temperature around the booth. "No," he said.

"It works well," Nastya said. She studied him a touch drunkenly, her head lolling. "And this daughter, she has friends? *Real* friends? Who like her for who she is, not just for"—she spread her arms, indicating the bright drinks, the canvas drapes, the VIP view—"*this.*"

Nate nodded.

Her gaze pinned him to the bench. "A mother?"

"Yes," he said. "She has a mother."

"And this mother takes her to lunch. They talk. She gives her advice."

Nate said nothing. The music thumped deadeningly.

"He is the only thing I have ever had," Nastya said. "You tell me I'm looking at a life sentence? I'm already serving one."

She blinked hard, stabbed her cigarette into the ashtray, and slid from the booth. By the time Nate rose, she'd vanished into the crowd.

Chapter 44

Bloody, crusted, and stitched up like an American baseball, Yuri's face resembled a Halloween mask. The cool basement gym smelled of the blue rubber mats on which Yuri, on better days, practiced Olympic lifts. The doctor checked his circulation in various places, poking his capped pen at the swollen flesh, then stepped away from the bench press he'd been using as an examination table. Pavlo handed him an envelope, which disappeared into the white coat.

The doctor said in Ukrainian, "I will return in the morning."

He exited.

Pavlo flexed his hands and stared down at his inked knuckles—crosses and diamonds, asterisks and bars. How many times had a needle stabbed his flesh while he'd gazed up at a prison ceiling? He'd gathered the pain prick by prick, swallowed it whole, stored it for future use.

Across the space, Dima and Valerik sat on the mats, smoking and playing their cards. Misha did push-ups, one after another, his lithe body plank-straight. He was shirtless, a Fila terry headband holding his swept-to-the-side blond hair at bay.

Dima glanced at Yuri's face. "Does it hurt?"

Yuri stood with a grumble. "No."

Contemplating Nate Overbay's escape, Pavlo ground his teeth. "He has the list still. Now we must chase. You are to call in more favors. I don't care how much you spend. Every flight, border, bus station. Understand?"

Yuri nodded. "We are."

"More," Pavlo said.

"He failed you," Misha offered. Not the least bit winded, he continued with his push-ups. "He was beaten by a dog."

"You did not see this dog," Yuri said. He walked over to Misha and glowered down. "Perhaps you think you could do better than me."

Misha did a few more push-ups, bouncing up to clap his hands between reps, then rose to confront Yuri. "That is why I am here. To do better than you." His shell of swoop-around hair remained perfect, unruffled from the exercise.

"No," Pavlo said. "Not yet. Let Yuri search through our channels. There are ways to locate someone here, many ways. Not just force."

"And if you don't find him?" Misha asked.

"We will find him," Yuri said.

"And if not in time for Anastasia's trial?"

"If I must, I will send an army of men with semiautomatics into DA's office a week before that trial," Pavlo said.

"This," Misha said, "sounds like a better plan."

He walked out to the balcony, knocking Yuri's shoulder. Though Yuri outweighed him by at least a hundred pounds, the bigger man did nothing. Misha stretched his muscles in the darkness, steam rising from his shoulders.

Pavlo heard the front door open upstairs, and a jangle of keys struck the wooden table. "Papa? *Papa!*"

He hurried up to the main floor and immediately knew something was wrong. Nastya stood in the open doorway, makeup smeared down her cheeks. Behind her the Town Car glided silently away.

"Come in from the cold," he said.

Her chest was heaving, her ribs faint outlines beneath her dress. "Is it true?"

"Is what?"

"That you're killing them. The people who saw me in the Jag." She held out her phone with a news story up on the little screen.

He caught a flash of the name—Patrice McKenna—and his blood ceased moving for an instant, his insides turning to concrete. "Who told you this?"

"Is it true?"

He tugged her arm gently, forcing her a half step into the foyer, then closed the front door. "Do not raise your voice to me."

"I don't care. I don't care! *Answer* me. Are you doing this? Are you killing them?"

He took her slender hand and led her into the sitting room, where he sat beside her on the recamier with its ridiculous scrolled cherry-veneer arms. The admission froze in his throat. He backed up, came in from a different angle. "You will not survive in prison," he said.

She seemed to break, as if someone had snipped the cords that held her upright. She sagged, boneless, her mouth spreading to emit a gut-deep moan.

"Many years, many times, I was in prison," he said. "I am *of* prison. Not my daughter. I would kill the world before I let my daughter go into a box."

She clutched at him. "That's not your choice."

He flung her back. "It is *all* my choice. Everything!" Spittle flew from his lips. "For you I betrayed who I was. I betrayed my code. In prison I remained unbroken, but for you—for *you*—I went against my own skin." He slapped a hand to his wrist, shoving up his sleeve, revealing the blue ink of the Zone. "Not for you to live a life behind bars like me. Like your *dedushka* in Babi Yar, starving and weak, made to carry a sack of wet salt across the yard and back. Across and back. A mockery of existence. A celebration of horror. You cannot understand. You will not live as we have lived. Every relative reaching back. All of us, filthy and marked. But not you."

"I *am* filthy," she sobbed. "I *am* marked."

"No. You are *pure*." Vehemence seethed in his words. "If I have to destroy the world, you will not go. I will bring *war*."

"I have no say," she wept, a hoarse whisper. "I have no choice. Stop, Papa." She'd switched to Ukrainian, something about his native tongue bringing the words home right to the pit of him, lifting the hairs on his arms. "For me."

"It is *all* for you."

"Please, Papa. Please." Pleading quietly, she pawed at him in desperation, pressing her palms to his chest. "Stop, Papa. Please."

"Stop this!" he roared. "Do not question me. I gave you life. I took you from the street. You *breathe* because of me."

She froze against the cushion, a startled animal. Not a sound. Not even the soft rasp of her crying. He was trembling, his powerful hands clenched. He loosened a fist, reached for her. At his touch she softened. Drew a shuddering breath. And then another.

He stroked her hair. She shifted so she was lying across his lap, the tension slackening in her neck.

"You will listen to me," he said gently.

She settled into him, her muscles surrendering. "Okay."

"It will be all right."

"Okay."

"I will take care of you."

"Okay."

"You will see."

She rustled a bit and then rose. Her face had gone flat, expressionless. "I'm tired. I need to go to bed. I need to forget all about this."

"Good. Forget all about this."

She paused before him. Holding his face, she leaned over and kissed him on the forehead. "I know you love me, Papa."

"Yes," he said.

She stepped out of her high heels, leaving them

empty on the pile carpet before her father, and floated into her room on stockinged feet. She put her back to the closed door and stared out her picture window at the magnificent view. Hollywood, the pulse of the universe. All those dreams and hopes bartered or bought for cents on the dollar, ground up and fed into the machine, fuel to keep the lights burning. People the world over drawn like moths to this strip of incandescence, yearning for a place, a home, an identity.

Her razor blade was out of her Coach wallet, in her hand, pressed to the top of her thigh, just shy of breaking the skin. She'd made no conscious choice, hadn't even known what her hand was up to while she'd taken in the view. She applied a bit more pressure, nylon and flesh yielding, freeing a quick endorphin rush. What a relief to feel *something*. To cut through the edge of herself, to reclaim her body as her own. Eyes watering, she bit her lip, an expression of ecstasy. Then she let the blade fall from her hand. She breathed, felt the thin tributary snake down the inside of her knee.

With effort she peeled herself off the door. She cleaned herself up, tissue and styptic pencil, a midsize Band-Aid. The care and healing were as much a part of the ritual as the cutting itself. She had promised her father she'd keep her body unmarred, and she would do so, even now, to the best of her ability.

Using her brightest pink lipstick, she wrote across the window, NO MORE. Then she drew her heavy shades across the brightness, blotting it out. Beneath her mattress she retrieved a hidden trove of papers, artifacts of her failed search for her mother. Genealogy trees with broken branches, chat-room threads that knit into nothing, leads that went nowhere—she let all the dead ends spill across her puffy duvet.

Her sturdy desk chair fought the carpet as she shoved it to the middle of the room. Swaying, she tilted her head, letting her long hair brush her arm. With a distant smile, she ran her knuckles up her swanlike neck, taking comfort in the smoothness of her skin. Her fingertips rose to the scar tissue, traced its faint ridges. She unbuckled her thin studded belt and snapped it once.

Then she stepped up onto the chair and tested the sturdiness of her ceiling fan.

Chapter 45

When Nate pulled off his T-shirt, grimacing, Janie regarded the fresh slice in his shoulder with disapproval. "Because between the ALS, the letter opener stab, and the butterfly stitches in your forehead, you didn't have enough problems."

"Price of entry," Nate said. "It was an exclusive club."

Aside from the reading lamp angled to spotlight the cut, the Silver Lake house was dark. With the heat turned off and the abundance of windows, the floor in the great room turned frigid. Janie stayed bundled up in a sweater. Nate sat in a leather armchair, Cielle and Jason dozing on separate couches in front of the TV. Nate had returned a few hours ago and shot off a text to Abara, updating him on his conversation with Nastya at the club. No response yet.

Though the cut had bled nicely, it was superficial. Janie patched it up with a few more butterfly stitches, Nate squinting at her through the glare.

She finished and said, "How're the symptoms?"

He rolled his head back, looked up at the dark ceiling. "Getting worse."

"Joints? Muscles?"

"Yeah. And I'm . . . I don't know, *fatigued.* Especially at night. Dizzy. Nauseated at intervals. Hands and wrists are bad, as you know. The ankle goes in and out."

"Sounds like fun."

"Regular laugh riot."

She regarded him, again with that bittersweet smile. "Can I get you something to eat, Husband?"

The old game. "No thanks, Wife." He matched her grin, though the exchange made his heart ache a little, too. "Being on the lam always makes me lose my appetite."

She set a hand on his cheek. "Maybe we should go to Paris. That honeymoon we never took."

"Dunno. I'm falling apart here. Not the best guy to be on the run with."

She leaned forward and kissed him. "Now the illness is going to your brain."

His cell phone chirped across on the kitchen table. Text message.

On the couch Jason groaned and sat up.

Nate said, "Abara," and tried to rise, but his leg complained and he winced and sat back down.

She moved toward the phone. "I'll get it. Maybe Nastya already got a confession from her old man. Maybe Abara's calling to say the whole gang's in jail and we won the Powerball, too, and NIH is announcing a cure for ALS—"

She stared at the LED screen, her words sticking in her throat. Her mouth came slightly ajar.

"What?" Nate said. "What?"

Jason stood and cracked his back, the sound loud in the quiet house. Cielle turned over and mumbled, "Gross."

Nate's focus stayed on Janie. Speechless, she crossed to him and held out the phone. "We gotta leave," she said.

Reading the screen, he felt a dull pain start up in his stomach, a beating drum. The words didn't fully compute, and he had to back up and read them again. ANASTASIA KILLED SELF. PVLO'S GONNA GO SCORCHED EARTH. I NVR SAID THIS, BUT FRGT THE TERRORISM CHRGES AGNST U + GET THE FUCK OUT OF DODGE. NOW.

A flood of guilt washed over him, leaving him shell-shocked, his ears ringing. She was a troubled girl in an impossible predicament. He pictured her in the booth, the weight of her denial melting away, her fierce words about her father—*He is the only thing I have ever had.*

Vaguely, through the haze in his head, he became aware of surging lights at the periphery of his vision. Blue and red, peaceful, almost angelic. And Jason by the front window saying something, his words fuzzed and shapeless.

Jason repeated himself, sharper, snapping Nate from his trance. "*Cops.* The cops are here. Right outside."

Indeed, those were patrol lights flickering through the gauzy curtains and rolling across the ceiling. Nate leaped to his feet, and then Cielle flew up from the couch, the blanket fluttering like a cape, Casper startling at her side.

Reaching to snap off the reading lamp, Janie nearly knocked it off the table. "They can't possibly know we're *us*," she said.

"Right," Cielle said. "Just break-in artists."

"Back door," Nate whispered.

"No," Jason hissed. "Two guys already headed through the side gates." He withdrew his finger from the curtain and flattened himself to the wall. "And two more are coming up the walk. *Right now.*"

They were frozen in place. Any move toward the kitchen or garage would put them in view through the beveled-glass panels bookending the front door. Fleeing down the hall would force them to cross a series of windows draped merely with silhouette curtains. Casper emitted a faint growl, and Nate snapped his fingers. *"Hush."*

Jason straightened himself. "I'll go out, make a run for it."

"They'll catch you," Cielle said.

"Yeah, up the block, though. It'll distract 'em, give you guys time to slip out. I'll just tell ' em I broke in as a prank."

Cielle said, "No way, Jason. Don't be lame—"

"It was my idea coming here. I don't care. I'll just get arrested, but you guys could get *killed*." He took a step toward the door, almost in sight of the glass panel.

"*Stop,* Jason," Cielle said. "You're freaking me out."

"They know you, too, Jason," Nate said, in as loud a whisper as he could risk. "Yuri saw you."

Jason paused, glanced back at Nate, and shrugged. "Then let it be me. Not Cielle."

Looking at the husky kid with his slouched shoulders and baggy hoodie, his hair swirled up in the back from sleep, Nate felt an undeniable pang of affection. Even regard.

They could hear the policemen's boots now and see flashlights strobing up the walk, rocking with each step. As Jason braced himself to step into view, Nate realized he was too far away to reach him in time.

But then Janie said, *"Wait."* She bounced on her feet, flipping off her shoes, then stepped out of her jeans. Beneath, she was wearing a pair of Nate's boxers. Then she tugged off her sweater, revealing a stretched T-shirt that showed the points of her nipples.

"Uh, Mrs. O?" Jason said.

Cielle had sagged back onto the couch, watching her mother, her mouth slightly agape. Nate had yet to formulate an appropriate question to ask Janie when the doorbell rang, the sound pronounced off the hard surfaces. A flashlight knocked wood a few times, hard.

Janie turned to Nate. A harsh whisper: "On the floor."

He dropped to the floorboards, the bottom two-thirds of the front door vanishing behind the half wall partitioning the foyer.

Janie's head swiveled to Cielle. "Lie down."

Cielle lowered herself stiffly on the cushions, disappearing behind the couch back, a vampire returning to its coffin. On the far side of the couch, Casper also lowered himself to the floor, following the same command.

Janie looked at Jason, frozen in almost comical surprise at the hinge side of the front door. "Stay."

He flattened to the wall inches from the panel window.

Janie mussed up her hair, blond spikes sticking out in all directions, and started for the door. *"Coming."*

Affecting a tired slump, she tugged the door open, stifling a fake yawn. "Yeah?"

The fresh-faced cop peered past her into the house. "Mrs. Newell?"

"You boys know what time it is?"

The two patrol cars at the curb seemed to light the neighborhood, but no one was up and about on the dark street. The faintest rustle issued from the couch cushions. The hidden dog made a barely audible whine.

"Yes, ma'am," the cops said. "We had a call from your neighbor, Mr. Sullivan? I guess there've been lights in the house—"

"Oh. Right. I forgot to tell Sully. I had to come back early from Maui. Family emergency. I must've left a light on out here." She rubbed an eye theatrically. "Look, I'm wiped out. Do you think . . . ?"

"Sorry, Mrs. Newell. But it's our responsibility to follow up—"

"And I'm glad you did. It's good to know you're here when we need you."

"We can give a quick check, make sure you're safe, and then we'll be on our way." His boot set down on the threshold, his knuckles pushing gently on the door.

Janie shuffled back a bit, swinging the door open a few more degrees. Two feet from her elbow, Jason stayed so still he might as well have been inanimate, nailed to the wall, a piece of art.

Janie halted, as if having second thoughts, the young cop moving forward, head down. Suddenly they were much too close.

"I'm fine," she said. "I really need to get some sleep."

The cop hesitated, unsure, reluctant to retreat but not wanting to force his way forward. The slightest lean on his part would bring Jason into view.

Janie looked into the young cop's face, inches from hers. "Boys," she said, summoning amusement and the slightest hint of scorn. *"Really?"* She gave him and his silent veteran counterpart the full-wattage smile, and both sets of eyes traveled briefly to her chest and then back up again.

Suddenly tongue-tied, they nodded and mumbled a few words, already backing up. The veteran gave a whistle, and a cop emerged from either side gate, nodding at her as they headed off the property.

Janie closed the door, lowered her head, and blew out a shaky breath. She stood there as one engine turned over, then another, and tires crackled slowly away.

"Okay," she called out, her voice tight with adrenaline. "We can go now."

Chapter 46

The slate-colored sky signaled either the birth or the death of the day, but Pavlo did not know which. He'd lost time, simply dropped out of it as if plunging through a sheet of ice into cryogenic waters. The first dot of sun nosed over the skyline to the east, casting straws of light through the grain and grit of early morning. Hastening along the fractured downtown sidewalk, he stared at the solitary point of light and thought, *So that's it. A new day.*

The venerable marble steps, worn by a million footfalls, stood out from the surrounding concrete and rotting wood. He mounted the brief flight of stairs and pushed through the imposing oak door. Contrasted with the gray morning chill, the humidity of the *banya* was startling, pressing itself into his pores.

He did not know what had drawn him here.

The memory returned, less a thought than a primal impulse, a fury of clawed impressions scratching at his spinal cord. Around midnight he'd entered her room to check on her. Those pale thin legs, the swaying feet—a familiar prison tableau. He'd stood breathless in the doorway, all the wrong details coming into painful focus. The dusting of drywall across her shoulders from where the fan had been wrenched from the ceiling. The rasp of the pull chain, still swaying. Those perfect teeth, gleaming above her slack jaw. The next he recalled, he had her down and across his lap. One of his hands rested beneath her slender, bruised neck, the other clutching his heart as if to hold it together. His chest convulsed, a silent shaking. He thought he might be dying. Choking on his own air, he felt the moisture on his cheeks. He had not cried since his boyhood and had forgotten the sensation. He made not a sound.

After the parade of paramedics and firemen, the cops with their endless questions and looks of thinly veiled suspicion, that spic Abara had arrived with another agent to sit on the couch—*his* couch—and make phone calls. The house was no longer his own; medics and officers stomped about and used the toilet and left the hand towels on the counter. Nastya was conveyed out finally in a white body bag, strapped to a gurney, and Pavlo was given a phone number to call in the morning.

He'd closed the door on the last intruder, listening to it click shut, the dividing line between the present and the rest of his life. He walked back into the kitchen, filled a glass with water, and drank it down. For seventeen years, every glass of water he'd had, each piece of bread, every bit of nourishment, he'd taken as a father. No more.

He rinsed the glass, dried it carefully with a towel,

and set it back in the cupboard. When he turned, his men had materialized behind him. It was safe now that the officials were gone.

With its seams and bulges, Yuri's face looked like a rotted piece of fruit. Dima and Valerik remained behind the big man, as was their habit. But Misha, Misha stood to the side, clear-eyed and well rested. His round, boyish face held a quiet contentment. He'd waited his turn, and now the bell was about to ring.

Pavlo walked over to him and brought his face close to Misha's. Misha did not flinch, didn't so much as blink.

"There is no trial now," Pavlo said. "No witness list. There is one thing only, one thing left in this world."

"I understand," Misha said.

"My daughter is gone. And his daughter lives." The skin of Pavlo's face tightened like a stretched hide, bringing a dull ache to his temples. "You take from him what he has taken from me. And then you keep taking, piece by piece."

"That is what you brought me here for," Misha said.

"There is no more *here,*" Pavlo said. "No more America. There is only *vorovskoi mir.*"

Misha nodded, keeping his head bowed an extra beat, a show of respect. With both hands Pavlo cradled his chin and lifted his head. He kissed him on one full cheek, then the other. Still he did not release Misha's face. Not until he'd leaned in and hissed, *"Let them hate as long as they fear."*

Now, sweating in the dense air of the *banya,* he passed several valets gathering plates and mugs from the night and preparing for the new day. All of them stepped aside and lowered their eyes as Pavlo walked by. Word had spread.

He entered the rows of lockers and stood before his own, removing one loafer, then the other. He laid his suit jacket beside them on the wide bench. A door banged open, and drunken voices echoed around the tile— club revelers, here to detoxify after an all-night drunk. They stumbled around the corner, unshaven and reeking of alcohol. Pavlo stood, facing his locker, pushing the buttons of his dress shirt through the holes.

"Move your shit over," one of the young men said in Russian. "You don't own the whole bench."

Keeping his eyes forward, Pavlo pulled off his shirt, revealing his blue arms and chest. At the sight of his tattoos, the young man backpedaled so violently that he lost his footing on the slick tile and fell back into his friends, who propped him up. Kowtowing, they retreated, calling out apologies and expressions of remorse. Pavlo kept undressing, his eyes never leaving his locker, and a moment later the door boomed a second time and it was silent again.

Once naked, Pavlo reached for a comb he kept on the top shelf of his locker and scraped back his hair, already wet from the humidity. He did it again and again, pressing the comb hard enough to bruise the scalp, feeling the plastic teeth scour his skull.

Then he padded through the antechamber, past the claw-foot tubs and icy plunge pools. Beneath a dripping faucet, a heap of thin birchwood branches soaked in a wooden barrel. He chose one with especially dense foliage and shook it in assessment, cool drops dotting his cheeks. It would do.

In the *banya* itself, the firebox glowed, the throat of a demon. A worker, half invisible in the steam, hurled logs in.

"Hotter," Pavlo said, and the mist-draped form nodded and fed the monster some more.

Pavlo set down the branch and stretched, first his hamstrings, then his groin. Leaning into the burn, he emitted a deep open-mouthed exhalation, expunging the swamp gas from his belly up through the tube of his throat. On the hiss of his air, he could smell his own insides, cigarettes and mortality. His skin was aflame, the heat at him with its pitchfork and horns.

"Hotter!" he roared.

The form bent and rose, hurling more logs into the mouth of the firebox.

Sweat beading on his skin, Pavlo snatched up the birchwood branch and slapped it against his legs. The sting was unearthly, divine, bringing up the toxins, releasing them through his skin.

He flailed and whipped at the tattooed shackles clamped around his ankles, purging the poisons of his body. That was what the birchwood was for, of course, but he knew now, in the hot center of the pain, why he had come.

In the Zone the worst sin a *vor* could commit was breaking the thieves' code, disgracing the brotherhood. If he did not stand by his decorations, they were taken from him. With sandpaper. Shards of glass. A lump of brick. Sometimes the offender was held by five men, a red-hot frying pan pressed to the back of his hand to black out the pigment beneath. So this, then, was why Pavlo had been drawn to the inferno.

With the branch he continued to strike at himself. His hands, the ring tattoos. Slapping at his chest, beating the eight-pointed star, the ornate church domes marking his internments, the scrolled lettering across his ribs—*LET ME BE DEAD TO YOU.* Sweat flew from his nose, his chin; it puddled at his feet. He flailed harder, slashed at the tulip thrice wrapped with barbed wire, tried to carve the bare-toothed scowl from the wolf capping his shoulder. And then, doubling over, whipping the branch over his shoulder, raking the leaves across the inked eyes on his back. His screams turned to animal roars, cords standing out on his neck, each blow intensifying the heat until·it seemed his entire body glowed like an ember.

"Hotter!" he cried, but the form was now lost entirely to the thickening steam.

The leaves shushed and rattled, a primitive instrument beating an age-old rhythm. Bits of foliage broke off, sticking to his red flesh. His sinuses burned; his lungs pulsed. He gasped in the heady scent of released pain and fresh-peeled skin, intoxicated on the taste of his own agony, choking on the knife-sharp purity of the air. He lashed at the abrasions, the sharp leaf edges finding greater purchase, rending the ink from his flesh. Screaming, he battered at his grief, beating the imperfection from himself, blood weeping from his brands.

Finally he paused in heart-arresting exhaustion, his chest heaving, his face awash with tears and sweat, and let the stained birchwood branch fall from his fist. Burgundy drops spattered the tile at his feet.

He stared down at himself through the swirling steam. His decorations moved, alive with veins of blood. They drifted on his skin, rippling and breathing, and the revelation lit him from within: He hadn't gouged the decorations from his body.

He had reclaimed them.

Chapter 47

"Nevada?" Cielle offered.

"Dude, the Grand Canyon is *epic*."

Janie rubbed her temples. "First of all, Jason, the Grand Canyon is in Ari*zona*—"

"Really?"

"Last I checked. And second, we're not really embarking on a *sightseeing* tour."

Leaving just before first light, they'd driven a short ways up State Route 2 toward Eagle Rock before pulling over to convene at a roadside diner. They required a game plan, but there was another reason Nate had opted for the early rest stop; his hands had grown loose and sloppy on the steering wheel, and he doubted his ability to hold the Jeep on the road. Forced to make a frank assessment, he had to concede that his body felt worse than it had yet, more in thrall to the illness. And not just the muscles, but dizziness, weakness, a dull throbbing in his stomach.

On the way to the corner booth now, he lagged behind with Janie to tell her softly that he needed her to take over at the wheel, and she nodded her solemn consent.

"Maybe we shouldn't risk going on the road," she said in a low voice. "We can't be running around with you if—"

"No way," Nate said. "If it gets to that, leave me at a bus stop."

At this, Janie grimaced, unamused.

"We have to get out of the state," he continued quietly. "As far away as possible. Besides, where the hell would we stay around here? Breaking and entering is too dangerous, as we just learned."

Cielle and Jason reached the table ahead, Cielle watching the heated if hushed exchange across the restaurant, and so Nate and Janie cranked neutral expressions onto their faces, forged forward, and sat down to order breakfast.

Sitting with his back to the wall, handgun in his jacket, and several thousand dollars in cash stuffed into his pockets, Nate kept watch of the truckers and postal officers at the counter, sipping their coffee and forking hotcakes. Cielle picked at her food. Jason stuffed another giant bite into his mouth; after asking if the eggs were organic (no) and if the biscuits were made with lard (yes), he had sanctimoniously settled on a salad. With bacon.

Nate set his pills next to his coffee mug in a neat line. The antibiotics again, another five-hundred-milligram surge to ravage his stomach further, and good old reliably ineffective riluzole. The Lovin' Spoonful caroled from the vintage-style jukebox: *Be-lieve in the magic that kin set you freee.* Would that he could.

Cielle looked across at Nate. "Why are you so quiet?"

"Don't mean to be." Troublingly, his voice was weak; he couldn't get any power behind it. With shaking hands he reached for the pills. It took some concentration to bring them to his mouth. He washed them down with a sip of decaf.

"He's fine," Janie said, too quickly. "Just exhausted like the rest of us."

The coffee's bitter aftertaste lingered, and instinctively he reached for the sugar packs. It wasn't until he had one in his weak, trembling grasp that he realized the challenge before him—of tearing it open, pouring the crystals, stirring. He flapped the pack against his knuckles, trying for casual, but Cielle's brown eyes remained on him, not buying the routine. He let the sugar fall, and her stare dropped to his shaking fingers. Too obvious now to take his hands off the table. He strained, willing them to be still, but was rescued by Janie, who reached over and clasped them as if romantically, firming them and hiding the tremor.

Thankfully, Jason's obliviousness could be counted on. "I still can't believe that chick—the dude's daughter—offed herself."

Behind the counter, sausage links landed on the grill with a sizzle and a puff of steam. "She was just seventeen," Nate said.

Cielle said, "She was a drunk-driving psychopath."

"She was still a kid," Nate said. "Like both of you."

Cielle looked away sharply.

Freeing his hands from Janie's, Nate reached for his coffee again but only succeeded in slopping some over the rim. He dried his hands on a napkin, all too aware of his daughter across from him. He did not want to look up, but finally he did. Sure enough, she was lasered in on his hands.

"There's this experimental therapy." She jerked in a breath. "In Switzerland."

"Oh, honey," he said. "No."

But she drove on. "I looked it up on the Internet."

"No, Cielle. There's nothing that'll—"

"No? Just *no*? If we live through this, you can't fucking try it?"

"Watch your language," Janie said.

Cielle glared at Nate. "God, you wonder why I hate you." She banged her fist on the table, making the plates and cups jump. A spoon bounced off into Jason's lap. The diner silenced, the patrons' collective focus pulling toward the corner booth, and then Cielle stormed out, leaving the door jingling cheerily. Nate tracked her through the window. Casper awaited her in the Jeep, tail knocking the headrests.

"At least she hates you," Jason said quietly.

Nate said, numbly, "Huh?"

Jason tugged his collar down in the front to reveal a necklace tattoo formed of words and letters: OLD BASTARD 1.23.70—5.10.2010. "Cirrhosis," he said. "Dying just made him meaner. I told myself I hated him, but I really wanted him just to fucking recognize, you know, something in me. . . ." He shook his head. "Never mind. I'm just saying. Hate's an emotion, you know?"

He scooted out and went after her.

Nate drank a sip of water. His face was twitching, and it took a moment for him to realize that it was not from being upset.

Janie's voice, as if from a deep well: "—okay?"

Hand pressed to his cheek, he nodded. He could feel the muscle jumping beneath his palm. Fasciculation, the doctors called it. He had been warned.

"Just need . . . bathroom." His voice, even weaker than before.

He weaved a bit on his feet but managed a course for the men's room, closing the door behind him with his hip. The room was dank, swirling with black flies. He regarded his face in the rust-flecked mirror, the twitch just below his right eye. He squinted, trying to make it stop, but still the skin rippled. A swell of light-headedness came on, static dotting his view along with the flies, and he staggered, banging into the hand-towel dispenser. The room blurred.

Fresh air. He needed fresh air.

Shoving through the bathroom door, he took a hard right and moved swiftly through the kitchen, nearly knocking the rear screen from its hinges. The smell from the Dumpster swarmed him, and he took a knee next to crates stuffed with rotting heads of cabbage. He tried to rise, but nausea kept him down. Refuse crowded in on him, his view swirling drunkenly, and then the ground came up hard against his cheek.

His blinks grew longer. Each breath rocked the

crumpled napkin an inch from his mouth. A masculine figure approached, off kilter and blurry, hoisting up his jeans like a cowboy. Blood pattered the ground before his combat boots. He had a hole straight through the middle of him, intestines dangling like marionette strings, the sun shining right through him. When he crouched, the hole disappeared and a shadow fell across Nate, the shadow of death. He looked up and saw Charles's face peering down, a hint of sorrow hiding behind the wise-ass scowl.

"See ya soon, podnah." Charles reached out and thumbed Nate's eyelids closed.

Chapter 48

"No hospital," Nate murmured, slumped in the passenger seat, the window cool against his cheek. The view outside scrolled by, a blur.

Janie honked and stomped on the gas pedal, veering around a Mercedes. "You lost your say in the matter when you passed out in an alley."

Cielle's voice, high and tremulous, came from the backseat. "Are you okay, Dad? Is he gonna be okay?"

"I'm . . . fine, honey," Nate said.

Jason: "He doesn't *sound* fine."

The noise of Cielle smacking him. "Shut the fuck up, Jason."

". . . where . . . ?" Nate managed between swells of nausea.

"We're going to my hospital," Janie said, "if this asshole in an Audi in front of us ever learns to drive."

"No . . . first place they'll look. . . ."

"I know the doctors, the intake nurses. I can get you in without putting you in the system. You'll be John Doe. It's our best bet."

Already they were redlining up smog-drenched Van Nuys Boulevard. Sure enough, the long white block of the Sherman Oaks Hospital zoomed past. Despite its unpromising location, the community hospital had top-notch staff who serviced a full gamut of the injured and the ailing. Meeting Janie here for lunch early in their marriage, Nate was as likely to stumble across a gardener cradling a severed, hankie-wrapped finger as a celebrity walking her kid out of the world-class burn unit.

". . . Cielle shouldn't . . . with us . . ."

"She can wait in the park up the street."

"I can drive," Jason said brightly.

"Fine." Janie tugged a wad of hundreds from her pocket and tossed it back at Cielle. "Take the Jeep and the dog. I'll call you every hour."

Nate tried to shape his mouth into another complaint but had to focus on breathing so as not to throw up. The Jeep lurched to a stop in front of the emergency-room doors, and then Casper was barking as Jason clambered forward into the driver's seat. Janie appeared through Nate's window, her fingers at the handle, and then he was tumbling out into her arms.

They headed in, Janie bearing half his weight, the glass doors yawning open before them.

"Antibiotics?" Dr. Griffin flipped the chart. "Who the hell put him on *antibiotics*?"

Janie looked across at Nate, who rustled on the stiff white sheets of the hospital bed and said, weakly, "She was . . . ER doc."

"ER doc. Terrific. With his condition she didn't think it necessary to pick up the phone to his treating physician? Or at least to consult Epocrates on her iPhone? What's he taking?"

"Keflex," Janie said. "Five hundred mg's qid."

"What for?"

"I keep getting stabbed," Nate said.

Dr. Griffin shot him a look over the top of his perpetually slipping tortoiseshell glasses. His brown eyes, nearly as dark as his skin, held a pinpoint focus that didn't match the saggy mien, the professorial potbelly, or the day-old scruff.

"We have an interaction?" Janie asked, getting the doctor back on task. Though Nate wasn't familiar with Dr. Griffin, Janie's working rapport with him was evident.

"Antibiotics raise the level of riluzole in the blood," the doctor said. "Not only do the liver enzymes spike—which can cause liver failure—but they increase the likelihood and severity of side effects. Which are—"

Janie cut in: "Weakness, fatigue, nausea, headaches, abdominal pain, dizziness—"

"—which in turn can exacerbate ALS symptoms."

Nate rolled his head on the pillow, keeping pace with the Ping-Pong match. An IV line pushed fluids steadily into his arm; already he was feeling a bit more clearheaded. As he untangled the medicalspeak, he felt a faint pulse of hope. "So it'll get better?" he asked. "The muscle weakness?"

"It should subside, yes, along with the dizziness and nausea once your blood levels drop."

Nate took a few cautious sips of air, relieved. "How long will that take?" he asked. His voice box felt feeble, no weight behind the words.

"Six to eight hours for Keflex to leave the bloodstream," Janie said. "Another six or so for the riluzole levels to back down to normal."

"But that's not the point." Dr. Griffin tugged at his jowls, which had surprising give. "You need supportive care. Fluids, rest—"

"Rest," Nate protested.

"You are *sick,* Mr. Overbay. I don't have to tell you that ALS is serious business. What you're doing to yourself—it's not tenable. You are dehydrated, hypoglycemic, suffering from lack of sleep. You can't do this given your condition." Dr. Griffin dropped the chart on the end of Nate's bed and turned to Janie. "Give your John Doe here another liter of saline and see if you can talk some sense into him."

Janie crossed her arms, shot a breath at the ceiling. "I've been trying for years."

The needle's pressure in his arm stayed constant, even when Nate dozed off. He surfaced from a brief sleep, blinking to consciousness, and focused on the tiny form at the foot of his bed. At first he thought it was a dream image hanging on, a vision from the spirit world. A painfully thin Hispanic boy, maybe six, with a bald, leukemic head that in combination with oversize eyes made him look vaguely alien. He wore black pajamas decorated with white bones—a skeleton costume—and clutched a starched pillowcase.

"Trick or treat," he said.

Nate sat up quickly. Charles he was used to, but this? He managed to say, "Uh . . ."

The boy shook the pillowcase imploringly. "It's Halloween."

Was it? Nate rewound the days, reorienting himself. It was. And the boy was real, or at least he appeared to be. The ceiling-hung dividing curtain had been partly drawn back so that Nate could see, above the unoccupied bed, dusk darkening the windows. Trick-or-treat time.

He glanced across at his food tray. "I have Jell-O."

"No. There." The boy pointed to a cup that had appeared on Nate's nightstand. "They leave you candy for us. See? So we can have Halloween even though we're stuck in here."

Nate reached into the cup, pulled out a mini–Three Musketeers, and with a trembling hand dropped it into the boy's pillowcase. "Want more?"

"You hafta save it for the others."

"Others?"

But the boy was already at the door, heading to his next benefactor. "My bones glow in the dark," he announced. His little hand clicked the light switch. Sure enough, there it was, a cartoonish skeleton with a faint green tinge. The light came back on, Nate making sure to wipe the astonished expression off his face.

A little girl entered next with fuzzy angel wings and a burn savaging her chin and throat. Fighting the knot forming in his throat, Nate produced a gentle grin for her and a bite-size Butterfinger. Next, a preteen pulling her own IV pole. They kept trickling in, one after the other, with their tiny voices and heartrending costumes.

After the last child departed, Nate carefully extracted his IV line and stepped into the hall. There they all were in the corridor, a ragged parade, standing in rough assembly under the benign direction of an immense, soft-featured orderly. Nate's hand quaked and his ankle had again gone numb, yet he refused to tear his eyes from the spectacle and withdraw to his bed. With their glow-in-the-dark bones and angel wings, the children seemed to point the way to where he was headed. Pixie faces lit with delight, they showed off their costumes and compared their hauls. All that hope and promise, uneroded even here in a hospital ward on Halloween.

From the nurses' station at the far end of the hall, Janie looked on, too. Nate managed a nod, and she gave a smile and a little wave.

"Come on, now," the orderly called out to her brood, "time to hit the next floor up."

They followed her to the stairs like a row of ducklings, a diminutive Darth Vader wrestling off his mask and taking a few genuine asthmatic wheezes as he passed from sight.

The tender display unlocked something inside Nate's chest, and all the anguish of the past week and a half rushed out, overwhelming him. Sagging against the wall, he pressed his thumb and forefinger to his eyes. But it was no use. The emotion came, swelling over him, and he hunched into himself, drawing halting breaths, struggling not to cry.

Janie was at his side, rubbing his back, somehow grasping the unexplainable, and, doubled over, he gripped her forearm. His mind spun, throwing out sense memories: his mother wasting away on that hospice bed in the dim air of the living room. The smell of decay on her breath. Abibas shading his eyes, staring back from the top of that dune. McGuire staring at his severed leg uncomprehendingly. *Don't leave me don't leave me don't you leave me.* Little girl with a burned face and angel wings.

For a time Nate and Janie held each other and breathed together, taking in the sounds and smells of the bustling medical ward in motion. A waft of iodine. Wobbly wheels on a gurney. A yielding cough, muffled by a closed door.

A set of clogs tapped through Nate's field of vision, a nurse calling out, "Good to see you again, girl. You been on vacation?"

"Sort of," Janie said. "Good to see you, too, Renee."

"Oh, I logged you in."

Janie stiffened in Nate's arms. "Wait. You what?"

"You forgot to sign in. Can't get paid if you don't—"

"When? *When?*"

"Relax, girl. When I was coming back from my coffee run, I saw you in here with Dr. Suspenders. What's that—forty minutes ago?"

At the end of the crowded corridor, the elevator dinged. A flush of heat rolled through Nate's face, the premonition of something dire to come. He straightened up, lifting his head to see the lit circle announcing the car's arrival, flicking in and out of view between patients and doctors.

The doors peeled open, and Misha stepped out.

Chapter 49

The security guard overflowing the folding chair next to the elevator glanced up from the *L.A. Times,* then returned his gaze to the print. Misha glided to the nurses' station at which Janie had been standing moments before.

"I am looking for Nurse Jane Overbay."

"I'm sorry, she's not working today."

Misha walked past the nurses' station, heading down the crowded hall. Still he didn't spot Janie and Nate, frozen in the bustling corridor.

"Sir, where's your visitor pass? I'm sorry, you can't go in here without a visitor pass. *Sir!*"

Without breaking stride Misha drew a handgun from inside his jacket, aiming over the counter as he passed, and shot the nurse through the hip point-blank. The force blew her straight off the chair onto the floor, where she began convulsing. Behind him the security guard could barely wobble to his feet before Misha pulled a second gun with his free hand and fired twice,

streaking the wall behind the man. A newspaper section fluttered down atop his body, soaking up blood.

A beat of stunned silence.

And then the medical ward erupted. Patients shouting, wheelchairs overturning, bodies stampeding for
the stairs. As Misha powered down the hall, kicking
aside gurneys and toppling IV poles, Janie shoved Nate
through the doorway into his room. He scrambled
across the bed and grabbed his jacket, flipping it
around, looking for the pocket, willing his weak hands
to work faster.

Footsteps. Screams. Another gunshot, followed by a
primal howl.

"He's just *shooting people,*" Janie said.

Nate had the gun out finally, in his trembling grasp.
He pushed Janie behind the dividing curtain and tugged
it. In the ceiling track, the nylon wheels gave a screech,
the sound lost beneath the crash of a cart overturning in
the hall and more shouts of panic.

The boom of a door being kicked in up the hall. A
startled shriek. Then a matching screech of a curtain
being raked back.

Seconds later another boom. Another screech.

Janie's panicked breaths against Nate's ear. "He's going room to room."

They waited, the scrubs-green sheet rippling before
their faces. With an unsteady thumb, Nate pushed the
safety off his Beretta.

Heavy footsteps—probably boots. The complaint of
a desiccated voice, a crash, then a faint moan. Boom.
Screech.

Dr. Griffin's voice, right outside in the corridor. "Don't, just *don't*—"

Gunshot.

Janie gave out a faint cry, pressed both hands across her mouth. They could hear Dr. Griffin's wet, labored breaths.

Now right next door. Boom. Screech.

Janie's whisper came again, a rush of hot air. "We should run."

Nate firmed his hands around the stock and mouthed, *No time.*

The door to Nate's room was open; they'd get no benefit of a warning. But the footsteps neared.

Tap tap tap.

Pause.

Somehow, even through the opaque curtain, Nate sensed a change in the quality of the air. A presence. Misha was in the doorway. One brisk pace into the room. Another.

Nate willed his forearms still. He took a silent step back and raised the gun. The barrel wavered ever so slightly in his weak grip.

Janie leaned against the wall, her face tense with anticipation. Nate aimed at the curtain, chest high, ready for the burst of movement.

A scream came from down the hall, then feminine footsteps skittering toward the stairs.

Misha stopped.

He must have been debating whether to continue on toward the curtain or go after the footsteps in the hall. Was he pondering whether the fleeing woman was

Janie? They could hear him drawing breath. Calm and steady. The guy's heart rate probably hadn't ticked north of sixty.

Nate sighted on the rubbery partition curtain, knowing that Misha was a few feet beyond but unsure where. A missed shot would be answered with a barrage.

The woman's footsteps in the hall grew louder.

Misha set down his boot again, the faintest scuff against the tile. Nate shifted the gun toward the noise and felt it slip soundlessly through his weakened fingers.

With all his focus, he willed his hands to clamp, but the muscles wouldn't obey. The gun spun in slow-motion rotation, the checkering on the handle grazing his fingertips. And then it was free, in the air, tumbling toward the hard tile.

He tried to suck in a breath but found his lungs already full. Bending, he lunged for the gun, missing, but then Janie's hand shot into sight and caught it two inches off the floor. She had made not a noise.

Crouching, they stared at each other, wide-eyed, neither daring to breathe. A squeak of Misha's boot on the tile, just beyond the curtain.

In the stillness they heard the woman's footsteps veer up an adjoining corridor, the sound starting to fade. And then another noise chimed in, that of distant sirens.

Misha retreated now, sprinting off, presumably after her.

Nate and Janie exhaled together, an explosion of relief. Moans reached them from the hall—Dr. Griffin, in agony.

Janie inched the curtain aside, and they peered

through the still-open door. Dr. Griffin lay in the corridor, hands across his thigh, blood spurting through his fingers at heartbeat intervals and painting thin lines on the floor.

"Arterial bleed," Janie said, pushing the pistol into Nate's hands. "I'll stabilize him and be right back. A minute, tops."

She started up, but Nate grabbed her shoulder. "Misha's still out there."

She pointed at Dr. Griffin. "He will *die* if I don't go."

The frantic look between them couldn't have lasted a second, but it stretched to an eternity, one objection after another shuffling through Nate's mind. The determination on Janie's face told him he didn't really have a say anyway. He removed his hand from her shoulder.

"Take the gun," he said. "I can't grip it."

Pocketing the Beretta, she was up and into the hall, a quick glimpse bringing into view only a few knocked-over patients and a resident hiding behind a gurney. No Misha.

Tearing a manual blood-pressure cuff from a cart, she sprinted across to Dr. Griffin. The slick red of his hands was all the more pronounced against his skin, which had gone dusty gray. He applied feeble pressure, too stunned to bear down on the wound. Supplies rolled in the growing puddle; he'd knocked over a cart on his way down.

"I think I went out from the shock," he was mumbling. "But I'm back now."

Janie tugged off his loafer and worked the cuff over his sock, sliding it up along his saturated pant leg and over the gushing rupture above his knee to the proximal side of the wound. His body went rigid with pain, but she ignored his reaction. Her hand pumping furiously, she inflated the cuff to full pressure, the bleeding slowing, slowing, then stopping.

Grabbing at the scattered supplies, she came up with a cylindrical pack, which she ripped open with her teeth. Crouching over him, she plugged the gauze into the wound, readjusting the doctor's hands. "Not outta the woods. Tamponade the bleed. Here. Hard. Harder." With one hand she thumbed an edge of paper tape up off a roll.

He looked up at her, his expression of gratitude turning to alarm. She didn't have time to turn around before a hand set down on her head, fisting her hair and ripping her straight back off her feet.

Chapter 50

Watching through the doorway in a state of suspended panic, Nate didn't see Misha's hand seize Janie's hair so much as he *anticipated* it—the fear of each torturous second finally realized. Misha himself never came into view, just his arm reaching into frame, the fist clenching, the tendons of the wrist flexing powerfully.

Janie was gone so quickly she might have been whipped off by a truck, the Beretta tumbling from her pocket to spin listlessly on the floor. He heard her make a noise like a roar—part pain, part rage—and then Misha's voice sang out to him. "Nate *Over*bay. I have your wife. Come out, please."

His steps plodded slowly down the hall. The sirens sounded closer, but not close enough.

Nate leaped up too fast, his weak ankle giving out. His chest no sooner slapped the tile than he was moving to rise again, shuffling forward.

Dr. Griffin's grunts of agony covered the noise of Nate stepping into the corridor. Facing away from Nate, Misha was literally towing Janie down the hall by her hair, dragging her slowly and calmly. She twisted and yelled, arcing with pain, the whites of her eyes impossibly big. Her hands, dark with the doctor's blood, were fastened on Misha's wrist, trying to relieve the pressure on her hair. In his free hand, Misha gripped one pistol; the handle of the second protruded from the back of his true-blue jeans.

He kept on, his heavy boots taking big strides, not noticing Nate stepping into the open behind them. The sirens were louder yet.

Ahead, an orderly opened a door, and, never slowing, Misha shot him in the shoulder. The man spun around, falling back and away, and the door wobbled closed behind him, a wet splotch marking the wood.

The Beretta was still, improbably, spinning on the tile where it had fallen. Nate stepped in front of Dr. Griffin and picked it up, his hand complaining against the weight of it. It wobbled severely in his grasp as he raised it, the tip jogging across the scene ahead like the sights on a video game with a broken control. No way he could take a shot.

Frustration rose inside him, driving him to a fury. He was about to cast the gun aside and limp in pursuit when something on the floor caught his eye.

A roll of paper tape with a short sticky length lifted from the end.

He stooped and picked it up. Digging a finger through the trigger guard, he wound tape around the pistol and his hand, fusing metal and flesh. The tape made a soft shushing sound as it peeled from the roll. He wrapped and wrapped.

"Nate *Over*bay! If I get to the elevator before you come out, I will shoot her through the top of her head."

Nate exhaled evenly through pursed lips. Janie writhed beneath the clenched fist, sliding backward, away from Nate, the shot getting harder every second. With her eyes she implored him. The sirens screamed outside.

Nate lifted the pistol, willing his elbow steady, willing his muscles strong. The gun wavered, the sights trembling across Janie, Misha, Janie, Misha.

Misha reached the end of the corridor and slapped the elevator button. He started to turn.

Nate closed his eyes. Took a single breath. Opened them.

Misha stared down the corridor at him, across the wreckage of carts, tipped-over wheelchairs, the bodies of the wounded. A western standoff. The Ukrainian's face was alight with surprise and something like amusement.

Nate watched him through the three elevated dots of white on the steel slide—the sights, perfectly aligned.

At Misha's back the elevator dinged open.

Misha started to raise his gun hand, and Nate squeezed.

A puff of red rose from Misha's shoulder. He released Janie, staggering back a step into the elevator, an instant of fear claiming his face before he regained his composure. He examined the tuft of raised fabric at his sleeve, flecked with blood. No more than a graze, but it had forced him to release Janie.

The wail of the sirens was matched by the roar of

multiple engines, vehicle after vehicle screeching around a turn, maybe a block away. The elevator doors began to slide closed. Janie rolled to the side, out of Misha's vantage before he could find his focus again.

The recoil had set Nate's arm on fire, fatiguing the muscle; he struggled to keep the Beretta raised, but the tip lowered to aim at the floor fifteen feet in front of him.

A smirk firmed Misha's features, and he lifted a hand and flicked the blood from his shoulder, a fuck-you gesture of carelessness, before the doors clamped shut, wiping him from view.

Janie scrambled up and peered over the counter to check on the nurse who'd been shot. Her face went limp—lost cause. Turning, she ran toward Nate and Dr. Griffin, stooping to swipe a bag of saline from the floor. Without slowing, she spiked the bag with a length of sterile tubing.

The doctor's hands were now firm around the gauze, the blood-pressure cuff holding. "I got it," Dr. Griffin said. "Get out of here."

But she was on her knees, fighting a catheter needle from its packaging, thrusting it into his vein with a single swift gesture. She screwed the free end of the tubing into the IV and slapped the saline bag in the doctor's palm. "Squeeze. Other hand stays on the wound. You understand?"

The sirens reached an earsplitting pitch. Dr. Griffin nodded briskly. "Good. Thanks."

Janie ushered Nate toward the back corridor, helping shoulder some of his weight when his foot dragged.

They reached the patient-transport elevator, and she swiped her ID card, then stabbed at the button repeatedly until the car arrived. As they started down to the ground floor, she dialed her cell phone.

"Meet us in the liquor-store parking lot, two storefronts south. Now. That means *now*." She looked at the screen—it had cut out. Her hand, crusted with the doctor's blood, swung at her side.

The elevator car whirred down with excruciating slowness. Nate used his teeth to tear at the tape around his gun hand. He ripped the Beretta loose, shoved it in the back of his jeans, then reached for her. "Your hair—"

"I'm fine," she said. "I'm fine." Her knee jogged up and down, a tic. "These doors open, we're gonna go left through the cafeteria, duck through the kitchen, and then stroll right out onto the sidewalk. Got me?"

"Yes."

They arrived and moved onto the well-lit floor. Not a soul in sight. Advancing briskly, they followed the prescribed route, Janie hiding her hands in her pockets before they stepped into the brisk night air.

A continuous line of squad cars flashed past as they shuffled up the alley toward the sidewalk, Nate barely keeping his feet beneath him. Ahead, a patrolman jogged by, disappearing past the mouth of the alley, not seeming to spot them.

Nate breathed through clenched teeth. They kept on.

The patrolman reversed back into view, staring down the alley at them. Nate's legs locked up. The patrolman's hand moved to his holster.

Janie rushed forward, stepping in front of Nate, her ID card flapping around her neck. "I'm a nurse here. Someone's shooting up the medical ward—"

"I know," the cop said. "We—"

"This is one of the patients. There are more who need help on the third floor and an injured doc."

"We've got plenty of paramedics. There's a back entrance here? We'll clear the building, then—"

"Hurry. Go."

The man obeyed, jogging past them, talking into his radio. He didn't give Nate a second look.

With some effort Nate started up his legs again. He put his arm around Janie's shoulders as they stepped out onto Van Nuys Boulevard. Just a couple out for a stroll. They put their back to the hospital. Nate could practically feel the heat from all those lights. They heard doors banging in, voices shouting, radios squawking. Janie was murmuring to herself, but Nate couldn't make out the words.

The liquor store was forty yards ahead and then twenty. A Jeep flew into the lot, bouncing one tire over the curb, and Nate caught a flash of Cielle's terrified face in the passenger seat.

He drew Janie closer, finally discerning her words: *"—it's over now it's over it's over—"*

It wasn't until she'd helped him up and into the backseat that she broke down sobbing.

Chapter 51

Beside Nate in the back of the Jeep, Janie remained stiff, leaning forward, straight arms pushing down on her knees, the hollow of her neck pronounced. They were twenty minutes from the hospital, but she was still fleeing it. Though she was done crying, each breath ended in a slight hitch.

Up front, Jason sang along incorrectly to the AC/DC disc he had taken from MonkeyBiz12's Silver Lake house, keeping time on the steering wheel: *The walls was achin', my heart was bakin', and we were shakin', 'cuz you—*

"Where are we gonna go?" Janie said. "They can track everything. There's nowhere. No one we can call."

"My father," Nate said.

In the front Cielle reached across and slapped off the radio. "Did you say your *father*?"

"I've never even met him," Janie said.

"That's exactly why we should call him," Nate said. "He's not on any of our emergency contact lists, phone records, nothing. No one will think to look."

"He still lives in your childhood house, doesn't he? Won't they look there?"

"He's got a cabin. Or at least he used to."

Jason took a corner too sharply, making Casper bounce to attention between the suitcases in the back. Nate put his phone in his lap and stared down at it for a moment. His skin prickled, all those memories buried in his cells. The tires thrummed across the road. Everyone stayed quiet, deliberately focused on the scrolling view past the windows, giving him space.

His thumb traced the familiar pattern on the number pad. A ring. Then another.

"Hello?" The voice was dryer than before, but even over the phone every subtlety of pitch and timbre found resonance.

"It's Nate."

"Who?"

The freeway flew past. "Dad. It's me."

The line crackled. Then his father, through the phone lines: "Nate."

The words came hard but he pushed them through. "You still got that place in Bouquet Canyon? With your friends?"

A beat while his father tried to catch up to the hasty conversation. "Just me and Ross now. Hugh passed. But I'm pretty much the only one who ever—"

"Is it under your name?"

"No. Ross set up one of those whaddayacallits. A partnership. What's this about, Nate?"

Nate pressed his forehead to the pane. Outside, headlights and red brakes streaked together, the whole world passing them by and them it. It took him a while to find the words and even longer to say them. "I'm in trouble, Dad."

The pause drew out, no sound but the faint rush of his father's breaths. Nate had no idea what was coming next.

The old man cleared his throat, an awkward prelude. "Then I'll be right there," he said.

They followed the directions to the outskirts of Santa Clarita, the freeway yielding to a smaller freeway, which in turn gave way to a two-lane road. Houses petered out, and traffic grew sparser, though Harleys roared by with enough regularity to suggest a biker bar tucked off somewhere behind the pines. They passed the mouth of the Angeles National Forest and the reservoir itself, the road winding more aggressively as they headed up Bouquet Canyon. Between the trees, fishermen flashed into view, their heads bent beneath khaki hats, toting poles and strings of rainbow trout that gleamed in the headlights' glow. Roadside, families loaded coolers and grocery bags of picnic residue into tailgates, kids braying and quarreling as the fathers pulled at longnecks, one last beer before the drive.

At the turnoff someone had jumped the gun and erected a plywood cutout of Santa on a chopper with the spray-painted rhetorical, WHAT'S *YOUR* WISH FOR THE NEW YEAR? Jason veered upslope, and they chased the creek, the not-quite-cabin houses spacing out more and more, and then it was all pines and oaks and the occasional tendril of smoke from a hidden chimney. That was one of the miracles of Los Angeles: less than an hour from Rodeo Drive, and you might as well have been transported to a square state. Nate felt his nerves rising with the altitude; he'd not seen his father in a decade and a half and was uncertain what he'd be confronting on just about every level.

Offering a cheery wave, Jason steered past a few forest rangers in their trucks.

Janie spoke for the first time in half an hour. "Thank God you have a license."

Through the wisps of his bangs, Jason's eyes flicked to the rearview. "I *don't* have a license. I just said I could drive."

A drawn-out silence. Cielle took care to stare straight ahead through the windshield. Finally Nate's scowl lightened a bit, and then Janie tittered, and they all laughed a little, Jason the loudest.

Jason said, "So I can keep—"

"Pull over," Janie said.

She steered them the final leg and down the driveway, a dirt slope leading to a Craftsman perched a stone's throw from a finger of the creek. A bowed footbridge arced across the ribbon of water like something from Disney. At the side of the enclosed porch, bent over the propane tank fussing with a knob, was Nate's father.

He straightened up, dusting his hands, and came toward the Jeep without waving.

"Really?" Cielle said breathlessly. "That's him?"

He was grayer, a touch stooped, the years heavy on him, but he had good healthy color in his cheeks and his eyes were clear and sober. He wore a flannel shirt fastidiously buttoned to the throat, and it struck Nate that he had never seen the man in a T-shirt. In a flash Nate was five years old again, strapped to the foam backseat of the LeSabre convertible, his father's elbow perched confidently on the windowsill ahead, holding the world together.

They climbed out, Casper bounding from the back and stretch-yawning with a curled tongue. Shuffling in the leaves, they confronted one another, Nate standing to favor his left foot.

"Cielle," he said, "this is your grandfather."

The old man's eyes crinkled as he regarded her for the first time. "Hello, then."

Cielle gave a self-conscious wave, all wrist. "Hi."

Janie gave Nate's father a quick hug, and then Jason strode forward. "I'm Jason. Her boyfriend."

With minimal interest Nate's father took the kid's oversize hand, looking past him at Nate. "They're not sleeping in the same room."

"You're telling me," Nate said. They studied each other from a safe distance. "I suppose you're wondering what the hell is going on."

"In due time. It's late. And you look tired."

For the first time in his life, Nate was pleased at his father's reticence. A rush of gratitude overtook him. "Thanks for coming, Dad."

His father turned for the house without so much as a nod. "No use in standing around out here," he said.

* * *

They showered and changed while Nate's father pan-fried some elk steaks, which he served with over-easy eggs and mugs of hot cider. Drying his shaggy hair and staring down at his plate, Jason said, "I'm sort of a veg-etarian," and Nate's father replied, "Eat the damn food, son."

For a man's getaway, the place was surprisingly cozy, with spongy carpeting, throw blankets over the chairs, and exposed wood beams bracing the vaulted ceiling. No television. Nate's father threw some cedar logs in the fireplace, and they ate on the surrounding couches, breathing in the sweet fragrance, letting the flames warm them. Casper lapped meat from a mixing bowl with enough exuberance to push it across the linoleum. His tags dinged against the metal lip, and then he gave out a tragic whimper that the elk was no more.

Wearing a borrowed sweater three sizes too big, Janie leaned into Nate, and he rested his arm across her narrow shoulders, and Cielle looked at them and for once said nothing cynical. He stole looks at his father, not quite believing that they were here under the same vaulted ceiling, and damned if the old man didn't al-most smile a time or two. Nate felt his muscles relax by degrees; maybe it was the meds starting to leave his system, or maybe he just finally had the space to let go a little. Cielle cracked a stupid joke and then giggled at it herself, leaning into her mom. Janie started laughing, too, and then Nate. He caught their reflection off the glass fireplace screen, something about the arrange-ment of the three of them tugging at a thread of a memory. And it struck him: the family portrait. Same pose, eight long years later. The sight of them was all different but somehow the same. They finished eating and talking, then sat for a moment in silence, basking in the afterglow, no one wanting the gathering to break up. It was magical, a momentary respite from reality.

After a while, as Cielle and Jason, with some prompting, cleared the dishes, Nate took his cell phone and started outside.

Janie caught his arm. "Where you going?"

"Find a signal. Abara. After the hospital—"

She plucked the phone from his hand and turned it off. "Not tonight," she said gently. "Just one night."

He could give her that.

Later, though it took some doing, Nate climbed the ladder to the open loft where Cielle was bedding down. Beyond the dormer window, black fangs of treetops bit into the star-patterned sky. He combat-crawled a few feet toward her pillow.

"Are you *stupid,* crawling up here with your muscles all tweaked?"

"Yes." He leaned to kiss her on the forehead, but before he could, she hugged him around the neck, holding on.

"What's gonna happen to us?" Her voice caught, and he felt her cheek growing hot against his.

He pulled away to answer, but she just squeezed tighter. He said, "I will let nothing happen to you."

"You can't promise that."

"Yes. I can."

"Are we ever gonna get home again?"

He thought, *I* am *home.*

He kissed her on the forehead and started to back out of the cramped space when she asked, "Why'd you and Mom split up?"

He halted, hunched beneath the low ceiling. "It took me a long time to come home from the war."

"How long?"

He considered. "Till now."

"So you fell out of love with her?"

"No. Never."

"But you . . . ?"

"Couldn't figure out how to love her right either."

"That's really what men are like? *This* is what I have to look forward to?"

He smiled a little.

She said, "If you loved her—us—then how could you stand being away?"

"I couldn't. I always thought tomorrow would be different."

"And it wasn't."

"No. But today was."

She smiled secretly and lowered her head to the pillow. "Dad? Will you . . . ?"

"Of course."

He inched forward and lay up there by her until she fell asleep.

After descending with difficulty, he searched out his father and spotted him just outside the back door, scraping leftovers into a composter. He started for him, but a neat row of framed photos hanging in the brief hall brought him up short—his own school pictures from preschool on, ending with his second-grade photo.

The year before his mother got sick.

He stared at the shrinelike display of himself. A collared shirt each time out, the neat side part, his small face not yet shadowed with loss. The abrupt end at second grade. He pictured those pen marks in Cielle's doorway, her heights marked at various ages. Where was the line at which childhood ended? His mind drifted to Nastya in her VIP booth, an ash-heavy cigarette forked between manicured fingers.

Despite our best efforts, we fail each other, he thought, *all the time.*

And yet there was still so much to keep trying for.

At once his father was at his side, looking on with him at the four small frames. "You deserved to have that wall filled."

By the time Nate could recover to reply, his father had moved on down the hall.

Nate stood for a while, leaning against the wall beside those pictures. He was about to start back when he heard the quiet plucking of guitar strings from the front of the house. He made his way through the kitchen and living room, Jason's form drawing into view outside on the porch swing. The kid sat Indian style, large shoulders bowed, guitar across his lap. Nate drew near to the window. Jason was singing so softly that the words were barely audible, but the song slowly resolved: McCartney's "Blackbird." Jason's voice was startlingly good, high-pitched and pure, almost feminine. Nate kept on toward the door, a snatch of lyrics coming clear—*"take these broken wings and learn to fly"*—but when he stepped onto the enclosed porch, Jason stopped playing abruptly, the guitar lying awkwardly across his thighs like a lapdog that could at any instant turn hostile.

They faced each other there in the light of the dark black night. The door clicked shut behind Nate, cold running up his sleeves and around his neck. "Why don't you play that instead of the other crap?"

"You really know how to pay a compliment."

"You really know how to play."

The kid actually blushed. "Yeah, well."

"I'm serious. Why don't you play more like that?"

Jason shrugged, jerking his head to flick the hair out of his eyes. "Dunno. Guess I figured I wasn't supposed to. You know. Be good at something."

Nate sat beside him, the porch swing rocking. "Maybe it's easier to just lump along sometimes."

"No," Jason said. "It's *exhausting* to be a fuckup."

Nate laughed.

Jason picked at his shoe. "All my life I was told no. Can't go outside to play. Can't do algebra. Can't date a smart girl. Well, I'm sick of it." A touch sharp—an accusation.

Nate thought for a time, then said, "You should be."

The crickets were at it out there in the blackness.

Jason nodded a bit to himself. "You know when you hear a song on the radio that you just *dig*? And it sticks in your head, right? So you download it from iTunes. At first you love it. Take it with you to the skate park. Go to the beach with it, everywhere. But then you have it, so you get sick of it. And later you hear it on the radio, it's not as exciting. Because you *own* it, right?" He licked his chapped lips. "That's how it was with other girls. But I never feel that way about Cielle."

They swayed a little on the porch swing, the silence growing awkward. Then Jason reached over and chucked Nate on the shoulder, a touch too hard. "Glad we had this talk, Pops."

Suppressing a grin, Nate rose. "Good night, Jason."

Jason threw his hands out, all smart-ass smirk. "C'mon. Shouldn't we, ya know, go throw a ball? Quick bonding game of catch?"

Nate passed through the door. Safely out of view, he couldn't help but crack a smile.

Janie lay across him in the sweaty aftermath, her lips at his chest, the blades of her shoulders forming an erotic ridgeline in the darkness. Starlight angled through the curtainless pane, blanketing half the bed in a faint blue glow. Her mouth worked up his neck and found his mouth. She lifted her head, catching the sheet of light, her face smooth and beatific save the inadvertent half sneer of her swollen lips. He tugged at her hair, damp and heavy at the nape, and she pulled forward into the gentle pressure, tilting her head as if to stretch her neck.

The moment was timeless—no, it was of a *different* time. It was before Fort Benning and the Sandbox, before the man-boy shackled to an outhouse and Abibas and a helicopter that capsized four feet above a dune. Before death notifications and a failure of will in the car outside Charles's childhood home. Before nightmares and ghosts and a Westwood apartment with two photographs thumbtacked to the wall. Before safe-deposit boxes and interrogation rooms and over-size footprints in the back lawn. Before neurologists and little white pills and a body that slowly and unpredictably betrayed him.

But of course it wasn't.

The muscle beneath his cheek rippled—a tiny bout of fasciculation—and Janie's eyes tracked down to it. Her breathing changed, ever so slightly. The mood, taking a turn, paradise interrupted by a twinge of the flesh. The illness had brought him home again, but it also meant that he wouldn't be able to stay.

His voice was husky. "I'm gonna die," he told her.

Her fingertips were at his face, fording his lips. "I don't care."

"Do you have *any idea* how awful this is gonna get?"

"I don't care." Her mouth trembled, then firmed with anger. "Your eyes can dry up and you can stop talking and lie there choking on fluid in your lungs—I don't care." She clutched at him, her nails digging into the skin beneath his collarbone. "You can stop swallowing and have a ventilator rammed down your throat and . . . and barely be able to blink, but I still want you there. Dying. For *me*. I don't care. I *don't care*."

She lowered her damp forehead to his chest and kept it there for a time. He held her and looked at the stars outside and thought how they'd be there the morning after he died and the morning after that. He stroked her back, and she fell asleep on him, and half his body went numb from the weight of her, but he didn't dare move, didn't want to waste a single instant of it.

Finally she stirred and shifted off him, raising her sleep-heavy face. "I don't mean it," she said.

He ran his fingers gently down her back and up again. "I know."

Chapter 52

Nate slept hard and awakened new. Beside him the quilt was flipped back to empty sheets; Janie had slipped out, letting him sleep. With wonder he flexed his hands, rotated his feet, clenched his jaw. Hints of weakness, minor aches. Not perfect, but a world better.

Standing, he stretched, straining for the ceiling, fingers spread, pushing as far and high as his body allowed. It felt divine. The drug interaction had given him a preview of the future. Testing the strength in his hands again, he realized that he now had a brief window before the decline happened again and with finality.

He vowed not to waste it.

He paced outside, nose to his cell phone, searching out a signal. Mistaking this for play, Casper ran at his side, thwacking Nate's legs with his tail. Nate wound up in the center of the footbridge, where two bars materialized and a third flickered moodily. The stream below was as clear as air, the rocks of the bed vibrant with mossy greens. He sent a text to Abara that simply read

YOU THERE? and seconds later got an answer: CALL ME IN TWENTY. And a phone number.

He wandered back inside, where his father handed him a cup of coffee, the morning newspaper, and a plate full of fresh blueberry pancakes. The rustic Martha Stewart routine continued to surprise the hell out of Nate, but he had to concede that years of living alone had made his father proficient in the kitchen.

Nate took a sip of coffee, closed his eyes into the pleasure of it, then handed the mug back. "I can only drink decaf now."

His father frowned at the curiousness of this but asked nothing. Janie was in the shower, the kids up in the loft. The hushed teenage voices were pleasant enough, though experience had shown that a petty argument was likely to erupt at any second.

Nate ate and swallowed his riluzole, glancing at the newspaper's subtle headline: HOSPITAL MASSACRE. He scanned down, finding little in the way of helpful information. Unidentified shooter, two dead, multiple injuries, all survivors now stable. No mention of Nate or Janie; the agency was probably withholding information for the investigation. Beneath the fold, photos showed the nurse who had manned the front station and the security guard. The two black-and-white pictures held Nate's attention.

What little regard Misha—and Pavlo—had shown for these lives. Obstacles to be obliterated in their pursuit. Scorched earth was right. With Nastya's suicide it seemed that every restraint and objective had fallen away; Pavlo wanted nothing now except vengeance.

From habit Nate flipped to the obituaries and was surprised to see the same photograph of the nurse reproduced there. Luanne Dupries's dedication to her profession and her leadership at the community level within the California Nurses Association were an inspiration to her many friends and colleagues. Nate's fingernail underscored the last two sentences.

LUANNE IS SURVIVED BY HER IMMEDIATE FAMILY: HER PARENTS, BROTHER, SON, DAUGHTER-IN-LAW, AND NIECES AND NEPHEWS. SHE IS ALSO SURVIVED BY HER FIANCÉ AND HIS FOUR CHILDREN.

Before her senseless death, Luanne Dupries had made a mark. She had been well loved, and she'd be missed. Nate made her a silent apology, tapped her photograph respectfully, and headed for the bridge with his cell phone.

A host of messages dating back a few days—Sergeant Jen Brown making clear he'd better get his ass in to sign that paperwork, several reporters who had somehow gotten ahold of his number, a few friends inquiring about the news story on the bank robbery. He deleted them all and made the call.

Abara wasted no time. "The fuck happened?"

"It's a conversation."

"Ya think? A hospital raid like something outta Fallujah. Have you seen the news reports on this thing?"

"No, actually."

"It's a big deal. Comment from the mayor and police chief, the whole nine."

"Can you connect it to Shevchenko?"

"Of course not. We pulled security footage. The shooter's a guy who doesn't even *exist*." Some muffled noise. "Hang on. . . . Okay. Sorry. It's all confusion right now, but at least eyewitness reports have you pegged as a victim. I think the DA and lead investigators are beginning to understand, now, the stakes. Why you did what you had to do—including the airplane threat."

Nate shot a breath at the cold sky. "So I'm off the hook."

"Not quite, not yet, but things are tilting that direction. You still got a lot to answer for, but I'm working on it."

"Is there an arrest warrant out on me?"

"No. You're wanted for some serious fucking questioning, obviously, but that's not even the main concern. We can't have you guys running around out there with what Pavlo and his boys are willing to do. This thing's quickly escalating. What if they catch you in a shopping mall?"

"We weren't exactly planning a trip to Crate and Barrel—"

"You know what I mean. We need to keep you safe to keep the *public* safe. In-house it's opened up the discussion again about protection. You and I need to figure out how to bring you in and negotiate all this so you guys are protected. Keep your damn phone on today. Let me be your guide through the shitstorm."

The line disconnected. Nate stared at the phone. Then he went inside to update everyone on the semi-good news. Tidying up in the background, his father took it in quietly, murmuring the occasional mm-hmm, and Nate gleaned that Janie had brought him up to speed on the other fronts as well. When Nate laid out Abara's plan, Janie and Cielle radiated a nervous hope-fulness that scared him a little. It didn't yet feel safe to believe that their lives could turn normal again. That they could find some shelter and protection from the chaos, find a way back inside the world they knew.

After, he went back out to the tiny zone of reception with his cell phone, sat on the edge of the bridge, and let his shoes dangle so the tips touched the stream. Casper stood beside him, smelling of wet dirt and musk, shift-ing his weight so he pressed heavily against Nate's side. Nate put his arm around the muscular stock of the dog's neck, across the twinning patches of lighter fur that the breeders called "angel wings." Casper's brow furrowed as he watched birds dart from tree to tree. After a time the wood creaked behind them.

"Quite a Greek tragedy you got on your hands," his father said. "And the Lou Gehrig's on top of it all." With an old-man groan, he lowered himself beside Nate, Casper reluctantly yielding ground, and they stared at the changing leaves, the breeze brisk, the air impossibly clean. "You got life insurance? For Janie and Cielle?"

That was his dad—pragmatics first.

"Yeah," Nate said. "As long as I don't kill myself."

"Was that a consideration?"

"Yes."

His father nodded once, solemnly. "Dying's rough. But so's living wrong, I guess."

Nate's shoe touched the stream, froth rising around the toe. "I've done enough of that already."

"As have I."

The air tasted of pine, a pleasant kind of smokiness. "How can I thank you for this?"

His father chuckled a little, though Nate didn't understand what he found amusing. "When your mom died, I was in no kind of shape. And I could tell that you just wanted to keep out of my way. But you couldn't figure out how to do it. And I couldn't figure out how to help you, help myself. It's a terrible feeling, knowing you're screwing up something so important and screwing it up anyway."

Nate thought about stumbling into Cielle's room in the clutch of a nightmare, blood streaming down his forehead. Janie crying in the bedroom while he'd listened through the thin bathroom door. So many ways he'd been frozen in place, well before the actual ice block.

"When I cleaned up later," his father continued, "I figured I owed you. To repay the favor, keep out of *your* way. I didn't figure you wanted me around."

This was the most Nate could recall his father speaking at one go, and he wanted to honor it by resisting anything trite, placating, or untrue. He said, "Maybe this is the one good thing out of this."

"What?"

"Sitting here together now."

His father made a muffled noise at the back of his throat and nodded, a sad grin crinkling the skin at his temples. Side by side they watched the patterns of the stream form and dissolve, each froth-flecked curl spending its lifespan of a single instant before getting swept away under the bridge.

The cell phone rested on Nate's thigh. Still nothing. He remained in the sole spot of reception on the bridge, a chained dog. But sitting with the scent of the pines and the rush of the stream, he didn't mind. Janie brought him a blanket and a few cups of decaf, affecting a waitress's demeanor, and he tipped her each time with a kiss. Now he closed his eyes and breathed the sharp air and waited for the damn text alert to chime.

On the porch swing, Cielle flipped through a magazine. Beside her, Jason enacted a comically fake yawn and stretch, landing his arm across her shoulders. She pushed at him. "Go *away*. You smell like *boy*."

The predictable squabble ensued, escalating until Jason harrumphed inside. Cielle noticed Nate on his perch at the bridge and rolled her eyes at him. He shrugged. Her boots clopped across the porch, and she walked heavily over, letting gravity tug at her shoulders. She slumped down next to him.

"Jay can be such a *asshole*."

"I thought it was *shithead*."

"What?"

"Nothing." Then Nate was surprised to hear himself say, "He's not so bad."

Cielle tilted her head, incredulous. "You're sticking up for *Jason*?!"

"I am just saying. You've always been so goddamned smart. So truthful. But you can use that to . . . you know, to bludgeon people."

Her mouth stayed open in a stunned half smile. "Like Jason. Jason as in My Boyfriend Jason."

"Yes. He's not . . . terrible."

"Hang on. Lemme get a tape recorder."

"Listen, Cielle—"

She appealed to an imaginary onlooker. "Court stenographer? Can you read that back?"

"—it is possible to be *too* smart. And it can get in your way. You can shoot yourself in the foot—"

Finally she broke character: "You're in no position to point fingers."

"Sure I am." He aimed his index finger at his chest. "Don't be like me." He risked a glance at her face. Sure enough, loosening into a grin. "I'm just saying, you deserve to have whatever you want."

"But he can be so *annoying*."

"No shit he's annoying. But he also has certain attributes which are . . . not altogether reprehensible."

In his lap the cell phone rang. Nate opened the phone, set it to his ear.

Abara said, "My house, midnight. Texting you the address now," and clicked off.

Nate slipped the phone into his pocket.

Cielle was chewing her lip, no doubt still contemplating his last words. The shiny row of her bangs was ruler-straight, of a single piece. The richest, darkest hair he'd ever seen. A triumph of nature. "I . . ." She trailed off.

"What?"

"Nothing. It's stupid."

"No," he said. "What?"

"I wish I was something you could be proud of." She kicked gently at the stream, specks of spray landing like ice on their cheeks.

"You're right," he said.

"What?"

"That *is* stupid."

Her wide cheeks grew wider—a grin, despite herself. She backhanded his shoulder.

"Proud of you?" he said. "You're the single best thing I can take *any* credit for." He hoped for some eye contact, but she kept her focus glued to the passing water. A blush came up in her cheeks, and it wasn't all from the wind. "I gave you up once already," he said, "and I'm gonna have to again sometime soon." He swallowed, and it took some effort. "Besides your mom, you're the only thing I'll miss."

Cielle looked away, and then she smiled a sweet, faint smile. "Shut up." She wiped her running eyeliner, and as a small gift to her he pretended not to notice. "But there's so much stuff"—she sniffled, dragged her sleeve beneath her nose—"so much stuff you didn't get to do."

He put his arm around her shoulder. "I got to do this."

The azure sheet of the sky dimmed a degree at a time. After a while she leaned her head against his shoulder.

Chapter 53

Rusted metal numbers nailed to a split-rail fence indicated Agent Abara's address. The long driveway sliced through a swath of eucalyptus, towering trunks that disappeared into the ink-black sky. No house in sight from the main road. Nate drove right past, parked a quarter mile up the street, and cut back on foot. The past ten days had taught him that he couldn't be cautious enough.

Abara's property was isolated here on a shoulder of the Santa Susana Mountains. Craggy boulders hemmed in the road. To Nate's back loomed Rocky Peak, and unfurled below was the apron of the Valley, Chatsworth in the foreground with its parks and porn studios, its family homes and crack dens. A little something of everything in a brief throw of land, a rural twist on downtown L.A. thirty miles to the southeast.

Curls of shed bark littered the driveway, softening his footfall. The cell phone in his pocket, now on silent mode, contained Abara's last text with the address.

The scent of the eucalyptus laced the breeze,

reminding Nate of the heavy air of the *banya*. A humble ranch house lurched into sight around the bend with every step, coming visible in vertical slices between the trees. Farther back among the gray trunks, a freestanding barn blended into the shadows. Much of the main house was dark, though lights glowed in a few rooms. A piece of paper fluttered from the front door, distinct beneath the porch lamp. Odd. Nate felt a stab of apprehension. A good ruse for an ambush.

He stared at the note, debating, then left the driveway, circled the ranch house as quietly as possible, and peered through the rear windows. The house, smaller than it appeared, was clearly a bachelor's place. No girls' rooms or purses or feminine jackets slung over chairs. In the main room, a TV and wet bar predominated. A single bedroom decorated with Lakers memorabilia. For a moment Nate questioned whether he'd approached the wrong house. But then he spotted the framed certificate from Quantico on the wall of the converted office and the badge resting next to a set of car keys on the desk. This was Abara's house, all right. But there was no Puerto Rican wife who misplaced her birth-control pills, no deceptive teenage daughters, no loyal dog who came home after Abara let him out through a gate that didn't exist.

Though Nate knew that Abara told his family stories as a manipulation tactic, the scope of the deception was pretty staggering. At the end of the day, he was a law-enforcement agent who lived alone and had invented an entire family life in hopes of eliciting rapport with suspects. Nate wanted to feel betrayal, even anger, but peering in at the single unwashed plate on the kitchen counter and the line of remote controls on the couch's armrest, he could summon nothing but empathy.

Still, it was odd that Abara had asked him here to the house where all the lies could be discovered. Had the direness of the situation made him abandon pretense? What else had he lied about? Was it possible that he might even be one of Pavlo's well-paid contacts inside the system? It seemed unlikely. In his gut Nate sensed that Abara was a good agent.

But he would find no firm answers here. He had to get to the note nailed to the front door.

Taking his time, minding each movement, he returned to the driveway. A twinge pulsed to life in his left ankle, the disease reminding him it still lurked in his nervous system, biding its time. Pushing down harder on the foot, he thought, *Not now*. After picking his way through the trees around the front of the house, he risked an approach to the porch. The words on the paper were visible even from a distance: *"Nate—I'm back in the barn."*

The unlit barn toward the rear of the property.

Backing away, Nate pulled the Beretta from the waistband of his jeans and began a cautious approach. With his other hand, he extracted his cell phone and thumbed in 911, but waited to push CALL.

He advanced on the old-fashioned barn warily. No windows. The considerable door in the front was slid closed, and there would be no opening it quietly. Moving to the rear, Nate spotted a second sliding door, this one already open a few feet, showing a sliver of dark interior. From what he could see, the barn had been repurposed, with half-built cars, tools, and dissected engines strewn about the concrete floor. In the far corner, a bare bulb hung from the loft, what little it illuminated blocked by a decrepit stall partition. Was Abara back there, working on something?

That stab of paranoia came again. Nate hesitated, not wanting to announce himself. Letting the gun lead, he eased inside. The foundation, tacky with oil, emanated a chill so intense it might as well have been air-conditioning. He planned each step, not wanting to kick a stray wrench. The stagnant air smelled earthy, a hint of rot.

Moving farther in, he tried to get an angle around that stall partition, but various machinery and the rusting husk of a vintage Mustang blocked him from spotting what was beneath the bulb. The smell grew stronger, became a stench. The toe of his shoe struck something light and delicate on the floor, and it skidded a few inches, giving off a faint metallic rattle. He went rigid, thumb tight on the call button, gripping the pistol with his other hand. He stopped breathing, tried not to make a sound.

Slowly, he crouched, keeping his gaze and the barrel on the darkness. His fingers patted the cold ground, searching out the object. His hand came up with it, lifting it before his eyes so he could make it out in the blackness.

A holy medal on a gold chain. Abara's necklace. The clasp torn.

Like the floor, the necklace seemed unnaturally cold.

Not just cold. Wet.

His senses revved to high alert, fight or flight kicking in, the grainy gloom suddenly swirling with unseen menace.

He pressed his trembling fingertips to the concrete foundation. A puddle. Frigid.

Melted ice.

With an industrial clang, the overheads went on, flooding the massive barn with daylight. His feet lost purchase on the slick floor. Down on his ass, blinking against the sudden glare, he took in the four men encircling him, the four hands gripping four pistols, each aimed at his skull. They'd been waiting, close enough to touch him in the darkness. But the Ukrainians weren't what was most fearful.

It was the sight beyond, finally visible behind that stall partition.

Chapter 54

The men were on him immediately, boots pinning his wrists to the floor, hands wrenching free first the Beretta, then his cell phone, which snapped closed. He was kicked once in the temple, his head snapping back, the sight beneath the bare bulb flashing again into sickening view.

Ice block. Abara, unattached from himself, displayed in parts. Rescue saw on the ground, utterly slathered, the circular blade gummed up and bent from overuse. Matte black handcuffs, now empty, dangled from a chain.

Woozy from the kick, Nate was hoisted to his feet. Two more ice blocks waiting at the back of the barn came visible, along with several rolls of plastic drop cloth. Reserved for him and his daughter.

Blind terror. Bile creeping up his throat. He had to remind himself to breathe so he wouldn't black out.

Pavlo stepped around the partition, sliding a hand along the edge of the ice block. Tattoos crawled up his neck, down his wrists, escaping his shirt.

"Mr. Abara was a sad man. No wife. No children. Alone." Pavlo approached, and there was no mistaking the animal rage simmering just beneath the sinew of his face. "It is hard to be alone. To have *nothing* worth living for." He wiped his hand on his pants, leaving a dark smear.

Valerik gripped one of Nate's arms, Dima the other, while Misha pressed a pistol to Nate's temple. His face a swollen mess, Yuri looked on, wearing gloves and another black guayabera. Blood flecked the front of his shirt, thighs, forearms, face, even the key fob hanging from his breast pocket. Struggling to find air, Nate turned away, wanting to see anything but the ice block and its gruesome display.

Pavlo grabbed Nate's face, grinding his cheeks painfully against his molars and forcing his head toward what remained of Abara. "This man was your last hope. He told *everything*. As will you." He leaned in, and Nate could smell the breath leaking through his teeth. "Where your daughter is. We will get her here."

"No." The word barely left Nate's lips.

Pavlo laughed. "You do not realize that before we even played this chess match, you had lost. Because we are in America, you think your laws cannot be bought? Your computer systems and watch lists? Every one of your movements. Each ATM withdrawal your wife makes." His hawkish eyes searched Nate for a reaction.

"I know. You buy people—"

"No. We buy people's *time*. In five-minute chunks. Little favors. One database search here. A bank report there. There is nowhere you and your family could have gone that my money would not reach. It was over before it began. And now we will have you and your daughter side by side. When we are done with you, you will *beg* us to hurt her instead of you."

"Either way," Nate said, "you're gonna kill me."

"Yes. You will die. But that is not the part that interests me." Pavlo's eyes reshaped, a squint of amusement and menace. "It is the hour before that." Keeping his stare on Nate, he gestured with a hand. "Bring saw here."

Yuri did as he was told, thrusting the dripping saw at Nate until the smell made him gag. Grabbing the handle, he shoved it away.

Yuri raised the saw, checking the set of prints on the sticky handle, the bent blade rasping against the guard bar. Content, he walked the saw over and set it at the base of the ice block. Exhibit A.

"He trusted you," Pavlo said. "Abara. But the other agents, they did not. They will be upset to learn you justify their suspicions. Would you like to hear recording of call he made to headquarters telling that he changed his mind over you? That he was concerned you were . . ." He turned and murmured a question to Misha, who said, "Unstable."

Nate fought another lurch of his gorge and forced out the words: "But the FBI has a file on you—"

"*Everyone* has file on me."

"They have evidence on the witness killings. They're building a case—"

"Let me be clear," Pavlo said, sounding out each word. "They can use team of forensic accountants, but they will *never* connect me to Danny Urban"—the name barely making it through the sneer—"and those killings."

The confidence blazing through Pavlo's glare removed all doubt. In that instant, Nate felt every hope collapse. His only law-enforcement ally lay severed on an ice block. Nate himself was captured, sure to be tortured, sure to die. And Cielle was next on the chopping block. He gagged some more on the wartime smell and the feeling of the residue on his hands. Choking on despair.

He reached for anything to give him strength. The impression of Janie came to him, her mouth at his collarbone: *Why'd you make me wait so long?* And then his vow to Cielle: *I will let nothing happen to you.*

You can't promise that.

Yes. I can.

He lifted his head, steeled with purpose. Stall, gather information, negotiate, redirect. Anything and everything to shake loose that grain of a chance.

Pavlo had turned to Misha, brushing against him. "Let us get started."

"You went to all this trouble to frame me," Nate said. "But once the cops find my carved-up body, they're gonna know I didn't kill Abara. And they'll come after you for it."

Misha flicked his yellow bangs from his eyes, the ridiculous Beatles mop moving as a single hair-sprayed unit. "No one will find your pieces. Only your fingerprints. And the agent. We will clean the scene. Prepare it."

"You will tell us where your fat daughter is," Pavlo said. "You will kill her with words from your own mouth."

"You broke the saw," Nate blurted. "What are you gonna use on me?"

Yuri: "We haff backup."

Pavlo nodded at him, and the big man ambled toward the door.

Nate said quickly, "I made a 911 call. Before I walked in here."

Misha looked bored. "You did not."

"Right before you grabbed me. Check the phone." None of the men moved. *"Check the phone."*

Pausing, Yuri reached into his pocket and raised Nate's phone, clicking through. "Two-second-duration call. A hang-up. So what."

He started for the door again, but Nate noticed a flicker of concern on Pavlo's face and pressed the advantage, hard. "My cell-phone number is red-flagged with the authorities. They've been waiting to track me down. Now they get a 911 hang-up that traces to a cell tower near Agent Abara's house? The same agent you just had call in to say he was concerned I was unstable?"

"They won't come," Misha said.

"Maybe not." Nate stared at Pavlo.

Yuri crushed the phone in his hand. Literally crushed it in one hand. It gave off a crackle, pieces of the tough plastic case sticking out of his fist at all angles. The remains hit the concrete floor with a thud.

Yuri took a heated step toward Nate, that key fob flapping in his breast pocket, but Pavlo held up a hand. "Pull car around. Quietly. We move him. Do this at warehouse, where we *take our time*." The last three words he spit into Nate's face.

Yuri glared at Nate, then hurried out. They waited in the chill, the ice blocks crackling now and again as they melted, Nate keeping his eyes from the red smear below the bare bulb. After a time an engine pierced the silence, growing louder, a car drifting up in front of the barn and then turning off. A key scratched in a lock, and then came the distinctive sound of a trunk yawning open.

A few seconds later, the immense front barn door shuddered back, Yuri's massive form framed against the opening. Behind him the dark Town Car waited. With no ceremony he crossed and seized Nate by the throat and shirt, hauling him through the space like a rolled carpet. Nate wheezed, air cinched off, legs dragging behind him. The capacious trunk awaited, a duffel bag taking up barely a third of the space. As they neared, Yuri hoisted Nate up and hurled him inside. His head struck something hard inside the duffel, and then the trunk slammed, leaving him in pitch-black.

Frantically, he twisted the key fob he'd managed to lift from Yuri's pocket. He fumbled it, heard it tap somewhere by his neck. Contorting, he searched desperately with his fingertips, finally nudging something. Seizing the key, he felt for the tiny buttons and hit the one with the raised bump. The car chirped twice, locking.

From outside came noise and confusion.

"—how did he . . . ?"

"—other keys?"

"—now you tell me he is inside the fucking—"

Nate rolled over, kicking at the front wall of the trunk, hoping to knock the rear seat backs down so he could squirm into the main cabin. His quick breaths bounced off the roof; his shoulder blades banged back against metal. Again and again he hammered his feet forward.

Zero give. Clearly, the Town Car didn't have the fold-down feature he was praying for; there'd be no getting through.

The duffel was lodged beneath him, something jamming his kidney, and he remembered that clank when whatever was inside had struck his head. Something hard enough to hammer through the division? As the voices outside grew angrier, he swung the bag around, fought the zipper open, and groped at the contents, trying to guess at what the hell he had.

His hands closed on a curved metal handle, and for the first time tonight he felt the advantage tilt in his direction. He ripped the cord, and the backup rescue saw roared deafeningly to life. The blade seethed in the contained space, all heat and teeth. One slip and he'd lose a limb. Bracing himself, he raked the blade against the trunk wall, sparks and shrapnel flying back into his eyes, his mouth. The smell of burned upholstery and greased metal clogged his throat. Under the strain he felt the weakness of his muscles; given his condition, he wouldn't be able to keep the pressure on for long. He stopped, the blade quieting, and kicked at the spot he'd carved out. His foot blew through, but the hole wasn't big enough.

From outside: "—locked in there with the—"

As he revved the blade inches from his cheek, he heard a percussion, and then a straw of light impaled the darkness.

A bullet hole.

Wrenching with all his might, he slashed at the dividing wall, then dropped the saw and smashed through the rear seat backs, a series of bullets skewering the cargo space behind him. Panting, he scrambled over the console into the driver's seat.

Misha stood five feet back from the driver's window, aiming for Nate's head. So it would end here in the front seat of a Town Car. Nate had only an instant to wonder why Misha was standing so far back when he pulled the trigger.

Flinching away, Nate heard himself bellow.

Inches from his temple, the driver's window wobbled and spit out a chip.

Bullet-resistant.

Of course the boss's car would be bullet-resistant.

Misha fired again and again, aiming at the same spot.

Nate rammed the keys into the ignition and floored it, the Town Car leaping forward, fishtailing around, clipping the rolled-open barn door. As the ass end of the vehicle swept past the men, they all leaped back except Pavlo. The rear bumper swung within inches of his knees, but he held his ground, unimpressed, glaring through the rear windshield, his craggy face and dead eyes promising, as the car accelerated away, that Nate's safety was only temporary.

Nate hurtled up the long driveway and careened onto the main road, spilling into the empty oncoming lane, wrestling the car back under control just in time to skid to a stop parallel to his parked Jeep. He stumbled out, across, in, his own set of keys at the ready.

The engine roared to life. Wiping sweat from his brow, his blood-sticky hands firm around the wheel, he aimed the hood at the glowing dotted line and clamped the pedal to the floor. Hurtling through darkness, he felt a sensation overtake him—that he was flying out of his own grave.

Chapter 55

Three in the morning and Nate had just finished scrubbing Abara's blood from his hands. He'd sneaked back into the Bouquet Canyon house, careful not to awaken his father or the kids. Janie had stirred as he'd slipped past into the bathroom, but he couldn't bring himself to wake her yet to tell her what they had done to Abara.

Beneath the punishing heat of the nozzle, Nate felt the reality of his situation settle in, and he emerged from the shower cloaked in a mood of black finality. Charles waited, holding his towel out for him and dripping blood on the clean tiles. Nate took the towel, his left arm quaking slightly. He refused to acknowledge the ache emanating from deep inside the muscle.

"I'm running out of options, Charles," he said. "And time. I gotta make a move. But I don't want to."

Charles took this in solemnly, chewing a cheek. "You were the guy on the beach," he said, "who dove into the waves and saved the girl."

"I was."

"But when we went over, you lost something."

Nate was almost afraid to say it out loud. "You mean the helicopter. When I didn't jump."

"And with my mom," Charles said. "You could've told her I was dead. You were right there, parked at the curb. But she had to hear it from a stranger."

Nate nodded. He was afraid to blink, to speak. When he did, his voice scratched his throat. "That's why you've been here all this time," he said. "You've never forgiven me."

"Of course I have," Charles said. "*You've* never forgiven you."

"I don't understand," Nate said. "What's that have to do with this? This decision, now?"

Charles's face was speckled with dried blood, his lashes heavy with sand. "You gotta decide for once and for all," he said. "Which guy are you? The guy on the beach or the guy outside my mother's house?"

Nate dried himself, taking a moment to flex his left hand. Charles's breath leaked through the blown-open lungs in his chest cavity. Nate dressed and hung the towel neatly over the rack. Placing his hand on the doorknob, he paused.

"The guy on the beach," he said.

He and Janie sat the way they used to as college kids, Indian style on the bed, facing each other. The mood tonight, however, was anything but hopeful.

Nate couldn't get the image of Abara out of his mind. He thought of that lonely house, the single plate resting on the kitchen counter.

"Good people keep getting killed because of me," he said.

"No," Janie said, her face still ashen from Nate's report. "People are getting killed because of Pavlo Shevchenko. Don't let guilt confuse the issue."

"It can't keep going this way. I won't let it. And at any minute the choice is gonna be taken away from me. As soon as my fingerprints are discovered on that saw, I'm done. I will have killed a federal agent—"

"You can go in, explain—"

"And they'll believe me? Even if it's true, I can't explain everything away. There's too much against me now, Janie. You know that. Abara was my best—my *only*—advocate. And before they killed him, they forced him to call in and say he was wrong about me. Then his body? My prints? Along with everything else? It's done."

"But the case they're building against Shevchenko—"

"They're not gonna be able to tie him to those murders. He covers his tracks too well. And we can't keep hiding forever. You know that too. It's only a matter of time before his men track down you and Cielle here. Or anywhere else. You can't live like this. Our daughter can't."

Janie's breathing quickened. "So what's that leave us?"

The starlight softened the room's edges, and he thought about the previous night here in this bed, how everything had been safe and promising then. A fantasy, sure, but one well worth having.

He touched her cheek gently. "No way out but through."

"What are you gonna do?" She pulled away. "Go to war?"

He said nothing.

She coughed out a one-note laugh and looked to the ceiling. "With what? Yourself? No weapons? You had one gun, and they took that."

"I'm going now to figure that out."

She covered her mouth, a gesture that might have looked prudish if not for her anguish.

"I've made so many mistakes," Nate said. "But the ones I regret the most are the things I *didn't* do. The things I let fear keep me from doing. But now, with this"—he lifted his left arm, rotated the weakened wrist—"and everything else. There's none of that. No more not doing." He moved her hand down away from her face and held it in her lap. "I will not go to my grave knowing that these guys are after you and my daughter."

She squeezed his hand, hard, holding on. "What are you gonna do?"

"Anything I have to."

His knuckles ached, but she didn't relent.

"You come back." She bit her lower lip hard enough that the color left beneath her teeth. "You come back and say good-bye first."

It took some effort for him to let go of her hand.

Casper followed him down the hall, his nails making too much noise on the floorboards. Nate tapped a knuckle against his father's door and heard a muffled answer: "Come in."

He stood in the doorway as his father rustled up against the headboard, pulling on a pair of spectacles. Early morning leaked around the curtains, a pale shade of gray.

"Dad," he said. "It's gonna get bad."

"Hardly call it a picnic now."

"Worse. Soon enough I'll be framed as a cop killer. The whole law-enforcement community is gonna come after me, on top of those men. I gotta leave and take care of some stuff. It's dangerous for you to stay around Janie and Cielle—"

"I got them."

"It's much safer for you to go back—"

"I'm not asking, Nate." The hard words rang around the room. He cleared his throat apologetically. "I can help protect them from those men. And anyone else."

"I don't want you to be at risk, Dad."

Nate's father pulled off his spectacles and rubbed his eyes. When he looked up, his weathered face was as vulnerable as Nate had ever seen it. "I haven't done anything worth anything in a long time. Don't take this away from me, son."

They regarded each other in the semidarkness.

Nate nodded once and withdrew.

Beneath the fan that had been half torn from the ceiling by the weight of his daughter's body, Pavlo spread Nastya's clothes across her luxurious duvet. With a razor blade—*her* razor blade—he visited a great, calm violence on her shirts and skirts, her bras and panties. He wore bifocals, his sole concession to his age, which lent him greater gravity and a dignified elegance he did not often display. He required them; it was meticulous and vital work. Firming the razor between thumb and fist, he dragged a dress across his arm, the blade's corner rising through the silk like a shark's fin.

Beyond the picture window, the lights of the Strip were on a low simmer, daybreak still barely a notion at the horizon. The spectacular city view had been freed once and for all, the curtains torn from the rod and shredded at Pavlo's hand. Traces of Nastya's lipsticked message remained, red smudges on the pane.

Yuri and Misha entered and stood like waiters waiting to be acknowledged. Plucking a red bra from the mound, Pavlo sliced through one cup, then the other. "What?"

"The police responded to Abara's barn," Misha said, "off our tip. They are processing the evidence now."

"Good." Pavlo cut the buttons from a sheer blouse, one by one. "And Overbay?"

Yuri said, "We are watching the airports and—"

"Find him." Pavlo's hands stopped, then resumed, making an incision down the length of the blouse, splitting it between the shoulders. "Don't watch. *Do.*"

"We have been spending money to gather addresses," Yuri said. "Overbay's buddy pals from the war. His friends. Guesthouses or second homes. The wife's parents have condo in Arrowhead. His father has cabin in Bouquet Canyon. A doctor friend of wife has

Malibu beach house. Those kinds of places. It is how they track criminals."

Pavlo said, "What of the wife's old boyfriend?"

"He drove east after crossing us. As of last night, he checked in to a motel in Ohio. No phone calls to or from him. He is useless to them."

Pavlo snatched the sheaf of papers from Yuri's hand and flipped through them.

"How much did this cost me?"

"Fifteen thousand dollars."

Pavlo handed the papers back and turned his attention to a pair of panties on the bed. "There are four of you. Split the list in half and go. Start with nearest places first." He pushed a strip of black lace across the blade until it frayed, then gave way. Misha had exited, but Yuri remained, his big swollen face the picture of concern. *"Go!"* Pavlo yelled. *"Leave me!"*

The door clicked quietly closed. Pavlo cut through more black lace, then shoved the razor savagely through the crotch, tearing, ripping. He was sweating, his arms straining against the fabric, and he realized he was burying a roar in his throat. A spasm of fury seized him. He raked the mound of sliced fabric off the duvet and watched the strips and ribbons scatter across the floor, the remnants of his broken daughter. But it wasn't until he turned the razor on himself, carving a furrow up his ink-sheathed forearm and releasing the pain that had been scouring his insides, that he finally understood the sweet agony Nastya had found in the blade.

Chapter 56

The 6:00 A.M. cold whipped through the imprecise seal of the not-so-weatherproof Wrangler's soft top, the stream blowing across Nate's forehead as steady and loud as cranked-on air-conditioning. Praying that Eddie Yeap would be as usual the first coroner at the morgue, Nate input the number into the cell phone he'd borrowed from Janie and stepped on the gas. Before he risked his next move, he had to know if he was wanted yet for the murder of Agent Abara, and Eddie was, he hoped, the guy with his hands inside the guts of the case. As the line rang, Nate ran through the reasoning he'd constructed as he'd flown down the freeway.

A murder in Chatsworth would fall under the jurisdiction of the Devonshire station, which meant the body and the crime scene should be processed by LAPD. Because Abara was an FBI agent, the case would go federal, but Nate was banking on the fact that no one would want to transport evidence across the country to the lab at Quantico, because of both the delay and the risk of deterioration of the chillingly fresh evidence. Which meant that his best bet for getting information on the case's status was from—

Eddie Yeap picked up. "Yullo?"

"Hey, Eddie. It's Nate."

"Nate Bank-Hero Nate?"

The greeting boded well—not a salutation offered to a cop killer.

"Listen," Nate said, "I caught a death notification for that agent killed out in Chatsworth. Abara. I have to go tell his mother."

"I thought FBI handled their own."

"I guess they're as short-staffed with this stuff as we are. Anyway, Brown asked me to handle it."

"You coming in?"

"Later. But I was wondering if you could give me a preview."

"Well, Jonesy's in bad shape. Heh. They used an honest-to-God rescue saw. You believe that?"

Nate parked at a meter a few blocks away from the Police Administration Building. If things went bad and he had to bolt, he didn't want to get stuck in a parking garage. "Any physical evidence?"

"I got bupkis off what was left of Jonesy, but scuttlebutt is the latent-print unit pulled something off the rescue saw."

Climbing out, Nate paused. Then slammed the door, a little harder than necessary, and started briskly toward the building. "Where are they with that?"

"Prints are at the lab now."

"Already?"

"Fast-tracked. Killed an agent, ya know. Heh."

"When do you think they'll have results?"

"I'd say any minute."

Nate picked up the pace, just shy of a jog. "Ask you one more question?"

"Course."

"I assume FBI's handling the investigation. But who's the detective liaison?"

"Ken Nowak."

By arriving unreasonably early, Nate hoped to dodge colleagues and complications. Even so, as he stepped out from the elevator with an empty duffel bag slung over his shoulder, he proceeded cautiously, unsure what he'd find. Sergeant Jen Brown's office was dark and most of the cubicles empty. Unnoticed, he picked his way toward his desk.

A loud voice startled him. "Surprised you'd show your face around here."

He turned, Ken Nowak drawing into sight around a partition wall. Leaning back in his chair, that hockey puck of a key ring resting next to his propped-up loafers.

Ken lowered his feet and settled forward with a touch of menace. "After that whole airport-terrorist incident, I mean."

Nate released a breath as evenly as he could manage. "It was just a mix-up."

"I bet. What you doing here?"

"Picking up my stuff."

"You don't need *that*." With a smirk, Ken gestured at the empty duffel hanging from Nate's shoulder. "They already took care of your shit for you."

Nate glanced over at his desk. Sure enough, his personal things were boxed and waiting. His *non*personal things—files, forms, research—appeared to be gone.

"Oh," he said, hoping he looked appropriately dismayed. "Well, I have to wait for Brown anyway. She had some stuff for me to sign, I'm guessing severance paperwork so I don't sue anyone."

Ken elected not to take up the feigned attempt at worker camaraderie.

Nate took a breath. "How 'bout you? Isn't this a little early?"

"I been here half the night. Big case, FBI agent iced out in Chatsworth. Literally. I'm waiting on print results from the lab." Ken turned back to his desk and took a sip of coffee. "We get our hands on the piece of shit who did it, ain't gonna be a pretty sight."

Nate managed a nod, staring at the phone just beyond Ken's knuckles. As soon as it rang, he was dead. He moved swiftly to his desk and powered up the computer. What he needed, what he'd come for, were weapons. Real weapons, as in assault rifles, handguns, C4. A virtual armory. Like the one Danny Urban had collected, the one that had been seized by the cops and put into an evidence locker down the hall.

The problem was, Nate didn't know *which* evidence locker. But the database did.

His muscles had gone tense, braced to hear the ring of Ken's phone. Typing furiously, he called up the log-in screen and keyed in his user name and password.

ACCESS DENIED.

Of course.

He pressed the heels of his hands into his eyes. Plan B. Now.

Rising, he crossed to Ken's desk. "I meant to ask, you still driving that gold Chrysler?"

"Champagne."

"Right. I parked near you. I think someone dinged you. Rear bumper's half off."

"You're kidding me." Already Ken was up, digging for his car keys, hustling out. "You'd better be wrong, Overbay."

Nate waited for him to pass from sight, and then he swiped the thick ring of work keys Ken had left behind. As he moved to go, Ken's phone rang, the caller ID screen lighting up: SCIENTIFIC INVESTIGATION DIVISION. The crime lab.

Nate lunged to lower the volume on the ringer, not daring to breathe. A frozen instant. But Ken's footsteps continued up the hall, and then the elevator car chimed its arrival. Nate blew out a shaky exhale. A moment later the voice-mail button blinked its red alert.

He tore his eyes from the phone and ran down the hall, readjusting the empty duffel across his back. He had five minutes, seven tops.

The evidence room was off the main corridor, just shy of the elevators. The reinforced door stood locked, the metal shutter rolled down behind the guard cage. Nate stared helplessly from the autolocking doorknob to the lump of keys sitting in his palm, maybe twenty of them. Had he hoped that one would have a big label on it reading EVIDENCE LOCKERS?

With fumbling hands Nate tried one key after another. The dead bolt stood firm, unimpressed with his offerings.

Another key failed. And the next. Sweat ran down Nate's forehead, stung his eyes. A memory surfaced—had he read somewhere that LAPD had changed the rules after Rampart so cops no longer were allowed keys to the evidence room? Which meant that even if he *did* have time to check every—

A voice from behind broke through his thoughts. "Help you there, Overbay?"

His hands froze. Hiding the keys, he lowered them into his pocket. Slowly, he turned.

Bernice Daniels, the evidence custodian, loomed behind him, holding up a gleaming silver key connected by a plastic clip coil to the front pocket of her overburdened polyester pants. She was a dense, squat woman, boulderlike buttocks providing a counterweight to a sturdy bosom. She was lovely and cheery, an oversize heart to match her proportions.

Flustered, he scratched at his head, feigning casual. "Yeah, actually. I was just waiting for you. Sergeant Brown assigned me to the Danny Urban case. And I like to . . . you know—"

"Look through every last piece of evidence. I know. But it's been a while since Homeboy Hit Man caught a bullet barrage. Why you serving the death notification now?"

Less than ten yards away, a set of elevator doors peeled open and Ken Nowak stepped forth.

Nate cleared his throat, regained his focus. "They just located a son. So I have to go let him know."

"Oh, dear." Bernice opened the door, stepping inside and hoisting the metal shutter behind the guard cage.

Annoyed, Ken walked briskly by. "The hell, Overbay? My car's fine."

"That's good. I must've had the wrong car."

"I'm surprised there's another. It's a rare color."

Ken continued past, heading toward his desk and the waiting voice-mail message identifying Nate as Abara's killer. Nate watched him walking away, every step one more tick of the countdown.

He turned back, debated making a break for the elevator.

Bernice's voice pulled him from his trance. "I believe the Urban case is locker 78B. Here. You'll need to sign the evidence log—"

"Of course."

The metal door swung open, revealing the promised armory. Drawing a deep breath, he stepped forward and started grabbing whatever he could, raking items from shelves and hooks into the open duffel. Assault rifle, handguns, magazines, boxes of ammo, blocks of C4, electric blasting caps, even a grenade. How much time until Ken charged through the door behind him? Ten seconds? Five?

He sensed Bernice hovering at his back, troubled.

"Nate?" She spoke slowly, as if to an insane person. "What are you doing?"

He zipped the bag and stood. Bernice's mouth was literally agape. No sound of footsteps coming up the hall.

"Can you give me a hand with this?" He slid a heavy evidence box from a wall rack straight across into Bernice's arms. She received its weight, cradling it against her chest.

Reaching down, he snapped the coil clip with the key from her pant pocket, stepped outside, and swung the autolocking door shut, trapping her inside.

He stared at her through the metal cage. "I'm sorry, Bernice."

Shouldering the hefty duffel, he ran for the elevator and thumbed the DOWN button. At the end of the hall, Ken appeared, wheeling around the last row of cubicles. He paused, his broad shoulders rotating as he scanned and locked onto Nate.

Between them Bernice began shouting and banging on the cage.

Ken started sprinting up the corridor.

Nate jabbed at the elevator's DOWN button again and again.

Ken hurtled at him, shoes slapping tile, a running back sensing the end zone. Bernice was hollering now, maximizing those impressive lungs.

The doors parted. Nate slid through, tapped the ground-floor button, holding it in so hard that his finger bent back. Though Ken was out of sight, his labored breaths and furious footfalls came through the closing doors and seemed to reverberate around the car.

Ken's fingertips flew into view just as the doors clamped shut, and then Nate staggered back a step, pulled by the weight of the duffel, and coughed out a chunk of air. Arming sweat off his brow and reconsidering his route, he clicked the button for the second floor so as to dodge security in the lobby.

He slid out at the first crack of light, letting the doors scrape him from either side, and then he hustled down two corridors to a rear stairwell, his left foot slightly sluggish. He took the stairs two at a time and shoved through an emergency door, setting off a shrill alarm. Stepping around a decorative hedge, he jogged for his Jeep, the weaponry clanking reassuringly against his back.

Chapter 57

Nate sat in his Jeep at the curb, staring up the steps of the front walk. Through the kitchen window, he watched her. Though it was almost noon, she still wore a bathrobe, and she fussed about the coffeemaker, her movements slowed by age. Even from here he could see she'd lost a good amount of weight, and he hoped that she wasn't ill.

He climbed out, making sure to lock the Jeep given what was in the cargo hold, then mounted the stairs and rang the bell. A delay. The shuffle of footsteps.

Grace Brightbill answered, one frail hand resting on the knob. She looked much older than Nate would have thought, but living alone could do that to a person. A whorl of puzzlement appeared in the wrinkles of her forehead.

"It's—" Nate had to clear his throat and start over. "It's Nate Overbay, Mrs. Brightbill. Charles's old college roommate."

Her face lightened with recognition. "Nate, of course. Come in, come in."

Thanking her, he entered, enveloped by warm air and the scent of cinnamon. Though it was barely November, a Christmas tray on the coffee table held a raft of desiccated brownies.

She followed his gaze. "Would you like one?"

"No," he said, too quickly. "No, thank you. I just ate."

A voice said, "Yup. She's still at it," and Nate looked up to see Charles reclining, one ankle hooked over a knee, arms spread on the couch back. Black, dried blood caked his hands, and sand dusted his hair. Through the hole blown in his stomach, Nate could make out the plaid upholstery behind him.

Grace gestured Nate toward the couch, then sat in a worn denim chair draped with a crocheted blanket. He took the cushion next to Charles, who watched him with keen interest. A dusty upright piano in the background held countless framed pictures of Charles, many from his boyhood. That dopey, optimistic smile.

"I'm happy for the visit," Grace said.

"I'm sorry I didn't come earlier." Nate laced his fingers, staring down, working up the courage. "I was with Charles. When he died."

She looked up and away, the skin loose at her neck. Her ankles shifted below the hem of the robe, the skin dry and white.

"I was afraid to see you," he continued slowly. "To talk to you. Because of what that might bring up for me. And that wasn't right."

She nodded a few times. "I'd like to know," she said. "Everything. I've been living in a haze of government-issue obfuscation for almost a decade now. And that's been the worst part of the grieving. Not knowing."

He'd forgotten her razor clarity, perhaps because it always seemed at odds with her chipper demeanor. A former teacher, she used her words precisely.

"Are you sure you want the details?"

"I think I'm entitled." She readjusted the blanket across her legs. "I've certainly had enough time to think about it."

Nate glanced across at Charles, who for once didn't say anything. He swallowed hard, his Adam's apple jerking.

Nate began, starting with Abibas and the little girl with the paddleball. How Charles had found the skinny man they were seeking, hiding behind a generator. The roasting walk out to the sand dunes. Abibas forgetting his notebook. Nate's moment of indecision and how Charles leaped on the rucksack.

At this, Grace's eyes moistened, and she lifted a tissue, produced from thin air, to her cheeks. Her eyes closed, a glow coming up beneath her grief-stricken face, altering her expression. It took a moment for Nate to identify it. Pride.

He kept on. How he recalled seeing the rotor blades kiss the sand and then not much of the minutes after. McGuire screaming, holding his severed leg. And Charles's gut, the morass of dark blood. How Nate had carried him over his back, running to get help, and how he couldn't let go even when the sergeant asked him to.

Somewhere in the telling, Nate realized he'd gone hoarse with emotion, the words a rush at his mouth.

" 'Don't leave me.' He kept telling me, 'Don't leave me.' "

At long last she rose with difficulty. She crossed and laid a fragile hand on his shoulder, light as a feather. "You never did."

The words went straight to the core of him, the simplest truth and yet one that redrew the lines of a picture he'd thought was carved in stone.

She walked slowly from the room, heading toward the rear of the house, and Nate understood somehow that she wouldn't be back.

When he rose, he saw that Charles was standing in the front doorway, forearms pressed to the frame on either side, a cowboy's lean. A playful enough posture, but it was clear that he was moved by what had preceded and was doing his best to cover up. He screwed on his crooked grin. "What next?"

"Sorry, podnah," Nate said. "From here I walk alone."

He brushed through him heading out the door.

Chapter 58

NEW ODESSA. The scrolled letters on the glowing yellow sign were visible from a block away. The parking lot sat empty until Nate pulled the Jeep in and slotted it into a front space. The vast bouncer—the one who'd shoved his face to the table—preened beneath the awning, peering at the dark glass inset in the oak door and making imperceptible changes to his cropped hair.

He turned as Nate approached and grinned broadly, showing off a gap between his front teeth. "You come back for more—"

Removing a handgun from the waistband of his jeans, Nate walked right past him, firing down through his thigh. As the big man grunted and began a slow-motion collapse, Nate pushed through the big door, never breaking stride.

The waitstaff flitted between the empty tables, changing linens and flatware, making the most of the pre-dinner break. They paused at Nate's entrance, the memory of the gunshot hanging in the dim air. In the TV mounted above the bar, he caught a picture of himself and a snip of a newscaster's chirpy declaration: *"—in a startling reversal, the former bank hero now wanted in connection with the murder of a federal officer—"* He kept on, pistol low at his side, weaving through workers. In the rear banquet hall, a band dressed in costumes suited to a medieval fair tuned their instruments, the shrill cacophony amplified off the brick walls.

Nate beelined for the VIP table encircled by pillars. Sure enough, the Georgian was there, poring over paperwork, one jaundiced hand poking at an accountant's calculator as the other groped blindly between a platter of pickled fish and a wineglass. He lifted his head at the sound of Nate's approach, his meaty lips twitching with disdain.

Nate kicked the chair straight out from under him, the hefty man toppling forward, his face smashing into the platter. The wineglass went sideways, his hands groping at the tablecloth, pulling himself up even as the cloth lost traction. Wheezing, he collapsed into the neighboring chair, hand cupped beneath his mouth, drooling blood through his fingers onto the starched linen. Red wine blotted his shirt. A piece of herring clung to the bulge beneath his chin. His eyes were wide, rolling, and his vast chest heaved. The lock of dyed black hair swooped up and away from his forehead as if aspiring to flight.

With his strong hand, Nate slammed the big head to the table, pressed Danny Urban's Glock 19 to his temple, and brought his clenched teeth to just above the man's ear. "Tell him I'm coming for him. Tonight. Understand?"

The Georgian's frantic nod against the tablecloth rattled the shards of the shattered platter.

Nate left him in the mess. The workers stood frozen between the tables. As he walked past, they lowered their eyes with respect.

Under the awning the bouncer was slumped back against the wall, each short breath blowing a string of saliva from his mouth. Bone glinted deep in the wound. His pant leg was lifted, snared on the ankle holster, and he leaned forward a few inches, reaching vainly for the gun. His trembling fingers were feet away and not getting any closer.

Nate stepped over his legs on his way out.

Yuri and Misha had taken the replacement Jaguar because the Town Car looked too conspicuous. A sheet of paper wedged on the dashboard and reflected up onto the windshield held numerous addresses, each a secondary residence of one of the Overbays' relatives or friends. The top two addresses were crossed out. Next up was the cabin belonging to Nate's father.

Flicking a cigarette out the window, Yuri turned off at the base of Bouquet Canyon and headed upslope. Wearing a sport coat and jeans bleached to within a shade of white, Misha reclined in the passenger seat, turning the map this way and that.

Blue and red lights flashed behind them, and Yuri lifted his eyes to the rearview, cursing under his breath. A Chevy Tahoe, raised on big knobby tires, with a light bar and a big black bumper guard like a shark's mouth. A Forest Service ranger. As Yuri signaled and pulled over, Misha removed a pistol from beneath his sport coat and racked the slide to chamber a round.

Yuri waved at him. "Not yet."

As the ranger approached in his pressed green uniform and the silly broad-brimmed hat, Misha slid the pistol beneath his leg and smoothed his hands down his thighs.

The ranger tapped the glass, and Yuri rolled down the window.

"Whoa there, pal. What happened to your face?"

"I haff climbing accident. The rope, it . . ." Yuri made a snapping noise.

The ranger whistled. "Well, I suppose you're wondering why I pulled you over."

"Yes, sir."

"You tossed a cigarette out the window."

Yuri smashed his palm to his forehead, a big show of self-recrimination, and swore at himself in Ukrainian.

The ranger bobbed his head, amused. "Where you boys from?"

"Ukraine."

"I got a sister-in-law from Russia."

"Different country," Misha said.

Yuri turned his head slowly and offered Misha a covert glare.

"St. Petersburg," the ranger said. "Beautiful."

"Yes," Yuri said.

"I tell you what. I know how you folks smoke there, so I'll just give you a warning. This is fire-hazard country. You can't be doing that here."

Yuri gave him a thumbs-up. "Okeydokey."

"And careful climbing. Watch yourself. I don't want to have to search-and-rescue you."

"That won't be necessary."

The ranger nodded and started away.

"Officer," Misha called out, the handcuffs hidden in his lapel pocket giving off a faint jangle as he leaned forward.

Yuri's hands clenched the wheel.

The ranger came back to the window. Misha held out the map and the piece of paper. He pointed to the address of the cabin. "We are looking for a friend's house. But the street is not on the map."

The ranger looked at it. "Oh, right. There's a turnoff here. See? Marked by a big stupid Santa Claus sign. Take that road a quarter mile and you'll see the house. No more'n five minutes."

Misha smiled. "Thank you very much."

Yuri rolled up his window and eased out onto the road. They drove awhile, finally spotting the ridiculous plywood sign of Santa astride a motorcycle——WHAT'S *YOUR* WISH FOR THE NEW YEAR?

The cell phone rang, and Yuri answered on Bluetooth, Pavlo's voice hissing through the speakers: "He's coming. Get here *now*."

The reception flickered in and out, and Yuri pulled over in the shade of the plywood sign to hold the connection. "What happened?"

"He went to New Odessa, passed threat to me through the Georgian. Said he is coming for me. I served time on the Arctic Circle, and he thinks he can say *anything* to threaten me?"

A rare show of outrage. Yuri and Misha looked at each other. "We will be right there."

Yuri clicked off the call.

Misha tapped the window with a knuckle, indicating the turnoff right beyond their front tires. "We are all the way here. Why not go and look?"

Yuri hesitated, casting a glance up the dirt road. "Because Pavlo did not tell us to."

"How long can one look take?"

Yuri weighed this, then slotted the gearshift into drive and started down the road. They coasted around the bend, the cabin coming into view way up ahead, a stream of smoke rising from the chimney. An older man appeared from the side of the house and started up the porch, bearing a stack of firewood in his arms.

Yuri's phone rang again, once, and then the signal went dead.

He touched the brakes. Stared down nervously at the phone. No bars.

Up ahead, the screen door banged shut, the man vanishing into the house.

Yuri exhaled through his teeth. "The father is alone. No sign of the Jeep." He considered a moment longer, then flipped the car around.

Misha made a sound of disappointment. "Okay, then. We will go to Pavlo's house and prepare for Overbay."

"Why did he go to the Georgian?" Yuri asked. "Why does he warn us?"

Misha lifted the pistol from beneath his leg, dropped the mag, then locked the slide to the rear so the bullet ejected. It spun shimmering in an arc before his face until he trapped it in a fist. "He wants us all in one place."

Chapter 59

During the drive back to his father's cabin, Nate's muscles hummed with energy. The weakness remained, sure, but the current of adrenaline seemed to be recharging them. He passed a few outsize forest ranger trucks, a fancy Jag, a minivan or two, but mostly the canyon roads were quiet.

When he arrived, Janie, the kids, and his father were playing Pictionary before the fire as Casper slumbered on the hearth. Janie's head snapped around at Nate's entrance, her face gentle and sorrowful; amid the greetings they shared a private understanding. He had just run a few errands, nothing more. And tonight he'd run a few more.

He quickly excused himself to the bedroom, the game raging at his back, Jason's booming voice drowning out the competition: *"It's a cat a cat with a wig dogs playing poker the Cat in the Hat chimney sweep CHIMNEY SWEEP!"*

Nate peeled off his clothes. His foot dragged across the bathroom tile, which did not bode well, and he had to take extra care stepping over the lip of the tub. In the shower he leaned his head into the stream as if trying to shove through it, warming his tendons and joints as a prophylactic measure against the strain to come. He spoke the mantra in his mind: *I can still feel* this. *My nerves still function. My muscles still work.*

After an appropriate delay, Janie appeared. He heard the door click, and she sat on the sink, and they shared in each other's company silently. After, he shaved, brushed his teeth, and dressed slowly, meticulously, Janie sitting on the quilt, knowing. He pushed buttons into place, threaded his belt, smoothed down his jeans over his socks, his hands trembling slightly but obeying.

The board game had broken up by the time they emerged. Jason and Cielle were out front on the porch swing, Nate's father cleaning dishes.

Nate found two cans of Campbell's tomato soup in a cupboard and cranked off the tops with a rusty opener. He cleaned the jagged circles of metal, dried them on the thigh of his jeans, and slipped them into his pocket. As he walked out, leaving the open cans full on the counter, his father just looked at him. Janie followed him to the front door, his father and Casper trailing.

Stepping onto the porch, Nate could feel his heart like a fist pressing up toward his throat. Jason picked quietly at his guitar, and Cielle sat sideways against one armrest, reading a vampire book, her feet wedged into him for warmth. Distracted.

Nate regarded her for a moment, the beat in his throat intensifying, then leaned over and kissed her on the forehead. A fine mist had come up, dappling the nodding leaves framing the porch. The Jeep waited, parked right off the steps. The sky grew darker by the second. He could feel the soup-can tops pressing into the meat of his thigh, and he thought of the brutal use he intended for them. Soon. Too soon.

"I'm gotta go take care of a few things," he said.

Jason looked up. "Want me to drive?"

The thing was, the kid was serious.

"If you run into Brobocop," Jason continued, "you might wish I was there."

"Right," Nate said. "Yellow belt, green stripe. Jeet Kune Do." Jason started to protest, and Nate held up a hand. "Kidding. I know, I know, tae kwon do. Chillax."

"Just sayin'. I got your back."

"I know, Jay," Nate said. "Thanks."

He brightened. "Jay," he repeated. "Right on."

Nate's father lingered near the Jeep, peering through the rear window. The barrel of an assault rifle poked up, barely in view. Nate saw the old man's posture wilt, his down-bent face loosening with realization, and something in his own chest gave way a little.

Cielle spread the book across her knee. "Where you going, Dad?"

Nate's father stepped in front of the window, blocking the rifle from her line of sight. Nate gave him a tiny nod of appreciation, and his father looked away, his mouth bunching.

Nate turned back to his daughter. "Just need to handle some business with the people who are after us."

"Like when you got all mad at those guys at the bank?"

"Oh, honey," he said, "I haven't gotten mad yet."

Her extraordinary brown eyes, set off by those long lashes, took his measure. "Is it gonna be okay?"

He remembered a trip they'd taken when she was four, their airplane shuddering over the Rockies. He'd been convinced they were going to drop out of the sky, but he'd told her it was all fine, that's just how airplanes flew sometimes, and she'd gone contentedly back to her coloring book while he and Janie had white-knuckled their armrests and braced for a plummet.

"Yeah." He smiled down at her. "It's gonna be okay."

Satisfied, she returned to her book.

Her take-it-for-granted faith in him was the most precious gift she could have given him.

He stepped from the porch into the mud, and his father came up off his lean on the Jeep. They regarded each other, his father's face shifting as he grappled whatever he was feeling back under control.

Nate said, "Dad, I want to tell you how much—"

"Don't you have somewhere to be?" He squeezed Nate's shoulder once, gently, then lowered his head mournfully and moved inside, the screen door banging after him.

Janie stood in the mud with Nate, before the Jeep. The mist had given over to a faint rain, her blond wisps turning dark at the points. Focusing to make sure his hand listened to what he was telling it, Nate put the key in the door.

"Bye, Dad!" Cielle called out from the porch swing. She waved, flashed a big smile, then went back to her book.

"I'm gonna tell her to come over," Janie said. "You should get to hug her at least—"

"No," he said. "This is perfect."

A few guitar chords vibrated the air around them, Jason working out the progressions of "Blackbird" on the porch behind them. Janie pressed her fist to her mouth, and her shoulders rose, but she was fighting everything down, not wanting Cielle to see. Nate lowered his hand to her as if asking her to dance.

She took it, her flesh cold and wet in the rain.

Water ran down her face, mixing with tears. The delicate lines of her collarbone, visible beneath her soaked T-shirt, rose and fell with her quick breaths. A smile tugged at her mouth but didn't quite take. "See ya around, Husband."

"Catch you on the other side, Wife."

She stepped into his kiss, and he gripped her narrow shoulders, raised and trembling against the cold. He savored the feel of her full lips and then pulled away, and they touched foreheads, the rain making them blink. Those translucent blue eyes. Her wide, lovely mouth. The sporadic band of freckles against her milk-white skin.

"I was drowning," he said, "and you saved me."

He tore himself away, climbed into the Jeep, and drove off, wiping at the wetness of his face. He didn't look back, because his self-control would not withstand another glimpse of her.

Around the bend he became aware of Casper galloping beside the Jeep, still favoring one front paw, and he skidded over in the slush and climbed out. He walked back, and they confronted each other in the road.

"Sit," he said, and the dog obeyed.

Nate put down his hand. "Shake."

Casper offered up a muddy paw.

Nate said, "Stay."

Casper's square head pulled back regally on his muscular neck. The yellow of his eyes shone through the brown, intelligent wrinkles furrowing his forehead, and it seemed in the way it has seemed for centuries between men and dogs that he understood precisely what was being said and what was not.

Casper withdrew his paw, let it drop to the wet earth.

Nate straightened up. "Good boy."

He kept the muddy smudge on his palm, not wanting to wipe it off. In the rearview he could still see Casper there, sitting in the down-slanting rain, watching him drive away.

Chapter 60

The grille of the Jeep pointed up the paved walk at Pavlo Shevchenko's front doors. A stretch of twenty or so feet, two drops of three concrete steps each, then the house itself, nestled into the hillside.

The engine ran, though Nate was not behind the wheel or even inside the vehicle. With an AR-15 assault rifle slung over his shoulder, a Glock 19 shoved into the band of his jeans, and a frag grenade wedged in his front pocket, he stood behind the open driver's door, holding in his hands a football-size hunk of fine-grained granite he'd pulled from Pavlo's own front yard.

Around the corner, parked under the protective cover of a neighbor's drooping sycamore, he had prepped everything. Danny Urban, with his militia-like sensibilities, had made Nate's job easier by acquiring gear familiar to an army grunt. Nate had wrapped two blocks of C4 with tape, adhered them above the gas tank, and sunk a military-issue M6 electric blasting cap into the white putty. Then it came down to junior-high physics, creating a simple circuit.

There was no leg wire in the duffel bag, an omission owed to Nate's haste in raiding the evidence locker. After pondering the dilemma, he'd removed one of the Jeep's rear speakers and stripped out several lengths of radio wire, which he'd connected to the blasting cap and the car battery before laying the two ends well apart on the ground before the front bumper. From his pocket he'd removed the two soup-can tops and taped one lead to each. When the jagged metal circles touched, they would complete the circuit and the Wrangler would go apocalyptic.

Now he needed a piece of paper to buffer the soup-can tops until contact. He searched the Jeep, finding nothing. No flyers, no CD jewel case from which to pull a cover. The service manual was long gone, his registration tattered and thin, and the proof-of-insurance slip too small to risk. How was it possible that there wasn't a single piece of sufficient paper in the vehicle? His concern mounted, edging on panic. He couldn't imagine coming all this way and having to deconstruct the bomb, drive down the hill, and go paper shopping.

A young father approached with his daughter, laughing and splashing through puddles in their rain boots. As they passed, the man stared at Nate curiously. The wires, C4, and duffel were not adequately indistinct even in the darkness. Nate forced a smile and said, "Engine trouble," and the pair hurried along.

Watching them leave, hand in hand, Nate felt a solution take shape. He reached for his back pocket, removing the two photographs. Cielle crouching beside her soccer ball, her grin punctuated by gaps. Janie laughing with him at their wedding. Closing his eyes, he kissed them each. Very carefully, he taped the soup-can tops around the pictures, sandwiching them, and adhered the makeshift pressure plate to the Jeep's grille. A collision of any force would tear the photographs and push the metal circles into contact.

He'd seen this make of car bomb a half dozen times at checkpoints in the Sandbox, and he knew what the aftermath looked like. Two point five pounds of explosives supersized by a half tank of gasoline should be enough to open Pavlo's front door.

Standing now at the end of the walk, his weakened arms straining under the weight of the granite, Nate said a silent prayer to Lady Luck and dropped the stone onto the gas pedal. The engine roared. Reaching across, he cranked on the radio, and Shithead Jason's AC/DC disc spun to life, Brian Johnson wailing from the remaining car speakers: *"—won't take no prisoners, won't spare no lives—"*

Below, the front door cracked open, Valerik poking his head out, the stub of his sleek ponytail wagging into view. The heel of his hand rode the stock of an AK-47. They were ready and waiting.

But not for this.

Nate yanked the gearshift into drive, and the Jeep rocketed away, knocking his arm.

Valerik's head reared back, the whites of his eyes pronounced, and the big door slammed shut.

The Jeep caught air off the first set of stairs, bounced off kilter, and hurtled toward the front door at a tilt,

Nate already walking behind, tugging on the sling, rotating the assault rifle into his hands.

"Gonna take you to—"

The explosion was expansive, the front door and surrounding wall obliterated, the front windows turned to shrapnel. Nate kept on through the blowback, heat and wind scorching his cheeks, his dropped left foot shushing across the concrete. The air stank of gasoline and burned metal. He sliced through a billowing wall of soot and drifted into the crumbled foyer, the Angel of Death. Cloaked in the swirling cloud, rubble loose underfoot, he listened for sounds of life.

A gurgle.

Squinting, he cut through the dense air and found Valerik slumped at the base of a blown-out wall. The blast overpressure had ruptured the air sacs in his lungs, thick dark soup pouring down his chin, drenching his collar. Nate pictured McGuire in his green-and-khaki ACUs, joking over a failed suicide bomber rustling and gagging on a dirt warehouse floor: *Looks like homeboy won the wet-T-shirt contest.*

Valerik burbled up at Nate.

"Hi there," Nate said.

Crouching over him, Nate pulled the pin from the grenade and nestled it under his body so the spoon held. He jogged a few steps into the powdered air, hid behind a burning cabinet, and waited.

Panicked voices, feet pounding a staircase, then creaking overhead. Pavlo, retreating to safety.

Nate was about to press on when he heard ragged

coughing coming from the kitchen, followed by hoarse cries. "Valerik? Valerik?"

Gun in hand, Dima jogged by, his form resolving briefly from the dust, though Nate couldn't risk stopping to aim and fire, not with his weakened left hand slowing his reaction time. He kept his back to the cabinet, the AR-15 at the ready. It was a low-end model—single-stage trigger, uncollapsible stock, and no floated barrel—and he reminded himself to use it calmly and carefully.

There came a moist choking as Valerik tried to warn his friend, and then a blast blew a tunnel of clear air through the foyer and partway down the hall. Shrapnel studded the cabinet and the adjoining wall. Nate heard Dima's body strike tile, then the sound of scrabbling limbs. He was up, moving; Valerik's body must have shielded some of the blast.

Nate pivoted out from behind the cabinet, fire licking at his sleeve, and headed toward the kitchen. Dima staggered away, a bobbing run, his silhouette framed by the lights sparkling through the floor-to-ceiling windows at the rear of the house. As Nate approached, Dima turned, broad chest flexing as he tried to lift the gun, and Nate stitched a line of bullets from groin to clavicle. Dima flew back against the blinds, knocking them flat, the bright skyline beyond disappearing. His body stood propped against the glass. Taking no chances, Nate unleashed a torrent of bullets into the standing corpse, the pane shattering, the blinds stretching to hold the body's weight and then ripping free. Dima tumbled through, vanishing into the abyss of the canyon, followed by a cascade of glass pebbles.

Nate released the mag, letting it clatter to the floor, and slammed in another with his quaking left hand. He was just starting to turn when it happened.

He felt the impact first, a sledgehammer swung into his shoulder blade, and he staggered forward, a bent knee barely supporting his weight. Ellipses of blood, his blood, sprayed the kitchen floor, giving off a pleasant shine. The sound of the gunshot registered vaguely, an afterthought. The AR-15 had flown from his body, sling and all, to spin at the kitchen's edge near the blown-out glass.

Nate pitched forward to the floor, bracing himself from total collapse with his one functional arm as Yuri approached from behind, chuckling. Nate could feel the handgun pressed into his belly, but his left hand was useless, his right bearing all his weight. If he dropped fully to the floor, freeing his good hand, Yuri would put a bullet through the back of his skull.

He closed his eyes, focusing through the throb in his shoulder. The Glock 19 in his waistband had no thumb safety, and the trigger pull was the same every time out. No extra double-action resistance at the front end. Which meant a quicker first shot.

Yuri said, "Now we can begin."

Nate whipped his right hand off the floor, his torso falling even as he grabbed for the gun at his waist. Through a miracle he hooked the handle properly, yanked, and twisted, squeezing off a shot before his bloodied shoulder struck the floor and sent a lightning bolt through his torso. The Glock bounced free as Yuri reeled back, one arm pinwheeling, and hit the floor. The big man's black guayabera grew even darker at his side, blood seeping through. Injured, handguns out of reach, they lay panting, staring at each other across the glass-strewn floor. The AR-15 still spun listlessly a few feet from them both by the window's edge, rasping quietly as it wound down.

Their stares pulled to the assault rifle. Back to each other.

They both scrambled for it, lunging and crawling. Four hands grabbed the barrel simultaneously. Not letting go, Nate pivoted, kicking Yuri, who slid to the edge, his movement slicked by the round pebbles of glass rolling beneath him. Yuri's grip firmed on the AR-15, and then one leg went over the brink, the weight tugging at him. His eyes widened in that swollen face. His other leg poured over the brink, then his hips, and then he grunted and sank into the open air, pulling Nate with him, the two men bound by their death lock on the assault rifle. Nate was dragged toward the edge, the tips of his shoes scraping across the tile, and he was just about to let go when they reached some magical equilibrium of friction and muscle and halted. His head and arms dangled over the lip. His left shoulder screamed in agony. Broken glass bit into his chest. But he kept his grip. The assault rifle was completely vertical, aimed straight down off the ledge.

Hanging on with bloodless hands, Yuri swayed back and forth, bucking and yelping, the canyon falling away beneath his feet. Then he stilled, realizing suddenly which end of the assault rifle he'd wound up with.

The wrong end.

Nate slipped his finger through the trigger guard. Yuri stared helplessly straight up into the bore, inches from his eyes, and, adjusting his grip, Nate discharged the assault rifle through the other man's head.

As Yuri plummeted, Nate jerked away painfully from the edge. He grabbed the Glock, stuffed it back into his waistband. It took a full minute for him to get up onto his feet, but then he was limping toward the stairs, leading with the AR-15. His weak left arm, further compromised by the gunshot at the shoulder, could do little more than prop up the barrel.

As he came up onto the concrete plain of the second floor, the vast open space with its walls of windows caught Nate off guard. Minimal cover. In fact, aside from a giant mattress with heaped sheets, several pillars, and a floating staircase, the great room was bare. Not a sign of Pavlo or Misha.

The staircase led to a hatch thrown open to the night air. Had they already escaped to the roof?

Nate made a snap decision to clear the floor before moving on. Breathing hard, he hurried behind the first pillar. Moonlight tumbled through the huge skylight, laying a distorted block across the concrete. Motes swam in the shaft of faint light. Every direction was pale, silver, gray, the red silk sheets on the mattress providing the only splotch of color. The walls of glass and evenly spaced pillars created a hall-of-mirrors effect.

The strain of holding Yuri's body for all that time

had cost him, his right arm, too, now weak and tingling. He waited, listening. Was that the faint sound of breathing he heard off the concrete and glass? Someone else's or his own, thrown back at him?

The pillars were broad, industrial; Pavlo could even be hiding on the opposite side of the very one Nate had shouldered into. Bracing himself, he pivoted around the corner and then the next, keeping an eye out for movement behind the other pillars as well. His left foot dragging, his shoulder complaining with every jolt, he broke cover, running to the next pillar. He made the same painful progress around it. When he sprinted for the third, he heard footsteps somewhere else in the room, echoes disguising the source. Gunshots blew out the windows behind him, and he arrived at the far pillar, panting, the fresh draft chilling the sweat on his face.

"I'm here, Pavlo," he called out.

No response.

The AR-15 rattled in his grip. Blood streaked down his left arm, dripping off the elbow. Each limb, skewered by pinpricks. He looked down at his fingers, willing them to hold on. A spate of light-headedness came on in a fury, then departed just as abruptly.

He risked a glance across the enormous space. Three equidistant pillars marked the long stretch of the opposing wall as well. The glow of the moon through the skylight cast ghostly reflections off some of the windows. Peering out, he studied the glass behind the far pillars for mirrored images, finally spotting a shard of a figure, barely visible given the angle. Narrow build, cap of blond hair, gun held in both hands, pointing at the floor.

Misha.

Which meant Pavlo was on the roof.

With the blood loss and the state of his muscles, Nate wouldn't have much time before he was too weak to be useful. Quietly, he withdrew the light Glock from his waistband. The AR-15 slipped in his left hand, almost clattering to the concrete; he'd have to do everything with his right. He set the Glock silently on the floor beyond the pillar, the handle positioned for a quick grab. Then he switched the assault rifle to his right hand. Easing from behind the pillar, he knelt in a shooter's position. Using his remaining strength, he tossed the assault rifle to the side of the pillar.

Before the gun reached the peak of its trajectory, he snatched up the Glock, doing his best to steady the pistol in his right hand. Insensate as a slab of meat, his left hand pressed to the base of the handle, propping it up. Static fuzzed his vision, and he blinked it away, and then everything went down in three quick claps.

The assault rifle striking the floor.

Misha darting from behind the pillar, firing at the blank air above the rifle.

And Nate squeezing the trigger.

Misha spun, a spray of blood painting the window behind him, then struck the floor, half concealed by the pillar, his shoes twitching.

Grunting, Nate started across, each step a fresh agony. His limbs felt so weak that it seemed he was moving himself with his core, dragging his feet along with his stomach muscles. The cold air of the room smelled of spicy cologne. He passed the mattress, rotating the gun barrel from Misha's feet to the square of black sky atop the floating staircase.

Step, pause. Step, pause. Keep moving.

To his left he heard a whisper of fabric, and, too late, he realized.

He flung himself away, landing on his back and firing as Pavlo reared up from the mattress, a silk sheet fluttering behind him like a cape. The room exploded with gunfire, each crack amplified, each muzzle flare multiplied off the walls of facing glass. Concrete chipped near Nate's face, flecks biting into his cheek, and he saw two holes open up in the still-descending sheet behind Pavlo, everything miraculously missing until a bullet slammed into Nate's side. The howl issuing from his lips was little more than a heated rush of air.

The old man leaped from the mattress onto the floating staircase and bounced toward the laid-open hatch, lunging two, three steps at a time. On his back, Nate aimed the trembling pistol and squeezed off one shot after another, the sparks catching up to the man until a round finally caught his calf just before it pulled up out of sight.

Pavlo's body thumped down on the roof, unseen. Not so much as a yelp. An instant of silence.

Then a scraping.

Nate looked down at his side. A quarter-size hole, leaking ink. He reached behind, found the exit wound. Through and through.

Rolling to all fours, he forced himself to his feet. The only way he could walk was in a half shuffle, tugging one leg along. His right hand held the gun, so he tried to clamp the wound with his left but could apply virtually no pressure at all. He mounted the stairs, drizzling blood in a neat line at his feet.

His vision spotted, his legs growing wobbly beneath him. He pictured Cielle with her coloring book on that airplane, bouncing over the Rockies.

Is it gonna be okay?

Yeah. It's gonna be okay.

Climbing the stairs took such focus that he barely noticed when his head pulled up into the sight line. A flash of light and a bullet wavered the air inches from his temple, the bark of the gun coming on a split-second delay. Across the roof Pavlo backed up, tender on his wounded leg, readying for a second shot.

Nate lifted the gun as far as his strength allowed and fired. A bullet embedded in Pavlo's thigh, tearing his pants, revealing the tattooed star on his kneecap. Pavlo's gun clattered to the rooftop, sliding to the edge and then off, and he clenched his jaw and took a few hobbling steps toward Nate, his sinewy face contorting with rage.

"I will not kneel to you."

Nate's next shot shattered his hip. Pavlo jerked ninety degrees, red mist puffing from his waist. He wobbled on his feet, then squared himself again, screaming, tendons standing out on his blue-inked neck.

"I will not—"

Hand shaking around the Glock, Nate shot out his ankle.

Pavlo collapsed onto the roof, his knees striking hard, jolting him before he fell flat onto his stomach. Then he started dragging himself away, elbow over elbow, toward the brink of the roof. Nate started after him.

The staggering openness and panoramic view snatched the breath from his lungs, and he paused for a drunken instant to regain his balance. It seemed he was standing on top of the entire city. Los Angeles unfurled below, a bejeweled blanket. The digital billboards and flashing club signs, green stoplights and stalled cars, all the stop-go, all that hot-cold, all those souls floating through the streets on gleaming rims, walking the corners on patched-up pumps, clogging the alleys gripping brown-bagged bottles. Everything was flayed open and laid bare, the gonna-bes and winged dreamers, the glittering lights coursing block to block, the blood of the city. Here Nate had soared and crashed. And here he had salvaged from the wreckage the slivers worth keeping, had pieced them together with trembling hands to form something better, something true.

The taste of the night air was oddly pleasing, wild fennel and sage of the canyon mixed with ash from the explosion. His blood felt warm against his skin and then quickly cold. He sent a signal to his legs, and a moment later they started moving again.

On his belly ahead, Pavlo grunted and scraped, grunted and scraped. Walking across the wide skylight, Nate left footprints of blood. He'd just reached the other side when a voice said, "Stop."

Nate halted, gun lowered, shoulders slumping, his

inhalations coming in weak rasps. For a moment he just breathed, and he heard Misha breathing behind him, too, waiting for a single wrong move.

Slowly, Nate turned. Misha stood on the skylight, aiming directly at his forehead. Nate's Glock remained at his side in his all-but-dead right hand; he couldn't raise it if he tried. Misha's boyish face looked smooth and innocent in the pale light. Blood gleamed on one of his hands, a pinkie finger sticking out at the wrong angle, but that didn't stop him from keeping the sights dead level.

"Did you really think you could do it?" Reluctant admiration found its way into Misha's voice. With his damaged hand, he reached slowly for a pocket, pulling out a pair of matte-black handcuffs. The pinkie, bent perpendicular to the back of his hand, looked like a snapped twig. "Even if you killed us all, a man such as Pavlo Shevchenko makes one phone call and ten more of us get on a boat in Kiev. And if you kill all *them,* he snaps his fingers and twenty more come to fill *their* place."

Nate's gun hand twitched, and Misha's eyes dropped to it. A single threatening movement and it was over.

Nate said, "Then I guess I'll have to kill him, too."

Misha's rosy lips pressed together. Amused. "You cannot even raise your hand."

Nate said, "Don't have to," and fired down into the skylight.

The center of the thick pane gave way, Misha lurching back, his arms flaring as his gun discharged, and then he dropped down into the break, fangs of glass biting into him. Sinking to his torso, he lunged to hold on, the handcuffs flying from his grip and skittering across the rooftop. He managed to clutch the crumbling edge, his fingertips sliding on the intact ledges of glass.

The points had raked through his body on its way down, one shard buried between his ribs. A tiny spurt of bright arterial blood splashed against the pane. As soon as the dagger of glass stopped damming that wound, he was done.

He stared at the tip of Nate's shoe. "A hand," he sputtered. His fingers slid another millimeter, leaving four streaks on the glass.

Nate raised his shoe, put it on Misha's shoulder, and sank him through the shattered skylight. Misha landed in the block of moonlight, his limbs twisted this way and that, glass tinkling on the concrete floor around him.

Nate swayed on his feet, summoning strength, the wound in his side drooling. He'd lost a lot of blood.

Behind him he could hear Pavlo grunting, still dragging himself away. The breeze carried the sound of sirens. Down at the base of the hill, flashing lights turned off Laurel Canyon. Winding their way up, they swept around a bend, vanishing for the moment.

Nate forced his body to turn, to walk. He caught up to Pavlo a few yards before the precipice. Despite his decimated lower body, Pavlo had reached a vent pipe and was prying at it, powerful forearm muscles flexing beneath their tattoo wrappings. Remarkably, he'd made some progress, the pipe rattling a bit in the flashing. His movements had slowed, but he was still at it, and Nate realized that he would stay at it until he tore free a weapon, pulled himself back to Nate, and staved in his head. Most shocking was how *unfazed* Pavlo seemed by it all—the still-smoldering house, his fragmented legs, the executioner stalking him across the roof. He grunted and tugged, his inked fingers relentless around the pipe, every last ounce of strength bent to dragging himself one inch closer to violence.

Standing over him, Nate aimed down at the back of his neck and pulled the trigger.

.The Glock gave a muted snap. No more rounds.

Pavlo never looked up, never stopped tugging at the pipe, but he registered the sound and gave a rasping chuckle. "You think this is pain?" he said, panting, the roof pressed to his mouth, muffling his words. He released a few notes of laughter, sweat shining on his cheek, the nape of his neck.

Nate grabbed the back of his shirt and dragged him across the roof, Pavlo's hands scrabbling for traction, his feet dragging limply. Nate's grip gave out just at the edge. A few hundred feet below, the canyon finally bottomed out in a seam of boulders and jagged rocks.

Pavlo's legs were a mess, streaming blood, one foot twisted around on the ankle. He couldn't rise or run, but he clawed his way up Nate's body, tearing at his shirt, grabbing his shoulders, bringing his face close. The warble of sirens grew clearer.

Mustering one last burst of energy, Nate braced himself to hurl Pavlo from the roof.

There was a click between the men's bodies, and Pavlo grinned maniacally up into Nate's face. A victorious leer. Nate glanced down.

Pavlo had gotten Misha's handcuffs and locked one cuff around his own wrist.

And the other around Nate's.

"Now if you throw me, I take you with me," Pavlo hissed.

The breeze came up, whipping Nate's hair, carrying the earthy scent of the canyon and soot from the dwindling fire on the first floor. He turned his head, regarding the drop. Way down at the bottom, spotlit by a preternatural throw of moonlight, Charles stood atop one of the boulders, the breeze lifting his hair and sucking the smoke from his decimated torso. He gazed up. Waiting.

"You actually gonna help this time," Nate asked, "or just stand there looking dead?"

"Help?" Charles said. "This is all you." Even across the ember-flecked distance, the words were clear as day in Nate's head. "It's *always* been just you."

Nate felt something that had been gripping his insides release, something so long forgotten that he knew it now only from its absence. Charles's stomach began to fill in, the edges of the wound stitching together, and the dried blood on his face and hands moistened and flowed backward, sucked into his body like a horror movie on rewind. Charles touched his intact stomach in wonderment. Then he looked up at Nate again and grinned.

"'Bout fuckin' time," he said.

Pavlo sputtered and clutched at Nate, forcing his focus back to the roof and the steel rings enclosing their wrists, joining them. The weight of the man hanging on him, the muscles glistening with sweat, blood, and ink. One step to the left, the plummet.

Nate felt the grainy night take itself apart, pixel by pixel, and reconstitute itself. He thought about Janie's body surrendering to him in the riptide. Wheeling her out of the maternity ward with that pink bundle in her lap. Cielle's saving up at the car wash to try to pay for private school. His million-dollar life-insurance policy. Sitting on the bridge above that stream, his daughter's head resting against his shoulder. Janie's mouth at his collarbone, her ankles crossed at the small of his back. Their house with the loose brick of the front porch mortared into place again. The family portrait hidden in the depths of Cielle's closet, waiting.

Pavlo held on with all his strength. He looked into Nate and must not have liked what he saw, for his grin ossified on his face, a skeletal grimace.

Nate tugged his wrist back, testing the strength of the handcuffs.

Then he gave the faintest of smiles.

WHAT WAS FOUND

Funny how fallin' feels like flyin'
For a little while.

—Otis "Bad" Blake

Shevchenko, Pavlo Maksimovich
? – November 2

Overbay, Nathan John

AUGUST 10, 1976 – NOVEMBER 2

NATHAN JOHN OVERBAY DIED FRIDAY OF INJURIES SUSTAINED IN A FALL. ON OCTOBER 23, NATE PLAYED A HEROIC ROLE IN THWARTING A ROBBERY AT THE FIRST UNION BANK OF SOUTHERN CALIFORNIA, LIKELY SAVING MANY LIVES IN THE PROCESS. THE AFTERMATH OF THAT EVENT FOUND HIM TARGETED BY THE CRIMINALS BEHIND THE FAILED HEIST. A STATEMENT RELEASED BY THE LOS ANGELES DISTRICT ATTORNEY'S OFFICE CREDITS NATE'S COURAGEOUS ACTIONS WITH LEADING INVESTI-GATORS TO A CACHE OF INCRIMINATING EVIDENCE THAT HELPED BREAK UP THE CRIMINAL RING.

BORN AND RAISED IN LOS ANGELES, NATE ATTENDED UCLA ON AN ROTC SCHOLARSHIP BEFORE SERVING IN THE U.S. ARMY. UPON COMPLETION OF MILITARY SERVICE, NATE BECAME A PROFESSIONAL CRISIS RESPONDER WITH LAPD, WHERE HE WAS HIGHLY REGARDED BY HIS COLLEAGUES FOR HIS EMPATHY AND COMMITMENT.

HE IS SURVIVED BY HIS FATHER, HIS LOVING WIFE, JANE, AND HIS DAUGHTER, CIELLE.

Epilogue

Morning light suffused the kitchen, bleaching the walls, buffing the counter to a high shine and lending the room a bright afterworld tint. Wearing the pressed blouse and plaid skirt of her private-school uniform, Cielle perched on one of the barstools, spooning oatmeal into her mouth and staring thoughtfully through the wide doorway into the living room. Above the mantel the old family portrait hung at a minor tilt. She and Janie had restored it to its rightful place the previous night in a quiet impromptu ceremony. There had been no words, just the two of them working in concert to balance on the stool, lift the heavy frame, and guide the hanging wire home.

Afterward they'd stood for a time gazing up, holding hands.

Now Cielle breathed the morning quiet and ate her breakfast. Her face was as pretty as ever, and full, though not as full as it had been.

Footfalls descended the stairs, and then Janie emerged, rubbing one eye with the heel of her hand and stifling a yawn. Passing behind Cielle, she gave her daughter's neck an affectionate squeeze, and Cielle caught her hand and clasped it. Janie paused, followed Cielle's stare across to the portrait, and they took a collective moment. The three of them preserved in a crisp photograph, cracking up, the frame still slightly askew.

Janie started up the coffeemaker, leaning over it on locked arms as it percolated, and then she filled her mug and sipped, her eyes wistful. Cielle finished her breakfast, washed the bowl in the sink, and they headed together for the garage. The door closed behind them.

A moment later it opened again.

Cielle came back in, crossed to the living room, and, lifting a solitary finger, straightened the family portrait. She studied it a moment, her features heavy with remembrance, and then a private memory flickered beneath the surface, firming her cheeks, bringing up an incipient smile. She jogged back out, lighter on her feet.

The door swung shut.

The sun lifted above the east-facing windows, softening the quality of light.

The house sat at peace.

Acknowledgments

As always, I consulted a number of experts in the course of writing this book, and I'd like to thank them for their time, support, and impressive brain power. Lauren Crais, for matters legal and prosecutorial. Melissa Hurwitz, M.D., and Bret Nelson, M.D., for matters medical. Philip Eisner and Maureen Sugden, for matters editorial. Greg Muradov, for introducing me to the culinary inclinations of our antagonists. Dana Kaye, my tireless publicist, who applied an even temperament and a dogged spirit throughout. Joseph Flueckiger, Omar Valdemar, and Alan Hill, security professionals who took me through the gritty realities of bank robberies. Scot Spooner, Green Beret and former member of the U.S. Army Special Operations Command, who helped me rig up a nasty IED. Chris Brenes, former lieutenant at SEAL Team One, who painted a picture and walked me inside it. It almost goes without saying that all errors in the book are mine alone.

Gratitude must also be extended to my attorneys, Stephen F. Breimer and Marc H. Glick, as well as to

Rich Green at CAA and my team at Aaron Priest. I am thankful daily for my editor, Keith Kahla, and the rest of the folks at St. Martin's, including publisher Sally Richardson and Matthew Baldacci, Loren Jaggers, Matthew Shear, and Martin Quinn. My UK publisher has done a spectacular job on my behalf—many thanks to Daniel Mallory, David Shelley, and the others at Sphere who have worked so hard.

A final tip of the hat to Delinah Raya, there for me in countless ways with a tranquil outlook and an irrepressible smile.

Read on for an excerpt
from Gregg Hurwitz's next book

TELL NO LIES

Available in hardcover from St. Martin's Press

The ridiculous thread count made the new sheets feel like warm butter, which is why Daniel had been luxuriating in them since the faux church bells of his alarm had chimed five minutes earlier. Forcing himself fully awake, he rolled to his side and watched his sleeping wife. Cristina lay on her back, dark tresses falling across her face, one arm flung wide, the other curled overhead like *Venus at Her Bath*. Smooth brown skin, bowed eyelashes, that broad mouth, always ready with a smile or a wisecrack. Her pajama top was unbuttoned to her cleavage, revealing three blue pinpoint tattoos on her sternum: the radiation therapist's alignment marks, finally starting to fade.

For whatever reason this morning, the familiar sight of those three dots caught him off guard, a first-thing splash of emotion in the face. Cristina used to talk about getting them lasered off—it *had* been five years since they'd served their purpose—but over time she'd taken a shine to them. Her war paint.

Just like that he was back in the swampy memory of

it. How she'd wake up breathless in the middle of the night, her heart racing, unable to draw a full breath. The bouts of nausea that kept her tethered to the couch for hours at a time, her athletic body softening. The doctor's appointment always a week away, rescheduled for this reason or that. And then the incident at the fund-raiser, Cristina in a pale tile bathroom, coughing until her white sundress was speckled with bright blood, her wounded elegance calling to mind a pellet-shot dove. He'd cleaned her up with trembling hands as she leaned over the sink, weak-kneed and faint, and she'd said, "We're at an age now that when people get sick, it doesn't mean they have the flu."

Their relationship up until then had accelerated without brakes. They'd fallen into each other with an instant intimacy, laughing about the right things and serious about the rest. He'd met her in front of a painting at SFMOMA. They'd found themselves side by side, admiring the same piece. She'd gotten him talking, and Daniel had mentioned how his mother loved Lautrec and how he'd been drawn to the bright, bold colors of the dancing ladies even at a young age. He was going on a bit about the Frenchman's debt to Japanese wood-cuts when Cris bit her lip thoughtfully, cocking her head to take in the row of paintings on the wall. "You can see how left out he felt," she said, and Daniel was brought up short with admiration.

Was it love at first conversation? Who could say? But after the drinks that followed their dinner, which followed their walk, which followed their spontaneous lunch in the museum's café, Daniel did know one thing:

She was the first good reason he'd had to want to live forever.

And now, half a decade later, his feelings were undiminished. At the cusp of forty, and still he got a heady schoolboy rush watching her twist her dripping hair up into a towel or sing under her breath while chopping cilantro or gather her pantyhose around her thumbs as she poised a foot for entry.

He set his hand gently on the slope of her upper chest over the three dots, feeling for her heartbeat. There. And there. And there.

She stirred, those lashes parting to show her rich brown eyes. She smiled, and then her gaze pulled south, taking in his flat hand pressed to her chest. A puzzled furrow of the brow as she frowned down. "What are you feeling?" she asked.

"Gratitude," he said.

Daniel ran the steep slopes of Pacific Heights with the same intensity with which he'd tackled them as a high-school wrestler trying to make weight, except now with the complaints of a thirty-nine-year-old body mediating the pace. Someone had once remarked that when you got tired of walking around San Francisco, you could always lean against it. He felt like leaning now. Instead he loped along Vallejo to the edge of the Presidio and jogged the regal Lyon Street Steps, lined with meticulously planted gardens and cast in the shadows of towering trees. He passed a cluster of teenagers up from the night before, smoking their cigarettes and practicing their pouts, and a few early-morning boot-campers he recognized, traders and i-bankers out to break a sweat before the market opened.

Ahead a younger man with rock-hard calves and tapered lats bounded up the steps, and Daniel dared himself to catch up. The stairs blurred underfoot, his muscles straining, taking two at a time, driving into the face of the challenge, and then it was no longer leisure but something more. The age-old urge fired his belly.

Be faster. Be stronger. Be *better*.

Whistling past the guy, he kept on, legs burning, breath scouring his throat, the hill like a wall stretching up and up. But he wouldn't stop, wouldn't slow, not even after the man's footsteps receded into memory. It was never about the man, of course, or this challenge on this day. It was about appeasing the chorus of voices in his head, the ones that had always told him that if he ever wanted a life he could call his own, he'd have to fight his way to it.

Sweat falls from Daniel's locks, dotting the wrestling mat at his feet. The gymnasium is packed, ridiculous for a junior-high meet, but it is that kind of school and these are those kinds of parents. The headgear's strap digs into his chin, and he tastes salt from where he nearly put his tooth through his lip on the last take-down. But he'd completed the move and gotten near-fall points to boot. If he has one thing going for him, it is that he won't allow pain to be a deterrent. His shaggy-haired, pale-skinned opponent is more developed, with real biceps, but even at age twelve Daniel fights as if his life is on the line, as if he is trying to escape from somewhere. He is winning 5–2 with less than a minute on the clock.

They circle each other warily. The kid takes a few open-hand swipes at Daniel's head, but they're half-hearted. His bowed shoulders and weary eyes show that he has already conceded the meet. But Daniel doesn't want to win like this. He wants to clash until the bell. He wants to hear the definitive slap of the referee's hand against the mat, announcing the pin, showing that he didn't back down from a challenge by coasting to the finish line.

A whistle halts the action—the kid's laces are un-tied. Daniel bounces on his toes to keep loose, his slender frame jiggling. Someone has the bright idea to enhance the time-out by blaring Kenny Loggins's "Danger Zone" through the antiquated speakers.

As the boy crouches to adjust his shoes, Daniel turns to take in the bleachers. There's his mother up in the stands, out of place among all those sweatshirts and done-up soccer-mom faces, her fingers doing an impatient caterpillar crawl along the sleeve of her fur coat, itching for a cigarette. Severe lipstick. Her pulse beating in the paper-thin skin at her temple. She notes his gaze, but her expression does not change, and he knows that her dead-even stare has everything to do with why winning by points is not enough.

The match goes live again, and they circle and slap, the other kid shuffling, exhausted. Their shoes chirp against the mat. The smell of rubber and sweat fills Daniel's nostrils. He watches the kid's legs, the angle of the feet, the bend of his knee. They shuffle-step some more. The clock ticks down, and then—there—he sees his opening. He lunges in for the fireman's carry, but his sole skids on an invisible puddle of sweat and then he is off balance, flipped on his shoulders, and the bigger kid is lying across him. Daniel bucks and flails but cannot wriggle free. Sooner than seems plausible, the referee's palm strikes the mat near his face and it is over.

In the locker-room shower, he replays the moment, except this time he doesn't slip—he hoists his larger opponent in the fireman's carry and dumps him on his back, and the crowd roars, and there's his mother, on her feet, cheering, her face lit with triumph.

He exits the building, his hair still damp. The sky is San Francisco slate, overcast and gloomy, and the air bites at him through the slacks and thin sweater of his school uniform. His mother waits, leaning against the car, her arms crossed against the cold, wearing an expression of disgust. No, not disgust—concealed rage.

"You had him on points," she says. "You just had to run the clock."

"I know," Daniel says.

"You could have had the medal."

"I know."

Evelyn's gloved hands light a slender cigarette, lift it to her bloodred lips. "You make things hard on yourself."

Daniel averts his gaze. In the car, behind the wheel, James is little more than a hat and a shadow. He stares straight ahead. This is not his business, and he has a paycheck to earn.

Daniel says, "I know."

Evelyn shoots a disciplined stream of smoke into the darkening evening and opens the rear door to climb in. Daniel takes a step forward, but she halts midway into the car and turns back to him.

"Losers walk," she says.

The door closes neatly behind her, and the car purrs up the street.

Daniel watches until it disappears. Blowing into his cupped hands, he begins the long walk home.

Pausing at the top of the Lyon Street Steps, panting, Daniel turned and looked back. Far below, the younger man he'd blown past struggled up the final leg of his run. Daniel took a few seconds to catch his breath, the raised sweatshirt hood damp around his head, eucalyptus clearing his lungs, stinging his nostrils. The summit afforded a view across the vast forest of the Presidio toward Sea Cliff, where Evelyn presided over her estate, looking down on the city.

He took the stairs hard back down and ran for home, dodging curbside recycling barrels. Victorian mansions alternated with Mission Revivals and the occasional Chateau, the gleaming façades making clearer than ever how Pacific Heights earned its nicknames—either the "Gold Coast" or "Specific Whites," depending on which demographic was weighing in.

Daniel and Cristina's place, though several blocks downsized from Billionaires' Row, was still stunning. Average-sized by the standards of any reasonable town, the midcentury house was a narrow three-story rise of concrete and dark wood with a square patch of front lawn, shoulder-width alleys on either side, and a match-book courtyard framing a black-pebble fire pit in the back.

Daniel entered, tossing his keys onto the accent table beside the miniature Zen garden with its white sand groomed into hypnotic patterns. Up the stairs to the wide-open second story, the view making its grand entrance through the floor-to-ceiling steel-framed windows in a fashion that—still—made his breath hitch. Backdropping the kitchen, a cascading vista down the hill to the Bay, the Golden Gate forging magnificently into the craggy headlands of Marin, Angel Island floating in an ice-cream haze of fog. And on the other side, beyond the little sitting area they called a living room, a panorama captured the dip of Fillmore and the Haight and the houses beyond popping up like pastel dominoes, forming a textured rise to the one visible Twin Peak. Sutro Tower loomed over it all, sticking out of the earth like a giant tuning fork.

He climbed to their bedroom on the third floor. Red pen clenched between her teeth, Cris was proofreading a printout and wriggling into a pair of jeans at the same time. Her eyeglasses were shoved atop her head, forgotten.

"Your op-ed?" he asked.

She nodded, distracted, not looking up.

"It was great two drafts ago."

"It has to be *better* than great. It has to be a brimstone avalanche of influence that convinces the planning commission that it is not worth their political while to displace sixty low-income families so their cronies can build faux-Italian town houses."

Cristina's job as a community organizer for non-profit tenants' societies had grown harder each year since the aggressive gentrification of the dot-com era. The hot-dotters had taken over vacant lots and home-less squats, pressing out each fold and wrinkle of the city like an expanding waistline. Now the trendy res-taurants and bars of the Divisadero were creeping into Western Addition, and developers were picking off build-ings not officially designated as projects and protected with federal subsidies. Including the sixty-unit apartment complex Cris was currently fighting to preserve.

She scribbled at the sheet. "They bought off the ass-hole landlord, who's helping drive the tenants out. No repairs, nothing. There's a family of six in there that's had a broken toilet for a month, so they have to use the neighbors'. Two black drag queens. You can imagine how *that's* working out. There are elderly couples with nowhere to go. I had a single mom in yesterday, crying, won't be able to afford to live in her own neighbor-hood. A five-generation Chinese-Filipino family on the third floor—"

"*Five* generations?"

"There's a great-great-aunt in there somewhere."

"Maybe the cupboard."

Her face lightened. For an instant. "This is boring."

"Not even a little."

She slashed out another paragraph. "I have two vol-unteers and a college intern. We spend six months organizing through churches and schools to get thirty thousand signatures, and then some *associate*"—she spit the word—"bundles two hundred grand in contributions to the right city supervisor and tilts the whole goddamned seesaw the other way."

Her accent edged into her words when she was mad. She sank onto the bed, chewing through the cap of the red pen. Having grown up in a similar apartment building in the Mission, she took her job personally.

"The power brokers," she said. "They matter more than we do."

"Don't say that," he told her.

She looked at him evenly, not a trace of self-pity in her eyes. "But it's true."

———

"Daniel Brasher, don't you run away from me!"

Session had ended, and the members finished filing out, mixing with a group of sullen teens from the juvie group up the hall. Daniel turned with a smile as Kendra Richardson, a mountain of a woman, ambled up the corridor after him, bracelets jangling about her wrists. The corridor emptied out, doors banging, elevator dinging, leaving them alone with the faint hiss of the heating vents.

Setting his satchel briefcase at his feet, he gave his program director a hug, disappearing into that delightful blend of Ed Hardy perfume and cinnamon gum.

"Did you sign your termination agreement?" she

asked. Then, off his blank expression, "Look, baby, I'm happy if you *don't*."

"What termination agreement?"

"The one that went out to you last month."

"Went out to me where?"

She drew back her head. "Where you think? Your work box, here."

"You mean they *haven't* been forwarding my mail to my house?"

She fluttered a hand at him. "That whole mess again? Remind me the problem?"

They'd been over it half a dozen times. The mail room in the bowels of the building had never been upgraded, the employee boxes no more than a bank of creaky wooden cubbyholes, each with a sedimentary layering of brittle, flaking labels—the remnants of workers past. Daniel had landed a box near the top, just beneath the outgoing-mail cubby, which was labeled OUTG IN MAIL. Which meant that folks accidentally shoved their mail into his box all the time. Which in turn had led him to make multiple requests that all his mail be forwarded to his house so he'd no longer have to sort through his colleagues' mail or the painstakingly addressed letters of various parolees just to get the occasional departmental notice. Kendra's administrative assistant was supposed to check his box to make sure everything was being appropriately routed, though she rarely showed interest in tasks aside from applying makeup and conducting cell-phone conversations at high volume.

"The problem is," he said, "that the only mail I get here is other people's."

"We'll get it straightened out. Just in time for you to head off to your fancy-pants private practice and forget all about us." She flipped her chin sharply away in mock offense. Kendra ran the perennially understaffed department like a benevolent matriarchy; affection and guilt were rarely in short supply.

He said, "First of all, I could *never* forget the woman who gave me my first break in the field"—a slight softening of her rigid neck—"and second, I'm still here another couple of months. Don't go writing my obituary yet."

He'd been steadily downsizing his workload so it would be a smooth transition for the program when he left. At one time he'd been juggling four groups, but he'd concluded three as the members graduated out. Kendra had begged him to stay on with this last group, though they'd need to phase in another therapist to see the members to the finish line. He'd have to tell them soon that he was leaving, give them time to adjust.

After promising Kendra that he'd dig out his termination agreement, he found the back stairs and descended to the mail room. He checked his watch; the hallway chat had put him behind for his already late-night dinner with Cristina, so he quickened his pace. The lights were on motion sensors to save money for the city, the corridors illuminating in swaths as he hurried forward. Sure enough, his mail cubby was stuffed with mail, so he stretched his satchel briefcase open and raked the envelopes in. He'd sort them out at home, bring back what wasn't his on Wednesday.

Sliding out a last stack of mail, he caught a splinter in his knuckle, and then the lights went out on him. He leaned back, balancing the briefcase on one knee and waving a hand to catch the sensor. He had to laugh a bit at himself. What a contrast with the new office suite he was checking out in the morning. Sleek marble and plush carpet and electricity that stayed on when you flipped the switch. After three years of blood and sweat, heartache and small triumphs, maybe he was finally ready to make it easy on himself.

He reset the burglar alarm behind him and headed up the stairs, which gleamed with Lemon Pledge—Cris's doing. Now and then they'd hire a cleaning lady, but every time they brought in someone regular, Cris would wind up tidying the place beforehand, making the woman lunch, and advising her son about college loans. Quickly, the convenience turned into a second job. She laughed about it—what a joke, you hear the one about the overzealous Pacific Heights housewife?—but at the end of the day, she preferred that the Brashers clean their own damn house.

She waited upstairs at the kitchen island, sitting over a glass of wine and a sliced loaf of Boudin sourdough, her hair up so a fan of caramel skin showed at her back collar. She turned at his footsteps, chin to shoulder. "Chicken reheating in the oven, *mi vida.* Five minutes."

He drew near, kissed her between the shoulder blades. "How was your day?"

Her head shook ever so slightly, and then she gave a faint sniffle. The heel of her hand rose to her cheek, and a spot of wet tapped the glossy photo on the counter in front of her. A birth announcement from a childhood friend. It showed a newborn swaddled in a blue hospital blanket, eyes no more than seams in a wrinkled face.

Daniel slid beside Cris, put his arms around both shoulders, and kissed her head as she wiped at her tears.

"Wow," she said. "Talk about self-centered. I should just be happy for them. I *am* happy for them, but I should *just* be."

He adopted his best commercial voice-over tone. *"Guilt: When feeling bad's not enough."*

She laughed a little, hit his arm gently. "Okay, okay. You know what'll make me feel better? Sending a gift." She reached for her silver laptop, across by the prep sink. "Babyregister-dot-com. I'm sure they have my credit card on file by now."

He waited, watching her.

"I'm okay." She kissed him, a peck pushing his face away. "I'm fine. Two minutes. Chicken."

He walked over to the living-room couch and dumped out his briefcase on the glass coffee table. Flyers and envelopes and junk mail. Sifting through the mess, he searched for the form—no, the "termination agreement." Who named these things? Last week he'd been stuck on hold with a "listening-care associate," which was enough to make him want to—

Finally. A clasp envelope in the distinctive gray of the department.

The timer dinged, and Cris clapped her Mac shut and padded to the oven.

He pinched up the metal clasps, ran a finger beneath the flap, and slid free a single sheet. At first he couldn't register what he was reading—the uneven scratch of the handwriting, the pencil-scraped letters cramped, then spaced, on the unlined white page—but the words came clear, one by one, and his heart did something funny against his ribs. The air had gone suddenly frigid, prickling the hairs at the base of his neck. He blinked hard and looked again, this time the sentences rushing at him.

admit what your done. or you will
bleed for it.

———

"Uh, hon?" Daniel's eyes, still fixed on the cramped handwriting.

Hoisting the roasting pan, Cris replied with a faint noise in the back of her throat. Then he heard metal thunk against Caesarstone, and she seemed to have levitated to his side, oven mitt on his back; his face must have mirrored the shock vibrating his insides.

She read over his shoulder. "Is that a joke?"

"Doesn't feel like one."

" 'Admit what you've done,' " she read. "What are you supposed to have done?"

"I have no idea."

"Disgruntled group member, maybe?" She tugged off the oven mitt, let it slap to the floorboards. "Whatever it is, it's creepy as hell."

Daniel turned the sheet over, his fingers leaving impressions. On the back, the same sloppy handwriting, pencil pushed hard enough to leave grooves in the paper.

you hav til november 15 at midnite

"Last Friday," Daniel said. "November fifteenth was last Friday. The deadline's already passed. That makes no sense."

Cris snatched the torn gray envelope from his lap and flipped it over. Through her teeth she shot a breath strong enough to flutter the envelope in her hand. "It's not for you."

"Not for . . . ?" He stopped, his brain still jarred out of gear. "Right." A rush of relief. "So it was outgoing mail that the person accidentally stuck in my box. Intended for . . . ?"

She lowered the envelope for him to read.

jack holley

And an address in the Tenderloin. The city, misspelled, with no state or zip code.

The stamp, unmarred by a postal mark. Not surprisingly, there was no return address.

"So Jack Holley, whoever he is, never got this ultimatum," Daniel said.

He looked up from the couch, and she looked down at him. Her hand, clammy against his neck.

At the same time, they directed their stares to the silver laptop on the kitchen counter.

Side by side, they walked over. Cris flipped the laptop open and keyed JACK HOLLEY TENDERLOIN into Google. Took a deep breath. Her finger hovered above the return key. A faint sheen of perspiration glistened on her cheek.

Reaching across, he clasped his hand over hers and lowered her finger to the key.

The little wheel spun atop the page as it loaded, and then the top search result slapped them in their faces.

LONGTIME TENDERLOIN RESIDENT
VICTIM OF BRUTAL KNIFE MURDER

November 16—Everyone in the **Tenderloin** seemed to know **Jack Holley**. Always a bright smile and a wave on his way to the second-floor walk-up where he'd lived for nearly thirty years. Which is why his vicious murder last night has left this community in shock. . . .

Heat rolled across Daniel's skin. He felt his face flush, his breath snag in his throat. "Not a joke," he said.

Cristina glanced down at the envelope still in her hand, then released it quickly onto the counter, as if it had burned her. Her throat lurched a bit when she swallowed. "Okay," she said. "Now what?"